# PRAISE FOR JOHN PEYTON COOKE'S
## DARK AND BRILLIANT
# *TORSOS*

♦          ♦          ♦

"Strong stuff. . . . The author creates brief, believable personal histories for the pitiful vagrants, prostitutes, and migrant workers, most of whose identities were never discovered and whose murders were never solved. But the true strength . . . surfaces when he steps back from the killings to survey hard times on a big city's bleak streets during the depression."
### —*New York Times Book Review*

♦          ♦          ♦

"A powerful and atmospheric re-creation of one of the most gruesome serial murders in American criminal history. Among the best novels ever written about a true crime."
### —Colin Wilson, author of *Written in Blood* and *The Criminal History of Mankind*

♦          ♦          ♦

"He writes moody understated prose and convincingly evokes both the depression and its erosion of the social fabric."
### —*Atlanta Journal & Constitution*

♦          ♦          ♦

"A compelling and an unsettling read."
### —*Library Journal*

*more . . .*

◆ ◆ ◆

"John Peyton Cooke skillfully sketches the hunt for the killer and provides his own solution to the mystery. . . . The author remains true to police, coroners, and newspaper reports of the crime." **—AP Serial Features**

◆ ◆ ◆

"An unflinching look at a horrifying episode. . . . Thoroughgoing research, attention to detail, and a muscular prose style mark this re-creation of modern America's fist serial killer in the days before the word 'serial' came into vogue."
**—Real Crime Book Digest**

◆ ◆ ◆

"Not for the fainthearted. Graphic sex and violence." **—Kirkus Reviews**

◆ ◆ ◆

♦ ♦ ♦

"*The Silence of the Lambs* gave us a serial killer whose effeminacy was blurred with his killer instinct. TORSOS superbly redresses the balance with a 1930's case based on facts far stranger than fiction. . . . Cooke succeeds where Thomas Harris failed, and the electrifying set pieces jingle the nerves more than any horror novel in recent memory."

—*Time Out* (London)

♦ ♦ ♦

"Not for the fainthearted or squeamish, Cooke's fact-based thriller takes a graphic look at a seamy side of 1930's Cleveland. . . . The talented Cooke has pulled an interesting switch by casting male characters in the classic women-in-peril roles of a typical slasher novel."

—*Publishers Weekly*

♦ ♦ ♦

**JOHN PEYTON COOKE** was born in 1967 in Amarillo, Texas. He is the author of two previous novels, *The Lake* and *Out for Blood*. His short stories have appeared in *Weird Tales* and *Christopher Street*. He currently lives in New York City.

# TORSOS

## John Peyton Cooke

**THE MYSTERIOUS PRESS**

Published by Warner Books

A Time Warner Company

First published in Great Britain in 1993 by Headline Book Publishing PLC.

MYSTERIOUS PRESS EDITION

Cover design and photograph by Richard Fahey

This Mysterious Press edition is published by arrangement with the author.

The Mysterious Press name and logo are registered trademarks
of Warner Books, Inc.

 Mysterious Press Books are published by
Warner Books, Inc.
1271 Avenue of the Americas
New York, NY 10020

 A Time Warner Company

Printed in the United States of America

Originally published in hardcover by The Mysterious Press.
First Printed in Paperback: May, 1995

10 9 8 7 6 5 4 3 2 1

This book is for
*Keng Kiew Leong*
my best buddy

smelled of must and mildew. He had inherited the office as well as the clutter from Inspector Cody—everything but

# 20 September 1935

**9:23 P.M.**

Eddie Andrassy sat on the lumpy narrow bed fully dressed. The partly opened door allowed some of the light from the hallway to filter in, but otherwise the small dormitory-style room was lighted only by a dim lamp on the nightstand. The men who came here tended to shrink from bright lights as if their wives were watching; they liked their encounters dark and indistinct. Eddie glanced at his pocket watch—time for the joint to start jumping.

He opened the window, lit a cigarette, and waited.

His line of vision was level with the Gothic pinnacles of Trinity Cathedral in the next block, barely visible through the drizzle and the gloom of the night. A streetcar clattered along on Prospect down below and screamed to a halt to let people off, amid the blaring of car horns. The damp breeze blowing into the room scattered the cigarette smoke up into his face.

A door creaked a ways down the hall; then came the sounds of two men greeting each other, one old and nervous and the other young and friendly, before the door was firmly shut and the key turned in the lock. Soon Eddie would hear

1

the creaking of bedsprings along with animalistic grunts of pleasure.

The seventh floor of the YMCA was open for business.

Strictly speaking, Eddie wasn't in that line of work, although he had a few such punks in his employ, some of whom were hustling here this evening. He had several small-time rackets going in this part of the city and had no need to sell himself for sex. Instead, he came here to peddle photographs and magazines to the men who came looking for fresh cock, for young guys they called "chicken."

Eddie opened up his cigar box and withdrew the stack of pictures he intended to sell.

His door swung open, but instead of a prospective customer, it was one of his boys, a kid named Danny.

"Hi, Eddie." Danny's grin was forced; for a slimy punk he had good teeth.

"Well, if it ain't Danny-boy. I was gonna come lookin' for you tonight, but here you saved me the trouble. You got somethin' for me, kid?"

Danny claimed to be nineteen but looked a couple years younger. He was a slender Italian boy with wavy black hair, an olive complexion, and a still-unformed body, as if his final mold hadn't yet been cast, which, Eddie suspected, was part of the boy's charm. Danny's greasy hair was always falling in his face, giving him the look of an innocent waif. He was clean and wore decent clothes, which was more than anyone had the right to expect in a hustler. Danny's skill and good nature had drawn many customers back for repeat encounters, and that was good for business.

"How about a smoke first, Eddie?"

"Sure, kid." Eddie tapped an Old Gold out of his pack and handed it to Danny. "Wanna light?"

"Thanks."

Eddie struck a match and lit the cigarette. Danny took a long drag and then blew out a cloud of smoke, which was sucked out into the hallway by a draft. Keeping the cigarette in the corner of his mouth, Danny reached into his trouser pocket, pulled out a small wad of bills, and handed them over to Eddie, who counted them up.

"This is it?"

Danny defended himself: "Things are slow."

"Things ain't never this slow. If I find you're holdin' out on me—"

"You know I wouldn't do that." Danny's voice was as sweet as molasses, high-pitched and angelic. "So maybe I've been a little lazy. You still make out all right, and you don't have to do nothing."

Eddie's hand reached out, grabbed Danny's flaccid prick through his trousers, and squeezed hard. "That's right, kid, but don't forget I own this—"

Danny winced, standing suddenly on his toes.

"And I can claim it anytime I want. All I need is a knife. Then you'll be worse than a girl, and nobody'll wantcha anymore, understand?"

"OK, OK!"

Eddie let go; Danny sighed, falling back on his heels.

"From now on whenever you get lazy, I'll just have to take a bigger percentage, teach you a lesson." Eddie snatched up most of the money, much more than his usual cut, and shoved the remainder back into Danny's pocket, reaching over and squeezing the kid's dick. "I'm making you hard." He chuckled.

Danny said nothing. He sucked down the last of his cigarette and turned to go.

"Hey, look at this," said Eddie, and grabbed his stack of photos.

One showed Danny totally nude from the front, leaning against a Roman pillar with one arm wrapped around it, one knee slightly bent, and his uncut cock poking its head from its sheath but not yet erect. He had a red rose tattoo, which showed up gray in the photo, on his right bicep.

Danny looked at the photos and smiled, as if mesmerized by the sight of his own naked flesh.

Eddie swatted his butt. "Go on, get lost. Get back to work."

Danny tossed the last of his cigarette on the linoleum floor, where it smoldered as he went back down the hall to his own room, leaving Eddie's door wide open.

This place was like the Central Market, except it was

flesh for sale, not meat and veggies. The working joes sat in their rooms, doors slightly ajar as an invitation to any old creep who might want to pucker his wrinkled lips around a still young prick, payment in advance on the nightstand. A different punk lay for sale behind every door, but Eddie was offering something different entirely. He had found that most of the men he encountered here were eager to fork over some cash for his "feelthy" pictures and publications.

Some of the men buying merchandise also wanted some action, but he resisted unless the guy in question offered him a lot of dough. Most of the men coming here thoroughly disgusted him. He could never understand how the hustlers could put up with them, aside from the fact that this was the only thing they had going—unlike Eddie, who sold his photos and magazines, engaged in pimpery and small-time swindles and also dealt hashish, marijuana, and opium when he could get it.

These various enterprises provided him with more than enough money to live on, but never enough to adequately fund him at the card tables and bookie joints he frequented. Most of his hard-earned money disappeared on the wrong poker hand or the wrong racehorse, which was the main reason he was still flopping at his parents' house on the near west side. He never seemed able to retain enough dough to expand his operations or move out of the house.

Eddie's cigarette was finished. He tossed the butt on the floor next to Danny's, stood up and ground them both with the leather sole of his shoe.

A young man, tastefully dressed in a black double-breasted pinstriped suit and a fedora, had been standing outside in the hallway. He looked in now at Eddie, smiled, and entered without a word. Eddie was suspicious of both the smile and the clothes; this might turn out to be a cop, in which case he would soon lose all the money he had just taken from Danny, and perhaps some of his better photos. There wasn't a cop in Cleveland that couldn't be bought.

"Whaddya want?" Eddie was brusque.

"Whatever you've got." The man closed the door behind

him, removing his hat and placing it atop the lampshade, which caused the light in the room to dim, illuminating his face only from below, casting shadows across his features and softening the glisten in his slicked-back black hair. He was movie-star handsome, with gleaming amber eyes and fine skin.

"Which is what?" Eddie asked.

"Photographs," said the man, "or so I've been told. Of men. Physique shots. Naked legs. Butts. Torsos."

"Easy, easy." Eddie realized that this guy was no cop, but more likely a local gangster. He was dressed to the nines and probably carrying a lot of dough. Eddie knew from experience that the Cleveland police were ugly sons-of-bitches, and no matter how dapper they might be able to make themselves, they couldn't do anything about their faces—the kinds of faces that only their mothers could love. So Eddie took the stack of black-and-white photographs and showed them one by one to his mysterious customer.

They were of sailors, swimmers, musclemen, and lithe-bodied youths, their flesh shaved and oiled, some completely naked, some dressed in G-strings. They struck statuesque poses—frontal shots displaying semihard dicks or large bulges in their pouches, rear angles showing their buttocks, some clenched, some spread—each photo shot in a professional photography studio somewhere, with dramatic backlighting and such props as an anchor, a ship's wheel, or a barbell. Some of these Eddie had got in Detroit during the summer, while others had been taken locally by an old queeny photographer who lived with his two spinster aunts just a few blocks from the Andrassy home. Eddie had supplied the photographer with some of his own boys as models.

"Yes, these are very nice," said the man. "I'll take them."

"Which ones?"

"How about all of them?"

"That'll cost a pretty penny."

"Is this pretty enough for you?" The man produced a twenty-dollar bill and handed it to Eddie, putting the stack of photographs in an inner pocket of his suitcoat.

Eddie was struck speechless and pocketed the cash. He

figured he would place it all on Max Baer in the Baer/Louis bout next week. The curly-headed Californian was going to cream the chocolate soldier from Detroit, and Eddie would make a mint as a result.

"There's more where that came from," said the man, taking a sudden step forward.

Eddie wished he had a knife on him. Then he could stick the guy and take whatever cash he could find. But that was how he had got sent to the workhouse a few years ago—not for sticking a guy, but for carrying a concealed weapon—and he had learned his lesson. It wasn't worth going back to Warrensville; he hadn't carried a knife since.

The man stood inches from Eddie's face. Eddie smelled the scent of expensive perfumed soap on his clean-shaven skin. The guy must have bathed and shaved just before coming over here.

Without warning, the stranger threw his arms around Eddie and embraced him. His fingers clutched at Eddie's back, curling inward like a vulture's claws, digging into his flesh. Eddie could feel the man's erect cock pressing against his crotch. His breath was hot and moist against Eddie's neck.

If there was some more dough to be had, Eddie wasn't about to turn it down, no matter what he had to do for it. The more money he could put down on Baer, the better.

The man rubbed his face against Eddie's cheek and then planted his lips on Eddie's mouth. His tongue tasted like a Chesterfield. Eddie could hear the sounds of spirited sex from the adjacent rooms. Then the man broke their embrace suddenly, flashing another twenty.

"Let's go somewhere more private," he said, and replaced the bill in his breast pocket. "Meet me in the alley back of Hessler's drugstore in half an hour."

Eddie forced a gee-whiz smile, trying to look something like Danny, and said, "Sure, fella. Whatever you say."


**10:16 P.M.**

The drizzle had made slick the bricks that paved the alleyway. The meager illumination came from the faintly glowing blanket of clouds overhead, and from either end of the alley, opening up on dim East Eighteenth and Nineteenth streets. The odor of neglected garbage was made worse by the damp.

But Eddie was accustomed to such smells in this part of the city, and indeed to taking back-alley routes under cover of darkness to avoid meeting up with police, who knew his record and liked to harass him. He always gave them a lot of lip, which only made things worse. On some weeknights, Eddie and his neighborhood pals on the near west side liked to get drunk and go gambling upstairs at McGinty's on West Twenty-fifth Street, sleeping it off in the dewy lawn over at Monroe Cemetery by the train tracks. Sometimes the Nickel Plate Railroad dicks came by and rousted them, roughing them up and taking their money; but since Eddie's parents locked him out of the house after midnight, the cemetery was usually the most comfortable place to sleep when the weather was good. Otherwise, he and his buddies had to take refuge in an alley much like the one he was in now.

Finding the back of Hessler's had been easy; everyone knew it was right on the corner of East Eighteenth and Prospect. He checked his pocket watch and saw that he was right on time, yet he was alone in the alley and all was quiet.

He saw no sign of his contact.

He dug a cigarette out of his pack and smoked it while he waited for the man to appear from around the corner. He wondered where he would be taken that was so "private." This alley would surely be a dangerous place for an encounter. Police could happen upon them all too easily, and then Eddie would be sent back to the workhouse for another long spell—only this time on a sodomy charge.

A Ford rattled past on East Eighteenth, and Eddie ducked back into the shadows hurriedly, leaning against Hessler's delivery entrance.

Suddenly, he felt the door give behind him. He lost his balance on the slippery bricks and fell backward, as the door opened and someone's arms caught him from behind.

A gloved hand clamped itself around his mouth and pinched his nostrils shut.

Eddie tried to scream out, but the sound was muffled by

the leather glove. He panicked, flailing his arms and kicking his legs as he was dragged backward through the unlighted doorway. He grabbed at the hand that was smothering him, but his strength failed him. His lungs convulsed. At last dizziness overtook him and everything went black.

## 10:57 P.M.

He awoke sometime later, staring up at an unfinished ceiling—at old crossbeams and the underside of floorboards covered with mildew and cobwebs, and at a single bright incandescent light bulb dangling from a cloth-insulated cord several feet directly above his torso, swinging back and forth as if someone had just pulled its chain to turn it on.

He had a headache and he was cold.

When he tried to get up, he felt the bite of fine hemp against his wrists, which were stretched out above his head on either side of him. Likewise his ankles had been spread and tied, but less tightly than his wrists, and his socks had been left on. His shoes and jacket had been removed and his shirtsleeves rolled up, but otherwise he remained fully clothed, bound securely to a butcher-block table in some kind of storeroom, probably in a basement. He saw no windows. Against the walls were stacked burlap bags each stuffed to the brim, and the air was filled with odd, pungent smells. No door was visible, so he assumed it stood behind him, somewhere beyond the reach of his vision.

The swinging light bulb reminded him of a scene in a movie he had seen a month ago at the Allen Theater—*The Raven,* one of those Universal thrillers with Boris Karloff and Bela Lugosi. In it, Bela had strapped a judge down to a table over which swung a great pendulum—a pendulum with a razor-sharp blade at its base that descended with each stroke, coming ever closer to slicing the judge in half as the seconds wore on. Now Eddie was tied to a table much the same way, and he couldn't keep his eyes off the goddamned light.

"Hey!" Eddie yelled. "Let me outta here!"

"Quiet," said a voice. The gloved hand closed itself over his mouth once more. "I'm not going to hurt you."

The face staring down at him—upside down—was that of the man he had met at the YMCA. The man smiled, but his pretty face was lost in shadow, so that what Eddie saw from his vantage point was a death's-head grin, wide eyes, and flared nostrils not unlike Lon Chaney's in *The Phantom of the Opera*. Eddie wondered if the man was a gangster—perhaps a hit man—and if he himself had done something to anger one of the local bosses. He had always been careful not to step on any of Cleveland's more important toes, to prevent just such predicaments as this from befalling him.

"I'll only remove my hand if you promise not to scream."

Eddie nodded in agreement. The gloved hand fell away, one finger lightly stroking his cheek.

"Wha-whaddya want?" Eddie asked, trembling.

"What do you think?" His captor's tone was conversational and cool. His gloved fingers undid a couple buttons of Eddie's shirt and reached inside, squeezing one of his nipples.

"Oh, Jesus." Eddie clenched his fists and pulled at his bonds. The pressure on his nipple was exciting him.

"What's the matter? Don't tell me no one's ever tied you up before."

"C'mon, lemme go."

"Relax! This is what I'm paying you for. You want the money, don't you? Then lie back and enjoy it."

"I'm not a whore," Eddie said. But as he said it, he realized that he was indeed. He was going to let this guy do whatever the hell he wanted with him, because twenty dollars was a lot of money and not easy to come by. This, however, would be the easiest thing in the world. All he had to do was lie here and let the man do all the work. And Eddie was already getting an erection. It would be different if the guy were rough trade, but instead he seemed to have a certain degree of sophistication. He was probably some rich kid with an appetite for the kinky.

"There, that's what I want," said the man.

He had both gloved hands on Eddie's nipples, twisting and

tugging them until they stood up from his chest. Then he moved one hand down to Eddie's crotch and clutched him through his trousers.

Eddie moaned, jerking against his bonds.

His captor unbuttoned his trousers, pulling both them and his underwear down to the top of his thighs, and began milking him, greasing up his leather gloves with his own spittle, while Eddie thrashed from side to side in ecstasy, his eyes shut tight against the bright light. Eddie's mouth was stuffed with an oily rag to keep him quiet.

The man pulled Eddie's balls up and clutched the base of his dick firmly from underneath the sac. Eddie felt something cold scrape the sensitive skin down there.

"Mmmph!" Eddie said, suddenly fearful of what was going on. He had known some hustlers who had had terrifying experiences at the hands of genuine sadists. The cold metal brushing the base of his balls felt like the blade of a knife. Eddie thrashed around on the table, trying somehow to get away.

But his captor grabbed his cock and balls firmly, and then Eddie felt white-hot pain shoot through his crotch and he screamed into the gag. His eyes welled up with tears. He struggled against the ropes and felt them cutting into his skin. Yet the only real pain came from the warm wetness between his legs.

He looked down and saw a pool of blood spreading from a hole where his cock and balls should have been.

The stranger stood grinning at him, holding Eddie's severed, bloodied genitals in one hand and a large machete-like butcher knife in the other.

Eddie managed to push out the oily rag with his tongue and screamed at the top of his lungs. He was feeling light-headed, ready to pass out at any second.

The man dropped Eddie's cock and balls onto his white shirt and lunged forward, grabbing Eddie by his hair and pulling his head back, stretching his neck taut. Eddie's eyes felt as if they would pop out of their sockets. He screamed as his captor raised the knife high, bringing it down swiftly in one clean stroke.

Then his screaming stopped.

All Eddie could hear was the sound of blood spurting from the table and gathering in a pool on the floor, and all he could taste was the blood on his tongue.

But he no longer felt any pain as the man held him by his hair at arm's length to gaze upon his own headless body. He witnessed the blood gushing forth from the bloody stump between his shoulders while his murderer stood there perfectly silent, until finally the room faded to black and the trickling noises went away.

# 23 September 1935

5:55 P.M.

Hank Lambert and Jack Finnegan stood knee-deep in thistle and scrub at the bottom of a dead-end ravine at the base
of Jackass Hill. Beyond this ravine to the west lay the Flats,
the industrial heart of the city, with its steel mills, oil refineries, and manufacturing plants. The smell of soot was preva-
lent. The Praha Avenue neighborhood up above was
composed primarily of the working class and the unemployed living in cheap company tract houses overlooking the
Kingsbury Run railway corridor, of which this ravine was
but a small part. The weeds were turning brown and corrupt
with the end of summer. Gnats and mosquitoes buzzed nois-
ily around the two detectives, while red-and yellow-winged
grasshoppers jumped from weed to weed, oblivious to the
detectives and railroad police searching the area.

Hank was just about to say something when a Cleveland
Interurban Railway train roared past in the main ravine of
Kingsbury Run fifty yards to the north, carrying a load of
commuters home from work to posh Shaker Heights. Because of the noise, he and the older detective simply stared at
the corpse for a few seconds. Hank tried to keep his eyes off
the blood-caked gash at the naked man's groin. He put his

hand in his pants pocket to make sure his own dick was still there.

"Self-inflicted?" wondered Jack Finnegan aloud, as the roar of the commuter train died away.

"Very funny." Hank was examining the neck, which had been severed neatly at the man's Adam's apple. The head was nowhere to be found. Hank removed his hat and wiped the sweat from his brow with a handkerchief. "Looks like a gang job, but then they go and take the guy's head. That's what bugs me. You ever seen them do that before? And Christ, the dick—"

Finnegan interrupted: "What bugs me is those goddamned socks. If they're going to lay a man out naked, why bother leaving his socks on?"

"Keep his feet warm?" Hank offered.

"Don't be a wise-ass."

"Cathy says I get it from you."

"Yeah," said Jack, "and you've got my eyes, too."

Once Hank had been tapped for Homicide four years ago, it was Finnegan who had shown him the ropes. Finnegan himself had been in Homicide for twelve years—as long as Hank had been on the force. Hank wondered if Finnegan had ever seen a body like this one before.

The corpse seemed in its late twenties, male, average height, slim build, tanned skin now bluish tinted, small brown nipples. Hank tried to picture him alive. Even without the head, he could tell the guy must have been a real looker. Hank felt sick at how the body had been maimed; he would have bet that it had once been beautiful. Now, with its bloody hole hidden in a thick nest of dark pubic hair, it was hideous.

No one had touched the body since it had been found an hour ago by two kids. Although it lay at the bottom of a ravine, Hank and Finnegan had already figured out that it hadn't been thrown over the side. Instead, it had been carried down the steep hill and carefully laid out, heels together, arms at the sides. The head and genitals were missing. Rope burns marred its wrists and all it wore was a pair of black socks.

Not a drop of blood could be found near the body. It

looked as if it had been almost lovingly cleansed prior to its being deposited here. It was at least a day or two old, although the Nickel Plate Railroad dicks said it hadn't been here Sunday night. That meant that most likely the suspect or suspects had carried the body down here sometime in the early morning hours before dawn and escaped unnoticed.

Hank looked up toward the railroad tower on the nearby hill and wondered what the Nickel Plate guys had been doing all that time—playing poker? jerking off?

"Let's get an officer over here to take care of this evidence," said Finnegan, motioning a few yards distant toward a metal pail and a stack of clothing they had discovered out in the open upon their arrival. The pail contained a filthy rag and an oily substance and possibly some blood. Finnegan had postulated that perhaps the suspect or suspects had wanted to set fire to the remains, but had fled for lack of time. The clothing had been neatly folded in a small pile and appeared to belong to the naked corpse. A cursory glance at the clothes revealed that the collar and front of the white shirt had been soaked with blood, which was now quite dry, the color of rust. No identification had been found, no wallet, no monograms, no laundry marks. So far they had turned up nothing that would identify the corpse, but Hank was pretty sure it was in good enough shape that they could get a decent set of fingerprints. Then he would just have to cross his fingers and hope they came up with a match.

"Detective!" yelled railroad patrolman Stitt ten yards away, standing behind a thick clump of scrub brush. "Come get a load of this!"

Hank took his time in following Finnegan to the patrolman's location. Stitt had probably come up with the head and dick, but there was nothing urgent about that. They had expected to find the missing pieces around here somewhere.

The area was buzzing with flies. The breeze shifted and Hank caught a whiff of the hideous smell.

"Jesus," said Finnegan.

"You said it," said Hank stupidly.

The odor came not from the expected missing head, but from another corpse. This, too, was a man, although older, shorter, and stockier than the first. He was completely naked and had been decapitated and emasculated as well, with neither the head nor the genitals in sight. He had been neatly laid out like the first, arms against sides, heels touching, plus he had lost a great deal of blood—yet not a trace of blood could be seen nearby.

"No socks," observed Finnegan. "Damn."

The corpse was in a much more advanced stage of decay than the first. It had been coated with some kind of brown substance that had given its skin a leathery texture and dark appearance. Hank wondered if this were the same stuff as in the pail.

"Self-inflicted again?" Hank said, but no one laughed.

Finnegan considered a moment, then seemed to come to a realization, and let out a curt chuckle. "Crime of passion, I'd say. Some kind of perverted love triangle."

"I still say it's a gang job," said Hank. "Probably a couple of policy men who came up short." Secretly, Hank hoped Finnegan was right; if it was in fact a gangland killing, they might as well write the whole thing off.

Suddenly Stitt called, "Here's the dicks!" At first Hank thought he meant the other detectives just then arriving from Central Station, but then realized he meant the severed organs.

Hank and Finnegan rushed to Stitt's side, no more than seven yards from the first body, and observed two pairs of cock and balls that had been neatly sliced beneath the scrotum, lying together in a heap. Soon the newly arrived officers and detectives were crowding around in a circle, staring at the dicks and passing rude remarks.

"Good work," said Finnegan to Stitt. "Find us the heads and I'll buy you a beer."

"Why don't these jerks help us instead of standing around gawking," said Hank. "You'd think they'd never seen a guy's dick before."

"Come on, fellas," shouted Finnegan. "What do you think this is, a cock fight?"

The policemen dispersed amid scattered groans, heading off to help collect evidence. Hank and Finnegan had already determined that the suspect or suspects had left no footprints, so they allowed the officers to tramp all over the hillside in their search.

Hank had already taken witness statements from the two kids who had found the first body while racing each other down Jackass Hill an hour ago. People seldom came to this part of Kingsbury Run. Had the two boys chosen to play elsewhere this evening, the bodies might not have been found for another week.

"Over here!" called patrolman Stitt.

Finnegan was directing Lloyd Trunk, the photographer from Ballistics, toward the bodies. Hank hurried over to Stitt's location to see what he might have turned up.

Stitt was carefully digging out sand from around a clump of human hair.

"Wait," Hank told him. "We have to get photos of this."

They waited there until Lloyd Trunk was able to join them. Hank performed the excavation work himself, gradually uncovering an entire head lying on its side in a small hole, pausing every so often so photos could be taken of the process. The mouth was partially open and caked with sand. The dust-coated eyes stared up at them, dried and shriveled. Hank wished he had brought some gloves.

The head appeared to belong to the first body. Its face was that of a thin young man with longish, brown wavy hair. Upon looking closer, it seemed to Hank that he had had past professional contacts with this guy.

"Go get Finnegan, will you?" Hank said to Stitt, who then hurried off in the older detective's direction.

Once the entire head had been uncovered, the bright illumination of Trunk's flashbulb gave a brief moment of life to the face, and at the same instant Hank recognized him as some pimp who operated in the Roaring Third, specializing in boys. His name was on the tip of Hank's tongue. . . .

"Goodness, gracious, Godness, Agnes," swore Finnegan, who had crept up behind him.

"Jesus Christ." Hank swallowed hard. Finnegan had startled him, just as the pimp's name had come to him.

*Eddie Andrassy,* thought Hank, though he would never be able to tell Finnegan. As he now realized, he had never had past *professional* contacts with him at all; their meetings had been more of a private nature.

## 7:41 P.M.

Danny Cottone lay on his stomach, waiting for Father Delvecchio to finish. Finally, the spent priest collapsed onto Danny's back, crushing him against the bed. Danny's ass was tingly and sore where the priest had spanked him during the fucking. He grabbed a pair of dirty underwear from the floor and wiped himself with it.

"Ah, my boy, that was well worth it." The priest slid off Danny and onto his side, in a precarious position at the edge of the single bed. He dripped with sweat and was out of breath. His round belly was overgrown with curly black hair, and his dick had shriveled back down to the size of a gherkin. He reached out with a flabby hand and stroked Danny's hair. "I certainly never expected to find such a beauty down at the market."

Danny said nothing, wishing to retain whatever illusion his customer might have of him.

"Goodness, I'm late." The priest leapt from the bed, grabbed his clothes, and scurried to the bathroom.

Danny had always had luck working the Central Market on Ontario Avenue, and today had been no exception. Father Delvecchio had been roaming around the market chatting with the younger male cashiers and laborers, when Danny caught sight of him and pegged him as a "possible." He followed him around for a while and then wormed his way through the crowd and positioned himself directly in the priest's path, leaning against a support beam near a fish stand. He lighted a cigarette and took several long drags before the priest stumbled across him, and Danny gave him a wink and said, "Hi, Father." They began talking, and Danny learned that he was Father Delvecchio from Philadelphia, in Cleveland for the Seventh National Eucharist Congress. The priest said he had a few hours on his hands and was hoping to find some young "lad" who could show him around the city, to which Danny responded, "For a few bucks I'll show you whatever you want," and then turned around and bent over as if to pick up a penny. His suspenders were cinched tight enough that his trousers crept high into the cleft of his ass and showed it off real nice. Danny had practiced this move in front of the mirror and got it down to a science. When Danny rose, the priest placed an arm around his shoulders, and Danny led him to his apartment a few blocks away on Bolivar Road.

"I hope I wasn't too rough on you," said Father Delvecchio from the bathroom. "Sometimes I get carried away."

"No, Father, I loved it," Danny yelled back. Flattery could sometimes garner an extra buck or two.

While Father Delvecchio was in the bathroom, Danny got up and stretched. He looked at himself in the mirror above his dresser, turning his torso so that he could see his ass. The glowing redness on his butt made him smile. He liked making other people happy, no matter what he had to do for them. Being spanked in itself was not so exciting, but the fact that Father Delvecchio had enjoyed it so much was. What Danny enjoyed most about sex was the intense pleasure he gave his customers. He was excited by the idea that they were excited by him, and he enjoyed himself the most when he knew they were enjoying his ministrations. Danny liked to be whomever or whatever his customer wanted him to be, yet during sex he saw himself through their eyes and was aroused by what he saw.

He took the three dollars the priest had given him and put it with the rest of his money in an old cocoa tin on a shelf in the kitchen. Though he preferred not to bring customers back to his own apartment, he figured he could trust a priest.

"I've really been very irresponsible," said Father Delvecchio, now fully dressed and putting on his shoes. "I must get back at once."

Danny stood before him naked. "Don't go, Father," he said, trying to sound convincing.

Delvecchio rose to his feet and planted a chaste kiss on Danny's lips. "Good-bye, my son." He pressed another crisp dollar bill into Danny's palm and turned to go.

"Next Eucharist Congress, I hope you look me up." Danny liked to encourage his customers. Sometimes they came back.

Father Delvecchio laughed and then left.

Danny didn't know what was so funny. He looked at his new wristwatch—Mickey Mouse's short arm was pointing at the seven, his long arm at the ten—and realized he had let the priest stay too long. He had more business to attend to. He threw on his clothes and pocketed the extra buck; he would need it for drinks at Charlie's, on the off chance he couldn't tease some guy into setting him up with a few.


**10:31 P.M.**

"Whew! Jesus H.!" said Hank Lambert. The stench as he entered the coroner's lab was sickening. Although he had partaken of the unique odors of an autopsy before, he had never in his life smelled anything as wholly corrupt as this.

"That's mostly from Number Two," said A.J. Pearse, the hefty, mustachioed Cuyahoga County coroner. "Number One ain't near as bad."

"Number One?" said white-haired Det. Insp. Cornelius W. Cody, following Hank in through the door of the lab. He held a piece of paper in his hand. "Not anymore. We've got a positive ID. Dandy set of prints, A.J. Matched up real nice with the jail records."

Pearse looked up from the corpse laid out on his table, lowered his glasses, took the page from Inspector Cody, and read: "Edward A. Andrassy, age twenty-eight, seventeen forty-four Fulton Road. Hmmph." He put the piece of paper in a pocket of his lab coat. His flabby, latex-gloved hands were covered in a gelatinous dark putrescence.

*Eddie, you little shit,* Hank thought. He looked down at the blue-tinted face, thin blue lips, and the wavy brown hair, and wondered why dead people's eyelashes were always caked together like that. Eddie's head was separated a few inches from his shoulders, propped up on either side by two stone bookends carved as owls, so that it wouldn't roll over onto its side. His chest cavity was opened, displaying purple muscle, white bone, yellow fat. Hank wondered just what Eddie had been up to that landed him here. He hadn't seen Eddie for months. Supposedly the stupid punk had moved to Detroit.

"Who was he," asked Pearse, "some hoodlum?"

"That's right," said Hank.

"Somebody didn't like him very much."

"I'd say that's a given."

*Lots of people didn't like Eddie very much,* Hank thought, but couldn't speak it aloud. It was true, Eddie could have been the target of just about anybody—rival pimps, gangsters, collection men, narcotics suppliers, rough trade, or even (the old standby) a jealous spouse—which in Eddie's case could have been either a husband or a wife. Eddie was as likely a candidate for murder as Hank could think of.

"It takes an awful lot of hate to cut off a man's head like that," the coroner added.

Hank enjoyed checking in with Coroner Pearse, although he could do without Inspector Cody's presence. Jack Finnegan had stayed behind at Central Station to pore over Eddie's criminal record, searching for names of Eddie's acquaintances and any other pertinent information, some of which Hank knew already but couldn't tell his partner.

"Parents are coming down to confirm the ID," said Cody. "You got a smoke, A.J.? Lucky Lambert here's all out."

That wasn't entirely true; Hank had three Lucky Strikes left in his pack. He had already given the inspector one back at the station, but he was damned if he was going to wait hand-and-foot on his supervisor. Cody was going to be retiring in a few weeks and collecting his big fat pension; he could afford to buy his own fucking cigarettes.

"Sure, Cornelius," said Pearse, and handed him a Camel.

Cody removed a gold lighter from his inner coat pocket and flicked the flint a few times before the gas ignited. He drew in a lungful of smoke. "So, A.J., what's the good word?" He held in the smoke.

"Decapitation."

Finally Cody exhaled, releasing a pungent cloud into the air. "Come on, we know his head was cut off. So what's the poop? How did he die? Shot or stabbed?"

"I told you, his head was cut off, see," said Pearse. "That *is* how he died. Allow me." The coroner beckoned the policemen closer and directed their attention toward the severed head of the corpse. "Reuben hasn't finished all the toxicology work yet, but all the same it's pretty clear what happened to Mr. . . . ." He fumbled around in his lab coat with his sticky fingers, looking for the scrap of paper.

"Andrassy," supplied Hank.

"Mr. Andrassy. Thanks. He's lost pretty near all his blood. If you look right here you can see his muscles all tensed up around the neck, see, and the shoulders, you see? His genitalia were removed either just before or just after the decapitation, but since I can't find any other stab wounds or other damage to the body, I can say for sure it was losing his head that killed him."

"Jesus," muttered Hank. "What are we talking here, a knife? A saw?"

Pearse's eyes beamed from behind his spectacles. "We know he was tied up. He got those rope burns struggling in the last seconds before the decapitation, and then *bam!*—his head was gone. The killer must have used some type of large knife. Butcher knife, machete, maybe some kind of cleaver."

"Butcher, eh?" said Inspector Cody, his interest piqued. He jotted the word down on his notepad.

"Now, Cornelius, I ain't saying the killer's a butcher. Could be. Whoever it is, he's got a certain knack for this kind of work. Could just as easily be a doctor."

"Doctor," repeated Cody, scribbling away.

"The head was cut off in a single slice, see, and if you think that sounds easy, well, it ain't. That's why the French build their guillotines so tall."

"Christ, A.J., don't go talking about guillotines to the press, all right?" advised Cody.

"So long as you don't say anything about butchers or doctors," said Pearse. "There aren't any hesitation marks on the neck here, see? If the killer had taken three or four strokes to do the job, we'd be able to tell. The guy sure as hell knew what he was doing. Hunter, maybe."

"Was it from the front or the back?" Hank asked. The mention of guillotines reminded him that when someone's head was cut off from the back they felt little pain, because the spinal cord was severed immediately. Having it cut off from the front was a different story; you could feel the blade going all the way through until it reached your spine.

"Front. But I think it all happened pretty quickly."

"Was he drugged?"

"Won't know for sure until Reuben's finished his tests, but right now it doesn't look like it. I'll cover all that in my report."

"A.J., the parents are going to be here any minute," said Inspector Cody. "Why don't you clean up now and make our little friend presentable so we can wheel him out?"

"You bet."

Hank's heart fell into his shoes thinking about the arrival of Eddie's parents and the ordeal awaiting them. This was the part of the job he hated the most.

## 10:38 P.M.

From the outside, Charlie's was nondescript, merely a gray door in a bricked-up storefront at the corner of East Twentieth and Central, with no windows allowing anyone to peer in and no sign proclaiming its existence. Such secrecy had been necessary during Prohibition, when Charlie's had thrived as a speakeasy, but in the two years since the repeal of the Volstead Act, no one had bothered to unbrick the windows or put up a sign. Business had slacked off, and Charlie's was now maintained by a steady but modest stream of regular customers, most of whom preferred the bar's lack of general renown.

Inside, the tavern was paneled in dark-stained wood that seemed even darker in the dim light. The few light bulbs dangling from the ceiling emitted a feeble yellow glow that was swallowed up by the thick smoky air. Candlestick lamps along the bar illuminated the bottles lining the shelves and gave the bartender some light to work by, but helped to push the booths along the far walls farther into darkness.

It was from this darkness that Flo Polillo emerged and sat upon a stool at the end of the bar. She sat in front of one of the lamps so that it would light up her face. Flo had spent the last hour drinking alone in a booth, staring around the bar and sizing up this evening's clientele.

"Hi, Flo." Mike the bartender set her up with another shot

of rye. Beads of sweat clung to his bald pate; what hair he had was loaded with Brylcreem. "How's tricks?"

"You think you're so funny." Flo tried to laugh, but what came out was a snort. She pulled a handkerchief out of her purse and wiped her nose. "Wanna come along sometime and find out?"

"Flo, I tell you, I'll try anything once, so long as it don't kill me and so long as it's free."

Flo replaced the handkerchief in her purse and took out a cigarette. "Got a light?"

"Here." Mike tossed her a book of matches.

"I'm no door-to-door salesman," she said, striking a match and holding it to the tip of the cigarette until it glowed, puffing on it the way she'd seen Joan Crawford do in the movies, then expelling a huge cloud of smoke befitting her husky frame. "I don't give out any free samples."

"You don't advertise on the radio, neither. Don't make you so special." Mike wiped off her corner of the bar and went down to the other end to serve another customer.

Flo put the book of matches in her purse and clasped it shut. The cigarette tasted good with the rye. She didn't know why Mike was giving her a hard time. She could never tell when he was kidding or when he was being a genuine heel. And she gave him enough business that he had little reason to complain.

Charlie's had begun to fill up, as much as it ever did on a Monday night. Except for the other whores, it was mostly men—typically older, half of them on Relief, the other half laborers in the nearby steel mills and oil refineries. They looked dirty even when they were clean. Some of that oil and soot just never came off, no matter how hard a person scrubbed. Enough of it had rubbed off onto Flo in the last couple of years that she ought to know.

Some of these men had lost parts of themselves to the machines they operated. The guy with the growth of gray stubble at the other end of the bar, talking with his buddies, had lost the thumb and first two fingers of his right hand to some machine, subsequently losing his job because he could no longer perform it. One of the guys down there talking to him had worn his eye patch ever since a tiny drop of molten steel had come flying out of the smelter and seared itself into his left eyeball. Flo knew another guy who had lost his testicles because of some freak accident or other. But he wasn't here this evening; it was just as well.

These guys were regular customers of Charlie's, but only occasional customers of Flo's, and certainly not on a Monday night. Friday or Saturday maybe, but never Monday. On Monday nights, Flo had to rely on other stragglers wandering in, the kind of guy who was simply feeling restless and looking for a party. And because Flo knew all the regulars so well, she could spot the other kind the minute they walked in.

Just such a one was now sitting at the middle of the bar, the collar of his jacket turned up, his fingers drumming the dark wood of the bartop. He was staring at the double scotch he'd just ordered, the drink Mike had left Flo's company to make. He had five o'clock shadow on his face, and his black hat hid much of his head, but he seemed rather young and handsome. Not many men with pretty faces hung out at Charlie's, except for the occasional pimp like Eddie Andrassy, but Eddie and the others usually came only on the weekends, and this guy didn't look like a pimp anyway, despite his nice jacket and hat. No, this guy was here for booze, and perhaps broads if Flo was lucky. Few other girls were working tonight, and they were all busy gossiping in a booth, so Flo figured she had the jump on them.

She placed her elbow on the bar and gazed off in the direction of the newcomer, adopting her Joan Crawford smoking style and staring him down. His eyes hadn't met hers yet, but when they did, it would be the moment of truth.

"Hey there, good-lookin'!" came a crusty voice from behind her.

"What?" Flo was startled, feeling a rough and calloused hand at the back of her neck. Both the voice and the hand belonged to the grizzled old cuss now sitting down on the stool next to her. His breath smelled of alcohol, for which she was thankful because the stench of his rotting teeth would have been far worse.

"Frank," she said in exasperation. "Go away! Why do you

always have to be coming around here bothering me, huh? I don't have the time to talk to you, so just beat it."

"You're lookin' awful lonely," said Frank Dolezal. He was one of the regulars at Charlie's. In the past he had been a paying customer of Flo's on occasion, though he favored spending his money on whiskey rather than women; sometimes Flo and the other girls even visited him socially. He could be a fun fella to get drunk with. Sure, he was rascally and mean sometimes, but what man wasn't?

"Well, it just so happens I've got something fixed up for this evening," said Flo, trying to look past Frank's crumpled old hat because he was sitting in the direct line of sight between her and the good-looking young man. "So . . . dammit! . . . so you'd best be on your way or you're gonna scare him off. Now, I don't mind talking to you, Frank, you know I don't. But not tonight, or so help me I'm gonna—"

"Whatcha gonna do, Flo?" said Frank, wheezing with laughter that whistled out through his teeth. "Whatcha gonna do, sit on me?"

"I'm gonna . . . I'm gonna—" Flo craned her neck and looked past Frank, and then sighed in disappointment.

That punk kid Danny Cottone was sitting—lounging was more like it—on the barstool next to the young man, and they were carrying on a most animated discussion. The young man was smiling at Danny, who was flirting with him like the little boy whore he was, sitting backward and leaning against the bar. The young man's hand crept up Danny's thigh and landed in his crotch. That kind of thing could happen in Charlie's, and people would just look the other way. But it was pissing the hell out of Flo.

"Dammit! Goddammit, Frank, you son-of-a-bitch!"

"Why, what's the—"

"Oh, hell, never mind."

Frank turned his neck to look down the bar at what Flo was looking at, and his wheezing, whistling laughter returned.

"Looks like you were fixin' yourself up with a nelly!" said Frank through tubercular gales of laughter.

He spoke loudly enough that Danny and the young man both turned their heads. Then, looking disgruntled, the young man nodded his head in the direction of the door, touched Danny on the shoulder, and tossed some change on the bar. He then led Danny through the front door, letting in a stiff autumn chill that freshened the stale air.

Flo lighted another cigarette and sucked some of it down. "I would have had him, Frank, if that bitch Danny hadn't sidled up to him like that. I'm gonna catch that kid one of these days and I'm gonna beat his sorry ass, put him out of commission for a while."

"Sure you will, Flo." Frank coughed a bit and turned a darker shade of purple. When he was through, Flo had finished her cigarette. "Listen, woman, I've got a decent bottle of Canadian in that back booth with Rosie. Come on over and join us for a snort."

"All right. Not much action around here, anyway."

**11:51 P.M.**

"Can you ID him?" asked Hank.

Pearse and the county pathologist, Dr. Reuben Strauss, were working on the corpse of the second man. The stench was even worse than before. Pearse and Strauss had opened him up and their examination table was slimy with a putrid syrupy substance oozing from the corpse. Number Two was decaying right before Hank's eyes.

"The easy answer is no," said Pearse. "Unless we can match up his dental records. That's a long shot, and it'll take some time even if we can find a match, see. But the guy has got perfect teeth."

"Do the best you can, A.J.," said Inspector Cody. "We need to find a connection between him and Andrassy."

"About all I can tell you is that he's approximately forty-five years of age, five foot six, hefty build, about a hundred sixty-five pounds, dark hair, brown eyes. But he's in pretty sad shape, see? I'd say he was killed at least three, maybe four weeks ago. There was some crude attempt made at preserving the body. I can't for the life of me figure out what this junk is on his skin. I thought it might be varnish, but it's not. I haven't got a clue. I'm sending a sample to the state crime lab for analysis. Can't get a decent set of fingerprints off those fingers, see, and I doubt if anyone who knew him could possibly recognize him now. I'm tagging him as a John Doe, and I'm going to have to bury him as soon as possible because of his condition."

"You're sure it's the work of the same killer?" asked Hank.

Pearse's bottom lip turned down, and he glanced at the county pathologist, deferring to him.

"Yes," said the bespectacled Dr. Strauss, holding his bloodstained hands away from his body. "They were killed the same way. There's no hesitation marks on Number Two's neck. He was killed by decapitation, no doubt about it."

"You guys ever seen anything like this before?" Hank meant his question partly in jest. As he stared at the grotesque mess of decayed flesh and bone that had once been a man, he thought that nothing like this could have ever happened in Cleveland.

"As a matter of fact, I have," said Pearse, and cleared his throat nervously. "The Lady of the Lake."

Inspector Cody's face went ashen. "Jesus, Mary, and Joseph. You don't think it's the same—"

"Hard to say. But the M.O. of our current killer jogged my memory a bit. The Lady's head was cut off in a similar fashion. And you might recall that her skin had been treated with some weird substance as a preservative."

"But that one was just a torso," said Inspector Cody.

"Two halves of the same torso," Pearse corrected. "I'm not saying I've made a positive connection. Lucky Lambert asked me if I'd seen anything like this before, and I have. Once, here in Cleveland, almost exactly a year ago."

Inspector Cody hurriedly thanked Coroner Pearse and Dr. Strauss for their good work, told them Detective Finnegan would be touching base with them tomorrow and reviewing their report, and bade Hank leave the lab with him. Once outside in the hallway, the old inspector placed an arm around Hank's shoulders.

"Listen, son. I want you and Jack to work your butts off on this one. You've got some good leads already. I hope you can have someone in custody within two weeks."

Hank looked askance at his boss. "Two weeks? You've got to be kidding!"

"I don't care how you do it, and I don't want to know. But I want you to have this whole thing wrapped up before my testimonial dinner. To which you and Jack are now formally invited." Inspector Cody's grin was broad. "Lucky, I want you and Jack to present me with something more than a gold watch on my retirement."

"Yes, sir. I understand, sir."

Hank understood, all right. His superior was asking him to arrest somebody—anybody—for the murders so that he could have one more trophy before he bugged out of the department. But Hank had no intention of trumping up a murder charge on anyone, and he knew Jack wouldn't go for it, either. They were both straight arrows. And there wouldn't be a damned thing Inspector Cody could do about it, because he would be inspector no longer come October.

Of course, Hank could play along and hope for the best. It was always possible that they might solve the case in a matter of days. There might have been a witness, or the killer might even turn himself in.

The one thing Hank had learned after so many years on the force was that anything could happen, and when it did, it could just as easily break in his favor. The other detectives didn't call him Lucky for nothing.

# 24 September 1935

**12:27 P.M.**

Danny Cottone was eating a Reuben at a café on Ontario Avenue, across the street from the market, when he learned of the murders. He had been thumbing through a copy of the *Plain Dealer* that someone had left on the counter, looking for today's installment of "The Tarzan Twins"—which never ran on the comics page and was sometimes a bitch to find—but instead he stumbled across the grotesque headline on an inner page, right next to a photo of Eddie Andrassy:

> FINDING OF TORSOS
> REVEALS SLAYINGS
> Headless and Nude Bodies
> of 2 Men Start Police
> on Mystery Case.

Above Eddie's photo, another bold heading read: "Slaying is Puzzle."

Danny felt his sandwich churning in his stomach. It had been greasy to begin with, but after reading the gory details

29

of the newspaper story, he could taste the bile rising in his throat and felt suddenly short of breath. His heart felt as if it were running the fifth race at Thistledown. The story said the bodies were found "headless and otherwise mutilated," that the older man remained unidentified, and that the police believed it was a "murder of passion." It said that Eddie had probably been killed three or four days ago. Danny realized he must have been one of the last people to have seen him alive.

"Freshen you up?" asked the waitress in her pink apron, holding a pot of coffee.

"Sure."

Danny squeezed the wad of bills in his pocket, smiling a crooked smile because he knew he would no longer have to fork over most of it to Eddie. At the same time, he broke out into a cold sweat.

The police didn't know who the killer was, and it might very easily be someone that Danny knew, or at least someone who knew him.

He rose from his seat in a hurry and downed the entire cup of coffee, scorching his throat. He grabbed the newspaper, tucked it under his arm, paid for his lunch, and left the café. The little bell above the door rang as he exited.

Stepping out onto Ontario, Danny took a deep breath and felt his heart begin to calm down. He looked straight up the street toward downtown and saw Terminal Tower basking in the noonday sun. If only they had given it a clock, Cleveland would have had its own Big Ben, he thought. Danny had seen picture postcards of London and found Big Ben more beautiful and impressive than his native city's colossal tower. But most of all, he hated the name itself, Terminal Tower. Danny figured that whoever was in charge of these things could have come up with a better name, even if the skyscraper was a part of Union Station.

When Danny was a kid, his mom's doctor had always said his mom's illness was "terminal," and ever since then, Danny had always associated the Terminal Tower with tuberculosis. It sounded like someplace where people went to die, not to catch the 5:42 to Youngstown. But the worst thing of all was that no matter where in Cleveland Danny went, he could never escape the sight of the thing, with its tapered, colonnaded pinnacles piercing the sky, casting its shadow across half the city.

A fat woman bumped into Danny, knocking the newspaper from his arms and walking on without a word.

"Excuse you," said Danny, but the woman didn't turn around. He retrieved his paper from the grimy sidewalk, folded it up, and put it inside his jacket.

He needed to hang on to the story about Eddie as a reminder to himself to be more careful. Even though Eddie's body had been found nearly forty blocks away at the southern end of Kingsbury Run, the murderer must have been someone from the neighborhoods where Eddie hung out, which were for the most part the same places where Danny hung out. It was possible that Danny had had contact with the killer in the past, and that he might in the future, and he would have to be on his guard.

As he crossed Ontario, a yellow Ford convertible nearly ran him down, blaring its horn. The last thing Danny needed was to be the victim of a disfiguring accident; if he didn't lose his life, he would lose his livelihood, which would be even worse. He liked his job and he didn't want to give it up.

Today he was going to try his luck at the Sheriff Street Market at East Fourth Street and Bolivar Road, just down the street from his apartment. It was the major competition for Central Market, and Danny found it was always healthy for his own career to have a frequent change of venue. He turned onto Bolivar Road, walking past the broken-down tenements.

The *Plain Dealer* had said that Eddie's wrists had been tied before his decapitation, which seemed strange to Danny. He couldn't see Eddie allowing anyone to tie his wrists; he must have had no choice in the matter.

Danny felt dizzy all of a sudden and leaned against a lamppost, blinking his eyes to clear his vision. Clutching onto the cool iron post, he felt his knees suddenly give way, then collapsed onto the sidewalk and began to cry.

# 1 November 1935

The office of Acting Det. Insp. Emmett J. Potts was a small glassed-in room overlooking the Detective Bureau, cluttered with stacks of files and loose papers atop his desk and filing cabinet. On the wall behind his desk hung a prominent photo of Potts with his arm around Mayor Harry Davis, a Democrat. Both of them were grinning wildly, staring into the camera like two deer caught in an automobile's headlights.

Potts himself was clearing some things from the seats of two wooden chairs before his desk just as Jack Finnegan and Hank Lambert entered.

"Inspector?" Finnegan inquired. "You wanted to see us."

"Oh, yes, come in." Potts plopped a messy stack of reports haphazardly on top of a Philco radio in the corner. "Sit down."

Hank followed Finnegan in, and they made themselves as comfortable as possible in the creaky old chairs. Inspector Potts sat opposite them behind his dusty desk. His office smelled of must and mildew. He had inherited the office as well as the clutter from Inspector Cody—everything but

32

Cody's personal files. It looked as if Potts had made no effort to straighten up the mess.

"You two are doing a fine job," said Potts, "but I'm taking you off the Andrassy case."

"What?" Hank bolted up from his chair. He felt Finnegan's hand touch his forearm, a tacit suggestion that he take it easy. But Hank wasn't having any of it. "You can't do that. We've invested too much time and effort to give up now."

"Sit down, Lambert." Potts stared up at Hank from beneath thick dark eyebrows. When Hank returned to his seat, Potts continued. "That's exactly my point. You two have been spending a great deal of time on this case, and our team is already spread too thin. You've come up with a few leads, but they've all led nowhere. I need you to help us on cases that we *can* solve."

"No case is unsolvable," said Finnegan simply. He looked not at Potts but at his fingernails, which he was cleaning with the small blade of his pocketknife.

"I'm not closing the case, you understand. I just can't afford to squander our resources on this one. Listen, Andrassy was a lowlife. Nobody particularly misses him. And we still don't know who the hell the other guy was. He doesn't match any missing persons reports, and nobody's come forward looking for him. If we can't find the killer and get a prosecution out of this case, there's no point in my sending you boys around on a wild-goose chase."

"Pardon my saying so, sir," began Hank, clearing his throat before continuing, "but I don't think it's our job to decide whose murder matters and whose doesn't. I want to find out who Number Two is and catch whoever's responsible. That's my duty as a—"

"Cut the crap, Lambert." Potts paused for a few seconds to light a cigar. The aroma quickly filled the small office. "We all know about your dedication to duty and so on and so forth."

"You can't just make this case go away," said Hank.

"At this point, there's not much you can do about it. If you want to continue to investigate on your own time, that's fine. But as long as I'm in charge here, I'm going to run an efficient bureau. I can't afford to promote two more detectives to replace you guys while you go searching high and low for this killer. And you know as well as I that this was probably the work of some gang. Try proving who did it. And then try bringing them to trial. The only way they ever got Al Capone was for not paying his taxes."

Hank offered a semblance of a smile. He was beginning to understand. He had always had his suspicions about Acting Inspector Potts. That photo of him and Mayor Davis together like fast friends was yet another hint that Potts, like Davis and much of the Cleveland Police Department, was probably corrupt beyond repair. No one had anything concrete on Davis, but it was obvious to any schoolboy that he was one of the slimiest politicians ever to sit in the mayor's office. Many policemen were receiving protection money and other rewards for turning a blind eye to certain crimes on their beats. Others were receiving salary bonuses and unwarranted promotions, solely because of their political bent or their loyalty to the administration. Hank even had some suspicions about certain lieutenants, but he had never been able to wholly convince himself that Inspector Potts had been bought. But if Potts was indeed in the pay of a mobster or a politician, and if he truly believed the Andrassy case was tied to the mob, that would be a good reason for him to ask his two investigating detectives to lay off the case.

"All I can say," said Finnegan, "is that I think you're wrong, but I'll accept your decision."

"Lambert?" Potts was guttural, barking his words like an old lazy hound. "What about you?"

Potts had called Hank's bluff. After what Hank had already said, he could easily take the next step and resign rather than acquiesce. But he was more practical than he was principled, and Potts had promised that he could continue to investigate the case on his own time. In the end he took a deep breath and said, "Yes, fine."

"I knew you would come around," said Potts. "You know, Inspector Cody was disappointed in you boys. Said you'd failed to solve his final case."

Hank held his tongue. He still resented the request Inspector Cody had made of him just before retiring. Since then,

Hank had been examining the history of the Lady of the Lake, as the trunk had been dubbed by the press, and recognized a similarity to the Andrassy double murder. If the resemblance was more than skin deep, that meant three had already been killed, while the killer himself was no longer in danger of being caught.

"But I want you to know how proud I am of you," Potts continued. "You boys have done a hell of a job."

"Thank you, sir," Hank said, but couldn't resist adding, "I'm sure the killer thinks so, too."

# 6 November 1935

**3:10 P.M.**

Danny Cottone thumbed through the magazines on the rack at Hessler's Drugs, looking for the latest issue of *Weird Tales*. Sometimes it was hard to find, hiding behind *Thrilling Wonder Stories* or *Spicy Adventure Stories* or *Secret Agent "X" Detective Mysteries*, but once he unearthed the familiar giant *W* in the upper left-hand corner and saw the typically gruesome cover, there was no mistaking he had found the newest copy of "The Unique Magazine." The artwork on the covers always verged on the pornographic but never turned him on; it usually featured nude or seminude female figures about to be assaulted by some hideous demonic beast, but never scantily clad young guys in similar straits.

The cover of the latest issue boasted a naked woman surrounded by evil-looking snakes. Looking inside, Danny noticed there was a new Conan story by Robert E. Howard, who was Danny's favorite writer. In fact, all of Danny's favorite writers were *Weird Tales* writers; he read little else. He devoured their stories of cosmic horror, supernatural detection, other-dimensional worlds, and sword-wielding barbarians. At twenty-five cents a copy, it was a little pricey compared with other magazines, but it was well worth it.

Danny snatched up the November issue and took it up to the soda counter.

"Give me a cherry Coke float," said Danny to Ted, the soda jerk, as he sat upon a stool at the bar.

"Sure thing, Danny," said Ted, who was about Danny's age and kind of cute, in a lean athletic sort of way, with short brown hair shorn up the sides. The rest of his hair was hiding beneath a little white cap. He was dressed in a pressed white shirt with a stiff collar and red bow tie; Hessler's soda jerks always looked spiffy.

But Danny wouldn't mind seeing Ted on the cover of *Weird Tales,* nude save for a tattered loincloth, chained to a stone pillar in some hideous dungeon and screaming for his life, a smoldering brazier in the foreground, with Conan or some such warrior having suddenly arrived on the scene bearing a sword against Ted's demonic captors, who stand poised with their raven claws to strike against the hulking barbarian or possibly to rend and tear at the hapless Ted's flesh.

"You sure do know how to make a good float, Ted," said Danny smiling. "And how about some whipped cream and a maraschino cherry on top?"

"How's about two cherries, Danny?" Ted grinned back at him, and then whispered conspiratorially, "Only don't tell my boss."

"Who, Hessler? What does he care?"

"Oh, he can be kinda funny sometimes. Say, you buying that?" Ted pointed at Danny's magazine. Danny nodded. "Mind if I have a look-see?"

"Sure." Danny slid the magazine toward Ted. It was in no danger of getting wet; the soda jerks at Hessler's always kept the marble countertop wiped clean.

Ted, eyes agleam, examined the cover and let out a wolf whistle. "That's some dame, ain't it? Boy, what I wouldn't want to do to her!"

"Hey, hey, hey! No drooling on my magazine, OK?"

"It ain't yours yet."

Danny took a quarter from his pocket and flicked it up in the air. "Here," he said. Ted caught it in midflight, then went to the cash register to ring up the sale.

"Now how about that soda?"

"Just hold your horses, will ya? I'm getting it."

The bell at the front door rang, and Danny glanced back over his shoulder to see who it was. The rest of the store was devoid of customers.

Flo Polillo was shambling in, like some wretched ghoul out of an H. P. Lovecraft story. Beneath a small pillbox hat, her graying hair streamed out in one big mess. She looked as if she hadn't had any sleep, and the threadbare coat she wore did nothing to flatter her figure. Her knees were wobbly, and she had bags under her eyes and far too much rouge on her cheeks. She didn't seem to notice Danny as she made her way to the prescription counter at the back of the store. No one was manning the prescription window, so she rang the service bell loudly several times.

"Hello!" she shouted.

"Jesus," Danny muttered. Last night had been election night; even though it had been a Tuesday, it had been a good night for business. Danny himself had hung out in the tavern at the Hollenden Hotel and ended up with more than his usual number of clients, as the drunken political hacks streamed out of the ballroom celebrating the election of a Republican mayor and looking for a good time. If Flo had played it smart, she would have entertained a similar number of johns, and at her age that was bound to leave her a little worn out. Danny himself had only woken up an hour ago, and a cherry Coke float was just the thing to start his day off right.

Ted was mixing the soda water with the cherry Coke syrup at the fountain. "Vanilla?" he asked wielding the ice cream scoop.

"You got it." Danny was trying to come up with some way he could land Ted in the sack. He didn't even want any money, just Ted's sweet soda jerk cock, with a touch of sarsaparilla on the tip.

Danny looked back over at Flo.

Mr. Hessler had come to the window and was taking the prescription that Flo had just retrieved from her purse.

Mr. Hessler was a fine-looking fellow, probably only six or seven years older than Danny, with beautiful shiny black hair and piercing eyes of a delicate amber color. In a matter of a few years, he had bought this old drugstore and built it up into the most popular in the neighborhood.

While Mr. Hessler went off to prepare Flo Polillo's prescription, Flo gazed blankly around the store until her eyes locked on Danny's. Danny smiled at her—poor old Flo!

"You!" she said. "What are you doing here?"

"Having a soda."

"You little runt. I ought to show you—" Flo came stomping past the magazine rack and café tables until she stood directly in front of Danny. He could smell whiskey on her breath. She suddenly grabbed him by the arm and shook him violently, knocking him off the stool and onto his feet.

"What's the big idea?"

Flo was still shaking him. "Stop stealing my men!"

"Aw, cut it out, Flo. I'm not stealing nobody."

"You're asking for it." Flo pushed Danny hard and he stumbled backward, knocking over an iron chair at one of the café tables and falling on the floor. "You little slut!"

"Flo, hey! Knock it off, huh? If they go with me, it's because they like me, OK? None of them even give you a glance! Is that my fault?"

Danny tried to get up from the floor, but Flo landed a kick to his ribs with the sharp point of her shoe. It hurt like hell. She kicked him a second time just as he was howling with the pain of the first blow.

"That'll teach you!" Flo landed another kick. "You fairy maggot!" *Kick.* "Stupid little whore!" *Kick.* "I don't want to see you around Charlie's no more. You're saying bad things about me. You're scaring them off, you two-bit cocksucker!"

"Ow! Shit! Jesus Christ, Flo! Stop it!" Flo's huge figure stood over him, her purse swinging back and forth from her right arm with every kick she planted. She stared down at him like a maniac, her eyes red and rimmed with tears.

"Oh, I'll stop it, all right. After I've cracked your nuts, you bitch!"

Just then, Danny saw Mr. Hessler and Ted both step in and grab Flo by the arms.

"Come on, Mrs. Polillo, I won't have that in my store."

Flo struggled a bit, but they soon had her seated in a chair on the other side of the room from where Danny lay. Danny rubbed his ribs where they hurt the most, and found that he was bleeding a little where she had broken his skin. The blood was spreading out and staining his blue cotton shirt. He sat himself up and leaned against a barstool; his ribs hurt too much for him to sit up so fast.

Flo broke down in tears, holding her hands to her face.

"I'm sorry, Mr. Hessler," she said through her sobbing. "I didn't know what I was doing. . . . I didn't mean to hurt the boy—please don't call the cops. My mama just died, I'm a wreck. . . . I've never hit anybody before in my life. I'm trying to figure out how to get to Pierpont for my mama's funeral, but I don't have the money. . . . If I can't see my mama, I'm going to die. I didn't mean to hurt him . . . honest, I swear. . . . I'm not trying to cause any trouble."

Mr. Hessler promised he wouldn't call the cops, but told her he wouldn't tolerate that kind of behavior in his store in the future. He also suggested she lay off the booze. "You're in no condition to be drinking."

Ted, meanwhile, came over and helped Danny to his feet.

Mr. Hessler sold Flo her prescription and hastily escorted her to the door. "She had no right," he said angrily upon her exit.

"You got a rag?" Danny asked, holding up a bloodstained finger he had wiped his chest with.

"I've got better than that," said Mr. Hessler, who ducked behind the far display case and came back with some gauze, bandages, and antiseptic. "Here, let me take care of you."

Ted helped Danny off with his jacket and shirt. The left side of his ribs was marked with redness and swelling that looked like the makings of some pretty good bruises, along with several spots where his skin had been gouged, where he was bleeding. Danny sat back down upon a stool while Hessler soaked his wounds with antiseptic and then fixed up some good bandages with gauze and adhesive tape.

"You should have a doctor look at that. You might have some cracked ribs." Mr. Hessler looked down at him with a friendly smile. He soaked some more gauze in the antiseptic and wiped off the areas around the wounds, and his fingers brushed up against Danny's nipples.

"Yes, sir," Danny said.

Up close, Hessler was strikingly handsome. Danny had noticed this before, but never under such intimate circumstances. To be sitting here now, having his wounds tended to by so beautiful a man, was making him excited. Every man, appealing or not, was a potential customer, but this man was something different. Hessler had a magnetic presence that seemed to suck Danny up. When Danny looked up into his eyes, he couldn't look away; he was ensnared by the strength of his gaze. He could feel himself being healed through Hessler's ministrations. The pharmacist was taking care of him nicely.

Ted handed Danny his float, complete with two maraschino cherries.

"Oh, is that yours?" asked Hessler. "Two ch——! Oh, well, I guess that's OK. Listen, kid, this is yours. On the house, you might say."

"Gee, thanks, Mr. Hessler," Danny said, grinning ear to ear. He knew how to make himself cute in the eyes of any beholder.

"Is that your magazine, too?"

Danny nodded.

Mr. Hessler handed it to him. "With my compliments," he said, and ruffled Danny's hair as one would a dog's.

"He's already paid for it," said Ted from behind the soda fountain.

"Well, go get a quarter from the register, then! Give him back his two bits!"

"Yes, sir," said Ted, scurrying off to the machine and ringing up No Sale.

"Just between you and me," said Hessler in a whisper, quite close to Danny's ear, "I'm sure Mrs. Polillo was dead wrong about you. You're worth a lot more than that."

"Yes, sir," Danny said with a wink, and took a powerful sip from his soda through the thin red-striped straw.

# 11 December 1935

**11:42 A.M.**

City Hall's polished mosaic tile floors echoed with the footfalls and friendly discourse of working men and women heading out for an early lunch, stuffing arms into greatcoats, tucking in scarves, and fixing hats just so before having to go outside and face the bitter wind coming off the lake. The skylights in the vaulted ceiling allowed the dull grayish light to filter in and gave the pillared and brightly painted interior a somber cast—a sample of the gloom that awaited them outside.

Eliot Ness felt like the odd man out, walking against the steady stream pouring out of City Hall's sluice gates. Hat in hand, he unbuttoned his overcoat and removed it, tossing it over one arm. He had to ask a uniformed security officer directions to the mayor's office. Harry Davis, the former mayor and a Democrat, had never invited him over.

When at last he turned down the correct corridor and entered the office, he found no one waiting in the outer room except the middle-aged secretary, who was probably anxious to get to lunch herself. She looked up at him with a polite smile and a cold stare from behind her steel-rimmed glasses.

"May I help you, young man?"

"Yes, I'm here to see Mayor Burton."

"I'm sorry, he's quite busy."

"He wanted me to come at once, but I guess I—"

"Oh," said the secretary, as if the thought had only then crossed her mind that this bright young fellow might be the one being interviewed for the position of director of public safety. She glanced at her calendar and licked the tip of her pencil. "I'm sorry, what was your name?"

"Ness," he said, and cleared his throat. "Eliot Ness. That's with one *l.* "

The mayor had telephoned Ness at his office earlier in the morning and asked him to come over as soon as possible for a meeting about a job. Yet despite Ness's interest, he had found himself embroiled in Treasury Department matters, and it had taken some time to get away. City Hall was a mere twelve blocks from his office at the Standard Building on Ontario Avenue; he had walked briskly to make up for lost time. He only hoped the mayor hadn't forgotten about him altogether and already gone to lunch.

"Oh, I'm dreadfully sorry. It's just that you didn't look like—oh, never mind!" The secretary's smile changed from polite to genuine. "The mayor wanted me to send you right in once you . . . arrived."

"I am late," he stated simply. He disliked excuses from others and never offered them himself.

"Here, let me take your hat and coat."

Ness obliged her and was shown into the inner office through tall dark-stained doors. Several cardboard boxes remained unpacked; Burton had been mayor for exactly one month. The windows behind the desk offered what would be in the summer a magnificent view of Lake Erie and the East Ninth Street docks, but was today a sober panorama of gray sky and dull choppy water, soon to freeze along the beach. After one year in Cleveland, Ness knew to expect a winter no less severe than those in Chicago.

Mayor Harold H. Burton rose immediately upon Ness's entering and stepped out from behind the desk, his hand proffered in greeting. He was a short man, and his suit had been tailored to fit a rather plain figure, neither fat nor thin. His hairline was receding and the hair itself turning silver, though he was yet neither bald nor old. He was clean shaven and wore no spectacles, and his dark-ringed eyes glimmered brightly from beneath a serious brow.

"Mr. Ness, please, have a seat." Burton was cordial.

"Thank you, Your Honor." Ness shook his hand and sat in the leather-upholstered chair opposite the desk, which squeaked as he shifted in his seat. "Sorry I'm late."

"No matter," said the mayor as he returned to his leather swivel chair. "This shouldn't take long."

"I came over as soon as I could get away."

"I understand." Burton seemed to scrutinize Ness the way a careful man might inspect a used car, looking beyond the slick paint job and checking under the hood, slamming the doors, kicking the tires. The open file in front of Burton held his attention. "Quite a résumé you've got here for a man your age. Ph.D. from the University of Chicago. Special agent of the Prohibition Bureau at age twenty-four. Selected to head special Justice Department task force two years later. Led the crackdown on bootlegging operations in Chicago, and had Al Capone behind bars before you were thirty."

"With all due respect, sir, it wasn't that easy. I nearly got myself killed, and I'm not solely responsible for nabbing Capone. I had a lot of help, and some of it was plain dumb luck."

"Nor am I solely responsible for everything that goes on in this city, Lord knows. But I am the mayor, and that does count for something. The city's facing a crisis. I ran on a law and order ticket—but I presume you're aware of that." Burton paused and his eyebrows came together. "You *are* a Republican."

"Oh, yes, sir."

"Frankly, I hadn't even heard of you until two weeks ago. I'd asked a lot of people for advice on this appointment— business types, community leaders—and they kept pitching me your name. Joe Keenan over at Justice said you'd be perfect—almost as if he were campaigning for you."

"I assure you I never asked anyone to go to bat for me."

"Yet your interest in the job is no secret."

"Well, to be frank, I've had my eye on it ever since your election, and I may have discussed it with one or two friends,

Joe Keenan among them. I'd be less than honest if I pretended otherwise."

"And I must admit that until your name came up, I'd had a hard time finding anyone with the slightest interest in tackling it. Just between you and me, I originally offered it to Joe, but he turned it down cold and gave me your name instead."

Ness grinned. "Joe's a swell guy. But he likes it pretty well over at Justice."

"And you don't at Treasury?"

"Well, sir, it can be damned frustrating to have the police working against you all the time—and not just the city, but the county as well. Cleveland's considered a safe haven for mobsters these days, did you know that? And as long as they can buy off the cops, we can't touch them. What we've got to do is two things: cut off their money and get rid of crooked cops. Only when they've lost their 'protection' will we have them licked. That's how we tightened the noose around Scarface Al. If you want to do the same to the Cleveland mafia, I'm the one who knows how."

"Is there really such a thing, Mr. Ness?"

"The mafia? You bet. If you had a couple of hours to spare, I could run down their whole history since coming to America in 1899. Remember those policy men who turned up dead a few months ago? And then there was that double murder in Kingsbury Run—a mafia hit if ever there was one. It's customary for them to hack off a guy's genital organs with a stiletto and toss them next to his body like that. We saw it all the time in Chicago. So you can't tell me there's no mafia in Cleveland."

"Yes, fine." The mayor seemed satisfied with Ness's answer. "You should see the file I've got on you, by the way."

"Oh? I imagine it's very complete."

Harold Burton had been a big wheel in local Republican politics for a long time, and now that he was the mayor of the sixth-largest city in the nation, he wielded a great deal of power. Luckily, nothing in Ness's decidedly uncheckered past could possibly do him any harm.

"You were the tennis champ at the University of Chicago?"

"Yes, sir."

"Ever play handball?"

"I'm no slouch."

"Good. I've been looking for a new partner. I take it the idea of being safety director appeals to you."

"Oh, very much," said Ness. "But you won't find the police and fire departments too keen on me."

"Really. Why is that?"

"They're complacent, inefficient, corrupt—just like in Chicago. Some are even inebriated on duty. If I were put in charge, I would mete out real discipline—reprimands, suspensions, what have you. I want to know I can trust my own men. Right now standard procedure is to shuffle them off to the Traffic Bureau, where they do even more harm, as far as I'm concerned. We've got far too many motorists killing people, and it doesn't make much sense to put drunken cops out directing traffic—"

"No, I suppose not." An enigmatic twinkle sprang to Burton's eyes. "I think you've misunderstood me, Mr. Ness. This isn't an interview, it's an appointment."

"Oh." Ness was shocked into silence.

"You do want the job."

"Yes, of course I want it." Ness spoke almost without thinking, but he would be stupid not to take it. At thirty-two, he would be the youngest man in the country to hold such a position in a major city. It offered him a chance to rid the police department of corruption and restore the confidence of the citizenry. His brain was spinning with ideas. Police science was brimming with new approaches and new technology, and he was eager to try them all out.

"Very well," said Burton. "Here's a copy of the city charter and some other things that might interest you." Burton handed Ness a sheaf of papers and stood up. "Congratulations."

Ness rose as well, and they shook hands.

Burton pressed a button on his intercom. "Send in Joe Crowley, will you?—and call the press room."

"Yes, Mr. Burton." The secretary's voice was squawky over the speaker.

"Might as well get you sworn in," said Burton, stepping

out from behind the desk and placing an arm around Ness's shoulders. "I want this in the evening papers."

Ness was taken aback. "But I haven't even tendered my resignation yet."

Burton shrugged. "So do it after lunch. In the meantime, just pretend that I gave you the job over the phone and you resigned before heading over to City Hall. Makes for better copy. Now smile, boy."

Ness was overcome by a strange feeling of déjà vu. The entire meeting reminded him of September 28, 1929—the single most significant day in his life—when, at age twenty-six, he had met with George Emmerson Q. Johnson, the U.S. district attorney for Chicago, and been asked to head the select squad of prohibition agents the press would later dub "the Untouchables." The task that lay ahead of him now was no less daunting, and this time he might not prove so lucky. He had the uneasy feeling he was starting from scratch—yet the very prospect gave him a much-needed boost of adrenaline.

Within two beats, the office doors swung wide open. The room filled with newsmen, and flashbulbs were going off all over—just like old times.

# 24 December 1935

**10:23 P.M.**

"Daddy?"

"Yes, sweetie?"

"Is Santa really going to fall through our roof and break his back?"

"Now who told you that?"

"Mommy did!"

Hank pretended to laugh. "Honey, she was just foolin'. I promise you our little roof can withstand ol' Saint Nick, plus his sleigh and his reindeer, too."

"Yeah, that's what I told her."

"Oh, did you?"

"Uh-huh." Becky Lambert nodded her head up and down in cute-as-pie Shirley Temple fashion.

Hank stroked Becky's curly locks, kissed her forehead, and tucked her in for the night. "There's a good girl. Now you go to sleep and dream nice dreams."

"I'm going to dream of sugar plum fairies!"

"Oh, really?"

Cathy had taken Becky and Luke to see *The Nutcracker* the other day, but the murder of a bakery delivery truck driver had prevented Hank from going, and he realized now that

he had never himself actually seen *The Nutcracker,* although
he had heard it on the radio. If a sugar plum fairy came to
him in his dream, he wouldn't be able to tell it from your
regular garden-variety.

Hank reached over to Luke's bed to tuck him in and found
him fast asleep already, his sandy blond hair tousled against
his pillow. Hank pulled up the covers, fixed them firmly
around his son's sleeping figure, and kissed him on the forehead.

"*Da*-ad!" said Luke upon being kissed. He opened his
eyes and made a yucky face. He was two years older than
Becky and perhaps had reached the age at which kisses from
his father were not devoutly to be wished.

"You were playin' possum," said Hank. "You're going to
get whiskered!"

"No, Dad!" Luke protested. "Stop!"

But it was too late. Hank was rubbing his cheek against
Luke's, his five-o'clock shadow tickling his son's fine
smooth skin. Luke was laughing now and cringing against
his father's onslaught.

"There," said Hank when he was finished, and thought,
*That's what you get for not wanting me to kiss you.* Luke's
covers were a mess, so Hank had to tuck him in all over
again. Then he turned off the lamp on the night table between the two single beds. The wind was whistling outside
the windows, blowing the snow into large drifts on the lawn
outside.

"Now, if I hear so much as a peep out of either of you . . ."
he advised, making his usual hollow threat. He never told
them what he might do to them should he hear so much as a
peep, but that only allowed their fertile imaginations to run
wild. Better for them to wonder. " 'Night, all."

"Good night, Daddy," said Becky.

" 'Night," said Luke.


**10:45 P.M.**

"Do you need any help with the presents?" asked Cathy,
lying in bed next to Hank, rollers in her hair.

"Naw, I'm going to wait till after midnight. I'd rather do it myself, anyway." Hank was staring up at the ceiling, imagining the cracks and bubbles widening and popping, crying out for replastering. He hoped it could last until spring without the roof crashing in on them. Somehow, he was thankful no reindeer would be prancing their little hoofs on his fragile escarpment this evening.

"Oh, then I guess we've got a little time to kill," said Cathy.

Under the sheets she rolled over, aligning her body against Hank's and placing her hand on his chest. He always wore pajama bottoms, but eschewed tops because they itched. His chest hair was fine and plentiful, a shade darker than that on his head, and Cathy loved entwining her fingers in the curls near his nipples, as she was doing now.

"Sorry, honey. I'm very tired," Hank said, continuing to stare at the ceiling. "Ness's shake-up has got the whole department on edge."

"Sure, but I know how to work out those kinks." Cathy's hand traveled down past his pubic hair and then her finger found his limp prick and began to stroke it.

"No," he said.

Cathy sighed and removed her hand, but did not sulk. During the first years of their marriage, Hank had surrendered himself to her strong sexual appetite, primarily because he wanted to produce children. Now that this had been accomplished, Hank found Cathy's behavior unbecoming. They had decided on no more children, and the risk of her getting pregnant a third time was too great. He loved her, yet sometimes in bed she could act downright whorish, and this only served to lessen Hank's desire.

"Dottie is having a fit," Cathy said, punching her pillow. "She says Jack hasn't done anything wrong."

"Maybe not," said Hank. But that didn't change the situation. Jack Finnegan had been transferred—which was a polite way of saying demoted—for unspecified offenses. If Finnegan was guilty of anything, he had managed to do it right under Hank's nose for four years and had never confided it to him despite their close friendship.

But then Hank had his own secrets that could easily damage his career, namely the street hustlers he met on the sly.

Smart guys kept their lips sealed and their eyes peeled, but Finnegan obviously wasn't smart enough to avoid being caught doing whatever it was he had been doing.

He wasn't alone. After Mayor Burton's election, the word in the locker room was that Chief Matowitz would be fired before you could say "boo," but instead Burton and Ness were using Matowitz as their hatchet man. One hundred twenty-two police officers had already been "transferred," including a delegation of sergeants and detectives, not to mention twenty-eight lieutenants and even one captain—and this was only the beginning. Each precinct captain had been put on notice that no misconduct would be tolerated among his men, and that he himself would be held accountable. The shake-up would continue until Ness could reorganize the department from top to bottom, and that meant that nobody was safe unless they had played it that way, as had Hank.

Hank could have had the money to fix his roof long ago. He could have bought that '36 Studebaker coupe he had been eyeing since September and rid himself of his debts. All he would have had to do was play the game the way some of the boys played it. Up until now, he had turned a blind eye to the corruption around him because he could do nothing about it. Now that the shit had finally hit the fan, Hank only hoped that none of it would land on him.

He wondered what Cathy would say if she learned about his dalliances with some of the young hustler punks in the Roaring Third. She would never understand why her husband would want to spend half the night in a cheap hotel room with a young gentleman, nor would she understand that these men weren't necessarily always so gentle.

"Does this mean a promotion?" Cathy asked.

"No, not really. But I did manage to get Joe Sweeney to put me back on the Andrassy case, and since poor old Jack's out of the picture, that means I'm in charge of the investigation. Doesn't mean I'll bring home any more money."

Cathy considered for a moment, lightly flicking Hank's elbow with her fingernail. "I always did wonder how Dottie could afford all those coats and hats and things."

"Well, now you know," said Hank. "Would you rather do

without the coats and hats, or would you rather have a crooked cop for a husband?"

"I don't know, Hank," she said with a laugh. "My closet's pretty bare. Maybe Dottie and I should swap men."

"You'd rather be married to a traffic cop?"

"One with a Packard? I wouldn't mind one bit."

"He's had to sell the Packard."

"Then I guess I'll have to settle for you."

Cathy reached for him, but Hank pushed her aside and got up off the bed. He stretched his muscles and yawned. "Guess it's time for Santa to make himself a fresh pot of coffee."

# 10 January 1936

**5:09 P.M.**

Mott Hessler watched the ball skip around the spinning roulette wheel until at last it came to rest on seventeen black, and a smile came to his lips. A small stack of chips was pushed over to join his existing pile. He scooped up his chips and was about to place half of them on thirty-two red when he saw one of the security men whispering into the ear of Jimmy Barnes, the young guy running the roulette table.

"The club is closing," announced Jimmy to the table. "Everybody please take your winnings to the cashiers' windows, and make it snappy."

A general groan of discontent welled up at the table, joining similar noises now coming from the thousand or so people in the huge gambling hall.

Hessler had been staring so intently at the roulette wheel that he had failed to notice what was going on around him. The tuxedoed and sport-jacketed members of the Harvard Club, along with their wives, mistresses, whores, or mothers, were hurriedly gathering their winnings or their losses and making their way to the cashiers' windows. Many could already be seen at the front entrance, the men putting on their overcoats and hats, some of the women wrapping themselves in mink and sable. "Security" men, big plug-uglies who looked out of place in their expensive duds, had come out of the woodwork wielding submachine guns. They guarded the joint from positions along a small wooden balcony that encircled the hall, just a few feet above everybody's heads. Other employees of the club were clearing off the tables and packing everything up.

Although everyone was working quickly, no one seemed to be in a panic, so Hessler theorized that the management had been tipped off to a police raid that had not yet occurred. Hessler expected nothing less from the Harvard Club, which always ran efficiently and had a reputation among its members—rich and impoverished alike—as a safe place to gamble, where no one would ever be in danger of being carted off to jail. The club was located just outside of Cleveland proper, in little Newburgh Heights, and Hessler wouldn't have been surprised if the local police department had been paid handsomely for keeping their mitts out of the club's business.

The lines were so long at the cashiers' windows that Hessler simply dumped his chips into the pockets of his tuxedo jacket, knowing full well that he would have ample opportunity to cash them in at some point in the future. Even if a raid were about to occur, he knew the club would reopen soon, if not at this location, then somewhere else. The police, all in all, could do very little about it one way or the other.

Hessler headed for the front entrance, past the throngs of Clevelanders who had been hoping either to add to their fortunes or rescue themselves from debt. He recognized many of the faces but spoke to no one. Although some of the club's members were poor suckers risking their entire Relief checks hoping to transform them into millions, the large majority of members came from the same social set as Hessler's parents—the rich bankers, businessmen, corporate lawyers, and politicians who showed up at all the same functions like a pack of lemmings, dressing alike and following each other around simply to keep up appearances.

They knew Mott Hessler as well but were unlikely to speak to him; although he was indeed a Hessler, he was *that* Hessler, the black sheep of the family, banished from Euclid Avenue like Cain to the land of Nod, which in Hessler's case lay several blocks west and one to the south, along Prospect, where he was making out splendidly with his drugstore without any help from his family.

Despite the best efforts of his parents to cut him off from their money, they could do nothing to touch the modest trust fund left behind for him by his late grandfather, Douglass Hessler, founder of the Ohio National Oil Company, who had passed away a few years before Mott Hessler's magnificent transgressions. Mott Hessler had been granted control of the monies and stocks left him by his grandfather upon his graduation from pharmacy school, and for the last few years had had few financial worries, despite the fact that he had lost a significant amount of his inheritance on these selfsame roulette wheels and blackjack tables at the Harvard Club. He had been attempting to double his inheritance and use it to launch a chain of drugstores across the state. Instead, he had struck upon a prolonged losing streak, but he had no doubt he could win it back.

Hessler nodded at a few people as he made his way smiling through the gathering throng, saying, "Pardon me . . . excuse me, sir . . . pardon me, madam." The faces stared back in shock, as if they had seen a ghost. They knew him for the most part by his reputation, but Hessler doubted seriously whether any of their number had the slightest knowledge of just what, exactly, had occurred to have so thoroughly emblazoned the scarlet letter, as it were, upon him. All manner of vicious rumor had been spread, little of which even approached the truth, but all of which he found wickedly flattering.

He gave each of them what he imagined to be a smoldering look of pity as he squeezed through the crowd. They were every bit as mad as the masked revelers in that story of Poe's, except that their faces were easily more hideous than even the most grotesque of masks. Hessler imagined himself as Prince Prospero as he strode from the main hall up the red-carpeted steps toward the coat-check boy, but unlike Prospero, he remained untouched by the all-consuming Red Death.

The pale skinny arm of the coat-check boy handed him his camel's-hair overcoat, plaid wool scarf, and black fedora. Hessler tipped the boy a one-dollar chip; the lad smiled keenly, showing no sign of the pestilence upon his face.

8:22 P.M.

Eliot Ness was attending the city council meeting, listening as they hashed out Mayor Burton's $10 million budget for 1936. It was of particular importance to him because it contained several provisions of his that would enable him to hire better-qualified policemen and improve the quality of the existing force. But the meeting was dragging on, and the council members had yet to even discuss the budget requests of the police department.

In the hands of these duly elected bags of wind now rested Ness's proposed police training school, which would not only educate rookies but also reeducate those already on the job. The current hiring procedure consisted of a simple written test, after the passing of which an applicant was handed a gun and assigned a beat. Little training was provided—the ultimate downfall of the current force. In his opinion, a police officer ought to be equally adept as a marksman, a boxer, a wrestler, a sprinter, a diplomat, a memory expert, and possess a thorough knowledge of various other subjects.

Besides the training school, he had a number of other reforms planned, but the school was the biggest-ticket item and the hardest sell.

Ness still felt uncomfortable in his new position as administrator. His new job tied him down to the desk too often, and he was constantly looking for any excuse to get out on the street and away from his stuffy office. But the previous safety director had left a mess behind, and Ness felt intimidated by the amount and scope of the work that lay ahead of him.

Ness was about to fall asleep with his eyes open when he

felt a tapping on his shoulder. He turned around to find John
Flynn, his executive assistant, bending over and whispering
in his ear.

"Phone call in your office," said Flynn in hushed tones.
"It's the county prosecutor. He says it's urgent."

Ness nodded, dismissing Flynn, and gathered up his papers before quietly slinking out of the city council chambers
and catching up with his assistant in the hallway.

Back in his office, he picked up the receiver. "Ness speaking," he said.

"Ness, Frank Cullitan," came the agitated voice of the
prosecutor.

Ness rubbed his eyes with his thumb and index finger, still
trying to shake the dull deliberations of the council from his
mind. "Frank, what can I do for you?"

"We're in a hell of a mess, and you're about the only one
left who can—"

"Calm down, Frank, calm down. What you got cooking?"

"We're raiding the Harvard Club."

Ness grinned from ear to ear and watched John Flynn's
eyebrows rise in curiosity. The idea of raiding the Harvard
Club was splendidly audacious and came as something of a
surprise. "Who's we?"

"Me, my staff, and twenty constables sworn in by Judge
Calhoun over in Cleveland Heights. Judge also gave us a
warrant for search and seizure, as well as warrants for the arrest of the proprietors, Misters Hebebrand, Patton, and Gal-
lagher. Old Shimmy Patton himself met me at the door but
wouldn't let us in. His boys came outside and drew their
tommy guns on us. Shimmy promised to mow us down if we
tried to break in, and we hightailed it across the street to the
Ohnoco station. I'm using their pay phone, matter of fact. All
my men are huddled here in the garage drinking stale coffee."

"Sounds like you could use some protection. But Newburgh's out of my jurisdiction. You should talk to the sheriff,
not me."

"I already tried to talk to Sulzmann. Deputies wouldn't let
me speak to him, but after a while they called me back and
said they couldn't spare any men unless the mayor of New-

burgh himself specifically asked for them. Some shit about 'home rule.' They said we're on our own. Of course, the mayor of Newburgh is nowhere to be found. Not that I expected anything from him. I tried to reach Chief Matowitz but couldn't track him down. So I'm calling you. We need some help down here—and as soon as possible."

"Hold everything," said Ness, absently loosening his tie. "I'll be there."

He hung up, toggling the cradle of the candlestick phone with his finger. He dialed for the operator and identified himself, asking her to get him the office of the Cuyahoga County sheriff. In his one month as safety director, Ness had not yet met the man: John M. "Honest John" Sulzmann, a Democrat who had been in office for five years and who was no fan of Mayor Burton's administration. If the sheriff wouldn't help, Ness was prepared to vent his whole goddamned Republican spleen at him.

"Sheriff's office. Deputy Murphy," came the sleepy-sounding voice on the other end.

"This is Eliot Ness. Get me Sulzmann."

"He's home, sick in bed. Who was this again?"

"Eliot Ness. Safety director for the City of Cleveland. Now you listen to me, Deputy Murphy, and listen good. At this very moment, Prosecutor Cullitan is at the Harvard Club with several of his staff, and their lives are endangered. As a citizen, I am calling on you and the sheriff to send some men out there to protect them."

"I'm afraid I can't do that, Mr. Ness. Mr. Cullitan should call the mayor of the village and let him ask for assistance if he thinks he needs it. That is in accordance with the sheriff's home-rule policy."

"Home rule!" Ness shouted into the receiver, grasping the neck of the phone and holding it inches from his face, while he paced behind his desk. "What the hell is that all about? Will you go out or won't you?"

"I'll have to call the sheriff and I'll call you back."

"To hell with calling back! I'll wait on the phone."

While Ness waited, he explained everything to John Flynn, whose curiosity had risen noticeably during the course of the phone calls. Finally, after nearly ten wasted minutes, the deputy returned to the phone. Ness could hear him chewing, either gum or tobacco.

"Well?" Ness prompted.

"Nope," said Deputy Murphy. "Sheriff doesn't see why everyone's making such a fuss over a little restaurant out in the boonies, and he says we're not going out there. He suggests you call Mayor Sticha over in Newburgh and—"

Ness hung up.

"Dammit!" He turned to Flynn. "John, I want you to go to the sheriff's department and see what you can do. I'm going to need all the men I can muster."

"Sure," said Flynn. "But what are you going to do?"

"I'm going out there," Ness responded, "but I've got to get Burton's OK first." He chuckled uneasily to himself. "This is one hell of a sticky situation."

"Then why are you smiling?" Flynn's smirk made his thin mustache look crooked.

"Frankly, John, I never could resist a sticky situation."

## 8:48 P.M.

It took some time to get Mayor Burton out of the city council meeting, but once that was accomplished, Ness was brief and to the point. He advised the mayor of his decision to assist Cullitan, but Burton counseled against taking any action.

"Cullitan's a goddamned Democrat," he said, "and besides, it's out of your jurisdiction. I don't want my safety director getting killed on some damn-fool crusade. Shimmy Patton doesn't play for marbles."

"Neither did Capone," Ness said, "and he's in Alcatraz."

This left the mayor speechless.

Ness continued: "Harry, look at it this way. Patton's ours. He's a Cleveland gangster. The money he makes in Newburgh makes its way into the pockets of our own police and officials. Unless we can cut off his income, he'll have more say over public safety than I do. I don't give a damn about jurisdiction. I'll go as a private citizen. We'll be there to protect Cullitan and his men and let them serve their warrants. But I won't do it if you say no."

Although Mayor Burton was a politician, he was also a reasonable man. In the end, he agreed with Ness and gave him the go-ahead, adding, "Just so long as no one gets killed."

"Harry, I give you my word. That's the whole point. Now, if you'll excuse me." Ness turned to go.

"Eliot," added the mayor, "don't let Patton pump you full of holes. I expect you to keep our date on the handball court tomorrow."

Ness gave him a thumbs-up, and then left City Hall as fast as he could, running down the grand staircase two steps at a time.

He drove his own Hudson 6 over to the Central Police Station on East Nineteenth Street, keeping his windows rolled down a crack to keep the windshield from fogging up. He had the car radio tuned to WGAR, which at the moment was playing a commercial jingle known popularly as "The Ohnoco Song," advertising Cleveland's own Ohio National Oil Company, sung in unison by some fey chorus boys who sounded as if they couldn't tell a carburetor from a cornhole:

> When your flivver has a shiver
> And her tank is running low,
> Drive on up and give her
> To the boys at Ohnoco!
>
> We'll fill her up and shine her up
> And make her good as new,
> And all of us will always have
> A smiling face for you!
>
> Oh, no! (beep-beep) Oh, no!
> It's time for Ohnoco!
> Oh, no! (beep-beep) Oh, no!
> It's time for Ohnoco!

"And now, Ohnoco proudly brings you Al Purlie and his musical hit parade—"

Ness turned the radio off in disgust, passing the *Plain Dealer* building on his left, which reminded him he ought to give the three major newspapers a call and tip them off to the impending raid.

Once Ness arrived at Central Station, he parked his car and went inside, heading straight for the patrol counter, where he found several uniformed officers, some with arrested persons in custody, others huddled over noisy typewriters completing reports.

"If I could have your attention," Ness called over the mass of voices and the *rat-a-tat-tat* of machines. All heads turned and stared at him. He withdrew his wallet with his special golden safety director's badge and held it up. "I'm Eliot Ness, director of public safety," he announced. "I'm going on a raid and I need some recruits. I want only volunteers, preferably men going off duty. If you're young and have no families, even better, but I won't turn down any capable officer. I need as many men as I can get, but none of you will be paid. There won't be any overtime in it for you, only the satisfaction of shutting down the Harvard Club and twisting the screws on Shimmy Patton. We're going to need some big guns and lots of ammo. Anyone interested should meet me back here in front of the patrol counter in five minutes. Now, gentlemen, if you'll excuse me."

Several police officers were already getting up, eager grins on their faces. Others simply continued to stare in Ness's direction over their coffee mugs.

Ness put away his badge and headed for the locker room, intending to deliver the same spiel to any man he could find, either there or in the gym. Then he was going to head for the toilet and empty his bladder, as he had downed two cups of cold coffee at his office before driving over here, and it had already snaked through his system.

**10:10 P.M.**

Driving his own personal vehicle, Ness led a stream of marked squads and motorcycles south of the city to 3111 Harvard Avenue in Newburgh, transporting three sergeants along with him so they could talk strategy. Each sergeant was to lead a contingent of volunteers, the first being twenty-nine uniformed patrolmen; the second, ten motorcycle cops; and the third, four plainclothes detectives. Their arms consisted of sawed-off shotguns, tear-gas pistols, and revolvers. Ness wanted the tear gas just in case things got out of hand. An old state statute still existed allowing for any citizen to make an arrest if a felony was committed in his presence; just in case anyone got shot, Ness would gas the bastards and storm the place.

They parked in the lot at the Ohnoco station across the street from the gigantic Harvard Club building. On the outside, the club was plain, perhaps thirty years old, but with new wooden cowlings around the windows preventing anyone from seeing inside. The outdoor lights of the club had been turned off, and Ness could see no one on the outside.

Ness got out of his car and told the sergeants to organize their men.

Immediately, Ness was swamped by three reporters and three photographers, one each from the *Plain Dealer,* the *Press,* and the *News*. They had all arrived before the police, thanks to the three phone calls Ness had made while at Central Station. Flashbulbs went off, and he tried to put his best law-and-order face forward.

"Where's the sheriff, Mr. Ness?" asked one of the reporters.

"Sick in bed," Ness responded. "Practicing something he calls 'home rule.' "

The reporters laughed as he pushed his way past them.

"Stick around, boys," said Ness, "and I'll give you a show."

Frank Cullitan's constables had left the relative comfort of the service station and spread out in locations around the front perimeter of the building, though a safe distance away from the entrance. Ness spotted the prosecutor himself standing by the gas pumps and talking with a young mechanic dressed in an oily Ohnoco jumpsuit.

"Frank," Ness called, and approached. "How does it look?"

Cullitan beamed when he saw Ness. He wore a black felt hat over his gray hair, and moon-shaped spectacles rested on his nose. He was a big man, though probably flabby under-neath his wool greatcoat. He and Ness shook hands.

"Well," Cullitan began, "they've managed to hold us off for five hours now. They've got one more load of equipment packed up on a truck in the back, but I can't touch it because our warrant's only for the building itself. I got Shimmy Pat-ton to let me in, alone, for a negotiation, but we just went around in circles. He tried to scare me off. A certified loony bird."

"Who exactly are these men of yours?" Ness asked. He wanted to know just what kind of force the good guys had amassed against the bad.

"Mostly private dicks," said Cullitan. "Calhoun swore them in this afternoon. I've got some more over at the Thomas Club out in Maple Heights. We've closed that one."

"Good work. Are they armed?"

"Pistols." Cullitan shrugged.

"OK." Ness scratched the stubble on his chin. "Mister Prosecutor, I think we'll do all right, you and me."

A worried look crossed Cullitan's face. "I don't want any bloodshed."

"Neither do I," said Ness, "but it may not be up to us."

The policemen from Central Station took their positions around the perimeter of the Harvard Club, staying as close to the trees as possible. Under ordinary circumstances, Ness would have had the squads park right in front of the club to provide some cover, but he was already overstep-ping his bounds by using city equipment, and couldn't allow the squads to get riddled with bullet holes. The sawed-off shotguns, pistols, and tear gas were also city property, and Ness would have to account for it all when this was over.

The men themselves had been warned of the risks they were taking. Ness had been unable to leave the station until ten o'clock when their shift had ended and they were off the police department payroll. If any one of these offi-cers, acting as private citizens, happened to be killed dur-ing this raid, their widows would never see so much as a dime of pension money. In the current economic climate, that was a great risk indeed, so Ness had been heartened by

the eager response he had received. These men were behind him 100 percent. It was enough to bring back the
heady excitement he had felt busting Capone's breweries
back in Chicago.

Ness stood in the middle of the Harvard Club parking lot,
Frank Cullitan a few steps to his side.

Ness himself was unarmed. The men surrounding the club
provided ample coverage, and a pistol in a shoulder holster
would have contributed little to his own safety.

Suddenly, the heavy steel front door swung open, creaking
on its hinges, and there upon the long darkened stoop stood
the fat, squat figure of James "Shimmy" Patton, dressed in a
green felt hat, a black overcoat, and a lengthy white scarf
that was whirled around his neck like a feather boa. He held
a submachine gun flat against his chest, pointed toward the
treetops. He rushed across the front stoop, cursing at the top
of his lungs.

"All right, you fucking coppers! Anyone that goes in there
gets their fucking head knocked off, understand? You've got
your fucking homes at stake, and we've got our fucking
property at stake. So back off if you know what's good for
you."

"I've tried every decent way I could," said Prosecutor Cullitan.

"No, you haven't!" Patton's tommy gun twitched.

"It's my job to close this place."

"Why don't you quit your fucking job?"

"Why don't you give up quietly?" countered Cullitan.

"You ain't making no pinch here. No pinches! Understand!" With that, Shimmy Patton withdrew and slammed
the front door behind him.

Ness glanced around to both sides of him and saw that
everyone was ready. He approached the steps of the club.

"Let's have a light here," he said, at which all the headlights of the police motorcycles and squads were trained on
the entryway. "All right? Let's go."

Ness took the steps two at a time, a contingent of shotgun-
wielding cops right on his heels.

He rapped on the cold metal door and observed a shadow
pass before the peephole, but heard no response from the

other side. "I'm Eliot Ness," he shouted. "I'm coming in with some warrants."

He tried the doorknob, but it was locked.

Nothing happened for the next five minutes. Ness wished he could kick the door down, but it was of thick metal set in a reinforced steel doorjamb. If nobody let them in, they would have to try their luck at an alternative entrance.

But at last, he heard a click and saw the knob turn, and the door was opened for them.

A tall Irish thug stood in the doorway, arms folded across his chest. "Who the hell do you think you are? You were only sworn in a few hours ago."

This hard guy had spoken his lines as if he had been coached. Obviously, Shimmy Patton knew how to obtain reliable information. He knew who Cullitan's men were and from where they had come, yet this stupid son-of-a-bitch had mistaken Ness for one of them.

Ness withdrew his special badge, which read: CITY OF CLEVELAND—DIRECTOR OF PUBLIC SAFETY. He smiled at the guy and stepped past him, meeting no resistance, and the rest of his recruits followed behind, covering every tuxedoed employee with their sawed-off shotguns. He saw no sign of the tommy guns Patton's gang had so enthusiastically brandished a while ago.

"All right, Frank," Ness advised, "let your men go in and serve their warrants. We'll back them up."

The whole place had indeed been cleaned out. It had been stripped of its notorious roulette, dice, and blackjack tables. Along the entire ninety-foot length of the right-hand wall was a huge race-chart blackboard, listing results from Santa Anita, Alamo Down, and Fair Grounds. Other than that, all that remained in the spacious gambling hall were streams of torn paper and a few framework baize dice tables.

Ness's men covered the scene while Cullitan's rounded up anyone they could find and gathered them in a corner near the counting room. Shimmy Patton was nowhere to be found, but they did managed to locate Arthur Hebebrand, one of the three proprietors named in the warrants. Hebebrand asked Cullitan if he and his aides could go into the money-counting room to retrieve their hats and coats, and the prosecutor allowed them to do so.

But when Hebebrand failed to return, Cullitan's constables rushed into the counting room and found the gangsters gone, having escaped through a small window near the ceiling. Somehow, this secret exit had gone uncovered by Cullitan's men outside.

As disheartening as this might have been for Ness, it remained Cullitan's responsibility, and the prosecutor seemed satisfied with closing the Harvard Club, which had eluded the grasp of the law for over twenty years. They found enough evidence lying around to close the place permanently as a gambling house: betting slips and change accounts in the counting room, as well as a storeroom housing an ample supply of ledger sheets and booking forms. The teletype itself had been removed from the teletype room, but ribbons of paper were scattered all over the floor, giving results for the races at Alamo Down.

Ness became occupied with the foyer of the club, whose ceiling was low and set with an odd glass window.

"Help me up here, will you?" he asked one of his detectives. He hadn't seen anything like this since his Chicago raids.

The detective cupped his hands and gave Ness a boost up. Ness placed his hands against the glass and tried to push it out, but it was heavier than he had figured. At last it popped free and he slid it off to the side. It was three-quarters of an inch thick and presumably bulletproof. Ness poked his head inside the hole but luckily saw no one hiding.

"Jesus Christ," said Ness. "An honest-to-God machine-gun nest."

He pulled himself up through the hole. Once inside, he found himself in a lighted cubby hole containing slits in the floors and walls that would have enabled Shimmy Patton's "security" men to fire their tommy guns directly into the foyer, the main gambling hall, or the counting room, in case of a raid or a heist.

This evening they could have had what the press would have referred to as a "wholesale slaughter." If Cullitan had tried to force his way in with his motley crew of constables, they would have been "mowed down" all right, just as Shimmy Patton had promised.

Finding the machine-gun nest made Ness more upset that they hadn't managed to nab Patton and his men. Thugs like that had no sense of right or wrong; they could shoot a cop in the back and then go home and kiss their mother good night without giving their crime a second thought. Ness had encountered gangsters who were family men by day and cold-blooded killers by night—people who, on the surface, were some of the nicest guys you would ever want to meet. They were real-life Jekyll-and-Hydes, scarier than any monster Ness had seen in a motion picture.

Ness jumped back down from the cubby hole and was immediately accosted by a reporter from the *Plain Dealer* seeking a statement. Rapidly his mind shifted gears, and he put himself into his public relations mode. He had had enough dealings with the press that he had developed a manner of speaking that would quote well, provided the reporter got it right. Sometimes he felt most at ease in front of a lanky guy in a cheap brown suit with a press tag stuck in the brim of his hat. These men were, for him at least, the bearers of good fortune.

A flashbulb went off in his face. He took a deep breath.

"Come on, Mr. Ness," said the reporter. "What's this raid got to do with rebuilding the police department?"

"Everything," Ness said simply, then paused for effect. "Shutting down these gambling joints can help us nail the lid on corruption, not just in the city but in the county, too. I hope you'll show this in its true light. It was a real victory for Prosecutor Cullitan, and I just hope the county people keep up their good work." He flashed a smile, and his picture was taken yet again. But he wasn't finished. "With their cooperation, my job of trying to keep Cleveland as free from crime as possible will be just that much easier."

The reporter scribbled down Ness's words with a pencil, grinning broadly, and Ness took a peek to make sure he was getting it right.

As the reporter walked away, Ness overheard him say to a photographer, "You ever heard so much canned corn?"

Ness smiled to himself; people thought he was a goody-two-shoes without also realizing how he could use this to his advantage. When Shimmy Patton read the papers tomorrow, he wouldn't be frightened one whit. He would remain over-confident and likely make a mistake. Then Ness would nab him to the surprise of everyone but himself.

# 26 January 1936

**11:37 A.M.**

Every few seconds, Hank Lambert had to use the cuff of his coat to wipe clear a small hole in the coating of frost on his windshield so that he could see well enough to reach the scene without causing another homicide in the process.

By the time he arrived, a crowd of about a dozen people had already gathered in the alley behind the Hart Manufacturing Company plant. Two beat officers were standing just inside the crowd waving their batons, trying to move the onlookers away from the site, while two big spotted mutts, one brown and one gray, ran around barking and wagging their tails with excitement.

Hank parked his unmarked detective car in the snow at the alley entrance, leaving room for the other detectives to park theirs once they arrived. Hank's immediate superiors had supposedly been following behind, but they must have gotten lost. Or perhaps they had had to stop to clean their windshields.

The weather report on the radio had told him it was all of ten degrees, with an expected high of about fourteen. The cold spell had hung over the Great Lakes region and the Northeast for two weeks and had been directly responsible for numerous deaths. The photo section of the morning paper showed a picture of Niagara Falls completely frozen over.

Hank fixed the muffler around his neck and fastened the top button of his overcoat before getting out of the car. The snow was crusty beneath his feet and crackled as he walked. His breath came out in a puff of steam.

Hank passed through the crowd and flashed his badge to the uniformed patrolmen, and saw before him the two half-bushel baskets the neighbors had found a few minutes ago.

Both baskets were draped with burlap bags. Hank knelt down, lifted the covering off the first basket and found himself staring at a human arm, severed at the shoulder and partially wrapped in a newspaper. Other body parts, similarly wrapped, lay beneath the first. Hank laid the burlap bag back across the top and checked inside the second basket, finding what appeared to be the lower half of a human torso, much of it covered with newspaper. All of the remains were frozen solid, with bits of frost and ice clinging to them.

"Jesus Christ," he muttered.

It was so cold outside and his nose was so clogged up that Hank could smell nothing. But the dogs could, and had; both of them were now lurking at the edge of the scene, tongues dripping with saliva as they stared toward the baskets, smiling in expectation with their ears pricked up.

*Sorry, boys,* Hank thought, *this isn't finders keepers.*

He stood up and scanned the crowd. "Which one of you is Charles Paige?"

A burly middle-aged man stepped forward. He wore no hat and his bald pate looked cold. "That's me."

Hank got out his notepad and pencil and took Paige's name and address. Paige was a butcher whose shop was around the corner. "You're the one who called us?"

"That's right."

"You the one who found the baskets?"

"No," Paige began, "I was just—"

A short, mustached Italian interrupted: "That was my dog, Lady."

"Oh?" Hank asked. "And who might you be?"

"Nick Albondante. It was Lady found the baskets."

"All right." Hank took Albondante's name and address.

"I thought they was some hams," said a colored woman.

"Yeah, and I figured maybe I'd been robbed," said Paige.

"That damn dog was barking all morning," said an older white woman standing behind the rest. "Wouldn't let up."

"Lady can track anything," said Albondante.

"Now, wait," said Hank. "One at a time. Let me see if I get this straight. Mr. Paige, you heard some barking and came out of your store to find—"

"No," said Paige. "I didn't hear it. It was that Negress come running up to me."

"I thought they was some hams," the colored woman repeated.

"Let me get your name and address," said Hank, and scribbled it down as she gave it to him: *Daisy Hayes, 2121 Charity Avenue.* "So you heard the dog barking. About what time was this?"

"Eleven or thereabout, but then I took my time a'cause of it bein' so damn cold out they."

"Let's say eleven-ten?" Hank offered.

"Sounds about right."

"I heard that damn dog at two-thirty in the morning," said the white woman who had spoken up before. "Kept me awake half the night with its yapping."

"That couldn't have been Lady," said Albondante. "She was with me all night, right by my bed."

"Well, maybe it was that other one," said the woman.

"Which one is Lady?" Hank asked Albondante.

"The brown one."

"They both yours?"

"No, sir. I never seen that one before." Albondante pointed at the gray one.

"Ma'am, is that the dog you saw barking at two-thirty this morning?"

"I don't know. I didn't get up to look. I just heard it yapping away, causing a ruckus all night."

"OK, enough," said Hank. He took the white woman's name and went on trying to figure everything out. "So Miss Hayes, you heard the dogs barking and ran out to see what was going on. What did you find when you came out?"

"They was these baskets in the ash heap, and I thought

maybe somebody forget they groceries or somethin'. That brown dog growled at me when I came up to take a peek."

"Hey, Lady never hurt nobody!" put in Albondante.

Daisy Hayes continued. "So I look inside, and I see all this meat. I thought they was some hams!"

"So I gathered," said Hank. "Go on."

"And I go down the alley and run into Mr. Paige at the corner, and I tell him about the hams, and he comes down and looks at it with me, but when we took another peek, they wasn't hams no mo'."

"Anything you'd like to add, Mr. Paige?"

The butcher shook his head, but then spoke. "That's pretty much how it happened. Like I said, when I heard there were some baskets full of hams, I figured some goon had come and pinched me during the night, so I went to see for myself. Then I came back to my shop and called the police."

Hank heard a car pulling up behind him, and he thought it might be Det. Lt. Harvey Weitzel and Det. Sgt. James Hogan, who should have been here by now. Instead, the second he saw a wiry fellow leap from the DeSoto wielding a camera and a flashbulb unit, he realized it was the press. This was no police photographer, this was a slobbering newshound.

"No pictures!" said Hank. "No one photographs anything until Lieutenant Weitzel gets here, understand?"

"What about the dog?" the photographer shouted.

"What dog?" Hank asked, annoyed that the press were already onto it.

"The dog that sniffed out the body." The photographer crouched to his knees and called the dogs over. "Come on, that's my baby!"

The dogs bounded across the snow toward him.

"My dog, Lady," said Albondante like a proud parent as the brown mutt sat before the photographer. "She's the one sniffed it out."

"Lady, huh?" said the photographer, scratching her behind the ears. He looked up at Albondante. "Why don't you stand right over there with her so we can get a shot."

Lady and her master walked over to the corner of the factory and waited.

The photographer rose to his feet and brushed the snow from his knees. He turned his attention to Hank while he popped in a fresh flashbulb. "You don't mind, do you, Detective?"

"Naw, go ahead," Hank said to him, beyond the hearing of the crowd at large, "shoot the bitch."

## 1:32 P.M.

Hank joined David Cowles in a laboratory at the Cuyahoga County Morgue over on Lakeside Avenue to help him inspect the material evidence gathered at the scene, while elsewhere in the building A.J. Pearse and Reuben Strauss were performing an autopsy on what was left of the woman's corpse.

It *was* the body of a woman; Hank had learned that much. What they had was the right arm, both thighs, and the lower half of the torso—which had been sliced neatly at the midsection. Pearse wasn't promising much at this point, but he had obtained what he considered a good set of fingerprints from her right hand, and it was still possible than an identification could be made by cross-checking the missing persons files.

Cowles, as the superintendent of the Ballistics Bureau, had been called in on his day off to perform a thorough examination of the items found among the remains. First among his priorities would be a search for the killer's fingerprints, though Hank expected they would find none. A close inspection of all the evidence could, however, yield a host of other vital information. And if any significant clues were to be found, Cowles would be the man to find them.

Cowles was probably in his fifties and completely bald, reminding Hank of that German actor who played the homicidal surgeon in that gothic movie he had seen last year—what was it called, *Mad Hands?*—no, *Mad Love*. Cathy disliked thrillers, so he had gone by himself.

"Let's see what we've got," said Cowles.

They began with the two burlap bags. Cowles could find

no printing on the bags themselves but did locate a paper tag still attached to one by a wire, reading DANCHES CO.——JANUARY 17, 1936.

"You ever heard of a Danches Company?" asked Cowles.

"Nope." Cleveland was chock-full of industry, and Hank wasn't surprised that he had never heard of it, despite his thorough knowledge of the city.

"Me, neither." Cowles pushed his thick round-framed glasses back from the bridge of his nose and held the tag up for a closer look, turning it over and saying, "Hmmph."

Because of the texture of the fabric, it was impossible to find any fingerprints. The bags were filthy, but Hank could see no visible bloodstains. Cowles scraped some samples into a white envelope that might turn out to be blood but were more likely oil or rust. Cowles did locate some bits of coal, however, along with a few small white feathers.

"Chicken feathers," said Cowles. "Two-to-one your Danches Company turns out to be either a coal or a chicken operation."

Hank nodded in agreement. "Pretty good odds."

Cowles sealed the coal chips and feathers in separate envelopes as evidence, then set aside the burlap bags for the time being. Hank would have to do the processing and property tagging later at the station.

The two half-bushel baskets offered little in the way of evidence, aside from some bloodstains at the bottom. No fingerprints could be found anywhere, again because of the textured material, and because the killer had been smart enough not to leave his thumb's impression in any of the blood. Hank took possession of the baskets for later processing as evidence.

The next items they examined were the newspapers the killer had used to wrap up the various parts of the woman's body. Some pages were white and appeared recent, while others were yellowed with age. The whitest, which had been wrapped around the arm, were a few pages from the Cleveland *News* dated January 25, 1936, just last night. Since the *News* was an evening paper, that meant the killer had wrapped up the arm less than twenty-four hours ago, although the actual time of death had not yet been determined by the autopsy surgeons. The woman could have been killed a few days ago, no matter how recently she had been wrapped up. The more-yellowed newspapers were dated August 11 and October 14, 1935. Although all of the papers were stained with blood, Hank was surprised at how little.

"Must have washed everything up pretty good," Hank said.

"Darn right," Cowles agreed. "I bet when we talk to A.J. he'll tell us the blood was completely drained from those limbs."

It was at this point that Hank first thought of the Andrassy double-murder case and wondered, fleetingly, if there was some connection. Eddie and his dead companion hadn't been so thoroughly dismembered, yet Hank couldn't help but recall how clean Eddie's body had been—as if it had been meticulously scrubbed down before the killer got rid of it—and how both bodies had been practically drained of blood. So far, he had no significant evidence linking the two cases. That would hinge, in part, on whether or not this woman had been killed by having her head chopped off. And the coroner would be unable to determine this until he had a chance to examine either the woman's head or her shoulders—if and when they ever turned up.

# 27 January 1936

## 9:28 A.M.

The unpaved road to the Danches chicken farm was full of deep ruts—hard reminders of the rainy season, when farm trucks had slogged to market through the mud and carved up these unnavigable tracks before the ground had frozen solid, not to loosen its grip until the spring thaw. The snow that had since fallen had coated the ruts with a slippery glaze of ice, allowing no one the freedom to climb out of their chosen path unless they had huge knobby tires and a hefty payload in the back to provide some traction.

"I hope we don't have to wake him up," said Hank's new partner, Vernal Quast, who had been transferred from Robbery to Homicide following the big shake-up. Quast was a good detective, if a trifle slow.

"Never knew a farmer who slept past five," Hank offered.

This rural backroad was not meant for a '36 Ford Deluxe, V-8 or no; still, Hank found himself thankful to be driving one of the departmental vehicles instead of his own.

"Any chance he might know something about the murder?" Vern asked, his teeth a-clatter. His gloved hands were shoved between his thighs.

"Doubt it."

76

The weather forecast claimed it might hit as high as twenty degrees this afternoon in greater downtown Cleveland, but they were currently several miles away from the city and the sun had yet to come out from behind the clouds. The car heater worked admirably, but they had had to crack open the windows to keep the windshield from fogging up. This had provided them with a steady arctic breeze as they made their way out to the boonies, and helped (along with three cups of coffee) to keep Hank from falling asleep at the wheel.

Hank had been up until the wee hours of the morning, waiting until they had come up with a positive ID on the woman's partial remains. The fingerprints matched those of a known prostitute, Florence Genevieve Martin Polillo, who also used the aliases Clara Dunn and Norma Crawford. She was forty-one years old, had often been arrested on soliciting and drinking charges, and was known to frequent the Roaring Third, the same area that had once been Eddie Andrassy's favorite haunt. However, Pearse had as yet no credible evidence linking Polillo's murder with the Andrassy case.

"Here we are," Quast observed.

"Yep." Hank had known Quast for several years and liked him all right, but the rhythm of their relationship had not yet been established. He and Jack Finnegan had complemented each other so well that it was now difficult getting used to the cadences of a new partner's thinking. Hank hoped his patience would hold up. They were stuck with each other for now, for better or worse, and Hank had better buck up to the fact that Jack was never coming back from Traffic Hell.

The ruts guided the car to the front lawn of the Danches farm. Hank saw a stout man in a heavy coat and blue jeans carrying a sack over his shoulder into the henhouse.

Hank and Quast got out of the relative comfort of the Ford and tramped across the snow-covered yard toward the open entrance of the henhouse, just as the man was coming out. He was perhaps sixty years old with a few days' growth of beard and a face as lined as the canals of Mars. His button eyes appeared to have no lashes.

The squawking of chickens came from inside the hen-house.

"Mr. William Danches?"

"Uh-huh."

Hank flashed his badge. Quast, flanking Hank on the right, followed suit. "Det. Henri Lambert, Cleveland Police. This is Detective Quast. We'd like to ask you a few questions."

"What for?" Danches's smile was friendly, showing off a craggy set of tobacco-stained choppers.

Hank pulled out the tag they had found wired to one of the burlap bags. "You recognize this tag?"

Danches's calloused hands grabbed the strip of cardboard and examined it closely. "No, sir."

"It's got the name of your farm on it."

"So it does."

"Does that date mean anything to you?"

Danches considered for a moment, then handed back the tag. "You find this on a bag of feathers?"

"Just answer the question."

"The seventeenth? that was a Friday. I think that was the last time they came and picked up my feathers."

"Who?"

"Cleveland Feather Company," said Danches. "They send a boy out here every now and then. Goes around to all the farms. Bet you he's the one wrote out the tag. 'Tweren't me. No, sir."

"What's this boy's name?"

"Johnny something." Danches scratched his unshaven chin. "Johnny Williams, Johnny Wilson—something like that."

"Is that the only company you sell your feathers to?"

"Yes, sir."

"Pay pretty good?"

Danches scowled and spat a gob of tobacco into the snow. "Pays shit, but they're the only ones buying."

"Mr. Danches, do you ever go into Cleveland for a good time?"

"I've taken the missus once or twice."

"You ever go by yourself, whoop it up a little?"

"Don't know what you mean."

"Does the name Florence Polillo mean anything to you?"

"No." Danches's head shake was firm.

"How about Clara Dunn?"

"No."

"Norma Crawford?"

"Ain't she some movie star?"

"Thank you, Mr. Danches." Hank looked him straight in the eye and could tell he knew nothing about the murder, much less why they were questioning him. "We may be back."

Danches shrugged. "I'll be here."

"Oh, one more thing. You wouldn't have the address of the Cleveland Feather Company handy, would you?"

"Be right back." Danches went into his farmhouse and returned a few minutes later with an old receipt clutched in his hand. He handed it to Hank. "Here, you can have this."

"Thanks."

Hank examined the receipt, which had the company's name and address printed in block letters at the top. As luck would have it, the Cleveland Feather Company was located at 1838 Central Avenue—a mere two blocks from where the assorted pieces of Florence Polillo had been found.

## 12:13 P.M.

Hank and Quast brought two patrolmen along and asked the owners if they would consent to a search of the premises. When told the reason, the manager was eager to oblige. Being in such close proximity to the site, the manager was well aware of the case and visibly shaken by the implication that one of his employees might prove to be a deranged killer.

"I'll need the name of one of your drivers," Hank told him.

"We only have one. That's John Willis."

Hank read the worry in the manager's face and asked, "Is there a problem?"

The manager swallowed hard. "He never showed up for work this morning. He was supposed to be here at seven."

"I'll need his address." Hank was matter-of-fact. He was

experienced enough to avoid excitement until they had a chance to question Willis.

Hank sent Vern back to Central Station to grab a few men, hunt for Willis, and bring him back to the station for questioning. They had enough circumstantial evidence to warrant a thorough interrogation.

But Hank still hoped to find evidence of a more conclusive nature, so the Cleveland Feather Company warehouse was searched top to bottom, saving the boiler room for last. Because of the bits of coal found in the burlap bags, Hank figured that some evidence might turn up in the coal bin or the ash heap—namely, Florence Polillo's head and other extremities. Borrowing pairs of overalls from the workers, Hank and the two patrolmen dug through the filthy piles, creating a huge black mess by the time they were through, but finding nothing relevant to the case.

Of course, if Willis proved to be the murderer, he may very well have disposed of all remaining evidence in the company's furnace.

By the time Hank declared an end to the search, the three of them were covered head to toe in carbon and soot. The two patrolmen, staring at one another wide-eyed and looking like a couple of vaudevillians in blackface, suddenly broke into a mock "Amos 'n' Andy" routine.

"What's the matter, Amos? 'Fraid o' haints?"

"I ain't 'fraid o' no haints, Andy. I's jess glad dey was no head down dey!"


1:56 P.M.

Hank opened the door to the interrogation room and found John Willis seated in a chair asleep, slumped facedown on the table, hands cuffed behind his back. Vern Quast and a couple of patrolmen had picked Willis up at a tavern near his home, drunk as all get-out.

He was dressed in a filthy undershirt and a ragged pair of blue jeans. During his five minutes alone, he had managed not only to fall asleep but also to stink up the room with the smell of cheap whiskey and the musk of his sweat. His torso was muscular, his arms scarred and sinewy. He struck Hank as someone at least physically capable of such a ghastly crime.

As Hank stood over the snoozing suspect, Quast closed the steel door behind them with a slam.

Hank grabbed Willis by the shoulder and forcibly sat him up. "Come on, you. Wake up!"

"Grrrrette," said Willis without opening his eyes.

"He wants a cigarette," Quast explained to Hank, as if he couldn't figure it out for himself.

"Well, he's not getting one," Hank said, lest Quast pull one out and hand it to him. Quast smoked Old Golds, for Christ's sake! Hank would have to break him of that. He couldn't have his partner handing him one of those when he needed a cig in a pinch. Jack Finnegan had smoked Luckies, so they had never had to face that particular problem.

*Like well-lubed gears, me and Jack!*

"Ssssss," said Willis, his bottom lip curling outward, "moke."

"No go, Joe," said Hank. "No cigarettes until you answer a few questions."

"Huh?" Willis raised his head and opened his eyes for the first time, looking up at Hank. His eyeballs were bloodshot and glassy, his pupils dilated. He seemed to have trouble focusing. He hadn't shaved in at least two days, probably not for the entire weekend. "I whassssn't drrriving . . . no, sssssir-rreee . . . Bob."

"Do you know the English alphabet?" Hank asked.

Willis nodded yes, his head lolling to the side as if a lead weight. Then, before Hank could ask him to recite it, Willis began singing it like a child: "A, B, C, D, E, F, T . . . Q, R, F, T . . . F, T. . . ." Willis stopped, crinkled his brow, closed his eyes, and began again: "A, B, C, D, E, F, T . . . H, R, L, M, N, O, V." At that, Willis stopped, a satisfied smile on his face. "Zat it?"

Hank sighed heavily and turned to face Quast.

"Vern," he said, "this man is in no condition to be questioned."

"He was OK when we brought him in." Quast defended himself. "I swear. It must have just caught up to him."

"Fine. I'm sure you're right. We'll put him in an isolation

cell and let him sober up. Won't be able to question him until tomorrow."

"Tough break," Quast observed.

"And don't you give him any cigarettes."

"Can . . . can I jussst go to jail now?" asked Willis.

Hank stared at the suspect's mussed, greasy hair, his stupid drunken smile, and cornflower blue eyes.

"Come on, Vern," he said. "Give me a hand with our little sweetheart."

## 4:09 P.M.

The rooming house at 3205 Carnegie Avenue was nondescript, a plain three-story structure with peaked roof and weathered white paint, a small porch on the ground floor and a second-floor balcony above it. The sounds of playful children came from within.

Hank trod with care the icy path leading toward the front steps. The steps themselves creaked under his weight. The screen door was ripped. Hank knocked upon it, and when the front door opened he found himself staring through the screen at the tired face of a woman holding a toddler.

"Mrs. Harold Ford?"

"Yes?"

"Det. Henri Lambert, Cleveland Police. I'm here about Florence Polillo. I understand Officer Jahnke paid you a visit earlier."

"Yes," she said without smiling, and pushed open the screen door. "He was very kind. Please come in."

"Thank you." Hank stepped inside the living area, where a couple of the older children sat rapt before the radio, listening to a kids' program, some western or "Buck Rogers" or something—he couldn't be sure, because he was always at work when these programs were on and never had a chance to tune in. The younger kids were running around, chasing each other and giggling. Hank counted nine children altogether.

"I baby-sit," Mrs. Ford explained, almost an apology, as she patted the toddler's butt. "Would you like some tea?"

"No, thanks. Like to ask you a few questions."

"Go right on ahead."

Hank had come here hoping to pry some new information out of the landlady. The beat officer, Jahnke, had questioned her briefly but had gone into no great detail. Meanwhile, Hank had sent Quast over to the offices of the Cuyahoga County Relief Administration, whose client Florence Polillo had been.

"How long ago did Mrs. Polillo move in here?" he began.

"Last May."

"Did she sleep here every night?"

"No, she came and went."

"You know of any other rooms she might have kept elsewhere?"

"Have no idea."

"Did she ever discuss with you how she earned her living?"

Mrs. Ford hesitated, then said, "Why, she was on full Relief. Paid her rent with her Relief checks, always on time."

"Did she ever bring anyone up to her room?"

"Just the kids and myself."

"Could I see her room?"

"Certainly." Mrs. Ford led him to the staircase, and he followed her up. "Like I told the young officer, she was always quiet."

"Except when she was drinking," Hank added, remembering what Jahnke had told him.

"Her only bad habit. She'd go out occasionally and get a quart of liquor—bad liquor, too—and drink it all by her lonesome up in her room. When she was drinking she was pecky—quarrelsome, you know. She never talked very much, exceptin' about her mother. Died three months ago. I felt so sorry for her. Drove her out to Pierpont for the funeral."

"You know about any surviving relatives?"

"None, exceptin' her ex back in Buffalo, and I don't suppose he counts for much. She was a fine roomer. The young ones loved her. I can't tell you what a help she was in the afternoons, playing with them and letting me get my cooking and cleaning done before Harry came home."

"Ah!" Hank feigned sympathy. "A woman's work is never done."

Once on the second-floor landing, Mrs. Ford led Hank

down the hallway to the room at the end and opened wide the door. "Here you are."

The small bedroom was sparsely furnished. The single bed had been made with the skill of a candy striper, covered with a clean pale quilt. The yellow window shades were drawn, yet the sun sneaked through to cast the room in a soft dreamy glow.

"Do you remember the last time you saw her?"

"Friday night."

"The twenty-fourth?"

"That's right. She was often gone for the whole weekend, so I didn't realize she was—well—" Mrs. Ford's voice trailed off, and she never completed her sentence.

Upon the squat dresser sat a dozen handmade dolls, each different from her sister, wearing simple hand-sewn garments and having different styles and colors of yarn upon their heads, masquerading as hair.

Officer Jahnke had said nothing to Hank about the dolls, and Hank found himself staring at them.

"Oh, yes," Mrs. Ford said, "the children loved Flo's dolls. She used to let the children borrow them, you know, as long as they promised to take good care . . . and all."

Hank approached the dresser and touched the hair of the first doll—a redhead—and observed in the mirror that his hand was shaking. He felt dizzy.

"That's Betty-Alice," said Mrs. Ford. "And that one is Sally, and—let me see now—Ruthie, Dorothy, Marie, Claudette, Heidi, Anna Mae, Rosella, Shirley, Beatrice, and Ginger."

"Jesus," Hank muttered.

He thought of all the lonely hours Florence Polillo had spent stitching them together, naming them, talking to them, sewing their clothing, and loaning them out to the rooming house waifs. He felt sick to his stomach. Until this moment, Florence Polillo had been little more than the bloodless remains he had seen unwrapped and lying upon A.J. Pearse's disinfected dissecting table.

Now Hank had to contend with the thought of a real woman, a flesh-and-blood human being, lying helpless beneath the killer's blade before being carved up like a Thanksgiving turkey, wrapped in newspaper, and dumped into baskets as if she were Little Red Riding Hood's goodies for Grandma.

"Mrs. Ford?" Hank queried. "I think I'll take you up on that cup of tea, after all."

"My pleasure. You do look a little peaked."

They left Florence Polillo's room, and Hank closed the door softly behind him, as if afraid of waking someone.

# 7 February 1936

**6:03 P.M.**

Sister Louisa bore no resemblance to those terrifying nuns who had taught Hank Lambert at school. Hers was a broad face narrowing down to a delicate chin, like that of a china doll, framed by the bleached cloth of her habit and made bewitching by a pair of eyes larger than any Hank had seen this side of Claudette Colbert. She wore no makeup but was possessed of a natural beauty. She ought to be under contract at MGM, not emptying bedpans at St. Vincent's.

"Come this way, Detective," said Sister Louisa, folding her hands in front of her and leading the way down the hall. They rounded a corner and entered the old elevator waiting there. A younger nun slid open the two iron gates as they stepped inside, and then closed them. The girl threw back the handle on the wall. The elevator lifted them up, gently, to the third floor.

"I guess he's delirious," said Hank, watching through the gate as the floors passed them by.

"Yes. He nearly died in the fire." Sister Louisa's statement was punctuated by the younger nun's slamming the lever back to the off position as they reached their destination. She manipulated it carefully until the floor of the elevator was level with the floor of the hallway, and then locked it back into place. She was as skilled at this as the elevator boys at the Hollenden.

"Here we are," said Sister Louisa, as the younger nun threw open the gates but remained mute.

Hank repressed an urge to tip the girl. He wondered suddenly whether you were expected to tip St. Peter as he let you through the pearly gates. But then what kind of a tip would St. Peter want?

"Thank you, Sister." Hank smiled, but the girl was not won. Sister Louisa offered him a scowl.

*That's right, Sister, men are wolves.*

"I'll take you to him," said Sister Louisa. She led Hank down the hallway and deposited him in front of room 318.

The young cop guarding the door tipped his cap to Sister Louisa. "Ma'am," he said, then went back to chewing his gum.

"Come with me," Hank said to the patrolman, flashing his badge. "I want you to witness this."

Hank halted before opening the door. He hadn't expected the nun to be present during the questioning.

"Sister, why don't you wait outside?" Hank asked, but was met with Sister Louisa's stone face. He continued: "This may get pretty gruesome."

"Forgive me, Detective, but it's customary for us to—"

"I should remind you this is police business," Hank interrupted, "and no place for a lady."

Sister Louisa smiled, as if privy to a secret Hank could never know. "I've read the newspaper stories about Mrs. Polillo. I know what this man did to her."

"Claims to have done," Hank corrected.

Sister Louisa's smile fell, as if she were disappointed her patient might turn out to have had nothing to do with the murder. Hank suspected that she was as interested as everyone else in hearing all the gory details. It was an opportunity she wasn't about to pass up. "After you, Detective."

Hank opened the door and the three of them entered.

A thin, gray-haired man, sick from smoke inhalation, lay

sleeping on the single hospital bed, his limbs bandaged where he had been burned in a fire at a rooming house two days before. Ordinarily, his injuries would not have garnered him a room to himself at St. Vincent's Charity Hospital, but he had been moved here under police security after having confessed to the murder of Florence Polillo.

"Mr. Daggett?" asked Hank in a loud voice.

Daggett's eyes sprung open and he sat up a bit. "Yep?"

"Det. Henri Lambert, Cleveland police." Hank offered him his badge, at which Daggett squinted noticeably. "Like to ask you a few questions."

"I done it!" Daggett's eyes were wide. "I killed her!"

"We'll get to that in a minute," said Hank, pulling up a wooden chair and sitting at Daggett's side. The young policeman and Sister Louisa stood at the foot of the bed.

Hank went through the routine questions first, discovering that he was Leonard O. Daggett, forty-five years of age, unemployed and on full Relief, and up until now a resident of the rooming house on Central Avenue that had burned to the ground on Wednesday. Daggett was hazy on some of these questions, which was Hank's first clue that he was a crackpot giving them a false confession.

John Willis, the truck driver for the Cleveland Feather Company, had proved to be another dead end, and since that time the department had already investigated and subsequently dismissed three false confessions to the Polillo murder. Hank suspected that Mr. Daggett would be number four.

"Where were you on the night of Saturday, January twenty-fifth?" he asked.

"With Florence Polillo, cutting and tearing and—"

"Hold on, now. About what time was this?"

"How the hell should I know?" Daggett snapped. "Take me away." He offered his bandaged arms for Hank to cuff, and winced visibly at the pain.

"Not yet," said Hank with a small laugh.

Sister Louisa placed Daggett's arms back at his sides.

"Was it light or dark outside?"

"Huh?"

"When you were with Mrs. Polillo."

"Oh, dark, I'd say."

"Before or after midnight?"

"Oh, I get on to bed along 'bout ten. Musta been afore that."

"You ever heard of a fellow named One-Armed Willie?"

"Can't say I have," said Daggett, " 'cause I haven't."

"All right." Hank had a number of witnesses who had seen One-Armed Willie get into a physical fight with Florence Polillo at around eleven-thirty that night—though none would admit where they had seen the fight—so it was unlikely she had been killed before midnight on the twenty-fifth.

"And exactly where was this?"

"Where was what?" Daggett looked bewildered.

"That you killed her."

"Oh, hell, I don't know. In front of some bar or somethin'."

"Right there on the street?"

"Naw, it musta been in some alley somewheres."

"What alley, where, Mr. Daggett?"

Daggett shrugged, cringed from pain. "Jess some dagnabbed alley."

"How did you kill her?"

"Whaddya mean?"

"Use any weapons? Your hands, what?" It was already clear to Hank that Daggett's "confession" was worthless, and he was growing impatient.

"Oh, yeah. Knife."

"Knife? What kind of knife?"

"Whaddya mean? Jess a dad-blamed knife!"

"Pocketknife? Steak knife?"

"Yeah, that's it. A steak knife. You shoulda seen me give it to her!"

"After you killed her, what did you do with the body?"

"Cut her all up, jess like it says."

"Like what says?"

"The dad-gummed newspapers! Whatsa matter with you?"

"You cut her up with a steak knife?"

"Yessir."

"How?"

"Cut off her arms and her legs and her head and then cut her in half, that's how!"

"You still got the knife?"

Daggett shook his head. "Done burned up like ever'thin' else. You jess have to take my word fer it."

"After you cut her up, what did you do with the body?"

"Tricky, tricky. I'll tell you what I done. I took—lemme see—I took her right arm, two thighs, and her lower torso, and I done put them in a bushel basket covered in burlap, and I done took them all back of the Hart Company building."

Daggett's answer was no less than Hank expected; he had lifted it right out of the Cleveland *News*. "What did you do with the other parts?"

"Threw 'em away."

"Where?"

"How the hell should I know? Jess some ashcan somewheres. What you waitin' fer? Why don't you arrest me?"

Just then there was a knock at the door. Sister Louisa opened it, and Hank saw that it was the elevator nun. She grabbed hold of Sister Louisa's hand as she addressed Hank.

"Are you Detective Lambert?" she asked in a nervous quaver.

"Yes, Sister." He smiled. "Problem?"

"It's the telephone for you, sir. An Inspector Sweeney. They've found the rest of that poor woman's body, no more than six blocks from here." The nun's face went ashen. "Everything but her head."

Sister Louisa crossed herself, but her eyes betrayed her fascination with the news—and at having been one of the first to hear it. "My goodness," she said in mock horror.

The other sister must have been pretty nosy herself to have learned so much. She must have asked Joe Sweeney a few questions, and Sweeney just couldn't say no—not to a nun.

Hank closed his notebook, got up from his chair, and motioned toward Sister Louisa and the cop. "Come on, let's go." Sister Louisa looked disappointed. Daggett had let her down.

"Wait!" said Daggett, frowning. "Where you goin'?"

"Out." Hank's patience had finally quit.

"You stinkin' sack of cow chips! Better not let me loose, 'cause I'm gonna kill again!"

Hank turned to Daggett and laughed harshly. "Don't worry. We're not giving up on you just yet. We might want to talk to you about some other matters."

Daggett was taken aback. "What other matters?"

Hank paused to light a cigarette, then allowed the match to burn itself out. "Like that rooming house fire, for starters."

"You think I'd do this to myself?" Daggett glanced at his bandaged burns.

"Stranger things have happened." Hank opened the door for the nun and the young officer and followed them out. "I want you to stand guard until you're told otherwise, all right?" he asked the gum-chewing cop.

"Yes, sir."

Hank was sure he wouldn't mind; it was easy duty.

"Excuse me." Hank pushed his way past the sisters and headed down the hall toward the nurse's station, where he could see the earpiece of the candlestick telephone lying upon the desk. Behind him he heard the pitter-patter of nun feet, as well as excited whispering from one habit to another.

6:29 P.M.

Hank drove as fast as he could to the corner of Orange Avenue and East Fourteenth Street—as the sister had said, no more than six blocks from St. Vincent's. The marked squads as well as the coroner's white Dodge panel truck were parked in the alley behind a vacant building, their headlights illuminating a weathered wooden fence. The fence's gate was open and various figures, uniformed and in plainclothes, were streaming in and out carrying flashlights, searching the ground. The bright glare of flashbulbs shot out through the slats of the fence every few seconds; all the action was clearly on the other side. Hank parked his department-owned Ford sedan behind the squad cars, grabbed his flashlight, and tramped his way through the snow and mud to the site of the discovery.

Lloyd Trunk of Ballistics was the one taking the pictures. Thankfully, no reporters had shown up yet. Several patrolmen's flashlights illuminated the scene in between the flaring of Trunk's flashbulbs, revealing a woman's upper torso, left arm, and lower legs—precisely the pieces missing from the Polillo corpse, not counting the head—each piece having been unwrapped from its burlap coverings and lying exposed in the snow. Two white-clothed men from the coroner's lab stood behind in the shadows, smoking cigarettes and awaiting their turn.

"Anyone touched anything?" Hank asked.

"No," said Det. Axel Bronson from Central Station. "It's just like it was when the guy found it."

"Who's that?"

"That guy over there, a truck driver name of Frank Gaeblein." Bronson pointed out a stocky fellow standing off to the side of the scene, and looked over Hank's shoulder while Hank scribbled on his notepad. "That's George Adam Edward Baker Lincoln Edward Ida Nora."

"Thanks. He made his statement?"

"Yeah, Lucky, I took it. He says he was cutting through the backyards at approximately six P.M. when he stumbled across these body parts, lying out in the open. Says he thought it was some hams at first, but then he saw her tits. Just a pair of fucking tits and some shoulders—Jesus Christ. Then he goes and hails an officer walking his beat, down near the public baths. I was sent down from the station, but they told me it's your case. I guess Sweeney got hold of you, huh?"

"No sign of the head?"

"Nope. How do you know this is her?"

"I don't, not until A.J. gets a look at her. But these are the missing pieces, all right. Looks like a match to me. Funny. People who found her last time said the same thing— thought they'd found some hams."

"Wishful thinking, huh? You think we'll find the head?"

"Probably. As long as no one mistook it for a pot roast."

"Jesus, Lucky." Bronson cringed. "You were paired up with Jack Finnegan for too damn long."

*Maybe not long enough,* thought Hank. Without Jack, it felt as if his luck had changed from good to bad.

# 29 February 1936

**10:20 P.M.**

Danny Cottone walked briskly down the shoveled side-walks of East Twenty-second Street, parts of which were well lighted, parts of which were dark. He had a way of walking quickly on any icy surface without slipping, by curling his toes within his shoes as if he were gripping the ground with a pair of claws, and stepping with the surefootedness of an alley cat. But on this night his socks had worn thin and his feet were freezing. His breath swirled in front of his face and his nose was running. He wished winter were on its way out. Business was bad and not likely to get better until things started warming up. It was about this time of year that Clevelanders came down with cabin fever, giving each other dirty looks on the street, bickering over nothing, and driving their cars as if they intended to kill one another. Neighbors fought neighbors, husbands wives, and mothers children. None of this insanity would be cured until the snow melted and the Indians set up shop in Municipal Stadium, yet baseball season was nearly two months distant and Danny had a funny feeling that since this winter had already been rough, March was going to remain decidedly lionlike.

Danny had tried his luck working the seventh floor of the

YMCA this evening, but after paying for a couple hours in the room and slipping the night clerk his cut, he hadn't made out so well. Clients had been sparse and competition fierce, so Danny had left early. He had considered maybe popping three blocks over to Charlie's and seeing what was happening there, but decided instead to head for the Orange Avenue Bath House, which was always a sure thing.

Danny had just passed St. Vincent's Charity Hospital and was coming upon Scovill Avenue when a tall, shadowed figure emerged from behind a building, dressed in a long coat, wide-brimmed hat, and muffler and carrying a burlap sack. The sack shifted and twitched, changing its shape as rustling noises came from within. Something inside was trying to get out.

"Hey, pal." The man's voice was deep and gruff. With his face half-hidden by the muffler and half in shadow from the hat, all Danny could see was the whites of his eyes glistening through the mist of his breath.

Danny was startled and came no closer, but the dark man approached him, breathing heavily and stepping forward with care as the black ice crackled beneath his boots.

"Come on kid. I . . . I know who you are. Don't play . . . play games with me."

"What do you want?" Danny took a cautious step backward. East Twenty-second had no traffic at the moment and the sidewalks were bare. He would have to run for it if this man proved dangerous. Danny had been keeping a watchful eye out ever since Flo's murder. What had happened to Eddie had scared him enough—and even though the papers hadn't caught on to it yet, Danny was sure the same guy had killed them both. That was the reason he was spending less time at Charlie's, because the killer might turn out to be one of the regulars, one of the real creeps like Frank Dolezal. Frank had known both Eddie and Flo, and he could sure get mean sometimes.

But the man standing in Danny's path was neither Frank Dolezal nor any of the other regulars at Charlie's. Now that he was getting closer, Danny could see his face, which was that of a thirty-year-old man, clean shaven with regular features.

"I'm not going to hurt you, Danny. I only want to . . . to be with you. I . . . I know you. I know who you are. I know all the . . . all the whores, and they . . . they know me. But I've never met you. I've wanted . . . wanted to for so long . . . to meet you."

"My name's not Danny," he said, frightened that the man knew his name. "I don't know what you're talking about."

The burlap sack rustled again at the man's side.

"They said you'll do . . . you'll do anything. They . . . they said you'd like me."

"Go jump in the lake, Mac."

"Hey, listen—"

Danny kept watching the sack and wondering about the rippling, shifting mass inside. Then whatever it was let out a high-pitched, horrible shriek, and all he could imagine was Flo's severed head inside, and he wondered insanely if she had actually, during the murder, screamed her head off.

Danny gasped and turned back, running in the direction of St. Vincent's.

"Wait, wait!" shouted the man, his boots picking up their pace right on Danny's heels.

But before reaching Charity Avenue, Danny slipped on the ice and fell headlong, landing on his palms and scraping them on the cement. As he tried to get up, he was snatched by his coat collar. The dark man had grabbed him with a single hand, his other maintaining its hold on the screaming sack. Danny tried to fight him, but he no longer had any footing on the ice.

"Hey, hold on there, little guy," said the man. "Don't be scared. It's . . . it's only a chicken. It won't hurt you."

"Fuck! Scared the shit out of me!" But knowing it was a chicken in the sack did little to lessen Danny's fears. The man was weird. "What do you want?"

"Name's Toby. I drive a delivery . . . delivery truck, make a few . . . a few stops each day at the Central Market. That's where . . . where I've seen you. This hooker Olive . . . she pointed you out to me."

"I don't know any Olive." That was a lie; Danny knew who he was talking about. He called her Olive Oyl, after that character in the "Thimble Theater" comic strip who liked Popeye, the sailor.

"Oh, I've seen you . . . seen you all right, hanging out . . . out by the fish stand on the corner, wearing those tight . . . tight trousers. You're a real slut, all right, and no mistake. No mistake . . . no, sir. You're no better . . . no better than any of the girls. You get fucked . . . fucked in the ass. Don't charge a whole . . . a whole lot, neither."

"Who says?"

"Olive," said Toby. "This hooker Olive."

"I don't have any friends named Olive."

"I've seen you with her."

"Just get away from me, buster!"

"Buster, eh? I'll bust you, my little . . . little chick. Come with me and I'll pay you . . . pay you five bucks."

"Tell me another," said Danny, though he was warming up to him a bit. Five bucks wasn't anything to sneeze at. "OK, show me."

"Jesus," muttered Toby. "Hold this." He handed the burlap bag to Danny, who took it warily. The chicken seemed to have settled down a bit and was only moving slightly. Toby removed his wallet and pulled out the five-spot. "But you've got to . . . got to understand I'm going to make you earn this. You'll have to . . . have to do exactly what Toby says."

"Like what? What does Toby like?"

"No questions. Just . . . just come with me."

"A secret, huh? That'll cost you seven."

"Done." Toby's eyes burned with a mad intensity.

Danny grinned and handed him back his chicken. The guy was big and mean looking, but Danny suddenly found him intriguing. He didn't feel as if he were in any great danger. He would keep his guard up, and if the guy made a move, he'd kick him in the nuts. "Where to?"

"The bathhouse," said Toby, "over on Orange."

"I was just going that way." Danny had been with weirder guys before, that was for sure, and based on his past experience, he figured this guy was probably harmless. If Toby wanted to kill him, he certainly wouldn't do it at the public baths. "OK, bub, it's a deal."

"You're going to . . . going to make me very happy, Danny-boy."

A shiver shot up Danny's spine, because "Danny-boy" was what Eddie had always called him.

## 10:54 P.M.

Danny and Toby shelled out five cents apiece for soap and towels when they went into the city-operated bathhouse, which had opened at the turn of the century. The city maintained several such houses in lower-income neighborhoods so that any city dwellers unfortunate enough to lack a bathtub or even indoor plumbing could get cleaned up on the cheap. Cleaner citizens spread less disease and simply smelled better. But naturally much more than mere bathing was going on at the baths, and among Cleveland's more sexually adventurous, places like the Orange Avenue Bath House were popular playgrounds. The sex usually came for free—which was why Danny sometimes had a rough time of it when he came here to work.

But tonight he was going to make out all right. His five-cent investment was going to bring him a seven-dollar return, once he'd satisfied big bad Toby with his chicken in the bag.

The three-story bathhouse had forty-nine bath cubicles and half as many private showers, as well as two larger shower rooms, a gymnasium, and a small swimming pool. Danny and Toby undressed in the locker room, fixed their towels around their waists, and went up to the top floor and down the hall, heading for the cubicle as far from other bathers as possible. Toby brought his chicken with him, presumably so no one would steal it from the locker room. Danny was wary of the idea of having a squawking chicken present while Toby was fucking him, yet he said nothing.

They passed a blond towel boy named Lefty with whom Danny had had sex on occasion just for fun. He didn't like charging people to whom he was genuinely attracted, especially when they were his same age and in a similar economic predicament. Sex without money could be fun, too, every once in a while. Danny winked at Lefty as he walked by, but Lefty looked at him quizzically, shifting his eyes to indicate Toby's burlap bag, to which Danny offered a shrug; he still had no idea what his customer wanted with a live chicken, other than perhaps tomorrow's Sunday dinner.

They entered a private room at the end of the hall, and Danny fixed the hook latch on the door to keep nosy joes from peeking in. The room was large enough only for a bathtub, a sink, and a wooden bench. Small ceramic tiles covered the floor, which had a drain in the center. The tub stood on claw feet, two faucets hanging over its lip, one painted red, the other blue. The walls were tiled in white, but the grout between the tiles was caked with mildew.

Toby set his chicken down on the floor and, facing away from Danny, removed his towel. The burlap bag formed a peak as the chicken raised its head within, then bobbed up and down. The chicken squawked. In the altogether, Toby was impressive. His buttocks were meaty but muscular, and his entire body was covered in thick, dark hair, except for his back, where only a few tufts poked up at his shoulders. Even a few feet away, Danny could smell his heady scent. When Toby turned around, Danny saw a trim waist and overly developed arms and pectorals, leading up to a thick neck and lean face with a lantern jaw. His body was truly that of a laborer. Hanging from the bush at his groin was a soft uncut dick sitting atop two huge hairy balls.

Danny dropped his own towel to the floor and found he had already attained an erection just looking at Toby. He took a few steps forward, no longer afraid. Toby was unarmed, and Danny felt in no danger. All he wanted now was to make his customer happy. He reached out and cupped Toby's cock and balls in his hands.

"No," said Toby, shrinking away. "Get out the chicken."

Danny drew back, silent.

Toby lay down upon the bench, his knees bent, his feet resting on the damp floor tiles. He grabbed his dick and began to stroke it. "Go on, kid, get it out. I'm ready."

"Sure," said Danny, beginning to realize that Toby's desires went beyond the normal suck and fuck.

Danny untied the piece of rawhide binding the top of the sack, and the chicken poked its head out of the bag. It flapped its wings and leapt free of the burlap, screaming and sending small white feathers flying everywhere. The chicken continued fluttering its wings and half-flying, half-jumping around the cubicle.

"Catch it," said Toby, manipulating his now almost hard cock.

But before Danny could get up to chase down the chicken, his eyes were drawn to a shiny glint at the base of the empty sack. He reached inside and pulled out a long butcher knife, its blade newly cleaned and polished. "What's this?"

"Put that back," said Toby.

Danny replaced the knife back in the sack. As long as it stayed out of Toby's reach, he figured he was safe.

In the small space, the chicken had little room to run, and in no time Danny had grabbed it by its wings and placed a hand firmly around its neck, preventing its escape. Its flappings had strewn feathers about the room, and many were still floating down to the ground. Several had landed upon the prone figure of Toby, sticking to his sweat amid the hairs. He now sported a fully erect cock of about eight inches in length, which he was stroking furiously.

"Hold it over my chest," said Toby. "But don't let go."

Danny bent over and set the chicken down. Its feet scratched Toby's skin as it struggled and shrieked.

"Chick, chick, chick, chick," said Toby. He spat on his palms and rubbed the saliva onto his dick until it was slick and slimy. "Here, hand her to me."

Toby grabbed hold of the chicken, and Danny let go. Danny was beginning to wonder what need Toby had of him, because it seemed all he wanted was the chicken.

"Thatta girl," said Toby to the chicken, and it seemed to settle down a little. "Just relax."

Then Toby lifted up the chicken and set it down slowly onto his erect prick.

The chicken screamed, craning its neck toward the ceiling and trying to fly away, but it was held firmly by Toby and was going nowhere but down.

"Oh, Mommy!" said Toby, closing his eyes. "Oh, Mommy, Mommy, Mommy! Here, little chick-chick. Daddy loves you. Chick, chick, chick, chick." He seemed to be in ecstasy as the chicken thrashed around upon him.

Danny shrunk away from the sight.

Toby's eyes sprang open and focused on Danny. "Come here, now! Come over here and pluck her."

Danny approached and sheepishly pulled at a couple of feathers. They came out with a little tugging, and the chicken squawked some more.

"Oh, Jesus!" yelled Toby, grinning with pleasure.

"I can't!" said Danny. His eyes were welling up with tears and his vision was becoming blurry.

Toby's hand grasped Danny by the wrist and squeezed hard. Danny could see the blue veins bulging along the length of his huge arm. Toby's grip was painful. "Yes, you can. Come on, pluck her!"

Danny caught his breath and then went about it, yanking handfuls of feathers and dropping them onto Toby's chest. With his free hand, Toby scooped up the feathers and rubbed them into his face.

"Oh, Mommy," he said with a moan in his voice. "Mommy, Mommy, Mommy!"

The chicken kept screaming, bobbing its head up and down and struggling against its captors.

Pink chicken skin became exposed as Danny plucked out more and more feathers, until it was nearly bald, with only the feathers on its head and some on its wings remaining.

"Chick, chick, chick," said Toby. The chicken tensed itself with each clump of feathers it lost. "Daddy loves you. Jesus loves you. Oh, Jesus, Jesus, Jesus!"

Danny's hands were covered with small feathers, which had stuck to his sweaty palms. He brushed them off, figuring he was finished.

"Get the knife," Toby said.

"No." Danny shook his head from side to side.

"Get it!" Toby snapped.

Danny thought about how badly he needed the seven bucks, and decided what the hell. He grabbed the butcher knife from off the floor and held it up. "Now, what?"

"Cut the little bitch's head off."

Danny grabbed the chicken by the neck with one hand and

swallowed hard. His grip on its neck was loose, and the chicken broke free and pecked at his hand. "Ow!" Danny said, but that was the final impetus he needed, and he grabbed her neck again, stretching it taut.

"Go on, do it!"

Danny swiped the knife across, just below his knuckles, and cut off the head, dropping it onto Toby's chest as the warm red blood shot forth, drenching him.

"Oh, Mommy, Mommy!"

The chicken continued to convulse, moving its legs as if it were running pell-mell across the barnyard.

Danny's hands were coated with sticky blood.

"Here!" Toby said, grasping Danny's hand that held the knife. His eyes were agleam. "Rub it across my neck."

Danny did as he was told, sliding the dull edge of the knife back and forth, back and forth across Toby's muscular neck. The blood from the knife dribbled down the sides of his neck, a thin ribbon spreading as if the flesh had been slashed.

"Oh, Jesus!" Toby shouted.

Suddenly, the headless chicken jumped up from Toby's dick and landed on the floor, squirting blood out its neck.

Toby's dick squirted a flood of come, which turned pink as it met the pool of blood on his chest.

"Chick, chick, chick! Daddy's coming! Jesus is coming! Oh, Mommy, Jesus is coming!"

The headless chicken leapt to its feet and ran around the floor spraying a trail of blood, bumping into the nearest wall and then bouncing back, scurrying around and returning to lay at rest alongside Danny's shivering feet. It pumped out the rest of its blood and then moved no more.

Toby's eyes were closed, a peaceful smile upon his face.

Danny stepped hurriedly into the tub and turned both spigots. He grabbed his cake of soap and scrubbed the blood from his feet, hands, and chest, and then wiped himself dry with his towel. Since both towels were now stained with chicken blood, he left them behind and fumbled with the hook latch on the door.

"Wait, where are you going?" said Toby.

But Danny was already out the door, running down the hall stark naked past the stares of dirty old towel-draped pederasts and taking the staircase two-by-two until he had reached the first floor and headed straight for the locker room, where he dressed and bundled himself up in his coat and left the bathhouse, exiting out onto Orange Avenue, where the wind was bracing and his breath froze in front of his face.

He no longer wanted Toby's money. He only wanted to get home and crawl into his nice cozy bed—by himself—and lay his head down upon his soft feather pillows.

# 22 May 1936

Mott Hessler was driving his Auburn 851 Speedster north on Ridge Road when his headlights picked up a ragged man several yards ahead standing alongside the road, at the edge of Brookside Park, trying to thumb a ride. All Hessler saw were the man's grizzled features and hopeful look before he whizzed past, sending him into the background. Hessler had wanted to pick him up, but was going too fast for such a sudden stop. He braked the roadster carefully and parked a short distance down the road, setting the emergency brake and leaving his engine running. He checked his rearview mirror and saw the man heading toward him, visible only in the faint red glow of the Auburn's taillights. This stretch of Ridge Road was isolated and unlighted, and Hessler could see no other traffic coming, either from up ahead or from behind. As far as he could tell, no houses stood nearby, for no glowing windows were visible through the dark trees of the park.

*How perfect,* he thought. *A peasant seeking a ride with the prince, in the middle of the enchanted forest.* He leaned across the front seat to open the passenger door.

"Come on, man," Hessler said as the peasant peeked inside.

"Thanks, mister." He was young, but his face was gaunt and unshaven, giving him the look of someone older. He had a small pack slung over his shoulder, which he removed and tossed on the floor before hopping upon the running board and climbing in. "Name's Tom Vandervest." He offered Hessler his hand to shake.

"Well, Tom! Mott Hessler, pleased to meet you."

Once Tom had shut the door and settled in, Hessler let up on the emergency brake and gave the car some gas. Soon they were zooming down the darkened road together through the woods.

"Gee, you sure know how to make a fella's day!"

Hessler dismissed the thought with a wave of his hand. "I had a craving for some company and suddenly there you were."

"Right place at the right time, huh?"

"Something like that."

Hessler glanced at his passenger and saw that his clothing was cheap but not dirty. He wore a rumpled gray suit— single breasted with matching trousers—over a sky-blue polo shirt, with black leather belt and black oxfords, and a charcoal-gray cap with dark stripes across the top that he wore high on his forehead, its brim pointing upward. He sat with his shoulders slumped forward, and he looked slim. With his lean features and beaten appearance, Hessler pegged him as a common laborer of some type, perhaps with the CCC.

"This is some car," Tom said. "How fast does she go?"

"A hundred and fifty horses."

"Holy Toledo!"

"I've had it over a hundred miles an hour."

"You're pulling my leg!"

"Not on your life."

"Must be some engine."

"Do you know about engines?"

"A little."

*Good,* Hessler thought. This was his chance to impress the poor bastard. "A 'supercharged' Lycoming straight eight.

Guaranteed to go over a hundred, or I never would have tried."

Tom's smile was enthusiastic. "Let's see!"

He was providing Hessler with a perfect excuse. Everything was falling into place splendidly. "Very well, but not here. This is the main road through Brooklyn, and the sheriff and his men are always around somewhere. We'll go up a ways and turn onto Clinton Road, where there's nobody to disturb us."

"Sounds swell."

"Are you looking for a job?" Hessler asked with feigned concern.

"Not yet," said Tom, and chuckled. "I was working for the WPA out at the airport, but I just quit today."

"Oh, really?" Hessler had come in on the night flight from Chicago, which was the only reason he was way out here on Ridge Road—and the only reason he had ever met Tom Vandervest. He had spent the last couple of days talking to some wholesale drug suppliers and looking over possible new fixtures for his store. His bed at the Palmer House had been oddly uncomfortable, and he had gotten little restful sleep as a result. He could have stayed until Sunday and done some sightseeing, but he had felt restless and decided to come home one day early.

"I been staying at this camp out there," Tom continued, "but since I quit I've got to find a new place to flop, in the city. Probably go to the YMCA, if they got any room."

"Are you from around here?"

"Naw, Pittsburgh. You live in Cleveland?"

"Yes. Matter of fact, the YMCA's only four blocks from my place."

"No foolin'?"

"None. But I'm sure the Y will be full up, it being Saturday night. You don't look like you have much cash on you, either."

"I do all right." Tom grabbed a folded red bandanna from his pocket, set it in his palm, and untied the four corners, showing Hessler his loose change. "I got four and a half bucks here."

"That will last you four days. I see a lot of men on the

streets who would give their eyeteeth for some work, and here you just turn and walk away."

"I needed a few days off, but they wouldn't give them to me. So I quit."

"Just like that. Over a few days off."

"That's right. I'm going to this convention, see."

"Don't tell me you're a Republican." In less than a month, the Republicans were going to be holding their national convention in Cleveland. Hessler's Drugs was prepared to do brisk business and Hessler had ordered his goods accordingly. A patriotic window display was planned. The boys in Chicago had helped him with some ideas.

"Naw, Socialist. Whole thing starts tomorrow, right downtown."

"You're kidding," Hessler said, but only because he was surprised to hear of the event; he had nothing against the Socialists. Yet if he had only known, he might have come up with something to cash in on their convention, as well— perhaps a window display done all in red, with product-boosting signs such as IVORY—THE WORKING MAN'S SOAP! 15 CENTS! or FIGHT OPPRESSIVE GREASE STAINS WITH CARBONA SPOT REMOVER! ONLY 23 CENTS! But on second thought, he doubted the Socialists had as much money to spend as the Republicans.

"Listen," said Hessler. "Why don't you stay with me for the night? I have a nice guestroom, and if it works out, maybe I'll let you stay for the whole convention. You look as if you could use a few good meals, and perhaps I could even find some work for you to do around my shop."

"No foolin'? You mean it?"

"I'll take that as a yes."

Hessler felt a smooth exhilaration fill him up. He had just engineered something beautiful, and he had no idea which way it would go. He was the master of ceremonies, in complete control of Tom Vandervest's destiny.

"That's Clinton Road on the left," said Hessler. "You want to see what this baby can do?"

"You bet!"

"Get ready." Hessler braked for the turn. "Hold on."

He made the turn onto Clinton and then began to accelerate, shifting up whenever the Auburn's tachometer showed the engine revving too high. The force of the acceleration was strong, and in a matter of seconds they were speeding along at a fast clip. Clinton Road lay straight for the first mile and a half, a smooth gravel surface, and the Speedster handled it with little difficulty, although the ride was a little bumpy.

On both sides of them the dense forest flew past, the car's bright headlights casting shadows amid the clustered trees.

"Holy shit!" said Tom, who had moved ever closer on the seat and was peering at the speedometer to the right of the steering wheel. The speedometer face went up to 120 miles per hour, but the needle wavered just below that. The car shimmied and rattled for a moment, but Hessler held it steady.

He slowed down in a matter of seconds once they reached the bend in the road. Clinton Road was only three miles long, and he had a decision to make before they reached the end: whether or not to spare Tom's life.

He rode the brakes and threw his arm around Tom suddenly, pulling him closer. He brought the Speedster over to the side of the road and parked, turning off the motor as well as the headlights.

Now everything was dark. Tom was nothing more than a silhouette against the gray background of the forest.

"Scared?" Hessler asked in a stage whisper, holding Tom tightly.

"No."

"You should be."

Hessler felt Tom's breath against his neck. He placed a hand on his thigh.

"Why?" Tom remained calm.

"You never know when a strange man might want to take advantage of you." Hessler stroked Tom's cheek.

"Listen, mister, I don't go for that stuff," said Tom.

"That's what they all say," said Hessler, knocking off Tom's cap and grabbing him by the hair at the scruff of his neck. He pulled his head back. Tom's lips parted as he took in a quick gasp of air, baring his teeth. Hessler planted his mouth against Tom's and thrust his tongue deep inside. Tom groaned a muffled protest that vibrated against Hessler's lips. But he offered no physical struggle.

"Stop," he said out of the corner of his mouth.

Hessler broke the kiss suddenly. "As if you really want me to. Don't tell me you never screwed around with the other guys back at the WPA camp."

"There were guys there that would suck you off," said Tom, his voice quavering. "But that doesn't mean that—"

"Come on, Tom, you fucked them, too, didn't you?" Hessler yanked him by the hair again. "Didn't you?"

"Y-yeah, I guess so." Tom was breathing hard, his face sweating.

"But that doesn't mean you're a fairy," Hessler teased.

"That's right."

Hessler let go of Tom's hair. Tom still had put up no real struggle, and even when Hessler let go of him, he didn't try to scoot further away on the seat. That meant Tom was waiting to see what kind of deal Hessler was prepared to pitch him. If he wanted to eat, he would have to play the game Hessler's way.

Hessler reached for his pack of Chesterfields. "Want a smoke?"

Tom took the cigarette Hessler offered him. Hessler struck a match and held it up in front of Tom's face. Instead of bringing the flame to the tip of the cigarette, Hessler let Tom lean toward it. The small orange glow gave a truer picture of Tom's age. He was young, perhaps twenty-three or twenty-four, a year or two younger than Hessler. His eyes narrowed. He kept his composure, staring at Hessler and sucking in the first drag of smoke.

Hessler lighted one for himself and leaned back against the driver's door, one knee up on the seat so that his legs were spread. He had a hard-on, but there was no way Tom could see that.

"I'll tell you a secret if you'll tell me one," Hessler said, breathing out smoke.

"Like what?"

"Like, do you like guys or girls?"

"Girls," said Tom.

"Oh, come on, be honest. Which do you like best?"

"I told you, girls."

"If you're going to lie to me, I won't tell you my secret."

"Well, guys are all right," said Tom and shrugged.

"A-ha!" Hessler was pleased; Tom knew how to play the game. "But that doesn't make you a fairy."

"No."

"Of course it doesn't."

"So what's your secret?" Tom asked. "Go ahead."

"And you're not scared?"

"Why should I be scared?"

"Come closer."

Tom complied, shifting over on the seat.

"Touch it," Hessler whispered. He grabbed Tom's hand and placed it in his crotch. Tom squeezed his hardness, just as Hessler knew he would.

Tom blew thick smoke into his face, but his smile was playful.

Hessler breathed in the smoke and said, "My secret is that I want my cock up your ass. But that doesn't make me a fairy, does it?"

"N-no, but . . ." Tom was hesitant.

Hessler grabbed Tom's hair with one hand and his crotch with the other. He could feel Tom's cock growing. It was nearly hard.

"Good. Very good," said Hessler, giving Tom a final squeeze. "I see you're accustomed to singing for your supper. Now get out."

"Huh?"

"Come on, I said get out." Hessler gave him a light shove. "We can't do it in the car. Someone might drive by."

Glancing behind him at the dark woods, Tom finally did look scared. "W-what about y-your place in the city?"

"No. Go on, now. I'll be right behind you. I just need to lock up."

Tom put his cap back on and got out of the car first. While Tom stood leaning against the fender, staring away from the car, Hessler reached under the seat and grabbed his machete.

# 3 June 1936

Pal Janssen had been watching the river for miles through the open door of the boxcar. As the train approached the city and slowed further, the monotonous click-clacking rhythm of the cars diminished, as if time itself were braking to a halt, while the snakelike river running alongside the tracks grew ever wider. The surrounding terrain changed from hilly farmland to industrial flatland, populated not with barns, silos, and windmills, but with massive factory works with spiraling brick smokestacks and great roaring furnaces. Thick coal smoke churned out of the mouths of the stacks, merging to form clouds of soot that dissipated into a thin brown film, dirtying the lower sky as it passed above the rooftops before settling upon them. Flames burned like an Olympic torch from the lips of tall pipes jutting up from the refineries, which were themselves a mass of intestinal tubing and conduits, blackened with grease and grime, peopled with men in hardhats climbing staircases and opening valves. Culverts running from the plants poured a mucky sludge into the river. Old useless machinery stood rusting in back lots, like the fossilized remains of prehistoric beasts. Some factories stood idle—windows shattered, smokestacks releasing nothing to the wind.

As the train wound its way through the industrial waste lands, Pal leaned against the rim of the boxcar door, soaking in his first look at Cleveland's innards while being jostled about on an empty stomach, with little change in his pockets and only a vague hope of finding work.

He gathered up his stuff and put together his knapsack. Once the train was moving slowly enough, but before it was fully stopped, he would ditch over the side and onto solid, steady earth once more. It was best to get off before the train had pulled into the station, to stay clear of the railroad dicks and their billy clubs. They had popped him a poke a time or two in the past, and Pal had had quite enough of that.

A dozen other ragged men stood behind him, preparing for their own opportunities to jump. Most were older and less nimble than Pal and would probably wait until the train was moving a little slower.

Pal gauged the speed of the telephone poles as they passed by, counting the seconds between them and trying to figure whether or not it was safe to jump. With a moving train, speeds could be deceptive, and a lapse in judgment could cost a leg or even a neck.

It was about four feet to the ground, but the red earth itself sloped downward into a long, troughlike ditch. At this speed, Pal knew he would be taking a bounce, but if he hit it just right and allowed himself to roll, he would escape with only some minor cuts and bruises—not with a dislocated shoulder like he'd taken in Charleston.

Nodding a farewell to his compatriots, Pal tossed out his knapsack, which tumbled into the ditch kicking up a cloud of dust. He took a quick glance ahead before jumping clear of the train himself, and fell free to the earth below.

He suddenly experienced that moment—that eerie, fleeting moment that felt like a century—when he wondered if he was ever going to hit the ground, if his heart would ever beat again. It was a longer distance than he had counted on, and the world seemed to disappear. The roar of the train vanished and all he heard was the blood gushing through his veins and the wind ruffling his hair. It was a moment of extreme panic and serenity.

Then he blinked. And hit hard—once.

The bounce sent him back into the air, into another split second of limbo. His heart stopped again, all sound gone as if he were tumbling within a vacuum.

Then his shoulders struck the earth and he was rolling. He tucked in his arms and allowed the roll to take him. Thistle scratched at him and tore his clothing. A cloud of dust flew into his face. His head struck some small rocks.

But when at last the world had ceased to spin, Pal found himself lying facedown against the side of the ditch, shaded from the sun, his limbs sprawled. He was banged up a bit, and felt pain from all corridors of his body; he had bitten his tongue and was tasting his own blood, along with a mouthful of grit. His hand was dangling in a stream of oily water that trickled slowly at the bottom of the ditch.

The train continued to rumble past, blaring its horn a few times to warn the yardworkers somewhere up ahead that it was coming in.

Pal spat, pulled himself closer to the stream, and plunged his face into it to cool off. He knew better than to open his mouth.

*Hello, Cleveland,* he thought, *how are ya?*


2:23 P.M.

Pal walked along the tracks through the barren railway corridor. The soles of his shoes were worn enough that he could feel every piece of loose gravel beneath his feet.

Directly ahead of him stood a huge skyscraper many blocks distant, half in sun and half in shadow, tapering to a sharp point at its tip. Not quite the Empire State Building, but it was OK. The tracks led straight toward this tower, which meant they would take him right smack downtown. Cities always put their best face out on the water, and somewhere beyond that skyscraper up ahead and all the squat buildings surrounding it, Pal knew he could find a Great Lake. Cleveland was going to be hosting some kind of expo-

sition this summer having to do with the lakes, and rumor
had it they needed men to help build things.

Pal imagined that the city looked much better from the
water than from the dusty tracks of the B&O. But from
where he was, he felt as if he was exploring the city's dark
back alley. He had never been to Cleveland before, but he
had seen his fair share of cities while in the merchant marine,
and it was easy to learn his way around a new one.

The hilly railway corridor was overgrown with weeds and
buzzing with noisy insects. Along the way, he spied empty
liquor bottles, rusty tin cans, cigarette butts—but no soda
bottles. Soda bottles were returnable, and someone had already picked the place over, looking for empty Nehis and
Coca-Colas and some easy pocket change.

Up ahead, along the side of a small hill, he found many
flimsy shacks made of scrap wood and cardboard cereal
boxes—a Hooverville, right where he would have expected
to find one. A few men were sitting around outside their hov-
els, soaking up the sun. Most of the residents of the shantytown were probably gone for the day, looking for work—but
they would return come nightfall. From the size of the camp,
Pal figured probably sixty or more men lived there.

He approached an old man with a gray beard leaning
against a shanty and nursing a bottle of cheap liquor.

"Hey, there," said Pal.

"How-dee." The man looked up at Pal, squinting into the
sun. He raised a hand to shade his sunburned face. "You just
come into town, didn'tcha?"

"Yep."

The old man wiped the lip of his bottle on the greasy tail
of his shirt. "Wanna toot?"

"Thanks." Pal accepted the bottle and took a small gulp,
wincing at the bite; the whiskey was awful.

"You'd be lookin' for work." The old man snatched his
bottle back. The liquid sloshed around, a dirty orange-brown.

"Yep." Pal stepped to one side, so that his shadow fell
upon the old man. He laughed—once, suddenly—and heard
it echo back to him: the laugh of a man adrift at sea, surrounded by miles and miles of ocean. "Heard I could find
work in Cleveland."

"That so?" The old man nodded and offered an understanding smile. He dusted off a spot on the ground next to him, which was nothing but dirt to begin with.

Pal accepted the tacit invitation and sat down beside him, looking across at the weed-infested railway corridor, squinting his eyes in the sun's glare. He took another swig from the proffered bottle. It tasted better this time.

"That's how it always is, ain't it?" Pal said, an edge rising in his voice. "There's always work just over the next hill, but once you get there, you find it's gone somewheres else."

Absently, Pal's fist grabbed a handful of earth. He loosened his grip and allowed the dust to fall through his fingers.

"Ain't no work nowhere," offered the old man. "No sense gallivantin' around lookin' for somethin' that ain't there."

The old man had been sitting out here for some time—perhaps all day—and was sweating in the fierce sun. His clothes stank, and Pal realized he hadn't had a bath himself in a couple of weeks. He also needed to tend to the cuts and bruises he had taken in his fall.

"Is there somewheres around here a guy can get washed up?"

The old man's thumb pointed behind, over his shoulder. "Over yonder. Get yourself to Broadway. It'll take you up to Orange. Bathhouse right there on the corner. Can't miss it."

"Broadway and Orange?"

"Now what'd I say, kid?"

"Okey-doke. Don't get all bent out of shape." Pal stood up. "You guys got room here tonight if I need somewheres to sleep?"

The old man shrugged and said, "Suit yourself. But don't 'spect us to feed you."

"No, sir." Pal parted company with the old man, going in the direction his thumb had pointed, over the next hill.

5:41 P.M.

Pal spent the entire afternoon at the Orange Avenue Bath House, picking up a buck here, a buck there.

He hung around the pool area, swimming to cool down and to show off his tattooed body, washing away the blood and dirt from his skin. In the bathhouse, totally naked, nobody could see his tattered, filthy clothing. Nobody had to see him with grime caked into his face. All cleaned up, he looked no different from anybody else, except he was younger and better built than most of the men here today. He struck up friendly conversations with likely clients, and they would go off to a shower or bath cubicle together once a deal was arranged.

Pal often had to resort to hustling just to feed himself. He preferred honest work, but well-paying jobs were few and far between, and he had had the worst of luck trying to find gainful employment. Hustling was easy, he was good at it, and it provided ready cash in a clench.

Pal was standing on the wooden diving board, preparing to plunge into the deep end, when he saw a new guy entering the pool area. He paused for a moment, his concentration broken as he stood at the end of the board, his toes gripping its edge.

The new guy stripped off his towel at the other end of the pool. He looked Italian, a year or two younger than Pal, olive complected—darker and more appealing to Pal than his own fair Norwegian skin. Although the Italian's legs were covered with black hair and he sported a thick bush at his pubes, only a hint of it had grown on his chest—a dark line up to his navel, thinning out to a mere shading across his lean pectorals. The black hair on his head was in need of a trim and fell in his face, nearly hiding his eyes. His dick was uncut and rested upon hairy balls. His steps toward the edge of the pool were graceful, as if he were being careful not to slip on the wet tiles. He mounted the ladder at the shallow end and, turning his back toward Pal, lowered himself into the water. His ass was beautiful, with a hairy cleft up the middle. Once he had touched bottom, the water came up to his ribs. He dunked his head underwater and plastered his wet hair back from his face.

Pal never found himself genuinely attracted to too many guys, but this Italian was an exception. Besides which, he had an air about him that suggested he had a little dough.

Pal dove into the water headfirst, arching his back and opening his eyes as the bubbles came up around him. He swam underwater for a few yards, noticing on both sides of him the flabby legs of old men treading water, the gray hairs on their legs like goose down. Pal rose to the surface and took a breath. He saw that the Italian guy remained where he was, lounging at the shallow end. Pal butterflied his way toward him, and when he stood up at the shallow end the water came up to his own belly button.

He stood face to face with the Italian kid, who was smiling.

"Oops," he said, "sorry," as if he had run into him by accident.

"That's OK," said the Italian. His eyes were dark, his voice musical, his smile framed by dimples. He looked as if he had never had to perform any physical labor in his life. "My fault. I'm in your way. I was just playing around over here. I guess I'm always getting in somebody's way."

"You come here a lot?"

The Italian shrugged. "Once in a while, you know. I've never seen you here before, though. What's your name?"

"Pal."

"Oh!" The Italian's face brightened. "Like on your arm."

"Yeah, sure," said Pal. The kid must have noticed the screwed-up tattoo on his right forearm, which read, "Helen—Paul." The tattoo itself was beautiful, the names well drawn, with a dove underneath. It was only that despite Pal's specific instructions, the artist had misspelled his name. This had been in London, after he'd arrived into port on a freighter. He and his buddies had gotten drunk and screwed a few whores before landing themselves in the tattoo parlor, and Pal had been too snockered to be able to pay any attention while the drunken artist worked on his arm. But there was nothing he could do about it now. It would be there until the day he died; at least his mother's name was spelled correctly. Of the six tattoos on his body, this was the only one that was flawed.

"I'm Danny," said the Italian, all smiles. He extended his hand for Pal to shake. Danny himself had a beautiful red rose tattoo on his skinny right bicep, its soft petals opened up invitingly. Pal felt Danny's middle finger stray into his palm, stroking it lightly back and forth while he looked into Pal's eyes. At the same time, one of Danny's feet had found Pal's underwater and his toes were brushing against them.

Pal withdrew his hand but maintained eye contact with Danny. "What do you want?"

"That depends on what you want," said Danny.

"I'm just looking for some fun," said Pal. "I'm new in town and I don't know anybody."

"You know me." Danny placed his hands on his hips. "I'm somebody."

"Maybe you and me could have some fun."

"I'd say there's a good chance of that."

Several men were hanging out in the shallow end, lounging about, discussing financial news and the war in Ethiopia.

"Why don't we go out to the deep end and talk?" said Pal.

"All I can do is dog-paddle."

"I'll teach you how to swim."

"Is that the kind of fun you're talking about?"

"It's good enough for starters."

"OK, go ahead. But I warn you, I'm lousy."

"You? Aww, come on! You gotta be kidding me! You'll be a natural."

"Just promise me you'll save my life if I drown, OK?"

"Scout's honor." Pal held up two fingers.

He took Danny out to slightly deeper water so that Danny could bend over just enough to get his face in the water, to practice on his arms. Pal demonstrated first, showing the form Danny should strive for, how to breathe, and how the arms should look when they come up out of the water. He watched as Danny attempted this, but Danny's arms were too loose and he couldn't coordinate them with his breathing. He took in some water and had to blow it out fiercely through his nose.

Pal took a position behind him. "Here," he said. "I'll guide you." He put himself above Danny, pressing his chest against the kid's back, and laying his own arms on top of Danny's, grabbing them by the wrists. His crotch was pressed up to Danny's butt. "Ready?"

"Are you kidding?" Danny said, and laughed.

"OK. Face in the water." Pal drew Danny's right hand down in a slow, sweeping motion, brushing Danny's thumb against his hip. As the right arm came up out of the water, he took Danny's left arm down and then guided it up toward Danny's ear. "Now breathe," Pal whispered, and Danny cocked his head to the left.

They continued the movements for some time, and Danny seemed to be getting the hang of it. At the same time, he had backed up and was pressing his butt harder into Pal's crotch, and Pal was getting an erection, which made its way in between the kid's thighs. Danny squeezed his thighs together around Pal's hard-on and, at the same time, began to choke. Danny's thigh muscles squeezed as he coughed and convulsed. Pal raised him back up out of the water.

Pal slapped Danny on the back a few times until the kid seemed OK.

"Paul?" said Danny. "Maybe we ought to get out of the water. You know, work on my stroke upstairs, in a room."

"A private lesson?"

"Yeah, something like that."

"You got any money for lessons?"

"No," said Danny, grabbing Pal's hand and guiding it down to his ass, "but I'll find some way to repay you."

Pal's fingers felt Danny's crack, and he found it hard to resist. But he had to. He couldn't afford to have sex without being paid for it in some way. He would be wasting his time. He'd already made several bucks here today, and he had the potential of earning much more, especially now that people were coming in after a hard day's work. If he went off with Danny just for fun, he would actually be losing money. He had never in his life had sex with another guy for the mere pleasure of it, and the thought of it scared him.

"You sure you don't have any money?"

Danny bristled at this. "Hey," he whispered huskily, "you're getting a bargain, buster. You can do anything you want with me, for free, see? All because you're so goddamned cute. You can have my ass all night. I don't care. I want you to fuck me, understand? But you won't get a dime out of me. You're the one who's supposed to pay."

Danny reached out underwater and squeezed Pal's dick.

"Get away from me, you faggot!" Pal shoved Danny away, out into the deeper water. Heads turned from around the pool, as Pal's words echoed off the walls. Danny fell backward trying to catch himself, right where the shallow end gave way to the deep. His legs were too short to touch bottom, as the motion of the water pushed him out into deeper territory.

Danny struggled, flailing his arms before finally plunging through the surface, choking on water and gasping for air.

Pal ignored him, swimming back toward the shallow end. He felt bad, because he really liked the kid, but if there was no money to be had, there was no point in going through with it.

As Pal climbed up out of the water, thankful that his dick had shrunk back down, he heard Danny call from halfway out in the pool, where he was dog-paddling: "Never try to hustle a hustler!"

Danny's voice carried far, louder than Pal's own harsh words to him. Laughter and cat-calls came up from the men in and around the pool.

Pal grabbed his towel from the empty bench he'd put it on, and left the pool area gritting his teeth. He was going to head for the locker room and grab his stuff. He was sick of hanging around all these stupid fat old queens.

In the outer hall, he nearly ran into a handsome young guy in a towel, sweaty from a workout in the gym. Pal moved to one side, but the guy followed suit, blocking his path. He smelled of sweat and man-musk, the kind of smells that had permeated the crowded berths on board ship, the kind of smell a guy worked up when Pal offered himself to him.

"Out of my way," said Pal, staring him in the face.

But Pal was caught suddenly by the peculiar amber cast of the fellow's eyes, and by his serene stare. The stranger's mouth parted and he smiled crookedly.

"I'm sorry," said the young guy, but did not budge. His breath smelled of cigarettes, which only made Pal hungry for a smoke. "What's the magic word?"

"If you want me to say please, you can take a flying fuck."

The guy's nice smile turned into a pout. "Oh, that's too bad. And here I had a ten-dollar bill with your name on it."

Pal's mind shifted suddenly into reverse, but he had missed the clutch and his gears were grinding. Finally, he found the spot and everything was OK, and he calmed himself and smiled. Ten dollars was ten dollars; a few hours ago all he had on him was forty cents. *This* guy was the one who had said the magic word!

"You just tell me what you want, mister," said Pal.

The man with the amber eyes led him upstairs to the third floor. A blond towel boy gave Pal a wink as they passed, and raised his eyebrows Groucho-style in approval.

## 8:10 P.M.

Pal had just finished cleaning his plate when Hessler asked him if he would care for seconds.

"Yes, sir," said Pal, eyeing the slices of pot roast on the serving platter, as well as the cooked carrots and peas, mashed potatoes, fresh bread, butter, and raspberry jam.

Hessler took Pal's plate and began filling it up, adding, "You're welcome to more wine, if you like."

Pal had eaten so little of late that his stomach had shrunk and he was already full, but he wasn't about to turn down another round of such hearty fare, even if it meant making himself sick.

"Thanks," he said, and poured himself another full glass of blood-red wine. It tasted rich, and he supposed it was a more expensive vintage than the crap he shared with his fellow hobos. It had been a long time since Pal had eaten such a civilized meal.

"Tomorrow, we'll get you started," said Hessler. "First we'll have to go down to Higbee's and get you some proper clothes. Do you know how to drive?"

"Yes, sir," said Pal, though that was a lie. Ever since he was fifteen, he'd been either at sea or riding the rails, and none of the meager work he'd managed to find had ever entailed driving a car. Not that it really mattered. Everybody knew how; even women could do it.

"Fine. Then you can also make deliveries for me." Hessler owned a canary yellow Chevrolet panel van emblazoned in red with the name of his pharmacy; Pal had noticed it parked in the back alley when he and Hessler had come in through the service entrance.

Pal would have said "Sounds great," except that he was too busy chewing a slice of roast. He washed it down with a large gulp of wine. Even though the glass was only half-empty, Hessler poured again and filled it back up.

"Eat up," Hessler said. "You're too thin, maybe too weak to help me with my storeroom."

Pal shook his head, swallowing a mouthful of food. "I'm strong enough."

"I'm going to need you to move several large bags—say, fifty to a hundred pounds each. Are you sure you can handle that?"

"You bet." Pal had already been told that he would be cleaning the store, stocking products, and helping straighten out the cellar storeroom. Now, apparently, he would be making deliveries as well, and anything else Hessler wanted. It was good work, and he was eager to have a steady job for a change.

Hessler had made the proposition back at the bathhouse, after they had fucked, after Hessler had learned that Pal was from out of town and also out of work. Since Pal had no friends or family in Cleveland, Hessler had offered to put him up in the guest bedroom of his apartment in exchange for his working in the store, and had also promised him a modest hourly wage, with the job starting tomorrow and lasting "indefinitely." There was also the implication of extra duties above and beyond those of a regular stock boy, and it wasn't difficult figuring out what those duties would be.

Pal had accepted the position; he wasn't stupid. Hessler might have thought that he was using Pal, but Pal was the one who would have the last laugh. To him, there was nothing easier than giving up his ass to some queer who wanted to shower him with money and gifts. Not that Hessler acted very queer. He was only a few years older than Pal, and seemed like a regular Joe, good-looking and well groomed, if a little snooty.

"This is terrific," said Pal. "You're a good cook."

Hessler dismissed the compliment with a wave of his hand. "Nothing to write home about. Which reminds me, where is home?"

Pal shrugged, taking a bite of mashed potatoes.

"Where are your parents?"

"Don't know. I never knew my pa, and I ran away from home when I was fifteen. For all I know my ma might be dead."

"Unfortunately, I'm not so lucky. My parents are still very much alive, lording over Cleveland like Louis XVI and Marie Antoinette. I can't wait until the Terror seizes them—and then, plop, plop, *plop!*"

Pal had no idea what Hessler was talking about, and he was too busy eating to care.

"Soon as you're finished, we'll go down and I'll show you the storeroom."

"Sure." Pal wondered what was the big rush.

# 6 June 1936

Three plain gray sedans—a Hudson, a Ford, and a Lafayette—turned together off Ivanhoe Road, pulling into the gravel parking lot behind the Black Hawk Inn, where they parked alongside spiffier Cadillacs, Packards, a LaSalle coupé, and an Auburn 851 Speedster. Six gray men in gray suits and hats got out of the Hudson and the Ford and moved toward the restaurant. Four more stayed behind in the Lafayette, rolling its windows down, lighting up cigarettes and waiting. One of the four took out his boxy camera and put a fresh bulb in the flash unit.

The leader of the six gray men removed his hat as they went up the front steps of the establishment. Before going in, he stopped and turned to the man next to him. "You just stand back and keep a level head, Mr. Vehovec," he said.

"You can count on me, Mr. Ness."

*If only that were true,* thought Eliot Ness, and reminded Vehovec, "Let me do all the talking."

Councilman Anton Vehovec assented. "Do whatever you have to do, but I want this place shut down."

"I'm just doing my job, Councillor. I can't do a thing un-

124

less we can catch them with the goods. We don't even have a warrant."

He had worse than that; all he was going on was a tip from Vehovec. The councilman claimed the Black Hawk Inn was running a gambling joint, which was believable enough. Less credible was Vehovec's assertion that the operation was linked in some way to Capt. Michael J. Harwood, commander of the Fourteenth Precinct, in which the establishment operated.

The enmity between Councilman Vehovec and Captain Harwood was well-known to Ness. When Harwood had recently closed down part of the Euclid Park Beach for no discernable reason, Vehovec had gone in with wire-cutters and cut the fence down, planting a sign that read THIS IS A PUBLIC BATHING BEACH. (SIGNED) ANTON VEHOVEC, COUNCILMAN, WARD 32. Harwood had countered by threatening, "If Councilman Vehovec cut the fence and I can prove it, I'll put him in jail."

The feud had begun after Vehovec had urged Harwood to crack down on suspected gambling and disorderly houses in their district, and Harwood had refused to do anything about it, saying, "Vehovec has made a mountain out of a molehill. This vice stuff is greatly exaggerated."

Getting no help from Harwood, Vehovec had turned to Ness, handing him a list of six houses that he demanded be shut down. Ness was now conducting an investigation as a result, but his first move was coming tonight against the Black Hawk Inn. He had no evidence at this point—only Vehovec's allegations—and he had better watch his step. If Vehovec was simply engaging in political grandstanding, Ness would end up with egg on his face, right on the front page of tomorrow's papers.

"OK," Ness said. "Let's go."

Ness opened the door and led the men through the foyer. The maître d' came from the bar bearing menus, his toupee crooked upon his perspiring pate. A tobacco-stained smile shone dully beneath his greasy mustache.

"Do you have a reservation, sir?"

"No." Ness should have thought of that; a reservation would have helped.

"Then I'm afraid there might be a significant wait."

Ness scanned the dining area of the restaurant, a darkly paneled room with few windows and many tables. Half the tables were empty but set up with china, silverware, folded napkins, and lighted candles.

"How about that table over there?" Ness had little patience for people who ignored the obvious. He saw no reason why they couldn't be seated right away. Plenty of tables were free.

"It's reserved, sir," said the maître d' with perhaps too much relish. "If you'd like a seat in the lounge—"

The plan had been to sit down and begin a meal in the restaurant, and then at some point to sneak toward the back rooms, where Vehovec asserted the gambling was going on.

"Where's your men's room?" Ness blurted. If they couldn't be seated, they might as well get down to cases.

"Through that door, to the left."

Ness went in the direction pointed out by the maître d'. His five men followed behind. He grinned to himself, thinking he'd give anything to see the look on the maître d's face as they all filed past together on their way to the john.

The door to the back hallway was propped open by a felt-covered brick. Once they were all in the hall, out of the restaurant proper, Ness grabbed up the doorstop to give them some privacy. He hefted the brick in his hand and decided to keep it as a weapon. They were faced with a staircase and four closed doors, one marked GENTLEMEN, another LADIES, and the final two unmarked. Ness looked to Vehovec for help.

"Do I have your permission to speak now, Mr. Director?"

"Listen, Councillor," Ness whispered through clenched teeth, "the last thing I need is a smart-ass crusader. Tell me which door."

"Well, this one's the cellar," said Vehovec, pointing out the door nearest them. "Those other two are the facilities, so that leaves us that one."

Ness stepped quietly toward the door at the end of the hall, the one Vehovec had pointed out. As with the Harvard Club raid, he carried no gun, yet he glanced over his shoulder to make sure Detective Walker had his drawn and ready. The three men bringing up the rear were reporters from the rival newspapers, armed only with pencils, for the moment concealed. Ness removed his safety director's badge and opened up the leather case to reveal the shiny gold shield within. He checked the doorknob without making a sound, but found it locked.

From the other side of the door, Ness heard men's muffled voices but couldn't make out what they were saying. He cupped a hand to his ear and placed it against the door. After a few moments of concentration, he distinctly heard a man say, "Straight-shooter coming in at thirty-two to one," and that was good enough for him.

"OK. Get ready," he warned his men. He pounded on the door with the felt-covered brick. It left no mark, but caused an enormous sound. Suddenly a buzzer sounded from within. "Open up in there! This is the police!"

"Let's break it down," said Vehovec.

Ness said nothing. It was best to wait, give them a chance to open the door for themselves. Ness had had enough experience in court to know how *not* to louse up a case. A shadow passed before the peephole in the door; someone was checking them out. Ness only hoped they weren't packing tommy guns, as had Shimmy Patton's men. A great commotion could be heard from inside the room, as people scrambled to hide things and flee out the back exit.

"They're getting away!" said Vehovec.

Ness could hear the sounds of the Cadillacs and Packards and other automobiles roaring out of the back parking lot.

He continued pounding on the door, repeating the order to open up and let them in. After a few minutes, he succumbed to the pressure from Vehovec as well as to his own frustration and, keeping in mind that the press was watching, lifted the brick and smashed it down with great force upon the old brass doorknob, sending the knob and several small pieces crashing down onto the floor. He rammed the brick once more against the lock, and the door at last swung open and banged against the inner wall.

"Police! Don't anybody move," said Ness, going in with his badge outstretched. Detective Walker flanked him, his revolver drawn and covering the men they found inside.

The door to the parking lot was open, and many cars were leaving in a hurry. Those who had gotten out had been quick about it; men had left behind their hats, women their scarves. A dozen remained, all men, holding their hands up high, disbelief written in their faces, cigarettes dangling from their lips.

"I'm Eliot Ness, director of public safety for the City of Cleveland. This is a raid, and you're all under arrest." Ness placed his badge back in his jacket pocket. His heart beat rapidly from a rush of adrenaline.

The back room of the Black Hawk Inn was set up much like the Harvard Club had been, though considerably smaller. It had room for perhaps 150 people, and from the looks of it at least 50 had been here this evening. Blackjack tables were plentiful, and they had their own well-used chalkboard to follow the horse-racing activity, probably from a teletype in the counting room. At least ten telephones could be seen on tables around the gambling hall. Betting slips covered much of the floor; no one had called in the maid for a while.

One of the reporters went out the back exit to give the OK to their photographers, who were waiting outside in the Lafayette sedan.

Once the photographers scurried in, Detective Walker secured the back exit, and he and Ness began taking statements from the twelve people they had cornered. The gleeful Councilman Vehovec stood by, examining the various gambling apparatus and letting out an occasional curt laugh of satisfaction.

"Don't touch anything," Ness told Vehovec. "This is all evidence."

"Yes, sir, Director, sir!"

Ness thought, *Facetious bastard.*

The occasional flashbulb illuminated the room for an instant as the photographers went about their business.

Three of the detained men agreed to give statements, but the other nine were uncooperative and belligerent. Ness and Walker questioned the three separately, in preparation for written statements that Ness would have them sign. Two of these three were older fellows; it was the third guy who caught Ness's attention.

Ness took a good look at him. Here before him stood a young man, decidedly dapper in a white summer suit of the finest cambric, his black hair slicked back and gleaming, his face smooth with a healthy tan, his teeth polished, his nails manicured, his eyes the color of a good, rich ale.

He identified himself as Mott David Hessler.

Without ever having met him, Ness could tell that his father was indeed *that* Hessler—Douglass Hessler II, chairman of the board of the Ohio National Oil Company. The elder Hessler was one of the richest Republicans in Cleveland, and Ness had met him at various fund-raisers and been introduced to two of his sons, who were following in their father's footsteps and would someday take control of Ohnoco. But Ness had never met Mott Hessler, and his appearance here, considering that he came from one of Cleveland's best families, was a mystery Ness would rather not try to unravel at the moment.

"I should hope that my name and picture can be kept out of the papers," said Hessler, as he signed his statement.

"Of course," said Ness. He would probably be releasing everyone and calling them back at a later date for questioning, and he saw no reason why any of their names had to appear in print. None of them, as far as Ness had been able to determine, was the proprietor.

As Ness was signing his name as witness to Hessler's statement, a heavyset man in a tuxedo came barging into the room, followed by two plug-ugly bodyguards.

"I heard something funny was going on down here," said the man. The collar of his tux was wide, to accommodate his double chin. "I own this place and you have no right to be here. I'll give you till the count of three to get out, or I'm calling the cops."

"Who the hell are you?" Ness demanded, his patience short.

"Edward Harwood," said the fat man, folding his arms and offering a haughty smile. "My dad's the captain who runs this district."

"Well," said Ness, withdrawing his special golden badge.

He was sure Vehovec behind him was eating this up, as were the reporters. Flashbulbs shot off in a flurry. Ness took a few steps forward so Harwood could read the badge for himself. "I'm Eliot Ness. I run the police department in this town, and you're under arrest."

**8:50 P.M.**

The line for *Mutiny on the Bounty* stretched out the door of the Circle Theater and halfway down the block. People from the last crowd were still trickling out of the exits and heading to their cars, and now—finally!—the line was beginning to move. Saturday-night crowds were the worst, but at least the night air was warm and pleasant, the sky clear and speckled with stars. Inside it would be air-conditioned, and Hank hoped it wouldn't be too cold.

"Here we go," said Cathy as the people ahead of them started to inch toward the box office.

"Don't worry," said Hank. "We got plenty of time."

"So, you think you'll be able to identify him?"

"Hmm?"

"The tattooed guy."

"I don't see why not," said Hank.

Two colored youths had found the head the previous morning while they were taking a shortcut through Kingsbury Run on their way to a fishing hole. They had spotted some clothing rolled up in a bundle at the base of a willow tree under the Kinsman Road Bridge and gone to investigate. The older youth later told Hank, "So we take a fish pole and poke the bundle, and out pops a head." They had been so frightened, they dashed home and hid until their mother came back from work, at which time they told her what they had found, and she called the police.

"We've got his face," Hank continued. "And we've got good prints, a distinct set of teeth, plus the tattoos. Haven't turned up anything yet, but we're going to start showing some photos around the docks tomorrow. He had some nautical tattoos. Looks like a sailor."

This morning, the Nickel Plate Railroad dicks searching Kingsbury Run had turned up the rest of the guy's body, nude and headless but otherwise intact, hidden under some sumac branches near the East 55th Street bridge, eight hundred feet away from where the head had been found. Pearse said the body was fresh, that he had been killed either late Wednesday or early Thursday, and that it was definitely the work of the same person who had killed Eddie Andrassy and Florence Polillo, as well as the still-unidentified older man whose body had been dumped with Andrassy's no more than a mile away from where the newest corpse had been found. No identification could be located on the body or on any of the clothing found nearby, so they were hoping the tattoos would help in identifying the man, who was good-looking and in his early twenties. The railroad dicks thought the head and torso had been deposited sometime after three o'clock in the afternoon on Thursday, the last time they had patrolled those particular areas. One railroad worker reported having seen what he described as a Cadillac parked beneath the Kinsman Road Bridge late Thursday evening.

Dep. Det. Insp. Charlie Nevel had theorized that the victim had been a hobo sleeping near the railroad tracks, when "this maniac attacked him, cut his throat, hacked away at his neck, and then undressed him." But Hank had had to point out to poor Charlie Nevel that no blood could be found anywhere in the area, so the victim had to have been killed elsewhere and then dumped, like the others.

Hank had stayed mum with reporters at the insistence of Sergeant Hogan, the spokesman for the Homicide unit, but Nevel had slipped and told the press they were dealing with "a maniac with a lust to kill." Jim Hogan had been furious and had taken Nevel to task. The Republican National Convention was coming up next week and the Great Lakes Exposition was slated to open at the end of the month, and Hogan didn't want any out-of-town visitors thinking there was a homicidal maniac loose on the streets of Cleveland.

Hank was so preoccupied thinking about the case that he failed to notice they had reached the head of the movie line.

"Hey, mister, you want a ticket, or what?" asked the blond gum-chewing girl manning the box office.

Cathy elbowed him sharply in the ribs. "Hank."

"Uh, yeah." He slid two quarters under the glass. The girl punched up the two tickets, and they headed inside.

Lewie Wasserman, the young fresh-faced manager of the theater, was standing right inside the lobby, greeting the patrons and ripping their tickets in half.

"Hi, Lewie," said Hank. He and Cathy came here often; the Circle was their neighborhood movie palace, on Euclid and 102nd Street, near Western Reserve University.

"Hope you enjoy the show." Lewie nodded them in.

Hank liked Lewie's offerings, which were always of the highest class. The Circle was popular with the college crowd. Never did Lewie show a silly Warner Brothers gangster epic or one of those lurid Universal thrillers.

Hank had needed a good diversion after such a long, grueling day. They had found the body of the tattooed man almost twelve hours ago, and Hank was bushed. Besides that, Cathy had been dying to see Clark Gable riding the high seas; Hank himself was partial to Franchot Tone.

"You think it's the same killer?" asked Cathy. They got in line to get a bag of buttered popcorn and two Coca-Colas. The cool air-conditioned air felt good after having waited so long in the early June heat.

"Jim Hogan's telling the press there's no connection, but that's just because he doesn't want to cause a scare."

"It's your case. What do you think?"

"No doubt about it. Coroner's almost a hundred percent sure. But don't go telling any reporters I said so, or Hogan'll have my head."

"That's not funny."

"Wasn't meant to be." Hank paid for the popcorn and Cokes and grabbed a straw for his wife.

They entered the darkened auditorium just as the newsreel was beginning, and made their way to a pair of empty seats toward the front, where Hank preferred to sit. The newsreel showed Benito Mussolini speaking to a cheering throng of Italians, followed by shaky footage of his infantry and fighter planes battling the Ethiopians.

"I don't see how you'll ever catch this guy," Cathy said, passing the popcorn to Hank.

"Shh!" said Hank. He wanted to get his mind off it.

A Silly Symphony cartoon came on after the newsreel, and Hank laughed until his stomach was sore and tears were streaming down his cheeks. It was the first really *good* laugh he had had all day.

Hank wiped his eyes dry with his handkerchief before the start of the movie, and then held Cathy's hand in the darkness for a moment as the lion roared and the opening credits began to roll.

# 8 June 1936

**10:39 P.M.**

Eliot Ness guarded his scotch and soda carefully against his chest while excusing his way through the clumsy elbows and laughing potbellies of Republican bigwigs. Cigar smoke was thick throughout the entire suite, and as the party filled up, the breeze from the open windows had been lost. The only way to grab a good draft of cool air was to maneuver next to an open window—and then you were liable to be accidentally pushed out and fall to your death twelve stories below—no doubt by some delegate for Senator Borah drunk on potato beer.

Ness shook his head, clearing the thought from his mind, and concentrated instead on the matter at hand, which was that while getting his drink, he had lost his wife.

He hoped Edna was all right. They had had an ugly argument on the way over to the Hotel Cleveland. Their marriage had nearly come to an end right there in the car.

A hand groped out, gold cufflinks glinting, and grabbed his arm. "Eliot!"

Ness turned and saw that Mayor Burton had made his way back. It was opening night of the convention, and Harold Burton was hosting a welcoming party in his vast suite.

"Harry, you throw a hell of a party." Ness had to shout in the mayor's ear to be heard over the general jocularity. "Say, have you seen Edna?"

"A whole gaggle of them just went to the powder room." Burton placed an arm around Ness's shoulder. "The smoke," he added. "Makes the mascara run."

Edna wore no mascara—besides which, she smoked.

Ness took a sip of his drink; the bartender had gone light on the soda, and that was the way he liked it. "You think she'll be all right?"

"Oh, gods, yes! They're all talking politics. Out here, it's only baseball. Here, I want you to meet somebody."

Burton led Ness through the throng, to the dapper figure of a businessman in charcoal gray pinstripes a shade darker than the streaks combed back from his widow's peak, wearing wire-rimmed Rooseveltian pince-nez and a button on his lapel proclaiming himself for Knox. Ness had met the man before and was amazed—only two days after his raid on the Black Hawk Inn—at the resemblance between him and his son Mott David Hessler, the only difference being thirty-odd years of wear and tear.

The mayor made the introductions. "Eliot Ness, may I present Douglass Hessler the Second, and, er, vice versa!"

"We've already been introduced," said Ness, shaking the hand of Douglass Hessler II, and trying to remember where it was, exactly, they had met.

Mayor Burton, being the good host he was, quietly vanished into the crowd to make further introductions, and to ingratiate himself with the machinery of the party.

"Yes, quite right," said Hessler, his flaming amber eyes magnified by the lenses of his spectacles. "Your speech to the advertiser's club. 'Round about New Year's, I believe. Very impressive."

*Yes, that was it*—Ohnoco had picked up an award for that inane little radio jingle. Hessler had been there with two of his sons. Ness had spoken of his shake-up of the police and fire departments and the fight against corruption, and had been well received by the group.

"Oh, that was nothing," said Ness, knowing his modesty was in fact false. He had literally dashed off the speech a mere hour before the luncheon and ad-libbed half of it on the spot.

"Harry tells me you're cleaning up the police force."

*For Christ's sake,* thought Ness, *doesn't he read the papers?*

"It's a bigger job than I thought it would be," Ness offered.

It was the last subject he wanted to discuss; the investigation was ongoing and growing larger and more cumbersome every day. It seemed Captain Harwood wasn't the only captain on the take, not to mention the vast number of crooked lieutenants—and they would all be getting the boot. So far his investigation had only revealed the tip of the iceberg. When Ness had told the mayor as much during their handball game yesterday afternoon, Burton had congratulated him on his early successes but, at the same time, urged him to keep the story out of the press during the week of the convention. Despite the fact that the corruption had bloomed during previous administrations, Burton wasn't keen for his pals in the party to know the extent of the problem—not until it was all tidied up. So Ness was watching what he said publicly and keeping a low profile with the press.

"You're a Chicago boy, aren't you?" asked Hessler.

"Born and bred." Ness resented being called a boy.

"Then I suppose you're for Knox."

Ness glanced at Hessler's button and prepared to lie. "Uh, yes, I am."

He was, in fact, for no-nonsense Senator Borah, the lion of Idaho. He knew Colonel Knox, publisher of the Chicago *Daily News,* all too well to be for him. At the same time, he saw the party's favorite, Governor Landon of Kansas, for what he was—a stooge of William Randolph Hearst. This convention was going to be a bloodbath. Knox's forces were slinging mud at the Landon camp, and Borah was taking on all comers. None of them stood a chance against Roosevelt, anyhow; most of the talk at the convention so far was about how they *might* have a shot at the White House in 1940.

"That's good to hear," said Hessler. "Harry's been telling me a lot about you. So you're really the guy who bagged Al Capone, eh?"

"That's right. It was my job."

"Listen, Ness, you're young. You got a bright future ahead of you."

"Well, I got my work cut out for me—"

Hessler's eyebrows drew together, making a furrow on his brow. "You got yourself a wife, son?"

"Why, yes." Ness glanced over his shoulder, looking for Edna's pink pillbox hat. "She's here somewhere."

"Fine, fine! Listen, Harry's not going to be mayor for long. He's looking statewide, maybe the governor's house, maybe the Senate. Got a good chance, too. But Cleveland's a Democratic city. Always has been, 'cause of all these Catholics. But we don't want to let City Hall slip through our fingers, if you know what I mean."

Ness knew what he meant, all right, and he was dumbfounded. Although he had studied political science at the University of Chicago, he had always told himself he never had any political aspirations, that his career was in law enforcement and that he would be an abject failure at anything else.

"You've got the wrong guy, Mr. Hessler." He had to be careful what he said. Douglass Hessler II held all the cards when it came to political support, not to mention money.

"Have I? The man who nabbed Scarface Al? The man who cleaned up Cleveland? Presuming, of course, that you—"

"Oh, don't worry. I'll clean it up, all right. But I'm no politician, you see, just a former G-man."

"Precisely my point." Hessler's index finger pointed straight into the air. "We don't stand a chance against FDR this year."

"Of course, everybody says—"

"Yes, everybody says! And they're damn right. The only way we could possibly win in this election is if we were to nominate Lindbergh."

"Fat chance." Ness had seen the newsreels; Charles Lindbergh was in Europe preaching peace and had already indicated his lack of interest in the presidency.

"My point is this," continued Hessler excitedly. "The people don't want politicians anymore. Politicians got them into this mess, and by the time Franklin Rosenfeld's through Socializing them they won't trust anyone in Washington. What they want are heroes, and it's no different in Cleveland."

"Mr. Hessler, I may like to think of myself as a hero, but the truth is, no one's ever heard of me. Everybody knows about Al Capone. Nobody knows I'm the guy who did him in."

Hessler shook his head. "Doesn't matter. You're still the guy who did it. You keep up the good work as safety director, and the mayor's office is in the bag. Trust me." Hessler clapped Ness on the back and grinned, showing brown flecks of chewing tobacco stuck between his teeth.

Ness was eager to change the subject. "Say, I met your son the other day—Mott, is it?"

Hessler's smile faded and his face grew pale. "Pardon?"

"Well, I assumed he was your son, but—"

"Oh, he's mine, all right. Wherever did you meet him?" Hessler's tone was derisive, and Ness wondered if he had trespassed into forbidden territory.

At the same time, he realized he had painted himself into a corner. He could hardly tell Hessler he had met his son in the gambling room of the Black Hawk Inn. He had promised his son he would keep his name out of it, and he had so far kept his promise; no names had appeared in the papers other than those of the arrested proprietors. It would have been best if Ness had never mentioned having met Mott David Hessler.

"Well, sir—" Ness began.

"I suppose you went into his drugstore," said Douglass Hessler II. "It couldn't have been in polite company."

*Good God,* thought Ness, *that's quite a thing to say about your own son. Perhaps he already knows about his gambling.*

Ness fortified himself with a swig of scotch. "Yes, actually, I did go in and pick up a prescription, and—"

The color suddenly returned to Hessler's cheeks. He was looking just beyond, over Ness's shoulder, at something that seemed to tickle his fancy. Ness felt a small arm squeeze his waist, and realized what had caught Hessler's attention: Edna had returned.

He placed his own arm around his wife and gave her a chaste kiss on the cheek. "There you are!" he said, relieved by the timely interruption. Edna had saved him from sticking his foot farther into his mouth and gnawing on it awhile. "Edna, this is Douglass Hessler. He runs Ohnoco."

"Yes, I know," she said with a laugh, as if he were being completely silly. Everyone knew who ran Ohnoco.

"Charmed," said Hessler with a small bow. "We were just discussing your husband."

"My favorite subject," said Edna.

Ness could feel himself turning beet-red. Edna was certainly putting her best face forward.

"Mrs. Ness, how would you like to become the first lady of Cleveland . . . someday?"

"Oh, don't be ridiculous. Eliot doesn't want to be mayor, do you, honey?"

Hessler turned to Ness with a piqued eyebrow.

"No, of course not." Ness laughed at the thought, and tried to firm up his smile.

It wasn't the first time he had ever lied to his wife.

# 22 July 1936

**11:40 A.M.**

Hank parked the unmarked Ford sedan on the slanting shoulder of Clinton Road, just ahead of the coroner's white Dodge panel van, which, in the rearview mirror, looked to him more like a bakery truck. His passenger, Det. Sgt. James Hogan, got out, and Hank decided to slide across the seat and exit from the passenger side as well, since the car was sloping in that direction and he was feeling lazy this morning. Vern Quast climbed uphill out of the backseat, getting out on the driver's side.

Hank took a whiff of the fresh Brooklyn air. The forest through which the road had been cut had grown rich and lush after the spring rains and summer sun.

Hank lighted a Lucky, hoping it would help with his digestion as the advertisements so loudly proclaimed. His stomach had been queasy all morning, and he was feeling out of sorts. Cathy had woken him up with the radio this morning, and the first thing he had heard was an unsettling news report about Fascist rebels taking Toledo. It wasn't until he had finished his shower that he realized they had been talking about Spain.

A number of marked squads from both the Brooklyn and

Cleveland police departments were parked on either side of the road.

"Must be through here," said Jim Hogan, pointing to a semblance of a path through the trees, along which various Brooklyn Village policemen were coming and going. In the distance could be seen two white-jacketed men from the coroner's office carrying a gurney.

Meandering through the dense forest, Hank kicked a bloated puffball out of spite, and it spewed its dark spores all around in a moldy green cloud.

No less than a hundred yards along the trail, they reached the site, in a clearing currently peopled by several uniformed policemen and a handful of others in plainclothes. Among them was a police photographer and the oversized coroner, A.J. Pearse, his jacket off, sleeves rolled up, hair and mustache greased up. He brushed aside several policemen and squatted before what must have been the corpse, while the photographer snapped photos.

"Excuse me," said Jim Hogan. "Sergeant Hogan, Cleveland Homicide. Excuse me, fellas."

The three detectives from Central Station had to push their way past the craning necks of the fascinated village police force, identifying themselves as they went.

"Detective Lambert, Cleveland Homicide."

From the wide-eyed expressions on their faces, these Brooklyn officers looked like babes in the woods as they stared at the object of interest.

Looking past Pearse's rotund figure, Hank could see for himself what all the commotion was about.

Lying facedown on the ground was a naked and badly decomposed body, *sans* head. The sweet, rotten stench of decay permeated the still air. The skin of the corpse had turned a sickly gray, mottled with colorful growths and slimy, gelatinous patches of flesh, out of which the bones of the ribcage were poking quite plainly. Flies and beetles crawled all over the body, nibbling.

"Jesus Christ." Jim Hogan cupped his handkerchief over his mouth.

Hank saw now why they had been called down: another headless corpse—a mystery the Brooklyn police would rather not have to tackle on their own, and which seemed to tie in with the other similar Cleveland murders.

"What do you think, A.J.?" asked Hank, squatting down beside the coroner.

"It's a man, I know that, at least. Been dead now, say, two months or so. That's my best guess before an autopsy."

"You think it's the work of our maniac friend?"

"Well, we'll just have to wait and see." The coroner's voice was clouded with uncertainty.

"Meaning what?" Hank didn't feel like playing games.

"Meaning, Lucky, that I'm not so sure we're going to need the services of your boys, after all."

"Oh, come on, A.J., look at this! How could a man get his head cut off without being murdered?"

"You know what would happen right now if I grabbed this arm?" Pearse pointed at the splayed-out limb of the corpse. "It would come clean off, see? Just like that. Now, what if this man died out here all by his lonesome, a couple months ago, and some dog comes along a month or so later and snatches up the head?"

"We haven't got the head?"

"Oh, no, we've got it, all right. It's over there in the bushes, waiting to get its portrait taken."

"No good for identification, I suppose."

"Are you kidding?" said Pearse, standing up. Hank heard popping sounds coming from the coroner's knees. "Not unless he's got some unique bridgework."

Hank rose to his feet as well. The noxious smell was doing little to alleviate his queasy stomach. He sucked down the last of his cigarette. "Do the best you can, A.J."

The coroner nodded, and waddled over to the department's photographer. Together, they went off in the direction of the head. Hank stayed behind. He had never before seen a face that had been decomposing in the warm summer air for two months, and he supposed he could wait a few minutes longer and enjoy another smoke.

Lighting another cigarette, Hank thought about the other murders and realized that in every instance, the killer had dispatched his victim somewhere other than where he later laid them out. But as he stared down at the rotten corpse at his feet, he noticed that the earth beneath the severed neck was a darker shade than the earth surrounding it. The darker shade spread out from the neck in a circular shape, and it was a subtle enough difference in color for Pearse not to have noticed it. Hank called the coroner back over.

"A.J., come look at this." He crouched down and dug out some of the darker soil.

Pearse looked at Hank's find and muttered, "Oh, dear."

"A.J., if your dog came around a month or so after this guy died, he wouldn't have bled like this, would he?"

"No, of course not."

"Then unless we can come up with this guy's wallet, I say we start referring to this one as Number Five."

Jim Hogan ran his fingers through his thinning hair, saying, "Jesus Christ," once more.

Hank stood up and went over to talk to him. This was the last thing Hogan wanted, that was for sure. He had been trying to deny all along that there was a connection between the five slayings. Hank could tell Hogan was worried, but he was less concerned about the killer than he was about the press. The Great Lakes Exposition was drawing people to Cleveland from all over the Midwest, and if the public knew that a mad killer had been stalking their streets for ten months now, it would be a public relations disaster for the Homicide Bureau. They would get heat from City Hall, worried about lost tourism dollars and a frightened populace. Jim Hogan seemed to want to delay the truth as long as possible. Hank, on the other hand, believed it had been put off far too long.

"What do you say, Jim? What are you going to give the press?"

"Listen, Lucky, we've got to wait until the autopsy."

"This is his fifth, you know."

"You're jumping the gun. Look, Lucky, all the other bodies turned up near the Flats. What's this one doing in Brooklyn, huh? Answer me that."

"Jim, it's the same guy, and if A.J.'s right, this one was killed before our tattooed friend. How many more has he killed that we don't know about?"

"It still could have been a dog that tore off his head. We don't even know if those are bloodstains."

"That's bullshit, Jim, and you know it." Hank exhaled a thick cloud of smoke. He was getting jittery, adrenaline flowing through his veins. "So when do we tell the city they're being stalked by a maniac?"

Hogan pointed a finger at him. "You'd better not use that word with the press. This may be your case, Lucky, but I'm the one running the show."

"OK, Jim, OK." Hank saw no point in pushing Hogan over the edge; he didn't want to lose the case.

Hogan smiled suddenly and placed his arm around Hank's shoulders. "I'll make you a deal," he said. "Next time. Next time, we'll tell them. But I just hope to God you catch him before there is a next time."

*Touché,* Hank thought.

# 10 September 1936

**12:32 P.M.**

"Mr. Harris, exactly where did you find this . . . trunk?" Hank didn't know what else to call it.

"Already told you, I didn't touch nothing."

Hank, of course, knew where the upper half of the man's torso had been found; his line of questioning was merely a formality, to make sure the witness's story gelled.

"Just tell me once more where you found it."

"Right there at the edge of the pool." Jerry Harris, who had discovered the remains, had purple rings of exhaustion around his eyes and a few days' growth of beard. His breath stank of alcohol, and his clothes could have used a good fumigating.

"Suppose you show me." Hank led the poor hobo back down the gully, toward the rectangular pool.

Sergeant Hogan was there, directing ten other detectives in their search for the rest of the man's body. A flock of policemen were performing their various duties around the garbage-strewn banks of the pool, setting up a perimeter, directing onlookers away from the scene, searching for evidence, plunging grappling hooks into the oily waters hoping to find more parts of the corpse. Despite their best efforts at crowd control, hundreds of people had gathered beyond the police line. Some watched from the bridge above.

The pool itself was the terminus of a vast underground sewer system that collected run-off from the nearby factories. The steel mills and petroleum companies in the Flats dumped their raw sewage, yellow ore-tinted wastewater, poisonous chemicals, and other industrial refuse into this sewer line. The deep man-made pool sat beneath the East Thirty-seventh Street railroad bridge, acting as a dam, allowing a steady flow of contaminated water to spill over its edge, feeding into a small stream that ran through a gully along the floor of Kingsbury Run and eventually emptied out into the Cuyahoga River.

Hank stepped gingerly through the swampy ground sloping down toward the edge of the pool. If he had known it was going to be like this, he would have brought a pair of galoshes. As it was, his shoes were caked with mud.

"Right here," said Jerry Harris, the hobo, pointing at the spot on the ground where the police had retrieved the trunk after photographing it. "I was up there by the tracks, waiting for this freight. I looked down here and thought I was seeing things. The train wasn't coming for a bit, so I came on down here to see what in tarnation . . ." Harris's voice trailed off, and Hank couldn't make sense of the mumbling that followed.

"Come on, Mr. Harris, speak up." Hank's patience was short.

"Well, there it was, plain as day. I knew right off it must have been the Phantom."

"The Phantom?" Hank was caught off guard. He scrawled the word down on his notepad.

It brought to mind an early date with his then-fiancee Cathy Lucerne eleven years ago, when he had taken her to the premiere of *The Phantom of the Opera* at the Allen Theater. Cathy had jumped a foot out of her seat when the poor opera singer girl had unmasked the Phantom. Men and women alike had shrieked at the grotesque revelation, but the part that had frightened Hank the most and had stuck with him all these years, creeping into his nightmares and leaping into his mind when he least expected it, was the masquerade scene in which the Phantom descended the stairs of the Paris Opera House disguised as Poe's Red Death—the crimson skull-face dressed in its gaudy costume, emerging from among the revelers to lay waste to all in the movie's amazing color sequence—that was the image that imposed itself upon Hank's mind at this particular moment.

"What do you mean? What Phantom?" Hank prodded, his fingers shaking. He told himself he had drunk too much coffee this morning.

"I don't know," said Harris. "I thought it was just a story the old boys told. You know."

"No, I don't."

"The Phantom of Kingsbury Run. I hear tell of him stalking around at night, in the dark, preying on the hobos. Head-hunting, they say."

"Has anyone seen this Phantom?" Hank was hurrying to write all this down on his notepad. His pencil lead was growing dull, his writing fuzzy.

Harris shook his head, laughing uneasily. "Not anyone I ever talked to. If 'n you see him, you're a dead man. I figgered it was just a story, but now I know different. You got a cigarette?"

Hank handed him a Lucky.

He got the rest of Harris's statement, but other than the bare facts the hobo had little to tell. He was from St. Louis and had come up to Cleveland riding a boxcar, looking for work. He had been here a week and was about to leave on a southbound train when he spotted the trunk and ran off to call for help.

Hank turned the hobo over to a uniformed officer to hold for further questioning.

He had already got a good look at what they had found of the body thus far. If the man's arms hadn't been severed at his sockets, he would have appeared broad-shouldered and muscular. His neck was thick, but he had no head. His pectorals were firm and well defined, covered with a fine light brown hair, and his nipples were blue and hard. The rest of his skin, naturally, had a bluish-white cast. His figure was trim right down to his navel, where he had been cut neatly in two.

Hank took a cigarette for himself and surveyed all the action around him. He wondered where all the people had come from. The surrounding crowd was growing with every minute: curiosity-seekers looking for thrills they could never find at the Expo.

Some people were simply thrilled by the gruesome; others weren't. Hank had never taken Cathy to another thriller after *The Phantom of the Opera*—she got no pleasure out of being frightened and couldn't understand why people lined up to see such "nonsense," much less paid money for it. So Hank had had to go see thrillers by himself.

"Holy Mother!" cried a voice.

Hank snapped his head in the direction of the voice and saw his partner, Vernal Quast, pulling something white and fleshy out of the brackish water with a grappling hook. He tramped through the mud to the other side of the pool, joining Quast and Hogan while other policemen looked on and the voices in the crowd grew louder with anticipation.

*This is what you paid for, folks!*

"Jesus Christ," muttered Hogan, predictably.

What Quast had found appeared on first glance to be the lower half of the man's torso.

"Good work. Looks like a match," said Hank.

As Quast pulled it onto the swampy banks, it revealed itself as a hairy man's buttocks. Rolling it over with the wooden pole, Hank saw where the thigh muscles had been cut and the femur bones wrenched from the pelvis. In between, surrounded by pubic hair, was a purple blood-caked hole where the cock and balls should have been. The abdomen had been skillfully sliced in half and looked like a perfect fit with the upper portion found earlier.

"Well, Jim," said Hank. "You want proof, here's your proof. I don't need A.J. Pearse to tell me what we got here, do you?"

"No," said Sergeant Hogan, holding his stomach as if he were about to throw up.

"This one's been cut up exactly like Florence Polillo," Hank went on. "And the emasculation's just like Andrassy and Number Two. What more do you need?"

"Jesus Christ."

Hogan removed his hat and wiped his sweaty forehead with a handkerchief. He looked up at the people watching from the railroad bridge and at the thick crowds of onlookers gathered upon the muddy hillocks of Kingsbury Run. The mumblings from the crowd had grown into a steady roar of noise from all sides.

"We'd better find the rest of this guy's body," Hogan continued. "I want his head, I want his hands, I want a positive ID. Let's get some divers down there, call the Marines or something. If that doesn't work, we'll blast it, dynamite the lower end and drain the damned thing. What is this now, number . . . ?" Hogan knit his brow.

"Six," Hank interjected without having to think. "This is Number Six. Sir."

# 15 September 1936

Hank poured himself a cup of coffee from the institutional-size pot on the counter in the police lab, where Eliot Ness was holding his "Torso Clinic." Thirty-odd men packed the room, and not everyone had a seat. Hank remained standing by the coffeepot; the room was small enough and the air so close that he felt no need to get more intimate with his colleagues.

Eliot Ness stood up. He cut an unimpressive figure in his close-fitting suit, and his haircut reminded Hank of Alfalfa in the *Our Gang* shorts—parted down the middle with bangs combed on either side. He looked like a slice of Americana from the cover of a *Saturday Evening Post*, like Tom Sawyer or some overgrown Boy Scout. Ness's tie was knotted snugly at his collar, and the sleeves of his shirt poked out of his jacket cuffs. Hank figured he and Ness were about the same age, which made them easily the youngest lawmen in the room.

"The last thing I want to do is step on the toes of the Homicide squad," Ness began, "but like everyone else, I want to see this psychopath caught. I'll give you all the help you need, but I'm leaving the ball in your court. With each new case, citizens are growing frightened. We're all getting calls from suspicious neighbors and the usual cranks. My idea is for us to sit down and hash this thing out, see if we can agree on a profile of the kind of man we're dealing with, something concrete to give the press."

Chuckles arose in the room. Unlike Ness, most policemen preferred keeping reporters at a discreet distance.

"Maybe we can show we're on the right track," continued Ness. "Maybe our man will get worried. Maybe this will smoke him out. Anyway, gentlemen, I now turn you over to Sergeant Hogan, who's been directing the investigation over at Homicide. Jim?"

Ness returned to his chair as the gaunt figure of Jim Hogan rose to speak. Most everybody else had already removed their suit jackets and were sitting around in white shirts, suspenders, and short fat ties that rested at the top of their bellies. Ness, however, remained completely dressed despite the heat. The room had no windows or air-conditioning, and with thirty-odd paunchy policemen, psychiatrists, and reporters packed tightly together, the temperature had risen noticeably. Hank had left his own jacket back at his desk in the Detective Bureau; he had been on the job since eight o'clock that morning.

"Gentlemen," Hogan began, his eyebrows knitting together above the rim of his glasses. His mouth formed a bitter scowl. "Tonight we're right where we were the day the first bodies were found. Our meager clues have led nowhere. We've tracked down too many false leads. And all we've got for our troubles is a total of six corpses and a hell of a lot of frustration."

Detectives laughed nervously. They had begun lighting their cigarettes, pipes, and cigars, using the floor as an ashtray. Hell, the janitors would clean it up.

Hogan turned the discussion over to Coroner Pearse, whose bulk dwarfed his bow tie and made his head seem shrunken by comparison. He had waxed his mustache anew for this occasion; he touched it absently as he stood up. For the next forty-five minutes, Pearse led a discussion of the circumstances surrounding each murder. Hank and the other Homicide detectives interrupted frequently with the various details of their investigations—the clues that had led nowhere, the suspects who had been picked up and questioned, the crazies who had "confessed" to the crimes, the rumors that had developed among the denizens of the Roaring Third. Each investigation had so far led straight into a brick wall.

Pearse set up a chart on a small wooden easel and asked Dr. Reuben Strauss, the county pathologist who had assisted him in each autopsy, to explain it. The chart represented the six victims, and just what, exactly, had been done to whom.

"As you can see here," Dr. Strauss began, pointing at the chart with a yardstick, "Numbers One, Two, and Six were all emasculated."

"Yee-ouch!" said a reporter standing at the back of the room. Eliot Ness turned and frowned at him.

Strauss continued unabated: "The genitals of two of the males were left intact, those of Number Four and Number Five. There was a gash several inches in length near the vagina of the female, Number Three, but the coroner and I determined it to be a mere slip of the knife as the killer set about cutting off her thighs, and not an attempt to disfigure her sex organs."

Pearse nodded his agreement.

Several of the detectives were visibly squirming in their seats. Hank was glad to be standing; he found such hard wooden chairs uncomfortable, reminding him of the chairs at the Catholic school he had attended. The coffee and cigarettes had left a dry, bitter aftertaste, so he unpeeled his roll of Life Savers and popped one of the little Pep-O-Mint candies into his mouth.

"We believe our killer is some kind of sexual pervert," said Coroner Pearse. "Probably a homosexual."

"If I may, for a moment," interjected Dr. Guy Williams, superintendent of the Cleveland State Hospital for the Criminally Insane, "I've had quite a lot of experience with homosexuals—"

Titters could be heard from several of the detectives.

"Professional experience," Williams corrected, his bearded face turning the deep red color of a good borscht. "And I must say, these methods of . . . mutilation do not fit into the established patterns of conduct of such an individual. Most homosexuals that I've had the occasion to . . . examine"—more titters, but Williams went on—"would have been incapable of this type of violence. Aside from their . . . illness, most homosexuals lead relatively normal lives and are impossible to tell from the rest of us. It may very well be, gentlemen, that your killer is some form of sexual degenerate and perhaps a homosexual, but I doubt very much that that alone is the root of his behavior."

"Excuse me, Doctor," said Eliot Ness. "But do you remember Leopold and Loeb?"

"Of course. A most singular duo."

"They were classmates of mine at the University of Chicago—and while I don't pretend to be an expert, still, I followed the case pretty closely. It seemed to me that their homosexuality was the central factor in their killing of that little boy."

"Why should it have been?" asked Williams. "They did it for the thrill of killing itself. There was no evidence of sexual . . . molestation."

"That's not exactly what I mean, Doctor. As homosexuals, these two could have been classified as mentally ill, yet they were prosecuted as if perfectly sane."

"Simply because someone is mentally disturbed doesn't make them insane, Mr. Ness."

"But how far can such an illness spread? Couldn't it conceivably grow worse and eat at the brain? Now, as a Chicagoan, I realize passions were running high during the trial, but to this day I still think Leopold and Loeb deserved treatment at an institution such as yours, Dr. Williams, rather than incarceration in prison. If the Torso Slayer is a similar kind of homosexual, couldn't his illness have affected his brain in a similar way? Couldn't that be the real reason he kills?"

"Homosexuality is a psychiatric disorder, Mr. Ness, not a cancer," said Dr. Williams. "It does not corrupt the flesh or 'eat at the brain,' as you put it. As to Leopold and Loeb, it is clear to me they were simply cold-blooded killers. Your man, on the other hand, is clearly insane. Now I gather that none of his victims were sexually . . . violated, am I correct?"

Pearse nodded. "As far as we can make out."

"Let's just say we found no evidence showing any signs of forced entry," said Strauss, who seemed surprised by the chuckles that accompanied his remark.

Ness sighed audibly, addressing the room, "Let's cut the clowning."

"If there was any consensual sexual intercourse between the killer and his victims," Strauss continued, "we found no evidence of such. However, there is the matter of the severed sex organs. I think Dr. Williams would agree with me that such a violent act would have to have a sexual pretext."

"You mean subtext," Dr. Williams corrected. "But that doesn't necessarily follow. This fellow cuts off arms as well as penises."

Ness made a quick survey of the room, but nobody dared laugh this time.

Williams glanced at his colleague, Dr. Royal Grossman of Common Pleas Court, daring him to disagree, but Grossman kept mum. Williams folded his arms. "Please continue."

The chastened Strauss returned to his chart. "You can see that no matter how else the bodies have been mutilated, the mode of death in each case is identical. He kills them by cutting off their heads. Four of the victims were left relatively whole, with only the heads and in two cases the genitals missing. These also happen to be the same bodies whose heads were recovered. The other two—Number Three and Number Six—were thoroughly dismembered, and these heads have yet to be found. Until we dredged up the man in the pool, we were going on the theory that the killer had done what he did to Mrs. Polillo—and Mrs. Polillo alone— out of his hatred toward women. But the latest case throws that theory out the window."

"It's half-baked, anyway." Dr. Williams's interruption was loud and abrupt. "I've seen nothing so far that would suggest this fellow is a misogynist. He's only killed one woman out of a possible six victims. Such simple answers, I'm afraid, are unreliable in this case."

"But it's obvious that—"

"Excuse me, Dr. Strauss, but I have dealt during my entire professional career with the criminally insane, and I must say that I cannot fit the activities of this murderer into any recognizable pattern of insanity."

*That hushed everybody up rather well,* Hank thought. The only sound he could hear was his own crunching of the candy in his mouth. The room was getting hotter. Beads of sweat had formed on the balding pates of his fellow detectives.

"But he is insane," said Ness, as if needing reassurance.

"Of course, of course." Now that he had everybody's attention, Dr. Williams paused for a moment to light his pipe. The sweet scent of his tobacco met Hank's nose, and he found it enticing. "But very little is known about this new type of insanity. The best-documented case is one that occurred in Victorian London—Jack the Ripper, also known as Red Jack, Leather Apron, *et cetera*—surely you've heard of him. He went on a . . . tear, shall we say, in 1888, killing several prostitutes and disemboweling them. His methods were distinctly different from this so-called Torso Slayer of yours, but their madness, gentlemen, is the same. And Jack the Ripper, by the by, was never apprehended."

"Don't jinx us, Doctor," said Ness with an uneasy laugh.

"Scotland Yard never had a clue as to his identity."

"But that was nearly fifty years ago," said Ness. "We've had a few advances in criminology since then. Fingerprints, lie detector tests, a better grasp of forensics. I see no reason why we can't catch him."

"Has your Torso Slayer ever left you a print?" asked Williams, but Ness must have taken the question as rhetorical, for he offered no response. Williams, meanwhile, puffed on his pipe. "The tricky thing about this type of individual is that he is not recognizably insane. By all outward appearances, he is as normal as you or I. He leads a perfectly ordinary existence, except for the occasional moment of sadistic passion that leads him to murder. Although six victims in the space of a year may seem like a lot, ask yourselves this question: what was your Torso Slayer doing the other three hundred fifty-nine days of the year?"

Hank had recognized all along that they were dealing with

more than a simple murder case, yet he still found Dr. Williams's words disconcerting.

"But you must have your share of psychopaths at the state hospital," said Ness.

"Oh, I've got plenty. Let me give you an example of how the typical insane murderer operates, sir. We had this one fellow locked up, but somehow he managed to escape. While he was out, he went to his former home and cut off his wife's head with a . . . well, with a carving knife . . . after which he returned to the hospital, babbling on and on about what he had done. It wasn't a guilt-ridden confession, mind you. He had no idea that he'd done anything wrong. He was simply showing off, recounting the adventures he'd had on the outside. That is the kind of insane murderer I deal with on a day-to-day basis. We've got no Rippers or Torso Slayers."

Hank was impressed by what he was hearing. Dr. Williams was making perfect sense. But if he was right, Hank was going to have one hell of a time finding the killer.

"What makes him so different?" asked Jim Hogan. "What if our man is a certifiable loony bird? Couldn't he just have been lucky so far in not getting caught?"

"Wishful thinking, I'm afraid," said Williams with a sigh. "Oh, your killer is quite different from the common variety who can be easily diagnosed and hospitalized. He contrives his plans with at least enough foresight to prevent his being seen in the company of his intended victims. He chooses them with care, and he's normal enough in his appearance and behavior that they come to trust him. He might befriend them for weeks, or even months, ahead of time so that he can gain their confidence.

"He commits his crimes in a secret place, which again suggests a measure of planning, as well as a desire not to get caught. He operates without any discernable motive. His only motive is the very act of murder itself. And his careful methods of disposing of the bodies once the killing is done show that he is in fact thinking quite rationally.

"He knows the full import of what he has done, and he makes every effort to avoid apprehension. He wipes the blood from their skin, scrubs them down, leaves no traces of himself behind. He even went so far as to wrap up the parts of Mrs. Polillo's body in newspaper and secure them with twine, placing them in baskets and practically laying them on someone's doorstep. Now, by the coroner's own account Mrs. Polillo was a large woman, and such a grisly enterprise would require many hours of difficult labor. Freud would say that your Torso Slayer is 'anal-retentive'—an organizer, neat and tidy by nature, probably lives a very ordered life. Cleaning up after his killings helps him get his life back in order. By the time he's back on the street, no one would be able to tell what he's been up to."

"So he could be a doctor," said Hogan, offering his own pet theory.

"Or a lawyer, a banker, a shoe salesman, anything," said Williams.

"I agree," said Hank jumping in. "I've always figured on him being of at least middle-class means and living somewhere private so he can cut up the bodies without having to worry about being disturbed. That means a house or else a very large apartment that he keeps to himself. You can't kill and dismember people in a rooming house or a crowded apartment building and expect to get away with it. Also he's got to own a car so he can transport the bodies. One witness saw this green Ford parked near Jackass Hill the night before the first two bodies were discovered, and another one spotted this late-model Cadillac beneath the Kinsman Road Bridge the night before we found the head of the Tattooed Man—"

"Number Four," supplied Pearse.

"Yes." Hank lighted another cigarette, but jumped back in quickly to prevent Williams from speaking. "The only victim who was killed where we found him was Number Five, and that was way out in Brooklyn near the airport. If our killer lives somewhere within the Third Precinct, as we believe, he would have to have a car to get all the way out there to Clinton Road. So I agree with Dr. Williams. Our killer probably holds down a regular eight-to-five job and probably lives alone."

"That sounds about right," Williams concurred. "I suspect he's not married, though he may be divorced."

"And there's absolutely no chance that our killer's a woman?" asked Police Chief Matowitz.

"None," said Dr. Strauss. "Except for Number One, who was tied up, the killer must have physically subdued each of his victims, or else cut off their heads while they were sleeping. He must be a man of great strength. I've never met a woman who could perform this type of physical labor."

"Thanks," said Matowitz. "Just wanted to rule that out. It narrows our field of suspects by half."

*That's one way of looking at it,* Hank thought. The chief was truly an odd bird.

"Have you linked any of the victims together socially?" asked Williams, addressing Hank.

"No," Hank said. "If we could, I think we'd be on the right track. But we've only been able to identify two of the six victims, and we can't make any solid connection between any of them. Andrassy was a pimp and Florence Polillo was a hooker, and they hung out in roughly the same territory, but there's no evidence that they knew each other. We've talked to hundreds of people in the Roaring Third. Those that'll talk won't say much."

"You think this reward might help any?" County Prosecutor Cullitan was referring to a resolution being considered by the City Council, offering a thousand-dollar cash reward for any information leading to the arrest and conviction of the Torso Slayer.

"No. All that's going to do is stir up more kooks. I already spend about ninety percent of my time tracking down false leads. Besides, I don't think anybody knows anything except the killer himself, and he's not going to be chomping at the bit for a mere thousand bucks."

Dr. Williams blew a smoke ring and then set about refilling his pipe. "Detective Lambert is right. This fellow is much too careful for anyone to know what he's been doing. And this matter of the prostitute . . . the other man was a pimp, you say. . . . How much do you really know about the other four?"

"We think they were all transients," said Hank, voicing the general conclusion reached by the Homicide squad. "The Tattooed Man was found June sixth, and we have yet to get a firm ID on him. A couple thousand people filed through the morgue to look at him, but nobody knew him. We've shown his photo in all the papers, and we've got a wax replica of his head on display at the Great Lakes Expo. Over a million people have gone through the Expo, and nobody's come forth to identify him. He had six very distinctive tattoos, yet nobody recognizes them. We think he must have been from out of town, probably just got into Cleveland. He may have been a sailor, maybe a hobo. The autopsy revealed a fresh meal in his stomach, yet he showed signs of malnourishment, am I right, A.J.?"

"Yes, that's right."

"We found the clothing of Number Five near his body, and it was worn out and threadbare, the clothing of a hobo. Plus he was found dead near an old hobo camp out there in the woods."

"Also malnourished," said Pearse, "with a bad liver."

"Number Six is the one we found in the pool. Inspector Sweeney found a felt hat about a hundred yards down from the pool, the only real evidence we've dug up aside from a few of the body parts. Maybe Lieutenant Cowles should tell you about it."

Cowles cleared his throat and stood up, dabbing his bald head with his handkerchief. He fixed his round thick-framed glasses onto his nose and began. "Well, it was like Lucky says, an old, beat-up hat, size seven and a half. The *Plain Dealer* put a photo of it in the paper, and this woman in the town of Bellevue recognized it and gave us a call. I went down there to talk to her, and she said she suspected it was the same hat she had given to a tramp who'd begged some clothing off her two weeks ago. When I showed her the hat, she made a positive ID, but she could give us no description of the tramp."

"The Ripper preyed on prostitutes in Whitechapel," advised Dr. Williams, "the most vice-ridden section of London, analogous to your Roaring Third. It seems your Torso Slayer hunts similar such lowlifes. It was also much speculated that the Ripper was a member of the middle class, if not the upper class."

"That's all very interesting," said Ness, glancing at his notes. "But the Ripper aside, Doctor, you say we're dealing with a new insane type. Now, I hate to bring up Leopold and

Loeb again, but let me ask you this. You said they may have been mentally ill but not insane. If they were not *recognizably* insane, couldn't they have been of the same type as the Torso Slayer?"

"The two cases are not analogous," Dr. Williams proclaimed. "You presume your killer acted alone, whereas Leopold and Loeb were a team, acting out a premeditated murder—and they only killed that one time."

"Ah, but only because they were caught—which in itself was something of a fluke. What if the Chicago Police hadn't been so lucky, and they had continued killing, selecting victims they believed inferior to themselves? Isn't that, in a nutshell, exactly the type of killer we're dealing with?"

Ness seemed to have caught Dr. Williams on this point. The psychiatrist sat back puffing on his pipe, and finally nodded respectfully, saying, "Yes, I see what you mean. You may be right."

Ness seemed greatly excited by his new theory and the approval with which it was met. "In which case, we are dealing with a highly intelligent man, probably college educated. He may think of himself as one of Nietzsche's supermen, as they did, and he is almost definitely a homosexual. I still think there is a direct link there between his homosexuality and his urge to kill."

This was one point where Hank's own views differed greatly. He could never accept that his own sexual tendencies were some form of psychiatric disorder, much less that his desire to have sex with men would lead to his wanting to kill them. It was obvious that this "new type of insanity" could not be explained quite so simply.

"I have a statement here from Michael J. Collegeman, head of the federal narcotics bureau here," said Jim Hogan. "He thinks our killer's addicted to some form of narcotic, probably marijuana, which inspires in its users 'an unreasoning desire to kill.' "

"Oh, that's ridiculous," said Williams. "I've treated my share of dope fiends, and none of them have ever displayed homicidal tendencies. Marijuana, in particular, seems to make them quite docile."

"Mr. Collegeman is an expert, Dr. Williams," said Hogan,

"and I'll not dismiss his testimony so easily. One thing we do know is that Andrassy sometimes sold marijuana. Maybe he was killed by one of his crazed clients."

"Folderol," said Williams. "That's simply ludicrous. This fellow kills because he's ill, not because of some drug."

"Gentlemen, gentlemen," said Ness. "I think we should be open to all theories here. That's what this meeting is all about."

They went on debating for another hour, at the end of which they all put their expertise together to draw up a list of seven "probable" conclusions. Hank agreed, for the most part, with the list, though he thought it was a meager set of "facts" to show after a year of investigation.

The Torso Slayer, the clinic decided, was probably a large, strong man. He was probably a hunter or a butcher and did not necessarily have any actual medical knowledge—though he might be college educated, as suggested by Ness. He used a large knife, perhaps a machete. He probably lived in the section bounding Kingsbury Run, somewhere within the Third Precinct, and knew his neighborhood well. He probably maintained a "laboratory" in this area, where he killed and dismembered his victims. He made a practice of associating with his victims for several weeks or months before killing them. He was probably some kind of pervert, homosexual, or sex fiend, possibly a drug addict. He was probably insane, though not recognizably so.

That was it, and it was little to go on.

"If all else fails," Hank suggested, "maybe we should plant a bunch of policemen and detectives in Kingsbury Run dressed as tramps—you know, as decoys. Maybe we can trap him."

Most everyone laughed at this suggestion, but at the same time, they agreed that it might be the only practical course of action left to them at this point, barring the discovery of any damning evidence.

"Lambert," said Ness. "I'm keeping you on this investigation full-time, with several other detectives at your disposal. But I expect results. I don't care if you do have to dress up as tramps. Whatever works, just catch him."

"Yes, sir. We'll do our best."

When the meeting was concluded, it was 10:30 P.M., and Hank felt giddy and lightheaded. He kept thinking about the million-odd people living in the sprawling city. During the course of his job, he came into contact with thousands of people each year, and he wondered if he had ever passed the Torso Slayer on the street, shaken his hand, or perhaps bought a pair of shoes from him.

Hank kept thinking about the proverbial needle in the haystack and wondering if the best solution was simply to set the haystack on fire.

# 22 September 1936

**2:14 P.M.**

Hank parked his car at the corner and stepped out into the downpour, yanking his hat down further over his forehead and turning up his trench-coat collar. It was a gray day and cool; the rain was cold. No lightning had come to heat up the sky, only the dull steady drone of rain and a weird, spectral fogginess.

The smell of worms was in the air.

The address on Bolivar Road was an old brick tenement, three stories tall with two sets of old-fashioned bay windows rising up in columns on either side of the central entry doors, which sat atop a half flight of concrete steps flanked by weathered limestone pilasters. All the wood trim was in need of new paint, and many of the soot-blackened bricks were cracking, as if the apartment building had done considerable settling over the years. The curtains in many windows appeared torn and useless.

On this block alone, Hank spotted three gaudily made-up women simply standing in the rain under the protection of umbrellas, waiting to hook someone. A couple of Italian youths were playing ball in the street, soaked to the skin.

Hank had brought no umbrella, and in the short walk from

his detective's car to the front entrance, his hat and trench coat had earned their keep. Only his shoes had failed him, when he had stepped into a couple of unexpected puddles. He only hoped no worms had spilled in with the rainwater.

Once inside, he checked the names on the mailboxes, and found what he wanted written on a yellowed slip of paper in block letters, affixed with cellophane tape on the box for apartment 301: D. COTTONE.

Pay dirt. Half the tips they got they failed to track down, but this caller just might be legit.

Hank slogged up the creaky narrow stairs to the third floor, dripping a small stream in his wake. Before knocking on the door to 301, he removed his hat and shook the last of the water from its recesses, and also ran his fingers through his hair, making himself presentable. Then he gave a couple of short, hard knocks on the dark, sticky-varnished door.

A cute kid answered, opening the door wide and smiling. He looked about nineteen—thin, but not too. "Yeah?"

"Mr. Cottone?"

"Yeah?" The kid's face was querulous, as if he were suddenly unsure whether he wished to be disturbed.

Hank held up his badge. "Detective Henri Lambert, Homicide. You gave us a call this morning. May I come in?"

"Oh," the kid hesitated, "sure." He led Hank into the large single room of the apartment, which had one of those front-facing bay windows. A clean pan sat in the middle of the floor, collecting a constant drip from the ceiling. "You can call me Danny."

Danny's place was a studio apartment with a half-kitchen off to the left and a bathroom that could partly be seen through an open door on the right. The main room was clean and pleasant, with a pretty purplish rug spread out across the floor and a single bed over against the bay window, neatly made and covered by an inviting quilt. Enough room was left over for an overstuffed chair, a few small tables and lamps, an old dresser with full mirror, a couple of secondhand Victorian chairs with padded seats and backs whose green plush upholstery was slightly worn, and tucked behind the bed, a square card table with its legs folded up. A shelf on the night table held a small pile of dusty books. At a glance they appeared to be boys' adventure tales.

Danny took Hank's hat and coat and placed them on a wall rack behind the door, then went over and turned on the lamp by the window. Hank sat on one of the sturdy Victorian chairs, for fear that the overstuffed one would become too comfortable and he might even fall asleep. Danny sat upon the bed, sinking into the quilt.

"Mind if I smoke?" Hank withdrew a half-empty pack of Luckies.

"Not if you give me one," said Danny "I'm fresh out."

"Here." Hank tapped one out and handed it to him.

"Light?" Danny asked, raising his dark eyebrows.

Hank popped open his lighter and sparked the flint until a flame appeared, which he drew close to the tip of Danny's cigarette, having to rise off his seat to do so. He lighted his own cigarette, as well.

"Mmm, thanks," said Danny, sucking in the smoke and blowing it out through his nose. He glanced at the printed end of the cigarette. "These are my favorite."

"Mine, too."

Danny was not merely cute, he was an angel—one of these olive-complected Italian kids with just the right features and a curly mane of black hair, long on top but trimmed short on the sides and at the nape of the neck. His cheeks were sunken, and his Adam's apple stuck out prominently beneath a well-shaped chin. His nose was Roman, his ruby lips full, as if sculpted by Michelangelo.

Hank had to stop staring at him and get on with it.

"You gave us some information, Danny," Hank began. "Would you mind repeating it for me?" He withdrew pencil and paper from his inner jacket pocket. By writing all this down, he wouldn't have to be constantly ogling the poor kid.

"Well, you see . . . I was at the Expo last night, and I come across this police exhibit, and I see this head and I do a double take, you know? 'Cause I know that guy. That's why I called. I figured maybe I could help you catch the Torso Slayer."

Hank shifted in his seat, and found that the chair was a little rickety. "Can you give us his name?"

"I told them on the phone. It's Paul."

"How do you know?"

"Because he said so."

"What about his last name?"

"I don't know, he didn't tell me."

"What did he tell you, exactly?"

"I remember I was looking at his arm when he told me his name, and right there on his arm was this tattoo with the same name on it. He said he was Paul. That's all."

So far, this information meant precious little. Danny could have read about the Helen–Paul tattoo and made up the entire story. Hank would have to grill him and make sure his story gelled—make sure it was aspic and not Swiss cheese. If this was for real, it would be the first solid lead they had had in the case of the Tattooed Man.

Hank asked Danny to describe Paul, and his description matched the corpse fairly well—but even that he could have picked up out of the newspapers and from the wax head Eliot Ness had set up at the Expo.

"Where did you and this Paul fellow meet?"

"At the public baths over on Orange."

*Ah, the baths!* Hank had gone to his own neighborhood bathhouse on occasion and found himself a few hours of sexual adventure. "Was he a regular? Had you seen him there before?"

"Oh, no," said Danny. His cigarette crackled as he sucked on it. "This was the first time."

"You go there a lot?"

Danny nodded and exhaled a cloud of smoke.

"When was this, when you met him?"

"Oh, a few months ago. June. Late May, early June."

"Do you remember the day of the week?"

"Yeah, it was a Friday afternoon. There's some bankers come in early on Fridays, and they were there."

"Maybe June third? That was a Friday."

"Yeah, maybe. I think so."

The third of June was when Coroner Pearse had thought the murder had taken place. If so, then Danny's meeting him on that date was more than mere coincidence. Even their meager clues pointed to the Tattooed Man's being a transient or a sailor or someone from out of town. He had probably just come into town, gone down to the baths, and was murdered that same day. He may have even met the killer at the baths.

"Do you recall the details of your meeting?"

"Sure, I was in the pool, hanging out, you know. And he comes swimming over from across the pool, almost runs into me."

"You remember what he said to you, exactly?"

"Well, not exactly, no." Danny went on to describe the encounter, and as it progressed Hank was shocked by the kid's honesty. It was increasingly clear that either Paul or Danny had been trying to pick up the other. "And then, I don't know, he just left."

"What do you mean, just left?"

"That was it. I kept swimming, and he got out of the pool."

"Oh, come on, now." Hank couldn't let him get away with that. The story of the encounter had been leading up to some kind of conclusion. Paul couldn't have simply got up and left. There had to have been a confrontation of some kind, and Hank wanted to know what it was. "He didn't just go. 'Fess up. What did he say to you?"

"Nothing. I don't know what you're talking about."

"Come on, kid, let's cut the bullshit, huh?" Hank smothered his spent cigarette in the ashtray on the lamp table and lit another. "One of you was cruising the other, looking for a pickup."

Danny said nothing; Hank had him.

"Don't take me for a fool. I've been to those baths." Hank chose the direct route. This lead was too important to let any details slip away. "I know the kind of pretty boys who go there. The pool's where they show off. You know that. You're just the right type. Now come on, Danny, be straight with me. I'm not here to arrest you, I'm just looking for some answers. You were trying to hustle him, weren't you?"

Danny spoke after a pregnant pause: "Yeah, but so was he."

"But you wanted him, too, didn't you? I mean, come on, kid, he was a real doll, don't you think?"

"Sure, but I didn't have any money."

"Are you telling me he didn't want you?"

"He needed some dough, and he couldn't get it from me. I would have let him have me, but he wanted me to pay, and I don't pay. He called me some name and then he pushed me away." Danny's eyes were wet, but he smiled crookedly, remembering something. "I told him never to hustle a hustler, and everybody laughed. You know, all the old men."

"Sure, I know." Hank had seen the old pederasts there before at his neighborhood baths, lounging by the pool—had even been groped by them.

"They laughed at him, and he got out of the pool and went away."

"Left the bathhouse?"

"I think so. I don't know. I was swimming." Danny sniffled. He seemed a little shaken up.

"And that was it? You didn't see him talking to anyone else? One of the old men, maybe?"

Danny shook his head no.

"When did you first learn of the murder?"

"Well, I'd read about the Torso Slayer, and I knew about Eddie and Flo, but didn't know about Paul until last night when I saw his head—"

*"Eddie and Flo?"* Hank was taken aback. If Danny had said what Hank thought he said, it would be a revelation. "Did you know them, too?"

"Sure, I mean Eddie was a pal of mine. We kind of hung out, sometimes. I don't . . . didn't know Flo all that well."

It didn't matter to Hank how well Danny knew any of them. Sitting here before him on that beautiful quilt was the only known link between any of the victims, outside of the killer himself. Here was a street-smart little hustler who just happened to have had contacts with three out of the six known victims.

Hank gazed around at the well-ordered room—the bed made just so, no small items cluttering the floor, the pan catching the drips, no dirty dishes in the kitchen—and remembered what Dr. Guy Williams had said about their killer being "anal-retentive." Despite the fact that Danny seemed too much the innocent and failed to match the physical profile they had put together of a big, strong individual, it seemed Hank had himself a genuine suspect.

"Danny," he said, standing up and putting away his pencil and notepad, "I'm afraid I'm going to have to take you down to the station. And if you don't cooperate, I'll have to handcuff you."

"Hey, I thought you said you weren't arresting me." Danny's tone was defiant.

"You're not under arrest. I just want to ask you some questions, OK?"

Danny said nothing, but his look was searing.

"Come on, kid, up off the bed. You're coming with me."

"Like hell I am."

Hank took out his handcuffs. "Get up now."

"You can't make me go. You've got to arrest me first."

This was not, in fact, true. Hank certainly could take Danny to the station if he so desired, and in handcuffs if he so chose. But he was more than happy to oblige the poor kid. There were a number of things he could charge him with.

"All right, then, you're under arrest. Now get up."

Danny stood, turned around, and held his wrists together behind his back; it was clear he knew the routine. "What for?" he asked.

"Oh, I don't know," said Hank, locking the steel cuffs on Danny's thin, supple wrists. "Prostitution, for starters. Sodomy. If you're lucky, maybe murder."

"Ow!" Danny shouted. "Hey, these cuffs are too tight."

"No, they're not." Hank grabbed the chain connecting the cuffs and gave a sharp tug. "Now come on, kid, let's go. Move it!"

"OK, OK! I'm going. Don't get pushy!"

# 23 February 1937

**9:24 P.M.**

"Disarticulation of the arms was neat and quick, right at the sockets, minimum of tearing. Shoulders possibly dislocated first, followed by a stroke or two with a large, heavy knife, probably a butcher or bread knife," said Cuyahoga County Coroner Samuel R. Gerber, who had replaced Dr. A.J. Pearse in that capacity as a result of last November's election, which the Republicans had considered an upset, the Democrats a rout, given Pearse's political, if not corporeal, stature.

Coroner Gerber bore little resemblance to his predecessor and was so slight of build, in fact, that he looked as if he could have been swallowed whole by Pearse and easily digested. Gerber's appearance was neat, his wavy hair trimmed in a dapper style, though it was already salt-and-pepper gray and yet he was only a few years older than Hank.

During the autopsy, Gerber had seemed to Hank at once horrified and exhilarated by the task at hand.

"Sounds like our man," Hank put in. The Torso Slayer had been quiet since September, and the investigation had run into a brick wall. The other detectives had been assigned

170

other duties many months ago, and only Hank and his partner Vern Quast remained on the case full-time. The public seemed to have forgotten about the case, and Safety Dir. Eliot Ness had apparently moved it toward the bottom of his list of priorities.

Gerber continued: "Head was cleanly disarticulated by means of a series of precise cuts around the flexure of the joint, between the seventh cervical vertebra and the first thoracic vertebra—"

"That's lower than the others," said Hank, who would never forget the anatomy lessons instilled in him by Sister Mary-Esther with the help of her palm-smacking ruler. The wired-together skeleton that had hung in the corner of her eighth-grade classroom, everyone thought, bore an uncanny resemblance to Father Al, who had met an untimely death the previous summer under the wheels of a milk truck.

"—followed by a strong twist wrenching the head out of the joint cavity. The torso itself was severed at the first lumbar vertebra and we found several hesitation marks."

"Also a deviation from the norm," said Dr. Strauss.

"We discovered blood clots in her heart," said Gerber, "so it is our conclusion that this one was murdered prior to decapitation."

"That's different, too," Hank noted. "But I still think"

"A couple more points of interest," said Gerber, raising a finger. "Her liver revealed no traces of drug use or alcohol intoxication at time of death, but her lungs are filthy with soot."

Hank had witnessed the gray tissue of the victim's lungs as Gerber had sliced open the organs in a stainless-steel bowl, but until now had failed to realized the significance of their unhealthy color.

"You're saying she lived in the city," Hank said.

"In a city, yes," said Gerber. "But not necessarily Cleveland. Pittsburgh, Detroit, Chicago—any of the bigger industrial cities, and probably a lifelong resident."

"How long would you say that was?"

"Twenty-five, maybe thirty-five at the outside."

Hank whistled. "That doesn't narrow it down much."

"I haven't got much to work with."

*That,* Hank thought, *is an understatement.*

What Gerber did have was lying upon the dissecting table before them: the upper half of a woman's torso brought in by Hank and Det. Sgt. James Hogan several hours earlier.

"OK, Sam," said Hank. "Give me the rest."

"She's anywhere from five five to five eight, about a hundred ten pounds, thin build, fair complexion, lighter brown hair—sort of a chestnut. The development of her breasts indicates she's been a mother at least once, possibly twice. She may have even been pregnant at time of death. Won't know until we locate the rest of her."

"Maybe it was an abortionist," said Jim Hogan. "He botched the job and then killed her to cover up his butchery."

Hank took a deep breath to calm himself; sometimes Hogan could be infuriating. All afternoon, Hogan had been trying to deny that this was the work of the Torso Slayer, just as he had denied all along the truth about the Lady of the Lake. All the "deviations" Gerber and Strauss had discovered were more fodder for Hogan's skepticism. It seemed to Hank unlikely the Headhunter was a mad abortionist, given the fact that most of his victims were male.

The upper torso had washed up along the frozen shore of Lake Erie at East 156th Street, onto the Beulah Park beach, and was spotted by a middle-aged local, Robert Smith of 10 Brown Street, at 1:40 P.M., who later told Hank he had "started to pick up some wood for the stove at home when I noticed a white object at the water's edge. At first I thought it was a dead dog or a sheep, but then I saw it was part of a body, so I figured I'd better call the police."

Hank and Jim Hogan had had to wade out a few feet into the freezing water to retrieve the damned thing. They wrapped it in a blanket and transported it back to the Cuyahoga County Morgue in the trunk of Hogan's unmarked Ford Deluxe. The chunk of torso had picked up gravel and weeds from the lake but seemed well preserved, considering.

Hank and several other detectives had combed the shoreline on either side of Beulah Park for much of the afternoon, searching for more body parts despite a bracing arctic wind coming off the lake, but had found nothing. Hank had been chilled to the bone and had actually found himself anxious to get back to the comparatively cozy morgue to witness Gerber and Strauss's handiwork.

During a cigarette break, Vern Quast had wondered aloud if a woman's severed head would sink or float. "Depends," Hank had responded. "Blonde or brunette?"

It seemed likely the torso had washed up on the shore after spilling out into the lake from a culvert, located fifty yards to the west, that ran from the storm sewer into Lake Erie. If so, it was likely more body parts could be found somewhere along the length of the culvert. But searching the culvert and storm sewers would be a long process and would have to wait at least a few days because of snow and ice blocking the inlets. It was equally possible the torso had been dumped into the Cuyahoga River, making its way along the eastward current of Lake Erie until it was beached.

Throughout Hank's investigation of the torso case, the Lady of the Lake had kept coming back to him, and with today's discovery she was brought yet again to the fore. One fact that Jim Hogan practically refused to discuss was that their current find (Hank already thought of her as Number Seven) had turned up at Beulah Park beach no less than a hundred yards west of the Euclid Beach amusement park, on whose sands the Lady of the Lake had washed up in September of '34. The Lady of the Lake had been a woman's lower torso with thighs still attached. Were it not for the two-and-a-half-year distance between the two cases, Hank might have wondered if they were parts of the same body—but Number Seven's remains were obviously recent. The Lady of the Lake was still officially discounted as a torso victim, but now that they had come up with a similar find at a similar location, Hank wished he could convince Hogan to allow the lady into the fold.

"Well, obviously there's no chance for an ID," Hank stated flatly, and Gerber nodded his agreement. "We'll have to cull through the missing persons reports again, see what turns up."

Hank was disgruntled, almost resigned to the fact that this one, too, would remain nameless, featureless. Without the head or the hands, a positive identification would be impossible.

# 1 March 1937

Eliot Ness stared at the bottom of his mug, where less than a sip of dark coffee remained, and pressed the buzzer on his General Electric intercom. "Betty-Lou?" he asked. He always waited for her response.

Meanwhile his new executive assistant, Bob Chamberlin, pointed to his own mug and said, "Me, too." His former assistant John Flynn, a Democrat, had resigned in a huff over political differences. Chamberlin was more to his liking.

"Yes, Mr. Ness?" came the squawky voice.

"Bob and I could both go for seconds, if you don't mind."

"Yes, sir."

Betty-Lou came in and took their mugs while they were finishing reading Coroner Gerber's report, hot off the Mimeograph machine and smelling strongly of duplicating fluid. As she turned to leave, both Ness's and Chamberlin's eyes strayed from the text and followed the young secretary out the door. Betty-Lou left the door open as she poured from the stainless steel coffeepot on a shelf behind her desk, bending over ever so slightly and holding the two men's rapt attention. Chamberlin craned his neck around the high-backed chair and removed his reading glasses.

175

Upon seeing his secretary returning, Ness averted his gaze back to the still-damp pages on his desk but didn't read them, although his eyes did pluck out the words "dismembered," "cartilages," and "intervertebral discs."

"Here you are, Mr. Ness." Along with the coffee came a smile. Betty-Lou was a true find, fresh out of secretarial school: a born typist, quick as a whip with the shorthand, and an expert in the art of coffee percolation. "Mr. Chamberlin."

"Gee, thanks," said Chamberlin, taking his mug. "But call me Bob."

Ness cleared his throat suddenly, catching their attention, and said, "Thanks, Betty-Lou, that'll be all. Hold my calls, all right?"

"Yes, Mr. Ness."

When she had gone, Ness chided his assistant: "And you a happily married man. Watch yourself—her boyfriend's built like Grays Armory."

"Duly noted."

Ness took a quick sip, not minding that the coffee burned his tongue. "Just when I think I'm through with this joker, he comes back to haunt me."

"Pardon?" Bob Chamberlin replaced his reading glasses on his nose and looked up from the coroner's report.

Ness held his copy of the report in the air. "This nut," he said, punctuating his epithet by backhanding the pages with a *crack*. "The Mad Butcher. I keep hoping he'll just go away, 'cause it sure as hell looks like we're never going to find him. We haven't got one solid bit of evidence."

"The perfect crime?" Chamberlin mused aloud.

"No such thing." Ness shook his head, driving the point home. "We're not dealing with Moriarty here, or Dr. Fu Manchu. This nut is a citizen of Cleveland, a home owner, a car owner, a taxpayer—probably looks like you or me. Hell, I've probably passed him in the halls, coming to pay his parking tickets."

"Then he's bound to screw up."

"That's what I thought about five bodies ago." Ness took an angry gulp from his mug to soothe his addled brain. "Did you see this?" He held aloft a copy of yesterday's *Plain*

*Dealer,* opened to the editorial page, and shook it violently in the air.

Chamberlin squinted from behind his reading glasses and shook his head. "No, I only get the *News.*"

"Then allow me to share it with you. This is from Philip Porter's column of yesterday morning, and I quote: 'The latest torso mystery failed to stir up a callous public that has fattened on Spanish war atrocities for six months, but to Detective Hank "Lucky" Lambert it's something to take very seriously. The Kingsbury Run torsos were not just a lot of John Does and this one, found in the lake, is not, to "Lucky," just Jane Doe.' Blah, blah, blah. 'The reason that the torso murders have not shocked the city as similar ghastly crimes have shocked England, says "Lucky," is that most of the victims have never been identified, and you can't very well get folks steamed up about a nameless midsection of anatomy.' And you know what, Bob? He's right."

Ness threw the newspaper down onto his desk, causing Coroner Gerber's report to fly up and settle a few inches away from the offending *Plain Dealer* op-ed piece.

"What I'd like to know," said Chamberlin, "is what this detective of ours was doing talking to Philip Porter."

"So would I."

Ness grabbed his candlestick phone and dialed the City Hall operator. "This is Eliot Ness. Get me Homicide over at Central Station, will you, and ask for Detective Lambert. Then ring me back." Ness hung up the receiver atop its cradle.

"I thought Sergeant Hogan was the spokesman for Homicide," said Chamberlin.

"Yes," said Ness. "But Lambert does have a point. This guy's killed seven people already, but he might as well have been putting slugs in pay phones for all anyone cares. Maybe we've been too successful at dampening hysteria. You realize that at the end of the fiscal year, we're going to have to justify all the overtime we've racked up. They're busting their balls out there on this case, and no one in Cleveland could care less."

Ness's phone rang. Chamberlin went back to reading Gerber's report.

"Ness speaking."

"Your call, sir," said the operator.

"Thanks. Hello?"

"Sir? Hank Lambert. I just finished Sam Gerber's report, and—"

"Never mind about that. I was wondering about that piece in the newspaper."

"Oh, that."

"Yes. I thought Jim Hogan was handling the press on this."

"Yes, sir, but—"

"But nothing. I don't need our detectives giving the press their personal opinions, understand?"

"Yes, but—"

"I mean, frankly, Lucky, I agree with you, but that's no reason to circumvent—"

"Excuse me—"

"—the established procedure. If Jim Hogan OK'd it, that's another thing, but—"

"Excuse me, sir. May I say something?"

"Yes, by all means. Go ahead."

"I don't know what my name's doing in there, sir."

"Oh?" Ness could feel it now: his foot preparing to raise itself up off the rug and into his mouth.

"Mr. Porter phoned me Saturday afternoon wanting to know what I thought about the case, but all I said was the investigation was ongoing and we were taking it very seriously. He embellished that a little and attributed his own opinions to me."

"Oh, I see." Ness was nervously tapping a pencil upon his blotter. "Well, in that case, I'm sorry. It's early yet, and I'm a little edgy."

"I understand why you'd be upset, sir. So was I."

Either he's telling the truth, thought Ness, or he's doing a magnificent job of covering his ass. "What do you think of his piece, then?"

"I think he's right, to a point. Most people don't care. The Roaring Third is pretty keyed up. I think they know the killer is one of them. None of the rest of the city is paying any attention. We've got a lot of homicides in this town and they get the whole front-page treatment, but all anyone cares about is what Little Orphan Annie is up to."

"Lucky, forget I brought it up. I've been misquoted a fair number of times, myself. Reporters can be a two-edged sword."

"Sir? About Sam Gerber's report"

"Oh, yes. Got it right here. A real bang-up job."

"I think he's making a mistake not including the Lady of the Lake in the torso cycle."

"You're the only one, then. Pearse, Strauss, all of them— they all agree she was not a torso victim."

"I realize that, sir, but I've examined the same evidence and I can't understand what makes her any different from the one we just turned up."

"Lucky, I don't know what difference it's going to make. We can't identify either one."

"Yes, I know, sir. But I'd like to know what proof he has that the killer is some deranged doctor who kills when he's drunk or pumped full of drugs. All the physical evidence shows that our man is cold and methodical in everything he does. A drunk or a junkie would screw up somehow. These murders show at least a certain amount of planning. I also question his inclusion of veterinarians on the list of probable suspects."

"Listen, I understand what you're saying. Nothing Gerber's said is written in stone. But I do think we ought to look more closely at any suspicious medical-type people."

"What do you want me to do, follow doctors around all day, see if they cut up anybody?"

"You know, Lucky, that's not a bad idea. Get on it."

# 6 June 1937

**3:42 P.M.**

Russell Lauer was an athletic youth who attended Scranton School. His big black eyes sat close together upon his face, his eyelids droopy and sensuous. His brown hair, though parted on one side, had grown long enough to hang low past his forehead and his querulous eyebrows. He had the serious, shy countenance of a dreamer, a boy who craved excitement and adventure. Well, today he had found it.

"How old are you, Russell?"

"Fourteen, sir."

"Why don't you start from the beginning and tell me what you were up to," said Hank Lambert, who felt like ruffling Russell's hair a little, like one might scratch behind the ears of a puppy dog, just to put a smile on the kid's sad, full lips.

Russell Lauer removed the gum from his mouth and tossed it on the garbage-strewn field. He spoke in a rush, as if he had to get it all out of his system: "I was over there by the river, see, 'cause yesterday there was this tugboat crew fell in and one of them drowned. You probably read about it in the papers. I didn't see it, but my pal Jody told me about it. They've been out there all day lookin' for the guy. So, I was watchin' the Coast Guard boats after church today, see.

My ma made me change, so these are my play clothes. So I'm just kinda sittin' around by the river, watchin' the divers all day, talkin' to some bums, throwin' rocks, you know. But I got to get home or my ma'd string me up, so I starts heading back goin' underneath the bridge. That's when I find this skull."

"Just tell me in your own words exactly what you saw."

"OK, OK. I didn't know what it was until I saw the gold teeth, see. Then I go and tell some guys down by the river, and we go call the cops. I knew it didn't belong to no dog, not with no gold teeth it didn't."

"No, it's a human skull, all right." Hank scribbled down Russell Lauer's statement as best he could. "I'm going to hand you over to my partner now, Russell. But I may have a few more questions for you later."

"OK." Russell smiled, showing a couple well-placed dimples. Hank wished he had a baseball card to give him, or something. "Sir, I really gotta call my ma."

"We'll call her for you."

"I mean, I'm really in dutch."

"Vern," Hank addressed Detective Quast, "can you contact Russell's mom for him, and just hang on to him for a while, all right? I'll be back."

A swarm of policemen had gathered around the discovery, in the shadow of the Lorain-Carnegie Bridge upon the vacant field of Stone's Levee. Along with a couple of unmarked detective cars were parked several of the newly repainted squads, of which Hank wasn't sure he approved. Safety Director Ness had ordered all the marked squads repainted from dull black and white to a garish red, white, and, blue. Ness's justification was that the Cleveland Police would be much more visible; whereas before the squads had been barely noticeable by the public, they now stood out more boldly than a taxi cab. Ness's theory was that people would feel safer, seeing the obvious police presence on their streets. Hank's own view was that it was always better to sneak up on crooks than to announce yourself.

The squads at the scene were parked haphazardly around the muddy plain. At the heart of the clustered group of uniformed officers stood Lloyd Trunk of Ballistics taking pictures. They were all standing near the base of one of the massive concrete abutments, halfway in between the river and the eastern approach of the bridge, where Russell Lauer had run across the skull. From overhead came the sound of motorists zooming across the tall span of the bridge.

"Excuse me, fellas," said Hank as he pushed his way through to Detective Sergeant James Hogan, who was supervising the scene and the taking of the photographs.

At the center of attention was a pile of bones loosely held together by what had once been a burlap bag. The skull must have rolled out some time ago and only now been discovered by the kid. Stone's Levee was a low area of the Flats, piled with refuse and poorly traveled, but all the same Hank found it surprising that a bag of human bones might remain here undiscovered for long. Either it was merely chance that no one had found it until now, or the killer had disposed of it more recently.

And Hank had a strong suspicion that this killer and the Torso Slayer were one and the same. The burlap bag was the first giveaway, but he was sure it wouldn't be the last.

Jim Hogan directed the officers to search the surrounding area for evidence, while he and Hank processed the scene. The bones in the bag were already mixed up, so they had no qualms about disturbing them further to search for evidence. Hank pulled apart the opening of the bag, which had been tied together tightly with a fine hemp. Immediately he recalled the hemp that had been used to bind Andrassy's wrists, and wondered if David Cowles's new ultraviolet ray could determine whether or not this was the same stuff.

"Holy Toledo," he muttered.

The bones clattered around while Hank peered inside. They were old enough that no sour smell remained.

All he could find along with the bones was a torn corner of a newspaper page, which he retrieved and examined more closely. Under the misprinted byline of W. Ward Mash, it was a review of a live Ziegfeld-like stage production, Nils T. Grandlund's "Radio-Cabaret Girl Revue," from New York

City, in a performance at the RKO-Palace Theater. The top
of the fragment read "Page Ten," and Hank knew that W.
Ward *Marsh* wrote for the *Plain Dealer,* but no date could be
found on the yellowed scrap.

Hank went to his unmarked Ford and brought back a canvas tarpaulin, which he and Hogan then used to wrap up the
bag of bones, along with the skull that had been lying a few
feet away. The skull was missing two molars, and Hank
searched the ground for any that might have fallen out *post
mortem,* but found none. They put the remains in the trunk of
Hogan's car.

After a thorough search of the area, officers and detectives found a ball of kinky black hair, the torn sleeve and
collar of a dress, and a woman's wool cap, all of which
Hank gathered up to process later as evidence back at Central Station.

"I have a bad feeling about this one," said Hogan unexpectedly, as they shared a smoke while the other officers
were clearing out. Vern Quast had gone to take Russell
Lauer home to his mother over on Scranton Road S.W.

"Oh, really?" said Hank, and sucked on his Lucky Strike.
Neither he nor Hogan had yet mentioned the possibility that
this might be a torso slaying, so as not to prejudge the investigation. It could most definitely turn out to be an unrelated
homicide. God knew they had enough murders in Cleveland
without counting the Headhunter's victims. "How bad?"

"You know very well how bad."

"Come on, Jim, where's that crusty old skeptic we all
know and love?"

"Don't butter me up." Hogan removed his hat and wiped
the sweat from his brow and bald pate with his shirtsleeve,
which was filthy from digging around among the bones and
dirt. "I think we've got ourselves Number Eight here, and I
don't know about you, but I'd say our prospects for identification are pretty damn lousy."

# 22 June 1937

"Mr. Ness?" came the voice of Betty-Lou over the intercom. "Detective Lambert is here."

Eliot Ness depressed the red "talk" button and said, "Send him in."

He rose behind his desk to greet the detective, who looked on first glance to be tired and overworked. But then, when Ness looked at himself in the mirror, he saw the same signs of wear and tear. It simply came with the territory.

"Eliot," said Lambert.

"Please, sit down."

They both sat. Ness rolled his chair back and turned his head to look out the window at the exposition along the beachfront, and Lake Erie shining in the late afternoon sun.

"Beautiful day."

"Yes, it is, sir." Lambert seemed distracted.

"You've got something for me?"

"Yes. Things are finally coming together in the torso case, sir."

"Give me what you got."

"We've got an ID on Number Eight."

"The pile of bones."

Coroner Gerber had had a hell of a time with Number Eight, but he had still come up with what Ness thought was some useful information. The victim had been a colored female in her late thirties, approximately five feet tall, weighing less than a hundred pounds. The skeleton was missing the arm and leg bones, as well as one rib, but was otherwise intact. The dental work, however, was unique, with a few gold crowns and a gold bridge, extracted upper wisdom teeth, and the first two upper molars missing—otherwise, Gerber had said the victim had good teeth. They had been hoping maybe to come up with an ID based on her dental work, but it had been a thousand-to-one shot that they would find a match.

"Yes, sir. Early today we got a call from a dentist in Cincy. He'd read about the case in the papers and recalled a patient who matched our victim, or so he believes. He's sending us up the dental records pronto, but I think there's a good chance we've got our ID. He gave us the name Rose Wallace, a colored female approximately forty years old."

"Are you sure it's her?"

"Not yet. He says his records match what we've got, and her physical descriptors match real well, about five feet tall, petite build."

"What else?" Ness could hardly contain his excitement. He wanted this case solved more than anything he had wanted in his entire life. It had become an obsession gnawing at the back of his brain, made all the worse by the fact that he was tied down to this goddamn desk. Secretly, Ness envied "Lucky" Lambert and wished they could switch places.

"Well, sir, I've had professional contacts with Rose Wallace in the past, in the Third Precinct area. She was a known prostitute, and in fact I interviewed her following the Flo Polillo murder. I checked back through my file, and she was the one who provided the alibi for One-Armed Willie, a colored guy who was a suspect at one point because he'd had a fight with Mrs. Polillo. Rose Wallace had witnessed the fight, and said she'd been with One-Armed Willie the rest of the evening, and we know that's the night Mrs. Polillo was killed, because we found her the next morning."

"Damn, I wish this wasn't all so circumstantial." Ness was inclined to believe the identification was correct, but he needed proof, not speculation. A homicide investigation had to be rock solid.

"OK, now get this." Lambert was speaking rapidly, thumbing through his notes with an excited tremolo in his voice. "Sam Gerber estimates Number Eight was killed approximately one year ago, though even he admits there's no way to be precise on this. I went to the morgue at the *Plain Dealer* and tracked down the piece we dug up with the remains. It's from June sixth of *last* year—one year to the day we found Number Eight. Also, this June sixth *Plain Dealer* was the issue reporting the discovery of Number Four, the Tattooed Man. Seems to me like too much of a coincidence that someone happened to find Number Eight exactly one year later. I think that sack was dumped there the night before, which means he's kept it lying around somewhere."

"If you're right, that means Number Eight was killed just after Number Four, maybe a matter of days."

"Well, no, sir. Not if it was Rose Wallace. She was reported missing last August twenty-first, and hasn't been seen since, but she was definitely alive and well last June. I think she was killed last August, her bones were dumped a few days before we found them, and the killer placed a scrap from last June sixth's paper in the bag along with her."

"Why?"

"To tease us. You know, I've been reading about Jack the Ripper. He used to send letters to the newspapers, taunting Scotland Yard, daring them to catch him."

"We're a little less fortunate," said Ness. If they had a letter from the Torso Slayer, perhaps they could find a latent print. Ness had supreme confidence in the infallibility of modern technology.

"Eliot, we've got a lot of disagreement on this case. You know that. Jim Hogan is real dubious of this identification, and Sam Gerber seems ready to reject it even before he's seen the dental charts. Jim thinks we're dealing with some kind of criminal genius, but I don't think so."

"Criminal genius?" Ness furrowed his brow to show Lambert he was on his side. "I've always believed that was a contradiction in terms. Capone was no scholar."

"Exactly," said Lambert. "Jim thinks the guy's a genius because he keeps preventing us from identifying the bodies. Without an ID, he knows there's little chance of his being caught. But this is what I think. He screwed up the early cases, right? We got IDs on Andrassy and Polillo. After that, he stopped giving us heads and hands, or else they were already decayed. The only exception is the Tattooed Man, and I'm sure he's just as shocked as we are that we never came up with an ID. We had the hands, we had the head, we had the tattoos—nothing. This seems too haphazard for the work of some mad genius. What I do think is that he reads about his crimes in the newspaper—"

"Of course he does," Ness put in.

"I think we've been telling the press too much. Now, the last thing I want to do is tell you or Jim Hogan how to do your jobs, but I think we ought to give the press the bare minimum from now on. We don't want the killer to know what we're up to."

Ness nodded his head. Despite some large gaps, the pieces were beginning to fall into place, and what "Lucky" Lambert was saying about the press made sense. He scribbled himself a note about it on his blotter. Maybe his reporter friends should be kept in closer check.

"Now," Lambert continued rapidly, "if Rose Wallace was killed last August, that means she was killed before Number Seven, and likely before Number Six. Rose Wallace had been picked up a few times on charges of solicitation. I checked our file reports on her and found she hung out at this speakeasy on East Nineteenth and Scovill. I went down there at lunch and spoke to the proprietress. She said Rose had been, quote, hustling for her, unquote, for a year or so. On August twenty-first of last year, Rose met a dark-skinned white man supposedly named Bob who the proprietress hadn't seen before or since. She said another regular in the tavern had seen Rose later that evening being driven by this same 'Bob' in some fancy convertible, but she couldn't provide a description. She described the dress Rose had been wearing that night, and it's a pretty close match to the fragments we found the other day. The proprietress was familiar with One-Armed Willie and told me he was one of the few people Rose was ever seen with on a regular basis, probably her pimp."

"Where's this One-Armed Willie now?"

"I don't know. We're working on it. But listen, she witnessed the fight between Flo Polillo and One-Armed Willie, and looking back over her statement, I get the impression she was at least acquainted with Mrs. Polillo. And I know from another suspect we interviewed last year that Mrs. Polillo knew Eddie—Edward Andrassy. Rose Wallace and Flo Polillo were both prostitutes, and Andrassy was a known pimp. They all hung out in the Roaring Third. I think this ID will stick, even if the dental records turn out a little sketchy."

"Sounds real good," said Ness. "What about this other suspect, the one who knew Polillo and Andrassy?"

"Oh, that's Danny Cottone, a male prostitute operating out of the Roaring Third. I'm going to track him down and see what he knows about Rose Wallace."

"And you've ruled him out?"

"Completely. There's no way he could have committed the murders, and that's not only my opinion but also that of Guy Williams at the asylum."

"Stuffed shirt." Ness was far from impressed with Dr. Williams. The state hospital he ran was simply an old-fashioned, dungeonlike madhouse, where ghastly new treatments were being experimented with. Ness tried to avoid calling out there. "Well, listen, Lucky, I don't want to keep you. Sounds like you really got something there."

"Well, it's added some new life to the case, at least."

"Oh, I almost forgot," said Ness, plucking through a stack of papers and interdepartmental envelopes on his desk. "I wanted to give you this. I talked with a Federal postal inspector recently, and he agreed to provide us a list of people in the greater Cleveland area suspected of unbalanced sexual tendencies. He brought it over yesterday afternoon."

Ness handed over to Lambert a thick manila envelope containing several pages of typewritten names and addresses.

"Jesus," Lambert remarked. "This is some list."

"I don't know what practical use we can make of it," said Ness with a shrug. "We can't surveil everybody. But if this Rose Wallace business doesn't pan out, maybe we'll have to give it a shot."

"Thanks." Lambert rose to leave.

Ness saw him to the door, then returned to the window behind his desk and looked out at the lake. Sailboats were rigged up and gliding across the water. A seaplane on the Detroit–Cleveland route had just landed and was propelling itself toward the East Ninth Street docks. Along the shoreline before him was splayed out the grandiose Great Lakes Exposition, now in its second season.

Ness grabbed a pair of binoculars from his bottom desk drawer and gazed out beyond the stylized smokestacks of the Industry Building to the exposition's newest and most popular attraction, "Billy Rose's Aquacade," a family show that starred Olympic diving champion Dick Deneger, Olympic "fancy diver" Aileen Riggin, backstroke champion Eleanor Holm, and Johnny "Tarzan" Weissmuller. Ness focused his binoculars and managed to get a look at some bathing beauties diving one after another into the lake from their floating stage, then swimming in synchronization to the live orchestra accompaniment, which he could not hear from this distance. Ness replaced the binoculars in their case and returned to his desk.

He had, naturally, taken a peek at the postal inspector's "pervert list" out of curiosity, to see if the names of any of his friends or enemies cropped up. Although he hadn't been looking for it, he had noticed the name "Henri P. Lambert" on the list, but without any notation indicating what type of material he had been sent. Ness had been disappointed by the discovery but merely filed the information away for future reference. After the shake-up he had put the police department through—and the subsequent firings—he needed every good man he had.

And Lucky Lambert was one of them, even if someone might have tried to send him some French postcards once upon a time.

**9:55 P.M.**

Danny Cottone was standing near the corner of East Ninth Street and Bolivar Road when the Ford sedan pulled up. He wasn't the only one hanging out; another male hustler and four female hookers were all in the general vicinity. But the driver of the Ford wanted him.

"Hey, you," came the voice, though Danny couldn't see the face until he went a little closer.

He sauntered over and threw his cigarette in the gutter, folding his arms and leaning his elbows on the open windowsill of the Ford's passenger side. He recognized the guy's face, but in the couple of seconds it took to remember who it was, the guy was flashing his badge.

"Detective Lambert, Homicide," he stated. "Remember me?"

"Fuck yeah. How could I forget?"

"Come on, kid, get in."

"What for?"

"Because I said so."

"You aren't taking me to the station."

"No, I'm not. How's about we just go for a ride, you and me, and talk?"

"I don't know, I kind of got plans."

"If you don't get in, I'll bust your ass for prostitution."

"Gee, mister, I wouldn't want you to bust my ass." Danny's tone was sarcastic and flirtatious.

Danny opened the door and sat on the seat next to the detective. "Hey," he said. "Where we going?"

"Around." Lambert put his foot on the gas, and they were off, heading north on East Ninth. Danny looked out the rear window and saw the other whores laughing at him.

Detective Lambert was real manly in his gray hat and black tie, with a growth of stubble along his chin and a cigarette dangling from his lips. The interior of the Ford reeked of smoke, and so did the detective's clothes.

"Do you know a Rose Wallace?" Lambert asked.

"Sure, I know Rosie. Don't know where she is."

"She's been missing. We just found another torso victim, and we think it's her."

"Aw, Christ!" Danny's heart sank. Rosie had always been real nice.

"Do you know anything about her acquaintances, anybody she might have been spending a lot of time with before she disappeared?"

They were turning left onto Euclid, heading toward Public Square, and in the opposite direction of the police station, which gave Danny a measure of relief.

"She was always tight with One-Armed Willie, but I don't think he would have—"

"Yeah, I know Willie. Do you know where I could find him?"

"No idea. Haven't seen him for a while, either."

The detective was taking him around the Square, past the gaudy Soldiers' and Sailors' Monument illuminated against the dark sky, and turning left onto Superior Avenue, heading west toward the bridge.

"Anybody else?" Lambert asked.

"Frank Dolezal," Danny said.

"How do you spell that?" Lambert asked, taking out a pencil and a small pad of paper. He put the steering wheel in control of his knees temporarily, while Danny spelled it out for him.

"They used to be roomies."

"Where might I find Mr. Dolezal?"

"At Charlie's, I guess."

Lambert put his pad and pencil away and put his hands back on the steering wheel. "That's the tavern you told me about, where Flo and Willie had their fight."

"That's right."

"Was Rose Wallace there that night?"

"Yeah, Rosie was pretty upset. Willie used to be her man, she didn't like seeing him getting pushed around like that."

"He was her pimp?"

"Sure," said Danny; that was what he had meant.

"When was the last time you saw her?"

"I don't know. Last summer, maybe. It took a few weeks before I noticed she wasn't hanging around. Can I have a cigarette?"

"You bet," said Lambert, and handed him a pack of Luck-ies and a book of matches.

Danny tapped one out and lighted it. It was yummy, espe-cially considering who it came from.

"Have you noticed anything suspicious recently? Any weird characters at Charlie's? Strange people in the neigh-borhood?"

"There's a lot of strange people in my neighborhood."

"You run across a dark-skinned white guy named Bob?"

"I know a lot of Bobs, too."

"Can you tell me where they live?"

"They don't make a habit of giving me their address."

"But some are regular customers?"

Danny nodded. "I get a lot of repeat business."

"Any of them ask you to do weird things? Any of them kinky or sick?"

"They're all kinky," Danny laughed. When guys paid money to fuck you, most were looking for something other than romance. Everybody had a fetish.

Lambert gunned the accelerator, and they sped across the upper level of the Detroit-Superior High-Level Bridge. Danny could feel the rumble of the streetcar rattling across on the lower level beneath them, as they passed under the arching iron girderage that kept them from falling into the Cuyahoga far below. The lights of Cleveland's west side could be seen across the river, far distant at the western end of the span.

"Did you ever find the Chicken Freak?" Danny asked, grinning as he remembered the detective's look of disbelief when Danny had told him the story at the police station.

"Yeah, you weren't kidding. He's sick all right, but he's no killer." Then, with a curt chuckle, Lambert added, "Of people, anyway."

"A lot of them are like that. Not all chicken freaks, but just . . . you know . . . they all get a kick out of something or other."

"And you're more than happy to oblige."

"Hey, if they're paying, I don't care."

"How much do they pay?"

"Depends." A smile crept onto Danny's face. He tried to

keep it down but couldn't. He didn't want Lambert to think he was too eager, which in fact he was. Besides, he was wary of a possible trap.

"Listen, kid, I'm not going to bust you."

"That's what you said last time." Danny was deliberately coy.

"This is different. Our business is over. I'm off duty and I've had a long day. Now what are your rates?"

"My rates are flexible." Danny leaned back against the car seat, suddenly feeling the need to stretch. "And so am I."

"I'll bet you are."

"Where are you taking me?" Danny wondered, realizing now the detective's real purpose in questioning him this evening.

"Oh, there's this old place I know over on Rowdy Row, the Connor Hotel. Cheap rooms, no questions."

"The Connor, huh?"

"You been there before?"

"Yeah," said Danny, looking out the window toward the dark squalid Flats.

Lambert downshifted as they came off the bridge, then reached over and squeezed Danny's knee. Danny grabbed the detective's hand and directed it further up his thigh, onto the merchandise itself.

## 10:18 P.M.

"Stuffy in here," said Hank upon entering the room. He set down his newly bought bottle of Jack Daniel's in its paper bag, and went to the windows, thrusting them both open and letting in a warm breeze that blew over West Twenty-fifth Street, four stories below. Hank saw no need to pull down the shades, for the buildings across the street were only three stories tall and no one would be able to see in.

Danny closed and locked the door behind them. Hank heard the creak of springs and a thud from behind him as Danny pulled the Murphy bed down from the wall. Hank tried to turn on a lamp by the bed, but nothing happened. Reaching under the lampshade to make sure the bulb was screwed in tightly, he found the bulb missing. Danny turned on the lamp on the other side of the room, producing a feeble yellow glow that richly illumined his olive skin, setting it aflame.

Hank grabbed his whiskey from out of the paper sack and took a swig. He took a five-dollar bill from his billfold and handed it to Danny, who plunged it into his trouser pocket.

"Come here," Danny suggested, patting the corner of the bed.

Hank loosened his tie and sat down, placing his hat on the bed and offering Danny the bottle. Danny smiled and took a gulp, then sat on the floor and started untying Hank's shoes, slipping them off and removing his black socks.

With a sudden, animallike ferocity, Danny leapt atop Hank on the bed and went for his trousers, unfastening the fly and the suspenders and yanking them roughly off of Hank's sweaty flanks, down past his knees, and off, before Hank knew what had hit him. Danny ground his knee into Hank's crotch and began licking his ear, rubbing a clothed thigh against the bulge in his boxers.

"Jesus." Hank had no idea where this was heading, but he was in no mood to stop it.

Danny was licking the underside of his jaw, scraping his tongue along the thick razor stubble and laughing. The kid's hands groped at Hank's dick, reaching in through the fly in his shorts and clutching it tightly, pumping it up to full hardness before withdrawing his hand and tugging at the elastic waistband, yanking the shorts down over Hank's ass and pulling them off while Hank assisted by bringing up his knees and putting his feet in the air.

"All right, mister, that's enough," said Hank, grabbing Danny's midsection with both hands and throwing him onto the other side of the bed. Danny yelped, giggling as Hank hastily began unbuttoning his shirt and exposing his dark chest sparsely covered with small black hairs, scooped by the curved neck of his undershirt, through which could be seen the protruding nubs of Danny's nipples.

"No, no!" said Danny laughing, but his resistance was clearly feigned. Hank removed Danny's shirt and unbuckled his belt, unzipping his pants, and grabbed both them and Danny's underwear and pulled them off, tossing the clothes in the growing pile on the floor. All that remained was Danny's tank-style white undershirt, but Hank chose to leave it, because it turned him on.

He bent over and kissed the rose tattoo on Danny's right bicep. The skin was as soft as a rose petal, and the color was so bright Hank worried some of it might rub off onto his lips.

Hank removed his own shirt and undershirt while Danny's head disappeared into his crotch and began sucking his cock.

"Oh, Jesus!" Hank muttered. Danny's sucking was so violent the mattress was bouncing and the springs were creaking.

He pulled Danny up, and his bright red dick plopped out of the kid's mouth with a slurping sound. Danny's undershirt was sweat-soaked and smelly. Hank placed Danny beside him on the bed and buried his face in his undeveloped chest, breathing in the musky, youthful scent. Danny was twenty if he was a day. Hank got on top of him, grabbed him by the wrists, and held his arms back above his head.

"Fuck me," Danny whispered, close to Hank's ear, digging fingers into his back. "Stud copper, come on, fuck me."

Hank rose, holding himself up with one hand while he spat on the other and lathered up his dick with it.

"Come on, Detective, do me like a girl," Danny begged.

Hank pressed his cockhead against the yielding flesh.

"Ah, ah," said Danny, wincing—a staccato cry of pain telling Hank to take it easy. "Ah . . . ah . . ."

Then, after some heavy intakes of breath on Danny's part, the wince turned into a rapturous smile, and Hank felt his balls pressing up against the kid's ass.

"Ooh," Danny cooed, his hand reaching down and cupping Hank's balls. "It's all the way in."

A voice from outside on the street was shouting: "Girls! Girls! Girls! Come on in, sir, see the burlesque show! You want girls, we got 'em, yes indeedy! We got girls of all shapes and sizes, to please any palate. Colored girls, too, if your tastes run to the exotic. An all-girl revue, yessiree Bob—"

*Bob,* Hank thought, and an imagined face popped into his mind, the face of Bob, Rose Wallace's killer, whoever he was—and who, Hank was convinced, was the Torso Slayer.

Then just as suddenly the image vanished and he was met with Danny's ecstatic face, awash in pleasure. Hank withdrew his entire length and then plunged it home.

He went slowly at first, feeling Danny's tight hole grip the girth of his rod in a milking rhythm—squeezing as Hank withdrew, relaxing as he went in.

Danny's own cock was rock hard and of a good size, brown and uncut with a bright pink, silky-smooth head.

Hank's hands were placed on either side of Danny's head, on the pillow. Danny was picking up the rhythm, prodding Hank's ass with his heels as if spurring a horse from a trot to a gallop. Hank thrust deeper and faster, arching his back and bucking his hips with more violence, to plunge as hard and as fast as he could.

"Ride me," Danny said. "Ride your pony."

"I'll ride you," Hank said.

Danny tossed his head to the side, and his curls fell back from his forehead. His hands clutched Hank's back muscles, which were tensed and strained from the exertion. His fingers roamed up and down, stroking, his fingernails lightly scratching.

Suddenly, Danny pulled Hank downward and kissed him, sucking Hank's tongue deep into his mouth.

Hank grabbed Danny by the ankles and held his feet up high, as widely spread as the kid could stand, allowing him to go even deeper.

"Oh, yes, please," said Danny. His hands reached up and tugged on Hank's nipples, squeezing and twisting the hardened nubs.

Hank let go of Danny's ankles and began jacking him off, while his free hand began toying with the kid's own nipples.

"Oh, God."

It seemed the instant he touched Danny's dick, it let loose a milky stream that splattered all over his chest, as far as his left nipple.

As Danny came, his ass muscles clenched, and that, along with the sight of him coming, brought Hank to the brink. He pounded firmly into Danny and held it there.

"Aw, man, fill me up," said Danny.

Hank groaned as the last drops came out and he felt Danny still squeezing his dick. "Jesus Christ."

He fell on top of Danny, leaving himself inside. He was breathing heavily, his muscles thoroughly weakened, his every ounce of energy spent. Danny was still hugging Hank against him. Hank rolled over onto his back, sliding out.

Danny snuggled against him and kissed his cheek. Hank turned and kissed Danny on the lips, once, briefly.

Danny stared him straight in the eye, stroking the hair on Hank's chest, and asked, "Do you love your little pony?"

# 6 July 1937

"Hank." It was a voice in his dream. "Hank."

His shoulder was nudged, and his eyes fluttered open to find Cathy staring down at him. "Leave me alone." His tongue felt thick and his words came out slurred.

"Get up," she said. "It's the phone."

"Phone," he repeated absently. He hated the phone.

"It's Jim Hogan."

"Jim Hogan. Shit."

Hank got up and scratched himself.

Cathy refixed her bathrobe and left the room, having done her duty and awakened him.

Hank went out into the hallway in his T-shirt and boxer shorts. He had a hard-on but he didn't care. He grabbed the phone from off the shelf.

"Hello?" he yawned, still scratching.

"Lucky, we need you down here," came Jim Hogan's voice.

"Oh, yeah?" *Oh, no, you don't.*

"West Third Street Bridge, south side of the river, by the Upson Nut plant."

Hank's mind finally kicked into gear and began to spin.

Upson Nut plant. That was Republic Steel. The steelworkers
were on strike. There had been a lot of violence, a couple of
people dead in recent clashes. The department had tried to
maintain order and ended up using tear gas and billy clubs. It
hadn't worked. The governor had called out the National
Guard three days ago and things had quieted down, though
Hank knew they were only simmering on the back burner,
ready to explode again.

"We got a riot?" Hank asked. "Somebody been killed?"

"No, no," said Hogan. "I'm afraid nothing so simple. Our
friend's at it again. He left us another torso, in the river."

"Maybe it's Amelia Earhart," said Hank, but Hogan didn't
laugh. He smelled bacon grilling, coffee brewing. "All right,
all right. I'm on my way."

"Hey, I need Lucky Lambert," Hogan said, "not Dick
Tracy."

"Would you settle for Spencer Tracy?"

"Frankly, Lucky, I'd settle for Joan Blondell in a pinch,
but that's neither here nor there, and right now I need you
here."

"I'll be there," Hank said, "with bells on."


6:37 A.M.

A smoky summer haze hung over the city.

Gazing a mile distant, north by northwest from where
Hank stood at the base of the West Third Street Bridge, the
gigantic Terminal Tower appeared as a ghostly apparition, a
purple silhouette of skyscraper rising from out of the earth-
bound cloud of soot and high up into the misty white morning light. The arch of the Detroit-Superior High-Level
Bridge was equally obscured, but the closer Lorain-Carnegie
Bridge had materialized more fully as the morning mist
burned off the smelly Cuyahoga.

Hank looked to the east, beyond the wide bend in the
river, to the other side where the railroad tracks wrapped
along the riverbank in a somewhat desolate stretch of the
Flats.

Over here on Hank's side of the river stood the Upson Nut
factory, surrounded by several pickets of striking workers

who were keeping their distance from the 147th Infantry of the Ohio National Guard, which was there protecting the perimeter of the plant and ensuring the safety of the scabs. The Guard had been there all night, as perhaps had been some of the strikers.

But, Hank conjectured, if the killer had dumped the torso on the opposite bank of the river at sunrise, while the mist was burning off the river, then none of the steelworkers or guardsmen would have been able to see a thing.

At least, not until around five-thirty in the morning, when Pvt. Edgar M. Steinbrecher of the Guard had looked out and seen floating underneath the bridge what turned out to be the lower half of a man's torso.

It looked much like the one they had pulled out of the Kingsbury Run pool last September: sliced cleanly at the waist and at the two femur joints, leaving a muscular pair of buttocks and, in this case, an intact set of male genitalia.

Before Hank's arrival, the guardsmen and Jim Hogan had retrieved the two upper halves of the guy's legs, which were of considerable heft—the thighs of a laborer.

Hank looked west from the bridge and saw something bob up in the water.

"Jim!" he shouted to Hogan, several yards away. "Over there, do you see it?"

Hank came running down off the bridge and along the shoreline, which was cluttered with garbage and colored a deep burnt-orange from the iron ore wastewater the factories routinely dumped into the river.

One of the guardsmen grabbed the rope they had been using and rigged up a lasso. Then, as if he were some fancy-pants cowboy, he whirled it around above his head and flung it out into the river, latching onto the object and tugging firmly on his rope. Another guardsman helped him pull it in to the bank, and by the time they had it, Hank was right alongside them with Jim Hogan.

"A burlap bag," observed Hank.

"That's his trademark," Hogan explained to the wide-eyed guardsmen. "He likes to wrap them up."

Although the bag claimed to contain one hundred pounds of Purina chicken feed, upon opening it Hank discovered approximately fifty pounds of human flesh, in the form of the man's upper torso, without head or arms, wrapped neatly in wet but unbloodied newspaper.

"Christmas in July," said Hogan from over Hank's shoulder.

"Hmm?" Hank said, thinking Hogan was trying to make some bad joke about the killer's latest present for them.

But Hogan had been reading from the newspaper wrappings clinging to the remains. "At Higbee's this weekend," he explained, as if defending himself. "Hey, my wife could use a new icebox."

# 2 November 1937

**10:14 P.M.**

"What'll you have?" asked Eliot Ness.

"Vodka martini," said Harold Burton.

"I'll tell the boy." Ness called over the waiter, a tall, slightly effeminate youth with wavy blond hair and a beaklike nose. "Vodka martini and a Bloody Mary."

When they got their drinks, Burton proposed a toast: "Two more years, God help us."

Ness thought his Bloody Mary a trifle strong.

"I'm making a run for the Senate," the mayor announced. "In 'forty."

"Well, good luck, Harry."

"The party has great faith in you, you know."

"I'm glad." Ness wanted to avoid committing himself to anything. He wasn't sure he would make a good mayor.

"You're still their man. They'll bankroll you all the way. This is still a Democratic city, and they think you're the only guy who can hang onto the mayor's seat for us."

"Who they?"

"The money men. The Hannas, the Hesslers." The mayor considered for a moment before adding, "Me."

"I'm not sure I can live up to that," said Ness.

Everyone always thought he was bearing false modesty, but he merely spoke the truth. Things were going poorly at home. His long hours at work, as well as his and Edna's failure to produce any children, had put a strain on their already precarious marriage, and he was worried they wouldn't last another year. Cleveland's Democrats were predominately working-class Catholic, and he would need their votes if he wanted to get elected mayor. A divorce from Edna would do little to win their support, but he hoped it wouldn't come to that.

"Listen, Eliot, if I'm reelected mayor in 'thirty-nine and then get elected to the Senate in 'forty, we'll get you appointed to serve the rest of my term, and then you run for reelection in 'forty-one. You've got three years to think on it. But if you want my advice, I'd say don't look a gift horse in the mouth."

*Three years,* Ness thought, and wondered if they would manage to track down the Torso Slayer by then. As Director of Public Safety, he was ultimately responsible for seeing the Headhunter apprehended and brought to justice, and if he still hadn't managed to do it by 1940, his own head would roll, politically speaking, and not even Harold Burton would be able to save it.

Ness was confident in Hank Lambert's handling of the case, but sometimes the department's combined efforts seemed futile and meaningless, not to mention expensive. It was as if their killer were some apparition, flitting unseen from one killing to the next and vanishing into thin air. His nameless victims seemed little more than shades themselves. The killer had succeeded, literally, in obliterating them—appropriating for himself not only their lives, but their identities as well—and, by cutting off their heads, perhaps had stolen their very souls. This aspect of primitive ritual violated Ness's twentieth-century sensibilities and left him groping for answers. The case preyed constantly on his mind, and this too was responsible for some of the friction between himself and Edna.

"Harry," Ness said, "I won't let you down." But underneath the table he kept his fingers crossed.

**11:51 P.M.**

Mott Hessler sat upon a bar stool at the Men's Café, just off the lower lobby of the Hotel Cleveland, and waited for the bartender to notice him. A nickel tip left by the previous customer remained on the mahogany bartop, just the other side of the brass railing. Hessler stood the nickel on its end and flicked it with his finger, sending it spinning like a top.

Les, the bartender, snapped up the nickel before it had a chance to fall over.

"Hey, Mott, what's it gonna be?" Les was drying a beer mug with a clean white towel. He had the pudgy, square-jawed face of an aging football player but looked rather neat in his black vest and bow tie.

"Gold Top."

"You got it." Les grabbed a glass mug from a refrigerated cabinet, placed it beneath the draft spigot for Pilsener Gold Top, and filled the mug until a fine head was dribbling over the side. Les wiped the spilled beer from the side of the mug and plopped it down in front of Hessler. "Fifteen."

Hessler gave him the change. He could have asked for a tab, but he wasn't planning on sticking around for too long this evening, and he'd rather keep his score with Les settled.

Hessler liked the Men's Café because its clientele usually looked smart. Many of Cleveland's younger set of unmarried businessmen dropped by for drinks on a regular basis, their hair slicked back from their foreheads, looking as pretty as guys in a picture show. Hessler had had reasonable success finding men to go home with him, though not everyone who came here was a pervert—not by a long shot.

The unfortunate thing about tonight was that the Men's Café was filled with politicians, and politicians were decidedly among the most unbeautiful people Hessler had ever seen. But aside from the election night crowd, there still remained many of the Men's Café regulars.

Hessler continued to sip his beer and to watch the crowd, looking for men sitting alone who fit a general type. He didn't like guys who were obviously queer, primped up and acting like girls—not that any of them would be allowed into the Men's Café in the first place. Hessler liked them young, his own age or younger, attractive, and with a touch of innocence or naïveté about them. They had to act like men, not girls, and they had to be somewhat passive, though at the same time eager.

As he scanned the room, however, he spotted something else that grabbed his attention: Mayor Harold Burton and Safety Director Eliot Ness sitting in a booth, celebrating.

Hessler had already met Ness, of course, during the raid at the Black Hawk Inn, but he felt it would be interesting to introduce himself under more appropriate circumstances—besides which, he wanted to meet the mayor.

Burton may have been in office two years and just been reelected for two more, but the Torso Slayer had been operating for longer and would continue to do so long after Burton was gone. Hessler rather liked the name the papers had given him, and he followed the Torso Slayer's exploits much the same way that ordinary people followed those of Flash Gordon. He was happy to see the police were nowhere near to catching him, and was certain that if the trail ever became "hot," the press would telegraph it way in advance and give him ample warning.

Ness had given himself a high-profile role in the case, commenting on it publicly and stating it was high on his list of priorities as safety director. Hessler thought it would be a lot of fun to meet him and shake his hand.

*Go on, I dare you. . . .*

Hessler downed the last of his beer and set it on the bar, his gaze zeroing in on Burton and Ness. Ness was pulling some cash out of his wallet, apparently about to settle their bill. If Hessler chose to act, he would have to do it now, before they left the room.

*I double dare you. . . .*

Hessler hopped up off the seat and absently brushed out any wrinkles in his jacket or trousers with the back of his hand, grabbed his hat, then began walking past the tables and down the narrow aisle alongside the booths, until he reached the one toward the back where Burton and Ness sat. The waiter was taking their money, and the two were just getting up to leave.

"Congratulations, Mr. Mayor," said Hessler, offering his hand to shake.

"Thank you," said Burton shaking his hand, his smile polite.

Hessler turned to Ness and shook his hand. "I suppose this means you get to keep your job, Mr. Ness?"

"Oh, yes," said Ness, his face suddenly beaming with recognition.

"Mott Hessler," he introduced himself, and watched them to see the effect of his name upon their countenances. "I'm sure you know my father."

"Of course!" Burton was now genuinely beaming. His hand slapped Hessler full on the back.

"I believe we've met," said Ness, his manner still reserved but not in the least offensive. "But I don't believe we were ever formally introduced."

"Why don't you join us?" the mayor asked.

"Oh, I don't think—" Hessler began, but was cut off.

"We were just heading upstairs to my party. Midnight's a swell time for a late entrance."

"Yes, the witching hour," Hessler agreed.

"I'm sure your father's there," said Ness, and Hessler wondered if he meant anything by it, or if the remark were purely innocuous.

"My father and I don't entirely get along," said Hessler, just to show Ness that there was no secret about it, and then to offer his own explanation: "He was miffed that I didn't want to follow in his footsteps."

"Oh?" asked the mayor, obviously perplexed at the thought of anyone not wanting to become part of such an enterprise as Ohnoco. "What exactly do you do?"

"I'm a businessman." *I'm the Torso Slayer. I chop people's heads off and cut them up, and you just shook my hand, sir.* "A pharmacist, actually. I've got my own store, Hessler's Drugs, and I plan on opening a chain, spreading out all over the Midwest. That's my businessman side, I guess."

"From small beginnings . . ." said Burton, and looked at his pocket watch. "Sure you won't join us?"

"Afraid not, Mr. Mayor. I'm meeting a friend."

"Well, bring him along. Room fourteen-twelve."

"I'll keep it in mind, sir."

"We'd better get going," said Ness, then turning to Hessler: "Nice meeting you, officially."

Hessler shook his hand again, this time clasping both of his hands firmly around Ness's. "Good luck to you," he said, looking Ness in the eye, and then added, "Both of you."

As Burton and Ness hurried out of the Men's Café and into the lower lobby, Hessler laughed aloud and thought to himself, *You're going to need it.*

He headed back toward the bar but saw that all the stools were taken. All the men sat facing the bar, their backs toward Hessler, except for one. This one was lounging back, leaning his elbows against the brass railing, his legs spread and dangling over the edge of the stool. His mouth was puckered in a whistle, though Hessler could hear no whistling above the noise of the crowd. But as Hessler neared and his vision at last cut through the haze of cigarette and cigar smoke, he saw the face and recognized who it was.

It was Danny Cottone, the young punk who came into his store every month to buy *Weird Tales.* The kid Flo Polillo had kicked in the ribs. The hustler whose naked photos he had purchased among that bunch from Eddie Andrassy. He could never forget a face like that, and right at this moment he was imagining Danny the way he appeared in the photos, his cockhead poking from out of his foreskin, the unfinished growth of hair along his legs and chest, the curves of his ass cheeks, the dimples in his smile, the little brown nipples, the rose tattoo.

"Hi, Danny," he said, turning on the charm. Not that he needed any charm to win Danny's affections. A few small bills would do the trick, so to speak.

"Hey, Mr. Hessler," said Danny, his face lighting up. "You want my seat?"

"That's all right." Hessler came closer and squeezed into the space between Danny and the next guy. "Buy you a drink?"

"Sure," said Danny. "Black Russian."

Hessler withdrew his wallet and opened it up, fumbling through the wad of bills ostensibly looking for a one, all the while intending for Danny to see the load of greenbacks for himself.

"Les, one Black Russian, and another Gold Top for me."

"Sure thing, Mott," said the barkeep, wiping off the bar.

"What's the occasion?" he asked Danny. He stood close enough that he could smell the kid's breath; he thought he detected the fishy odor of cock. He knew Danny hadn't been in the bar even ten minutes ago, and decided he must have just come from entertaining a john, probably some politician upstairs.

"Election night," Danny said, and shrugged.

"Are you a party member?"

"I like the excitement."

"Republicans aren't exciting people," Hessler observed.

"You wanna bet?" Danny's dimples were showing.

Les set down their drinks. Hessler handed him a buck, and Les gave him back his change. Hessler handed Danny his drink and said, "Here, this'll get that bad taste out of your mouth."

Danny looked at him with a start. "What taste?"

"What is it our dear departed Flo Polillo called you, a 'two-bit cocksucker'?"

Danny laughed, and Hessler saw they were finally on the same frequency. "You can tell?"

"From ten paces."

"Shit, I'd better have some of this." Danny took a healthy gulp of his dark drink.

"I imagine the price has inflated since then." Hessler riffled through the bills in his wallet.

"You want to make a deal?" Danny's eyebrows went up.

Hessler leaned into him, cupped his hand around Danny's ear, and whispered, "Kid, what I want is your ass," at the same time placing a folded ten-dollar bill into his palm.

"OK." Danny pocketed the cash.

"Come on, then." Hessler tugged Danny out into the lower lobby and led him through the foyer, out onto the sidewalk along Superior Avenue and around the corner onto Public Square, where they approached the base of the brightly illumined Terminal Tower, where Hessler had parked his Auburn. Beyond the tapering pinnacle of the skyscraper, the clouds passed swiftly, backlighted by the glow of the gibbous moon. The night air was chilly.

"Where to?" Danny asked, his teeth a-chatter. He glanced up at the skyscraper and seemed apprehensive.

"My place," Hessler said, opening the passenger door for him. "Now get in."

# 8 April 1938

4:07 A.M.

Hank Lambert was being chased down a long winding tunnel, circular in shape like a subway tube and tiled throughout with baby-blue polished ceramic squares. The tunnel was brightly illumined, its curves sinuous as if the tunnelers had had no idea where they were going. Hank could certainly hazard no guess as to where it was taking him.

Hasty footsteps echoed from behind him, as well as sinister laughter. No matter how fast Hank ran, the footsteps grew ever louder. His pursuer was gaining on him.

"Daddy?" he heard a voice say—Becky's voice—but it was more distant than the footsteps and its echo merely a ghost.

At the end of the tunnel, Hank found a blue-tiled crawlspace. With the footsteps right behind him, this was his only possible escape route. Hank got down on his knees and squeezed into the hole, crawling through the claustrophobic passage for about fifteen feet, and emerging inside a square room tiled in the same baby blue, brightly lighted but without any visible means of illumination. The room was a dead end.

The footsteps stopped when they reached the other side of

the crawlspace. Long-legged shadows were cast into the room from Hank's pursuer pacing back and forth outside. His pursuer's footfalls had become steady but light, like the ticking of a clock.

"Daddy!" Again came Becky's far-off voice. Hank felt somebody poking his shoulder, but no one else was in the room.

He noticed a tube of grout, a trowel, and other assorted tools lying on the floor next to a stack of loose tiles, and realized the tiling of the room had yet to be completed. It was hard at first to discern, but as he approached the objects, he noticed a round hole in the floor, large enough for a man to squeeze through. The hole was framed by a circle of several broad tiles whose lips curved neatly past the edge of the hole.

The patient plodding of footsteps echoed from outside. The shadows passed to and fro. His pursuer was waiting for him to come out.

Hank knelt and looked over the rim to see what was inside the hole, when suddenly he felt the tiles loosen beneath him, and he realized the grout was fresh and had not entirely set. He lost his balance and fell headlong into the hole, the loosened tiles raining down on him, and saw beneath him, as he fell, a cavernous room filled with a bubbly white mudlike substance that he somehow knew to be boiling plaster.

*"Ahh!"* he shouted, and awoke with a start to find himself back in his bed, Cathy sleeping soundly beside him, and his daughter Becky's moonlight-blue face staring down at him from beside the bed, with tears in her eyes.

"Hm?" he said, bewildered. He had broken out in a cold sweat.

Becky was shaking his shoulder roughly, her face screwed up into a look of grave concern. "Daddy, wake up!"

"What?" Hank asked, dazed. His eyelids were heavy and he had a hard time keeping them open. He held Becky's hand; her palm was clammy. "It was only a nightmare, sugarplum."

"Daddy, it's for you," she said. "Hurry!"

"What is?" he asked, and wondered if she were walking in her sleep.

"There's a weird man on the phone."

*A man? At four A.M.? No, hon, you mean Sergeant Hogan.*

"Oh, crud." He had only gone to sleep three hours ago, and if Jim Hogan thought he was getting out of bed just for some goddamned murder or something, he damn well had another think coming. Let him shake Vernal Quast out of bed, for Chrissakes! Let Quast earn his fucking keep for once.

"Hurry, Daddy!" Becky jumped up and down, but she looked fearful rather than excited. Her small fingers grabbed more tightly onto Hank's hand as she tried to pull him out of bed.

"What is it?" asked Cathy, turning over in bed.

"Just the phone," said Hank, tossing his portion of the bedcovers aside and planting his feet on the floor. "Probably Jim Hogan. Go back to sleep."

Cathy turned away toward the far wall. She had made a practice of no longer answering the phone in the wee hours of the morning, since it was always for Hank, anyway. Hank only wished Becky hadn't been awakened. If it hadn't been for his nightmare, he would have heard the ringing himself and gone to answer it before it could disturb his little girl.

Once Hank had his house slippers on, Becky led him out of the bedroom and down the hallway to the phone on its little shelf. The handset hung over the edge, swinging a few inches above the floor.

"Daddy, I'm scared," said Becky, her eyes wet.

Hank ruffled her blond curls. "I told you, it was only a nightmare. Daddy has them, too." *Boy, does he!* "Now back to bed." He patted her behind. Normally, she would have scurried off as he'd asked, but this time she stayed put.

"That man," she said, pointing at the dangling handset. "I said you were sleeping with Mommy, but he told me to go wake you up or he'd cut my head off!"

Hank grabbed the phone and placed his hand over the

mouthpiece. "Becky, go get in bed with your mother!" he ordered. "Now! And close the door."

Becky ran crying back into the bedroom and slammed the door shut.

Taking his hand away, Hank said, "Hello? Who is this?"

"Three guesses," came the voice, deep yet smooth.

Hank had to assume from the outset that this guy was some kind of crank. It wouldn't be the first person who had claimed he was the Torso Slayer.

"What's the meaning of this?" Hank asked. "What do you want?"

"It's not what I want that matters, it's what you need."

"Oh yeah? What's that?" Hank's tone was the same he used on door-to-door salesmen.

"I've got something for your investigation."

"C'mon, get to the point."

"You really don't believe it's me, do you?" The voice sounded disappointed.

"Me who?"

"You know." The voice laughed. "All those ingenious names. The Mad Butcher. The Phantom. The Headhunter. The Torso Slayer. Torsos, torsos, everywhere, yet not a drop to drink. But what, my friend, do you think?"

"I'm not your friend," said Hank.

"Can't take it, can you? You don't like what I said to your daughter."

"Stop it."

"You'll have to catch me first."

"Oh, I will, you can count on it." Even if this were a crank, Hank thought it best to play along.

"Hi-ho, hi-ho, it's off to work I go," the voice sang, in a grating mockery of the popular song, followed by some maniacal whistling. Hank had taken Luke and Becky just the other day to see *Snow White and the Seven Dwarfs*, with which he had been more impressed than they, and now this joker had gone and ruined it for him. He wondered if the caller had followed them to the theater.

"If you're the Torso Slayer, where have you been? You haven't killed anybody in nine months."

"That's what you think."

"I thought you said you had some information for me."

"Oh, I do. It regards my sexual peccadilloes, about which you all seem so fascinated. I thought you, in particular, might be interested."

"Is that so?" Hank wondered what he meant by that.

"You're the detective," said the voice.

"Go on," Hank prodded.

"Have you ever stuck your cock in somebody's asshole?"

"Listen, I've had just about enough of—"

"I never get enough. If you believe everything you read in the papers, I'm quite the pervert. A sexual degenerate. A dope fiend. A drunken surgeon, *ha-ha!* A butcher even, just like Leather Apron. Do you know, some people even think I'm Jack the Ripper himself? He might still be alive, you know."

"Shut up."

"If he were twenty when he went wassailing, he'd be seventy today. Unless of course he's been drinking the blood of virgins all this time."

"I said shut up."

"Do you realize it's been fifty years since Jack took his first bride? Emma Smith, I believe, was her name."

"Yeah? So what?"

"Fifty years last Sunday, as a matter of fact."

"That was London, fella, this is Cleveland."

"Golden anniversary, you might call it. Fine excuse for a celebration, let me tell you. I went walking around near the market Sunday night and bought myself a little whore for the evening. Had a ripping good time. She proved a real cut-up. That's why I'm making this trunk call—"

"You think you're pretty clever, don't you?" Hank was still treating it as a prank. Even though the caller was probably sick, he had as yet said nothing that proved he was the killer. He had displayed no intimate knowledge of the case beyond what anyone could have read in the papers.

"Cleverer than you, detective. My head count is slightly different from yours. You're only up to number nine."

"How many more have you got?"

"You mean in Cleveland proper?"

"Yeah, let's stick to that."

"That's for me to know and you to find out."

"Give me a rough estimate."

"More than the Ripper."

"Congratulations."

"You know, Detective, I get the distinct impression that you aren't taking me seriously."

"You're not the first Torso Slayer I've talked to, buddy."

"Hacks, all of them, I assure you."

"Listen, buster, I don't want you calling here again. I'm going to be writing up a threats report on this, and don't think there won't be any follow-up."

"Go ahead. You've been unable to catch me so far."

"Don't flatter yourself." Hank was about to hang up.

"Oh, Detective?" came the voice. "One more thing. I've sent you a present."

"What kind of present?"

"A memento of last Sunday. An anniversary present, you might say. In honor of Jack and Emma."

"You disgust me."

"You might want to make note of the fact that after killing Emma, Saucy Jack didn't rip again until August—"

Hank slammed the receiver down upon the cradle.

When he returned to the bedroom, he found Cathy sitting up in bed comforting Becky, who was pressed against her chest.

"It's all right," Cathy was saying, rocking her back and forth.

Hank got in bed beside them and stroked Becky's hair. "Honey, that was just someone playing a bad joke. He can't hurt you. I'm here to protect you."

"That's right," said Cathy, giving him a cold look across their daughter's curly locks. "Your Daddy's got a gun."

Her lips mouthed *You bastard!* as if Hank had been somehow responsible for the phone call. She had often expressed her concern that Hank's homicide cases would intrude even further into their home life, and now it seemed she had been proven right.

Hank wanted to apologize to her, but now was a lousy time to discuss it.

"C'mon, Becky," he said, settling down against the pillows. "Why don't you sleep right here between me and Mommy?"

Becky turned to face him and snuggled against him, kissing his stubbly cheek. "Daddy, I love you."

Cathy and Becky both managed to fall asleep within minutes, but Hank kept replaying the phone call in his mind. The more he thought about it, the more it troubled him. If indeed the caller *had* been the Torso Slayer, then he likely knew not only Hank's home phone number, but also where he lived.

### 7:38 P.M.

Hank Lambert had invited Eliot Ness down to the morgue to join them for the autopsy. Before them upon the coroner's dissection table lay the lower half of a human leg, disarticulated at the knee and ankle joints.

"We think it's from a woman," said Coroner Sam Gerber.

"You *think?*" asked Hank.

"We can't tell for certain. We're going to have to have it X-rayed, and even then we may not know. We're not even positive if it's right or left."

Laborer Steve Morosky had thought it was a dead fish before pulling it from the river. Spring storms and winter runoff had flooded the Cuyahoga, and the disembodied shin had washed up against a cluster of old pier pilings at the mouth of a storm sewer beneath the eastern span of the Detroit-Superior High-Level Bridge. Morosky, a WPA worker on his afternoon break, had waded out into the murky water and retrieved the thing at 2:15 P.M., then gone and phoned the police.

"The piece is thirteen inches long," Gerber continued, replacing his glasses and withdrawing a measuring tape so the policemen could see for themselves. "My preliminary estimate is that this is from a mature adult female approximately five foot two or three, with a slim build, no more than a hundred ten pounds, probably twenty-five to thirty-five years of age. The piece has been in the water up to seventy-two hours, and from that and the condition of the flesh,

I'm estimating time of death at between three and five days ago."

"Five days ago, that was Sunday," said Hank, thinking aloud. Ever since the discovery of the gruesome leg, he had begun to believe his early-morning phone call had been the real McCoy, and he cursed himself for his stupidity in thinking otherwise. "Sunday, April third," he said aloud.

*Happy anniversary. . . .*

Hank had decided the Torso Slayer had called him purely for practical reasons. He was bound to realize the many hours Hank worked and the erratic schedule he kept, and that Hank might appear in the Kingsbury Run area at any time hoping to see something suspicious. The killer had probably planned on dumping the remains and wanted to make sure the detective was at home. Hank imagined the Mad Butcher had driven onto either the Detroit-Superior High-Level or the Lorain-Carnegie Bridge to dump his load into the drink.

"Gentlemen, these crude knife marks indicate the slayer was in a hurry," said Gerber, "and the hesitation marks at the knee joint show the killer was right-handed."

"That's a big help," said Eliot Ness. Nobody laughed.

After responding to the scene of Morosky's discovery, the detectives had spent all afternoon searching the swollen banks of the river for further body parts, but met with no success. Eliot Ness had phoned the U.S. Coast Guard and enlisted their aid; tomorrow, the detectives would be climbing aboard a patrol boat and scanning the breadth of the river for chunks of flesh or for a tell-tale burlap bag.

"I must warn you," said Gerber, "this is all Dr. Strauss's and my best estimates. The leg might still prove to be from the body of a slightly built man. Dr. Magid is going to take some X rays for us. The skin's very smooth, and I'm going to conduct a test to determine if the hair was shaved."

"How's that going to tell you anything?" asked Ness. "If the victim *was* a man, couldn't the killer have shaved the hair off to throw us off the track?"

"Could have," Gerber agreed, "but there's also the possibility the hairs have been plucked."

"You mean one by one?" asked Ness.

"Sure," Hank agreed, "Dr. Williams said the slayer's 'anal-retentive,' very neat and orderly. All evidence shows he goes to a lot of trouble to cover his tracks."

"Precisely." Gerber's grin was incongruous. He seemed almost giddy in his work. "We also found a few strands of long blond hair wrapped around the shin, which we believe are from the victim's head."

"What about med students?" Ness asked. "Couldn't this be some prank, say an amputation? Some students tossing the leg in the river just for laughs?"

"No, sir, I don't believe so," said Gerber.

"But how do we really know it's the Torso Slayer?"

"I'd recognize his work anywhere."

"C'mon, Sam, how many ways can there be to cut up a body?"

"Are you questioning my abilities?" Gerber asked.

"You know me better than that." Ness sounded hurt.

"I'm having some experts come down tonight from Western Reserve University, but I'm confident they'll confirm our findings."

An uncomfortable silence fell over the room.

"Well," said Ness, rubbing his hands together. The morgue laboratory *was* rather cold, Hank thought. "We'll see what we can come up with tomorrow. Lucky, I want you and Vern to track down all the missing persons reports for the past two or three weeks and meet me in my office. No one's going home tonight until we make a little headway."

Hank wondered what use missing persons reports would be at this stage, when they knew so little. Even if they came across one matching Gerber's rough description, they could hardly ask family members to make an ID from a disembodied shin. Hank wondered if Ness realized the futility of this exercise. It would be better to cull through the missing persons reports at some later date, once they had found a few more body parts and had a better idea of who exactly they were looking for, including such minor details as the person's sex.

Aside from the current find, the Torso Slayer had murdered six men and three women—four if you counted the Lady of the Lake. All Hank or anyone else really knew at this point was that the sexless shin had passed the coroner's test and become officially known as Number Ten.

# 9 April 1938

**9:03 A.M.**

Snow flurries were being blown about by a fierce wind outside Eliot Ness's office window. Down the hill from City Hall, toward the lake, he could see a throng of burly WPA construction men along with their bulldozers, road graders, and dump trucks, hard at work building Lake Shore Boulevard just on the other side of the railroad tracks, through the land that had been filled three years ago and used as the grounds of the Great Lakes Exposition. Now the futuristic buildings of the exposition had been torn down, leaving only a desolate vacant space this side of Municipal Stadium, as if it were some vast parking lot for the Indians. The snow flurries seemed to be scattering fairly well, the construction workers only dogged by the cold wind. Out in gray Lake Erie, large breakers were being whipped up, causing a bubbly spray as they crashed against the East Ninth Street docks.

Ness took a sip of his coffee, which had grown tepid but tasted strong. *Thanks, Betty-Lou.*

The buzzer sounded on his intercom, making him jump. The thing was damned loud and never failed to give him a start. Betty-Lou's voice came over the speaker: "Sir? It's your wife on the phone."

Ness picked up the receiver. "Yes, Edna."

"Some mail came for you. You want me to come by tonight and drop it off?"

"I may be working late on this torso case."

"Yes, I saw the paper. Gruesome."

The newest murder had, naturally, been front-page news. The *Plain Dealer* featured a map of Cleveland marked with the ten official torso slayings, with small black dots strewn from the village of Brooklyn all the way up to the Beulah Park beach, most located south of Public Square, clustered around Kingsbury Run and the Flats, along the snakelike Cuyahoga. Ness had a similar map on the wall of his office, his with little red stick-pins where the bodies had been discovered.

"It's always puzzled me," Ness said, "how he managed to get rid of all those bodies without ever being seen. When I looked at the map this morning I got to wondering if there might be some method to it, perhaps certain paths he'd taken with less chance of being spotted."

"Maybe he took the trolley," Edna said.

Ness failed to appreciate her sarcasm, and his way of dealing with it was to ignore it. "If we can trace those paths," he continued, "they should cross at some point and show us where he lives, or at least where he kills."

Edna sighed on the other end of the line. "Eliot, honey—"

"Colonel Zistel at the National Guard is going to send up four planes from their Observation Squadron and take some aerial photographs of the torso sites. Then we'll have their experts sit down with us and analyze the pictures, see if we can come up with something. We might be able to see something from the air that we're missing on the ground."

The headline above the map in the paper read, "Hunt for More Torso Evidence," followed by the subhead, "Police Seek Clews From Severed Leg," followed by a whole column-length story on the latest find. Ness was somewhat afraid the map in the paper would cause undue hysteria, since it gave the impression that all of Cleveland was equally vulnerable, when such was obviously not the case. Their killer only preyed on those who were down and out and easily victimized. He certainly didn't select them from the social register.

Ness heard nothing on the other end of the line. "Edna? Are you still there?"

"Yes. Do you want me to bring over your mail?"

"Why don't I pick it up after I get off?"

"Are you through unpacking?"

"Mostly."

"I'd like to see what the place looks like without all those boxes cluttering it up."

Ness yawned suddenly and excused himself to his wife; he had been getting little restful sleep. He and Edna had decided to try a separation for a while, and between that and the torso case his nerves were jangled. He had rented himself an apartment in the Lakewood neighborhood and let Edna stay at the house for now, but the apartment felt too small and the bed too big with only himself sleeping in it. He found, though, that he still kept to his side of the bed rather than flailing across its entire breadth; he had been accustomed to the left side for eight years now, with Edna always there on his right, ever since their honeymoon. Edna's absence kept him awake, staring at the ceiling, as if he were waiting for her to come home. He supposed he would get used to the apartment in time, as he would the separation, which he agreed, on the whole, was a good thing.

"Well, sure, Edna, come by if you want. Give me a ring first. Don't want you to waste the trip if I'm tied up at the office."

"All right. Do you need anything else? Stocked up on food? I'm going by the store."

"No, I'm fine." Ness tried not to snap at her, but now that they had made a break, he didn't want her mothering him.

"Well, OK, then. I've got to go run some errands now, but I'll ring you before I come by tonight."

"OK, hon. Have a good day." Ness hung up. Luckily, Edna had ended the conversation before he could complain about how busy he was; that was one of the reasons behind their separation. He put in sometimes seventy hours a week, and had done so for years.

He had known Edna since high school, and in retrospect

perhaps it had been naïve of them to think a marriage could work. After he had finished his dissertation and joined the Justice Department, she had stood by him and even put herself at risk when he and his band of "Untouchables" had taken on the mob. On occasion, Ness had been tailed by Capone's men while he and Edna were out driving around on a date. Even the lives of Edna's family had been placed in jeopardy by her association with such a high-profile gangbuster. Looking back, Ness thought he had married her out of a sense of duty—as if, after subjecting her to such danger, he owed her something.

The marriage had long since proved a mistake, but it had taken them both some time to confess to the fact. He had no time for her because of the hours he put in at work; she had been unhappy for years. Perhaps children could have saved the marriage, yet for whatever reason they had never been able to have any, and the doctors seemed at a loss to explain why. For the first time, Ness was grateful they had failed to start a family. If the separation indeed led to a divorce, it would make things easier for both of them.

Ness stood up from his desk and went over to the map on his wall. He hadn't yet stuck a pin in for Number Ten, so he grabbed one and searched the streets for the proper place along Superior Avenue, on the north side of the bridge. He stuck the red pin through the paper and into the cork at a bend in the Cuyahoga.

Ness wondered how he was going to tell Harry Burton about his and Edna's separation. Harry wanted his potential successor not only married, but happily so, preferably with kids. Ness was keeping it secret from the press, and perhaps he should keep it from Harry for a while, too, in case nothing came of it.

But considering the state of things, that was probably wishful thinking.

# 2 May 1938

Hank felt as nervous as a schoolboy on his first date, standing in the hallway outside Danny's apartment. His day had been exhausting. He had a headache, and his face felt warm because of a terrific sunburn. His shirt beneath his jacket was damp with perspiration, and he could smell himself; he smelled like lamb. Drops of water fell onto his gray coat sleeve from the leak in the ceiling and spread into a small circle before he could draw his arm back.

He could hear nothing on the other side of the door. He hoped Danny was alone. He knocked.

His foot tapped absently in the small puddle of water at his feet. Behind him, he clutched several red carnations in a neatly wrapped bundle.

He stood there for a minute or so before he heard the creak of footsteps on the other side and saw a light click on through the slit at the base of the door. Danny opened the door with the chain lock still on. Hank could only see a dim, narrow view of him; the hallway was poorly lighted.

"Hank," said Danny with a surprised smile.

"I had to see you," Hank said. "Are you alone?"

"Sure." Danny hurriedly closed the door and removed the chain lock. Then he opened it fully and let Hank in.

Danny was wearing a short brown bathrobe that was tied rather high on his waist and came down to above his knees—probably the same robe he had worn since he was a kid at the Parmadale Children's Village. The robe opened up clear down to the tie, showing nothing underneath but bare olive skin and dark curly hair.

Hank handed him the flowers.

Danny laughed, tossing his head back, and at first Hank didn't know how to take it. But Danny quickly reached out and grabbed them and said, "They're wonderful. My favorite color," and Hank was relieved.

Danny went straight into the small kitchen area just off the room, filled up an empty Coca-Cola bottle with water, and stuffed the carnations into it. He carried the makeshift arrangement to the bay window and set it down upon the ledge, in front of the dark windows dripping with rain from the storm outside. Hank could see both their reflections in the glass before Danny pulled the curtains shut with a few quick yanks along the curtain rod.

"It's been a month," said Danny. "You should have called. I though you weren't coming around anymore."

Hank closed the door to the apartment and stepped into the room, removing his hat and tossing it on the bed.

Danny turned around, saying, "There," and motioned toward the flowers. "How's that?"

"Super," said Hank.

Danny came out from around the bed and retied his robe; it hugged him more tightly and showed less of his chest hair. Hank remained where he was and watched as the face drew nearer—the greasy hair perpetually in need of a trim, the sharp line of Danny's underfed chin, the dark eyes and full lips heading straight for him. And suddenly Danny was embracing him, eyes closing, lips parting—and Hank looked briefly into the tooth-guarded abyss before Danny's pink tongue poked out and into Hank's mouth, and they consumed each other in a long, sloppy kiss.

Hank grabbed the lapels of Danny's threadbare robe and pulled them over his shoulders, allowing Danny to pull out his sinewy arms as Hank untied the cloth belt, helping the robe fall in a heap at their feet. Hank caressed the warm flesh and held it against him, running his hands down and around Danny's ass.

"You got to promise me you'll stop hustling."

"Sure, I know."

"You can't do this forever." Hank brushed aside a lock of Danny's hair and kissed his forehead. "You won't always be so pretty. What are you going to do then?"

Danny shrugged. "I don't know. But nobody lives forever."

"You're twenty-two. You've got a lot to live for."

"I don't know about that."

"What's the matter with you?"

"A lot, I guess."

"Come on, that's not what I meant." Hank grasped the back of Danny's neck and planted a kiss on his cheek. "How can you let people do this to you?"

"That's just how it is, ever since the orphanage."

"Did the other boys abuse you?"

"Naw," said Danny, laughing. "I guess I traded favors with them. They'd do things for me if I let them fuck me. I got what I wanted, they got what they wanted. I was the richest kid around."

"They didn't steal your money?"

"No one tried. The other guys protected me. That's one of the favors I traded for. I was never that big, in case you hadn't figured that out."

"Will you let me do that?"

"What?"

"Protect you."

"Sure."

"Then take this." Hank pulled twenty dollars out of his pocket and handed it to Danny. It was all he had on him. He didn't have much in the bank, and on his salary he was unsure exactly how he was going to be able to keep Danny afloat, but he would have to try, somehow.

Cathy had begun talking to him about their marriage, and about her disappointments. She still had no idea about Hank's commerce with young hustlers, yet she knew there was something wrong with him. He could not satisfy her sexually. She had tried to allay his fears of her getting pregnant by buying him a box of prophylactics, and he had tried one on but hated it. He had understood her feelings but was uncomfortable talking with her about sex. He feared that further discussion might lead to a divorce, which was the last thing he wanted. Yet their current troubles had only driven Hank further away from her, and into Danny's arms to find solace.

"Thanks," Danny mumbled, as if ashamed to be taking Hank's money, and put the bill in the pocket of his robe.

"When you need more, call me. You've got my number at the station. Just don't call me at home, all right?"

"Yes, sir."

"It's just plain Hank."

"I'm sorry."

Hank hugged him tightly, wondering what was happening to the poor kid. When Hank was lonely or tired or needed to talk, he looked for Danny—and more often than not was unable to find him. He had been working so hard on the torso case during the last month that Danny had fallen by the wayside, but today's discovery of more parts of Number Ten had altered the equation. He needed someone to hold and couldn't go to Cathy.

The parts had started showing up in the river this morning: the rest of the leg, both halves of the torso. She had been small and thin, young, about Danny's age. She had had two babies, one they had had to cut out of her. Coroner Gerber had found drugs in her blood, and they thought she was a junkie, though without the arms that was impossible to confirm. Hank imagined she was probably a whore, too.

All afternoon alone in the rowboat upon the fast-moving Cuyahoga, Hank had stared into the murky waters, thinking. After their initial discovery, no more burlap bags had turned up, so Hank was left scanning the rippling surface of the river for hours, during which time he had thought mostly about Danny. Flashes of Eddie Andrassy's severed head and the head of the Tattooed Man kept presenting themselves as the sun beat down on his face, and he kept imagining Danny's severed head popping up from the ore-tinted water, staring back at him.

As he sat there being tossed about, his arms sore from fighting the current, he had had the urge to row ashore and run to find Danny and make sure he was all right. After completing his search, he had had to go to the morgue to see the last of the autopsy and get the good word from Sam Gerber. Once his duties for the day were done, he went off to find Danny, and purchased the carnations from a flower girl on Euclid, near Public Square. He had wanted red roses, but all she had had were these carnations. Hank had never needed anyone the way he needed Danny now.

"Let's turn out the light," said Hank.

Danny reached over to the lamp on the end table and turned the switch, putting the room in darkness except for a dim blue light filtering through the curtains.

Danny was already removing Hank's tie and unbuttoning his shirt, placing his hands inside and stroking Hank's chest. His lips came up and they kissed once more, falling against the bed. Hank kicked off his shoes, and in no time Danny had him totally naked.

"You'll be my only one," Danny whispered in Hank's ear, and gave his earlobe a nibble. "I won't let you down."

"That's a promise?"

"Cross my heart—"

Hank put his hand over Danny's mouth to keep him from finishing the phrase. "Shh." He tried to be soothing. "Shh. There, that's better. Now there's a good pony."

# 3 May 1938

**1:29 A.M.**

Once Hank was gone, Danny got up off the bed and reached for his robe. He fumbled around in the dark until he found the right pocket, and pulled out the crumpled bills. Twenty bucks! Hank had really made with the dough this time.

He got up and stretched and went to the kitchen.

Danny pulled the old cocoa tin off the shelf and pried open the lid with a spoon. The rest of his money tried to pop out, and he had some trouble stuffing these twenty bucks inside. If this kept up, he might have to get himself a larger tin.

Danny's heart had dropped when he had opened the door and seen the detective standing out there in the hallway looking so sad. He liked the idea of Hank taking care of him.

Mr. Hessler had been offering him a similar proposition as of late, wanting Danny to give up hustling so he could have him to himself. But Danny had been teasing him, drawing him out until he made the best possible offer. Hessler wanted him to come work as a soda jerk, for which he promised to pay a far better wage than the average. All Danny had to do was satisfy Hessler's every need, no matter how kinky. The pharmacist said that Ted was no longer the best soda jerk and had to be let go, but he wasn't going to fire Ted until he had a proper replacement lined up.

Aside from the money, the offer had held little appeal. Hessler was too demanding and wanted more from Danny than he could ever possibly give—besides which, Danny had no feelings whatsoever for the man. Hessler was cold and heartless, but he had cash like it was growing on trees. Danny had been taking his money, and in addition to his other regular business, had been making out real well the last few weeks. Still, he was wary of setting up any kind of permanent arrangement with Hessler. He didn't know if he could take it.

But now Hank wanted him to get a job, and if he did, Hank would pay his rent money and he would at least be able to survive. If he went to work for Hessler, he would be getting Hessler's money as well, but he would have to ask him not to be so rough on him. Hank had to think he wasn't still hustling, if Danny wanted to win his heart, and if Hessler left any marks, it would give the game away.

Since Hank was unable to see him that often, Danny would have plenty of time to meet Hessler's demands, and Hank would be proud that he had such a great job and was turning his life around. Hank would also be glad that Danny wasn't going to meet up with the Torso Slayer on some midnight rendezvous in a dark alley somewhere, and Danny himself would feel a little safer not seeing quite so many strangers all the time.

Danny placed the lid back on top of the cocoa tin and pounded it shut with his palm. Then he went back to bed, fluffing up his feather pillow and climbing under the covers.

As he lay there staring at the faintly glowing curtains, he decided to go see Hessler first thing in the morning and take him up on his offer. If it didn't work out, he could always quit, and he would still make out ahead, with the kind of money Hessler was prepared to part with.

But no matter what happened, he would wind up with Hank, and then he would be happy at last, for the first time since his mother was still alive.

# 16 August 1938

**5:12 P.M.**

"Good night, Mr. Ness."

"Good night, Betty-Lou."

Eliot Ness waved halfheartedly at his secretary as she turned to leave and closed the door behind her. He looked at his wristwatch and decided he had better pack it in himself.

The heat wave showed no sign of letting up. Though his windows were open, no breeze came in. The humidity and the stillness of the air made him sticky and uncomfortable. The fan seated atop his filing cabinet did little to help.

Ness stopped what he was doing, put his fountain pens back in his drawer, and tidied up his desk. All this unfinished business would have to wait until tomorrow morning.

He was trying to teach himself how to leave his work behind at the end of the day, which for him was no easy task. He was accustomed to putting in long hours and to working harder than the rest of his staff. Since his separation from Edna, he had on occasion worked until the wee hours of the morning and then slept on the couch in his office. He had kept a clean, pressed suit and some shaving supplies on hand in the closet and used the men's room down the hall to get spruced up before the start of the day.

Other evenings, he had simply packed papers into his briefcase and taken them back to his apartment, where he took them back out and worked until he dropped dead on his bed. He had managed to accomplish a great deal this way, yet it had taken its toll, as evidenced by his bedraggled look when he woke up in the mornings.

Those days, he had now decided, were officially over.

Whatever he didn't finish by the end of the day, he now saved for the next. Weekday evenings were time to relax with a cocktail and catch up on his pleasure reading, with no one around to tell him to get his feet off the coffee table; and weekends were time to go out and have a little fun. Hell, he deserved it after working so hard all these years.

Plus, there was the matter of women. Ness's old friend Evaline McAndrew of Chicago had recently moved to Cleveland, and they had already gone out dancing at the Vogue Room at the Hotel Hollenden. It seemed everywhere he went, he was surrounded by beautiful girls, but Evaline was the only one he wanted. She knew him from the old days and could always make him laugh.

But today was Tuesday, which meant he would be heading home to his stuffy apartment, coming up with excuses to go into the kitchen and open up the Coldspot for a breath of refrigerated air. Perhaps tonight he should go to the movies, not so much for the entertainment as for the air-conditioning. *Algiers* was playing down at the Loew's State, starring an alluring new actress with the unlikely name of Hedy Lamarr. Having seen her photos in the newspapers, Ness frankly could not care less whether the girl could act.

Ness pulled the chain turning off his desk lamp and rose from his chair. As he turned to close the window behind him, he noticed a curious sight across the way, toward the lake.

Cars were packed bumper to bumper all along Lake Shore Boulevard, which in itself was nothing extraordinary at this time of day. It was the cause of the traffic jam that was so puzzling. The cars in both east-and west-bound lanes were slowing at the intersection with East Ninth Street, at the same point where a crowd was gathered a few yards to the north, in the rocky wasteland that had last year been the exposition grounds.

Ness's own red-white-and-blue squad cars were pulling up at the scene, and at first he thought it must have been an accident—probably a pedestrian struck while trying to cross the busy drive at rush hour. But now he recognized several unmarked detective cars pulling up, as well as the coroner's white panel truck.

He grabbed his binoculars from his desk drawer to take a closer look.

He focused the lenses and saw that the crowd was blocking his view of the scene, but as he looked toward the unmarked cars he saw Jim Hogan, Hank Lambert, Vern Quast, and other Homicide detectives getting out and making their way through the crowd, and then he realized what was going on.

"Damn," he said. There went *Algiers*.

Ness lowered the binoculars, mesmerized for a moment by the distant scene of the gathering crowd, then lay them down on his desk and hurried out of his office, grabbing his jacket and hat without bothering to close the windows. He would return later to close up, once everything was over.

He swore under his breath. This time the bastard had dumped one right under his nose—practically within spitting distance. It was a direct challenge: *catch me if you can!* This point was not likely to be lost on the press, which meant Ness was in for a bumpy ride. If the police failed to catch the killer, he as safety director would now be held personally responsible by the people of Cleveland.

The torso case was now about to become his baby.

### 5:20 P.M.

Some of the uniformed policemen had to draw their nightsticks to persuade the crowd to move back from the scene. The noise from the mass of people was an excited murmuring, with an occasional gasp as one of the onlookers got a look at the remains.

But what Hank hated most was the smell. With the air this humid and still, there was no avoiding it. The former exposition grounds were already cluttered with garbage that people had been dumping here all summer long. Along with the crowd, seagulls had gathered on nearby trash heaps, and Hank had already had to scare one away that had tried to peck at the flesh of their new torso.

"What the hell's the matter with these people?" asked Hogan.

"Morbid fascination," said Hank.

"So what's so fascinating about it? We got a dead girl here."

Lloyd Trunk of Ballistics was snapping pictures. Quast was a few feet distant, interviewing the three colored men who had made the discovery.

When the detectives had arrived on the scene, she had still been wrapped in brown butcher paper and tied with twine, over which had been draped a man's navy suit coat. The men had found her that way, hidden underneath a tattered patchwork quilt laden with rocks. They had immediately contacted the police and left the detectives to handle the unveiling.

Photos were made every step of the way as they removed the rocks, the quilt, the coat, and finally cut through the butcher paper. Trunk was finishing the job now, snapping shots of the exposed body, which was badly decomposed but intact from neck to crotch, with dark stumps of dried blood at her pelvis, shoulders, and neck. Her breasts were small, her figure trim. Her flesh was pale blue in spots, and in others a jaundiced yellow, spattered with purple lesions and green funguslike growths.

After retrieving the rocks, quilt, coat, butcher paper, and twine for later examination by Lt. David Cowles, Hank called over the boys from the morgue in their bright white suits. "Get this thing out of here," he said. "And put it on ice."

While the coroner's helpers placed the torso on a gurney and carried it to their truck, Hank and Hogan set about searching through the many piles of debris. Hank heard the snapping of picture taking and suddenly realized the press was upon them. It was the uniformed policemen's job to keep them back from the scene, and they were doing it well; so far no hot-shot photographer had tried to break through the crime scene. They were only getting shots of bewildered policemen.

Hank used a piece of driftwood to turn over rocks and pieces of scrap metal. Underneath a small pile of tin cans and beer bottles, he found a round object newly wrapped in brown butcher paper and tied with twine.

"Jim!" he called to Hogan, who came running.

"Holy Jesus," said Hogan. "Open it up."

Hank wanted to say "You open it!" but could hardly say such a thing to his superior. He waited until Trunk could come over to take a picture of it still wrapped, then withdrew his pocketknife and cut through the tight cords and ripped open the heavy paper. Under the wrappings was a woman's head, the rotted flesh covered with purple postmortem sores and torn swaths of gray skin. Her sandy brown hair was coming away from her scalp, and from out of her blue lips squirmed little white maggots.

Hank called "Hey!" to the boys from the morgue. They had just gotten in the truck and were about to drive off. Hank walked briskly to their location, opened the back door to the van, and carefully placed the head upon the gurney, atop the woman's shoulders. Retrieving the butcher paper and twine as evidence, Hank accidentally caused the head to roll over onto its face, and some maggots spilled out. Several strands of hair remained stuck to the paper. Hank had to pick them off and place them back on the head; Sam Gerber would need them, just in case one of them belonged to the killer.

Hank approached the driver and said to him through his open window: "Maybe you guys ought to stick around a little longer, have yourselves a smoke."

"Sure thing, pal. I'm on overtime." The young driver grinned a Good Humor grin, and in this heat Hank suddenly found himself wishing the coroner's van was an ice-cream truck instead. "Whatcha got there, another torso murder?"

"No." Hank sneered. "The bride of Frankenstein."

"Oh." The driver lighted a cigarette, passed it to Hank, and lighted another for himself.

"Thanks." Hank took a healthy drag from the cigarette, and immediately tasted that it was a Lucky. He needed it real bad; his hands were still shaking from handling the poor woman's head. Immediately the toasted tobacco went to work soothing his nerves.

"Kinda came unglued, didn't she?" cracked the driver.

"Well," said Hank, "without her makeup I guess she isn't much to look at."

"Lucky!" came the voice of Eliot Ness from around the front of the van. He held his jacket draped over one arm, his hat shading his face. Dark sweat stains were bleeding out from under his arms. "Is this what I think it is?"

Wondering where Ness had come from, Hank looked from Ness's face to City Hall behind him, just across Lake Shore Boulevard and up the hill. Ness's office was one of those windows reflecting the glare of the sun.

"She's in back," Hank said, motioning over his shoulder with his thumb. "Go have yourself a look-see."

Ness went toward the rear of the truck, and Hank heard him open the door.

"Jesus!" said Ness, closing the rear door with a slam. He returned to face Hank and the driver, removed his hat, and wiped the beads of sweat from his forehead with his handkerchief. A green pall had consumed his face.

"Go on," said Ness to the driver, rapping the side of the truck with his knuckles. "Take this stuff to the morgue, pronto."

"We may still find some more remains," said Hank. "Maybe they should wait."

"I don't care." Ness loosened his tie and took a deep breath, unbuttoning his top button. "If we need them back we'll have them dispatched over the radio."

Ness had had two-way radios installed in each police car, and now every squad in the city was radio-dispatched from a powerful transmitter at Central Station, cutting down considerably on response time. Cleveland was the first city in the nation to fully implement such a plan citywide, and Ness was being called on as a consultant by other communities that wanted to make a similar change. Hank loved the new system; it was a big improvement over finding a call-box or plugging a pay phone. Even though he was officially on the torso case full-time, he now found himself responding to assist other officers on a number of other calls. The new radio setup was giving everybody more work, which meant they were catching more crooks. That could only be a good thing.

The coroner's van started up and turned onto Lake Shore Boulevard turning on its lights and siren to help it cut through the slowly passing traffic.

Hank and Ness started back toward the crime scene. A press photographer took their photo from amidst a crowd of onlookers. The seagulls overhead squawked, circling the sky like vultures.

"This is a nasty business," said Ness, as they met up with Jim Hogan. "Jim, I want a full account of what you've found so far. I just saw the head and the trunk."

"We've just found her arms and lower legs in a cardboard box belonging to the International Biscuit Company. Still haven't located the thighs."

"Well, let's get cracking. I want this crowd out of here. We're going to turn over every rock in this goddamned dump, and if we don't finish it tonight, we'll be back tomorrow. Get Sergeant McDonald over here, and Quast, too. I want a little confab. We're stepping up the investigation, and I'm going to supervise it personally."

Hogan's face was growing red with anger. With the heat, along with the twenty-odd years Hogan had on Ness, Hank wouldn't have been surprised to see Hogan punch the safety director smack in the face. Ness might be well versed in law enforcement, but he was an administrator, not a detective, and if he put himself in charge, he was liable to make serious errors in judgment. Hell, he might even remove Hank from the case.

If Hank had been the Torso Slayer, he would have wholeheartedly approved of the new arrangement. Anything that threw a wrench into the machinery of the investigation was a good thing, if you were the killer.

As the detectives gathered around Ness for their "confab," Hank suddenly realized that this was precisely why the killer had placed the eleventh victim at this location, right by the new busy highway, in front of City Hall. He *wanted* to rouse the public. He *wanted* Ness to take over the investigation, perhaps assign a new detective to the case.

Perhaps Hank was getting too close. That was one of the problems with an investigation such as this. Hank's role was very public, and simply by reading the newspapers the Torso Slayer had a huge advantage over the police.

This actually put Hank in an enviable position. With Ness publicly taking the lead on the case, Hank could slink back into the shadows. While the safety director played cops and robbers and got his picture in the papers, Hank might be able to gain the element of surprise.

## 8:05 P.M.

The sunset over Lake Erie was dull—a simple wash of salmon across the horizon, the sky itself having turned a dusky shade of blue. Even at this hour the heat remained stifling.

"Hey, police!" someone called from an easterly direction. "I found something!"

Hank saw a wiry man with a gaunt face heading his way, followed by two women, and pointing back in the direction from which they had come. The women hurried close behind in high heels and summery flower print dresses, stepping carefully among the rocks and speaking excitedly to one another.

"I parked my car down near that billboard to watch," said the man, breathing heavily. "When I come upon this pipe and there's this awful stink, so I look and it's coming from this pile of bones! I swear! Come on, I'll show you."

*Probably a dead dog,* Hank thought. *Everybody's getting hysterical.* He lighted a cigarette and followed the three citizens back toward their blue Pontiac, which was parked next to a billboard advertising Jantzen swimwear.

"Over here, sir," said the stringy man. "Right by that pipe, there!"

The smell was indeed rotten, and as Hank approached, he saw a scattering of yellowed bones, as if newly unearthed from some archaeological dig. At once, he saw that these were not canine but human bones, though by no means did they make a complete skeleton. He recognized a human pelvis, several ribs, assorted vertebrae, a clavicle, a femur, and several smaller bones probably from the hands and feet.

Hank disturbed nothing before calling over Ness, Hogan, Quast, and Trunk.

"What the hell—" Ness began, removing his hat and scratching his head.

"Number Twelve," said Hank simply.

"Jesus Christ," said Hogan. "I hope those are all from the same person."

"What do you mean?" asked Ness.

Hogan motioned all around them, at the vast piles of stone and concrete rubble left behind by the demolition of the Great Lakes Exposition, with twisted iron supports poking out.

"I hate even to think it, but we might have just stumbled upon a torso graveyard." Hogan was nothing if not dramatic.

"Here," said Ness, pointing out the scene for Trunk, who was fumbling with a roll of film as he loaded up his camera. "Get some shots of this before we start gathering up the pieces."

Ness went off among the nearby piles of rock, apparently looking for more bones. Hank saw Trunk rolling his eyes and heard him expel some air through his nose in frustration; he didn't need the safety director telling him his job. He set about photographing the find, while Hank began his interview of the citizens who had made the discovery.

Suddenly, from the other side of a garbage heap, Eliot Ness emitted a snort of surprise, as if someone had sneaked up behind him and tapped him on the shoulder. But Ness was alone, standing there holding on to the rim of an institutional-sized tin can, and looking inside.

"What is it?" asked Hogan, whose smile was serene. He seemed pleased by this development.

Ness's laugh was nervous, embarrassed. "I picked this up thinking we might use it to put the bones in."

Hank followed Hogan over to Ness's location, yet long before he looked into the can he knew what was inside. Before Ness could tell him to do so, Lloyd Trunk was taking a picture of it.

Hogan was snickering, patting Ness on the back. "You should have known better," he said. "That's the first place I would have looked."

Ness said nothing. Hank felt sorry for him; Hogan was trying to make him look like a fool.

The skull inside the can was grinning broadly up at them, as skulls tended to do even on their worst days.

# 18 August 1938

**1:10 A.M.**

Eliot Ness had gathered all the men he could muster—detectives, uniformed officers, firemen, even some of his own staff from the safety department. They were gathered around at the fire department headquarters at the east end of the Central Viaduct, while he outlined his plan on the blackboard.

"We'll take Canal Road down through the Run," he said, pointing with a yardstick to his crude chalk map, "until we reach the hillside here overlooking the Interurban railroad tracks. This $X$ represents the main hobo encampment, just off Canal and Commercial. There's at least thirty shanties down there, probably two or three men to a shanty, so we're looking at maybe a hundred men, all told. A lot of them are drunks, and they'll probably try to resist. Most of you have experience in this sort of thing, but all the same I'd like to remind you to use extreme caution. Some of these people might be carrying weapons. Some of them might simply be crazy. One might even be our killer. So be careful."

Ness took the chalk and drew lines in several directions,

each heading toward the hobo camp, rather like a football coach outlining his strategy before a game.

"Each squad will come up from a different direction to block their exit. We're going to sweep down and enter each hut, one by one. They've got no lawful right to be squatting on this property, so feel free to kick in their doors if they refuse to let you in. Each man is to be handcuffed and escorted to one of our vans, which will be parked up here on Canal Road. Once we're through up here, as long as everything goes according to plan, we'll send a few squads deeper into the Run to raid the smaller shantytowns down there. I want every man detained as quickly and in as orderly a fashion as possible.

"Once we've got them in the vans, we'll search each and every shack. We're looking for evidence. Any knives, bloodstained clothing—"

"Heads," added some smart-ass from the sea of blue uniforms and gray suits and hats. Ness was well aware that not everyone was happy to be here at such an ungodly hour on a Thursday morning.

"Yes," Ness agreed. "But I don't expect we'll find any. We don't honestly know what we're looking for, but you'll recognize it when you see it. No matter what you find, package it up and send it back to the station. We'll look everything over again later. Now, are there any questions?"

No one spoke up.

"OK then. Fix yourself up with your squad leader and let's get going."

He dismissed the crowd and they all gathered outside into teams, led by people such as Lt. David Cowles, Sgt. Jim Hogan, Sgt. James McDonald, and Ness's assistant Bob Chamberlin. Ness followed them outside the station and headed toward his car, which would be the lead vehicle. He would be directing the raid from the hillside at Canal and Commercial.

As Ness had expected, the press had had a field day with the latest news. The *Plain Dealer* had run a bold streamer across the top of the front page Wednesday morning:

## TWO MORE TORSO VICTIMS FOUND

followed by a smaller headline:

### POLICE PUSH HUNT AS
### 11TH AND 12TH SLAIN
### APPEAR ON E. 9TH DUMP

which in turn was followed by the subhead:

*Scrap Iron Pickers and Volunteer Searchers*
*Discover Body Fragments Near Lake Front;*
*Both Dead for Months, Coroner Says; One*
*Covered by Rock Pile, Second Found Not*
*Far Away, Head Placed in Tin Can.*

By now, Cleveland was known the world over as the stomping grounds of the famous Torso Slayer. The British press had played it up as another series of Ripper-like murders, while in Germany, Joseph Goebbels's propaganda organs had laid blame for the killings on democracy itself and the "Communist influences" that pervaded American society.

Ness was determined to put an end to all that.

Their biggest stumbling block to date lay in being unable to identify nine out of the twelve victims. Since most of the bodies had turned up either in Kingsbury Run itself or in the nearby Cuyahoga, and since most of the victims seemed to be vagrants or some other type of lowlife, these men living in shanties along the Run would be the most likely potential victims in any future torso mayhem. After being rounded up tonight and taken back to Central Station, they would each be fingerprinted and identified before being questioned. Even if no new clues arose as a result of their interrogations, even if no new evidence could be found, they would have fingerprints on file that would prove useful if one of these hobos turned up later as Number Thirteen or Fourteen.

Of course, if they accidentally caught the killer during the raid, Ness wouldn't mind one damn bit.

Once all the law enforcement and fire personnel were in their respective vehicles, Ness addressed them over a tactical channel: "OK, let's go!"

**1:31 A.M.**

"Police!" Ness shouted. "Open up!"

He heard rustling from within, but no one spoke up.

"I said open up!"

"Fuck you!" came the craggy voice from the other side of the door.

Ness wasn't going to take that from anybody. He raised his foot and gave a sharp kick to the middle of the crude wooden door, busting the plank in half and knocking the door half off its hinges. As usual, he carried no gun, but he had a uniformed officer backing him up armed with revolver and nightstick. Ness shone his flashlight ahead of him as he entered.

Inside the shack lay an old man with a gray bird's nest of a beard, in a torn felt hat and wearing no shirt. He had no meat on his bones. His skin looked tough as leather, a deep reddish brown, wrapped tightly around his ribs and covered with thick wisps of white hair that grew even on his shoulders. The top button of his trousers was undone, and even from six feet away Ness could smell the odor of cheap wine. The shack itself had been crudely constructed of weathered, worm-eaten planks, papered over on the inside by cardboard boxes of corn flakes and raisin bran to keep the wind from whistling through. Broken bottles and the odd cigarette butt littered the dirt floor, and that was all. No knives. No severed heads.

"On your feet!" Ness commanded, lightly tapping the old geezer in the ribs with the toe of his shoe.

"You can't do this," said the man.

"Come on, just cooperate and everything will be all right."

"What's this about?"

"Violation of city ordinance. Come on, get up."

The old man groaned as he rose to his feet. His trousers were too big for him and rested on his hips. It appeared as if he wasn't wearing any underwear, because all Ness saw was skin.

"Why can't you leave me alone?" the man mumbled, heading toward the doorway.

"This is for your own safety," said Ness, grabbing hold of his arm and escorting him outside. The officer backing him up took a pair of handcuffs and slapped them on the man's wrists, behind his back.

Ness made a quick scan of the shack's interior, but saw nothing of any evidentiary value. A small bundle of dirty clothes lay where the old man had been. Ness gathered them up and handed them to the policeman; the clothes stank, and Ness preferred taking charge of the man. He clutched the chain linking the two cuffs, and began leading the hobo up the hillside, toward the trucks.

"What's your name, sir?" asked Ness. As they walked, the man stumbled and nearly lost his balance several times, but Ness prevented him from falling over.

"Jim MacReady, that's M-A-C."

Below them the shantytown was utter chaos, like nothing Ness had seen since the steel strike last year, when he had reluctantly had to send in some police units armed with gas and clubs. Most of the hobos were being less agreeable than Mr. MacReady, raising their voice and trying to struggle loose from the officers' grasp. Wild, mangy dogs were barking incessantly, snapping at the heels of the policemen, and generally taking the hobos' side. Many cops had drawn their nightsticks, though Ness had witnessed none actually used. Still, the possibility existed that the men could get violent, which was why they had some tear gas on hand in the trucks as a last resort.

"Here we go. Step up." Ness led Mr. MacReady to the back of a van rapidly filling up with men.

MacReady muttered curses under his breath as he ducked his head and climbed in. Ness had the policeman place MacReady's property in a canvas bag and tag it with the hobo's name.

A large truck from Fire Station No. 1 was pulling up, a little later than Ness had hoped for. He went over to speak to the fireman climbing off its running boards.

"Eliot Ness," he introduced himself, flashing his golden safety director's shield. "How fast can you set this up?"

"No time at all, sir."

"Excellent. Just shine it right down there when you're ready."

Ness motioned toward the dark Hooverville down the hill, a haphazard collection of dilapidated shacks, looking more like a field of outhouses than of homes. Amid the flimsy structures were numerous dim flashlight beams and many more silhouetted shapes of men. The din of police, angry hobos, and stray dogs was something, even up here.

Atop the special fire truck was a huge arc lamp of the kind used at Hollywood premieres. With a loud *clang* the lamp suddenly came to life, shining its beam upward into the hazy, humid sky. Two firemen on either side grabbed the thing and shone the stark white light upon Kingsbury Run below, illuminating the entire encampment.

"That's perfect!" said Ness. "Just hold it right there."

A steady stream of grizzled men were being led up the hill and into the trucks. Ness ran back down the hillside toward the camp to supervise the searching of the huts.

The arc lamp from atop Canal Road cast long shadows across the shantytown. Men would suddenly appear from out of the shadows and into the glaring rays, being led by detectives. Everyone squinted and blinked their eyes as they were headed up the hill, toward the light.

Outside one of the larger huts Ness recognized the bald head of Sergeant Hogan, ringed with short-cropped white hair.

"How does it look to you, Jim?" he asked.

"Just a lot of junk," Hogan said. "Haven't found anything important. I don't think we're going to turn up much."

"Damn poor luck."

Hogan shrugged, looked about to speak, but in the end seemed to change his mind, and then said, "Well, who knows? We've tried everything else."

Ness took that comment as being conciliatory. Hogan had been none too pleased with Ness's new hands-on approach to the case. Ness had decided no plan was too desperate if they wanted to catch the killer. He was willing to try anything that hadn't yet been tried.

"Keep up the good work," said Ness, slapping Hogan on the shoulder. "Let me know if you turn up anything."

Hogan led Lloyd Trunk inside one of the shanties and had him snap a few photographs. Ness poked his head inside, but saw nothing of importance, aside from the general filth of the interior. In the corner was what seemed either human or dog feces, and a foul odor emanated from within.

Ness left them alone and took a walk down the main corridor of the shantytown, poking his head into huts and shining his flashlight inside, and seeing that most of them by now had been cleared out. As far as he knew, no men had escaped their clutches and all were now being loaded into the trucks. One truck was already pulling out of its spot up on Canal Road and heading back to Central Station, where the hobos would be booked.

Everything was proceeding faster than he had planned. They would be out of here within the hour, and then everyone could go home.

The hobo jungles of Kingsbury Run were located not far from Central Market, to which investigators had traced the cardboard carton of the International Biscuit Company. The other box containing the woman's thighs had been disposed of at the Sheriff Street Market on Bolivar Road, also nearby. Men from these encampments were well known to take discarded boxes from the markets and, like packrats, use them to help reinforce their meager dwellings. This is what had led Ness to the idea of the raid in the first place, though even he had been dubious of its eventual success.

For one thing, he was well aware that the Torso Slayer could hardly live in such an environment. If Sam Gerber's estimates were correct, several of the victims had been stored for months before being discovered. The woman who had turned up Tuesday along Lake Shore Boulevard had, in fact, shown signs of having been refrigerated.

No, it was clear their killer lived somewhere other than a hut in Kingsbury Run. He almost definitely had a car and positively had an icebox or freezer of some kind. Hank Lam-

bert was right; the killer had to be someone of at least middle-class means.

A hand touched Ness's shoulder, and he jumped.

"I think that's it," said Hank Lambert, scanning the
crowded field of huts unnaturally illuminated in the stark
white light. "We've searched them all, didn't find much."

"All right, then." Ness walked toward the nearest hut and
gave it a firm kick with the heel of his shoe. The tired wood
creaked and the hut settled off-center. Another kick sent it
falling over and collapsing in a heap of broken boards and a
cloud of dust.

He bent down and felt that the wood was very dry.

*Perfect.*

"Lucky, can I borrow your lighter?"

"Sure."

Lambert handed it to him. Ness opened it up and flicked
the flint a couple times, until the flame leapt forth. He allowed the flame to kiss the brittle wood, until a much larger
fire was spreading across the weathered timbers, brightening
the shadows left by the arc lamp.

"Oh, here you go," said Ness, handing Lambert back his
lighter. He grabbed a burning stick and set the next shanty
aflame.

By morning, there would be nothing left of the encampment, and the area of Central Market would be considerably
safer—if not from the Torso Slayer, from homeless men that
citizens considered a public nuisance.

"I don't see why we need to burn the place down," said
Lambert, gazing thoughtfully at the blaze. "I mean, it's not
as if—"

Ness interrupted him: "Public health. Look at the condition these things are in. Human excrement, filth, probably all
kinds of diseases. Besides, these men won't be needing them
anymore."

"I thought we were just taking them in for fingerprints and
questioning," said Lambert.

"Sure, but then we're sending them all off to Warrensville
for a while so they can learn a useful skill."

"Out of harm's way?" Lambert asked, making no effort to
veil his sarcasm.

"Something like that."

"Out of sight, out of mind?"

Ness was surprised at Lambert's taking the side of the hobos, and fleetingly wondered if his main torso detective was in reality a closet Communist.

*Christ!* Ness thought, *Herr Goebbels would love that one!*

# 5 September 1938

"Mr. Ness, is it true your wife is divorcing you?" asked the reporter from the *Plain Dealer,* who sat in the leather high-backed chair opposite Eliot Ness's desk, taking notes and peering out through black wire-rimmed spectacles.

Ness decided to deal plainly with the subject. "It's public knowledge," he said, knowing full well this was the first the public would hear of it. "Edna and I are separated and in the process of seeking a divorce. It was a mutual decision. We both realized a mistake was made, and we set out to correct it."

This stopped the reporter dead in his tracks.

Ness had recently developed an antipathy toward newspapermen, his former comrades-in-arms. He felt as if they had turned against him, raking him over the coals with their vituperative accounts of the hobo raid. They had called him a misguided zealot.

"Who's this young lady you take dancing at the Vogue Room?"

Ness's reply to this question was curt: "That is none of your business. And I would advise you to be well versed in libel laws before you go spreading any salacious rumors."

The last thing he wanted was Evaline McAndrew's name getting dragged into this.

"Well, sir, forgive me, but as you say, it's public knowledge."

"Then there's no point in printing it, is there?"

"My city editor might see it differently," the reporter said smugly.

"He certainly might," Ness countered, "after I give him a call." His threat sounded hollow; it made him feel small; he wasn't sure he liked himself very much these days. Immersing himself in the torso case had only succeeded in wearing him down. The hobo raid had been at best a hollow victory; he still believed he had done the right thing.

"How does the mayor feel about all this?"

"You would have to ask him that question."

"Word around town is you'd like a shot at his job."

Ness laughed, sitting up taller in his seat and staring the reporter in the eye. "I work for Harry Burton. Harry Burton's a friend of mine. Harry Burton's a fine mayor. As long as he's there, I'll be here."

"Come on Ness," the reporter said, as if to say, *It's all right, you can tell me!* "Everyone knows he's going to run for the Senate."

"He'll do a fine job."

"You can't tell me you don't want to run for mayor."

"I'm a lawman, not a politician."

"What if the party asked you?"

Ness caused his brow to furrow, and said, "Do you know something I don't know?"

"Well, we *are* a Republican paper."

"I don't want to hear it. I've got too much work to do. I don't have any time to think about being mayor. I'll leave that up to you folks."

The reporter closed his notebook and stood up. Ness came out from behind the desk, shook his hand, and showed him to the door. On his way out, the reporter tipped his hat to Betty-Lou, who offered an annoyed smile.

"It's out," said Ness. "He knows about the divorce."

"Oh, that's too bad." Betty-Lou seemed to have little sympathy for him. She was tearing through the morning mail with her stiletto-like letter opener. "What about Miss McAndrew?"

"Naw, they haven't caught on to that."

"Not yet," she cautioned him. "Seems like you could at least wait until the divorce is final."

"If I wanted your advice, Betty-Lou, I'd—" Ness caught himself. He liked his secretary and tried to treat her with respect.

"It's purely a professional concern," she said, ripping through another envelope. "I wouldn't mind being Mayor Ness's secretary, you know."

"Who else would I pick?" he said lightly.

"The last thing you need is a scandal. I'll tell you once and then I'll keep my trap shut." At this she pointed a finger his way. "Watch your step."

"I'll take it under advisement." He turned to head back inside his office. "Hold my calls, will you?"

"Oh!" Betty-Lou's eyes lit up as she scanned a piece of correspondence. "You might want to look at this. Another secret admirer."

She handed him a small piece of linen notepaper on which a message had been scrawled in a crude hand—probably a right-handed person using his left:

Sept. 2, 1938

Mr. Safety Director,
    You may have had your fill, but I'm not
finished yet. Did you have fun in the Run?
You managed in one night what would have taken
me years! But then my method is more
selective. Don't feel bad about what you've
done to them. Nobody will miss them, least of
all yours truly. You've given us all quite a
good laugh.
    See you in the funny papers!
                         Your Paranoidal Nemesis

Ness felt a compelling urge to crumple up the note and throw it in the garbage. It wasn't the first crank letter he had received in the torso case. Chances were this was a phony, the examination of which would only waste the department's time; yet disposing of it was something he could ill afford. He would have to send it over to David Cowles in Finger-prints and have him check for latent prints, though it was un-likely they would find any on the textured paper. A handwriting analysis would prove useless, given the author's inexpert use of his left hand. Such an analysis would also have no evidentiary value unless they had a suspect against whose own handwriting they could compare it.

"Goddamn waste of time," Ness said, taking from Betty-Lou the envelope the note had arrived in. It bore a Cleveland postmark of September 4, but naturally no return address.

"Now why would somebody want to write a letter like that?" asked Betty-Lou.

"You'd be surprised," said Ness. "The killer's probably got more fans than I do."

"Really?" The end of Betty Lou's pencil was placed thoughtfully between her teeth. "Then maybe *he* should con-sider running for mayor."

# 6 October 1938

**6:00 P.M.**

The first Hank Lambert heard of it was over the radio, while he sat in his parked detective car eating a ham sandwich on his dinner break.

"This is Jack Paar bringing you WGAR news of the day. The Torso Slayer has been captured. This from Sheriff Martin O'Donnell, who announced half an hour ago that county deputies have apprehended one Frank Dolezal, fifty-two-year-old Cleveland bricklayer, as chief suspect in the brutal slayings that have kept city police baffled for three years running. Dolezal has confessed to the hideous murders and is being kept under close watch at Cuyahoga County Jail—"

Hank nearly choked on his sandwich.

"Bastards!" he said aloud, turning the key in the ignition and putting the car in gear. He maneuvered out of the parking space into the heavy traffic on Euclid Avenue, making his way to the left lane and making a U-turn once the oncoming lanes were clear. He had to get to the jail, fast.

The sheriff's department had never shown any official interest in the torso case. Whenever Homicide had asked Sheriff O'Donnell for some help, he had always come up with some excuse for not getting involved, usually citing reasons of jurisdiction. Hank had always assumed they were either too proud or too lazy to lend a hand to their floundering colleagues, but now he saw the truth behind their traditional policy of "home rule."

Sheriff O'Donnell was a Democrat who had already made it known that he intended to run against Harold Burton for the mayor's office in '39. If he caught the Torso Slayer himself, without assistance from the city, he would be sure to win, without having to share the glory with Eliot Ness.

All that aside, the sheriff had the wrong man.

Hank had questioned Frank Dolezal following Florence Polillo's murder, and again after the identification of Rose Wallace. Even though he had known both women and hung out with them at the same tavern, Hank had eliminated him as a possible suspect. For one thing, he had no permanent address, no place private enough to cut people into bits and hide their remains for months on end. For another, Dolezal had an alibi for the evening previous to the discovery of Florence Polillo's corpse. Danny Cottone and several other regulars at Charlie's tavern had already attested to Hank that Dolezal had gotten drunk and eventually passed out on the night of January 25, 1936, the last night Florence Polillo had been seen alive.

Even if he had, in fact, "confessed" of his own free will, it would never hold up in court. Dolezal was clearly innocent.

Hank stepped on the gas and weaved his way in and out of traffic heading westbound on Euclid. He had to get to the jail and find out just what the hell was going on. Surely Sheriff O'Donnell didn't think he could get away with this.


7:40 P.M.

Hank stood in the crowded corridor outside the jail, smoking a cigarette and looking out the window onto busy Ontario Avenue down below. The streetlights had come on, and most motorists had turned their headlights on, though the sky was not yet black. Hank had the window open for some fresh air, and his smoke was being sucked outside. The hall was filled with tobacco smoke from the countless reporters and lawmen crowding the place, to the point where there seemed no air to breathe. Hank had already gone through half a pack of Luckies. All this waiting was making him stir-crazy.

Suddenly he felt a tap on his shoulder. "Hey, Lucky."

Looking up, he saw Eliot Ness's face reflected in the plate-glass window, his summer tan already faded, his hair parted down the middle in that out-of-date way of his. All in all, Hank had come to like the man.

Hank turned around to face him. "What's the scoop?"

"They won't let us see him, but I did talk to O'Donnell and he filled me in from their end. Damn fools, that's what they are," said Ness.

A diminutive man was lurking behind Ness—bald, silver haired, slumped shoulders, sunken cheeks, lips curving inward over his teeth, presumably dentures.

"Lucky, this is Mr. Smith," Ness said, introducing them. "He's the attorney they let speak to Dolezal."

"Funny. Got a dog named Lucky," said Smith, shaking Hank's hand.

Hank ignored the comment. "What about this confession. Is it legit?"

"Not on your life. Couldn't keep their hands off him, the cowards," said the lawyer.

"They roughed him up," said Ness, prompting Smith. "Go on, tell him."

"I took a doctor in with me. Not the first time they've done this. My client's got, now let me see . . ." Smith pulled out of his pocket a cocktail napkin on which some words were illegibly scrawled. He squinted at it and read, " 'Bruises lower abdomen, chest, back.' Doctor thinks he's got four busted ribs. He only confessed after they blindfolded him, knocked the wind out of him, threw him to the floor, and kicked him. They've had him since last night. Interrogation lasted clean till this afternoon. Says he only confessed to make them stop."

"He's retracted his confession," Ness put in.

"Yes," said Smith, wetting his lips with his gray tongue. "Got it right here." His withered hand patted his leather satchel.

"He only ever confessed to killing Florence Polillo," said Ness. "And that's where we've got them."

"He couldn't have killed her," Hank said.

"Exactly. And he refuses to talk about any of the other torso killings."

"Mr. Ness showed me your police reports," said Smith. "When I told Dolezal where he'd really been the night that whore was murdered, he changed his story and retracted his confession."

"They can't pin any of the other murders on him," said Ness, grinning wickedly. "They know they haven't got the Torso Slayer. But they're still going to pursue charges on the Polillo murder."

"That's ridiculous," said Hank. "You can't separate one from the others. If they can't link him to any of the others, they haven't got a case."

"Then they're screwed," said Smith, displaying his to-bacco-stained dentures in a rictus grin.


## 8:43 P.M.

"You can see him now," said Deputy Martin, leading them into the jail.

"It's about fucking time," said Ness. Hank had never seen him this hot, and his respect for him only mounted.

"This way." Deputy Martin walked ahead of them, his keys jangling on his belt. He was a big man, broad shouldered but beer bellied, who stretched his brown county uniform to its limit. He walked, Hank thought, as if he had a nightstick shoved up his butt.

"We'll speak to him alone," said Ness.

"Oh, no, you won't," advised Deputy Martin as he opened the first iron-barred gate leading to the main part of the jail. "He's our man, our responsibility. I promise I won't get in the way."

"That's what you think," said Ness. "We don't want him to feel intimidated."

"So who's intimidating him? We haven't even charged the son of a bitch yet."

Deputy Martin led them down the hall past rows of prisoners in their jail cells, most awaiting trial. Once they reached the end of the hall, the deputy took them through another locked gate and they turned the corner. They passed a corridor lined with solid iron doors set with small windows. The whole wing was eerily quiet.

"Isolation cells," said the deputy, as if the two city lawmen couldn't figure it out for themselves. They used the same jail, and Hank had come up here on plenty of occasions to interview arrested persons. "Dolezal's in the next wing over."

Along the way they passed other county deputies stationed as guards, each watching over a different wing.

Deputy Martin next took them through another series of gates until they reached what appeared to be the end of the line. This was the maximum security area, with cells containing one prisoner each. The walls were concrete, to minimize contact between prisoners, with doors of double-barred iron. Here were kept the rapists, murderers, and armed robbers, left to their own devices under heavy guard until they had the opportunity for a full jury trial, after which they would all most likely be going to the "big house."

"He's at the very end," said the deputy. "Last one on your right."

Oddly, the deputy stopped for a smoke and allowed Hank and Ness to continue.

"You think he'll remember you?" asked Ness.

"You bet," said Hank.

They came to the end of the hall. The cell opposite Dolezal's was unoccupied, the only empty cell in the wing.

Frank Dolezal himself was pressed against the bars of his cell with a black eye and a cut to his forehead, his tongue hanging out the side of his mouth, his unshaven face a pale blue, his knees bent, his body limp and hanging by the neck from a series of rags that had been tied together and secured to the uppermost crossbar of the door.

"Deputy!" called Ness down the hall. "Call an ambulance and toss me your keys!"

"What?" said the deputy. "What's the matter?"

"Now, dammit!" The muscles on Ness's neck tightened.

The key ring came sliding down the hallway to Hank, who

fumbled with it until he found the right key, while the deputy called down the hall for someone to get an emergency team up here. Hank unlocked the door and Dolezal's body snapped free from the makeshift noose, falling into his arms. Ness helped him lower Dolezal to the floor, where they laid him on his back.

Within minutes, paramedics responded and tried to revive him, but it was no use. He had been dead for some time now.

"Did any of you see what happened?" Hank asked the other prisoners in the wing. Deputy Martin gave them all cold looks, and Hank was nonplussed by their silence.

"Take him to the morgue," Ness told the paramedics. "I'll call Coroner Gerber."

"No, I'll take care of calling the coroner," said the voice of Sheriff O'Donnell, who was coming down the hall. "The jail's my jurisdiction."

"Right, I forget," said Ness, and pointed at the figure of Frank Dolezal being covered with a sheet. "That's also your responsibility."

"I guess the guilt was too much for him," said the sheriff, with a sorrowful shake of his head. "Can't say that I'm sorry."

"He was innocent," said Ness, raising his voice, "and we can prove it."

Ness was taking the words right out of Hank's mouth, but Hank never would have had the balls to talk to the sheriff in such a manner.

"Now I'm going to go out there and have a word with my reporter friends." Ness stepped past the sheriff, and Hank followed, eager to get away from this place.

"I wouldn't stir up any trouble, if I were you," said Sheriff O'Donnell.

"Thank God you're not," Ness called over his shoulder. "As far as I'm concerned, we've got the thirteenth torso victim right here."

"Not the luckiest number in the world," Hank said to Ness, as the jailers let them out through the gate. His admiration for the safety director had just grown tenfold.

# 12 October 1938

**11:33 P.M.**

*It's only a game,* Danny kept having to remind himself. *Only a game.*

He lay on his back upon Hessler's bed, ankles securely bound to either bedpost. The hemp felt as if it was cutting into his skin, and his toes had become tingly from loss of circulation. He felt a mild pulling in his groin muscles from his legs being so widely stretched. The smooth pink head of his erect cock lay slightly to the left of his belly button. His lean stomach was stretched taut.

"Here, have a cigarette," said Hessler, staring down at him, fully dressed. He made Danny lean his head forward and placed a Chesterfield between his lips. He lighted it with a match, holding the bright flame before Danny's eyes for a moment before placing it against the tip of the cigarette.

Danny sucked in until the smoke was thick in his lungs, then expelled the air. He preferred Hank's Luckies.

Hessler removed the cigarette from Danny's mouth and held it out between his thumb and forefinger like a dart. Thin gray smoke wafted up from its glowing tip.

"Where would you like it?" Hessler asked.

"No, please!" Danny begged. *It's only a game.*

"How about here?"

Danny followed the tip with his eyes as Hessler lowered the cigarette toward his exposed armpit. His wrists were secured with short lengths of rope to the posts at the head of the bed, so that his arms were stretched behind him and the wavy hair under his arms was standing up. The bed was pulled away from the wall so that Hessler could work from all directions. Hessler touched the smoldering tobacco against the tips of the hairs. They caught aflame for an instant, curling up, disintegrating, and sending a sharp aroma into the air. As Hessler poked closer and closer with the cigarette, Danny could feel the heat radiating from the orange embers.

"No, don't," Danny pleaded.

But Hessler continued singeing the hairs, smiling as he incinerated them further and further, until the hair was so short it appeared as if it had been closely cropped with a pair of shears. He reached out and touched Danny's armpit, lightly brushing the ashes away and blowing on it. This contact with the sensitive skin sent Danny into a sudden fit of laughter.

"Oh, you like it."

"No, please."

Hessler placed the half-burnt cigarette in between his own lips and smoked on it. He turned around and grabbed something from a nearby chair. It was a foot-long length of dowel. He came around the bed, almost out of Danny's sight.

"What are you doing?" Danny asked.

"Shut up."

Hessler placed the dowel against the rope tying Danny's left wrist, holding either end of the dowel, one hand above the rope, the other below. Then he gave the dowel two sharp turns, stretching Danny's limbs much further than before.

"Ow!" Danny shouted, surprised by the pain. "Jesus!"

Hessler tied off the dowel with a short length of rope, then performed the same operation on Danny's right wrist, tightening a second dowel and then tying it off.

Danny winced. His breathing became deeper, his heartbeat faster. All circulation was disappearing from his wrists. His fingers clutched at the air, helpless.

"Tell me what you know about the torso murders," said Hessler.

"What?" asked Danny, before the full weight of Hessler's words struck him.

*Oh, Jesus!*

He looked up at Hessler's upside-down face, with its fiery amber eyes and death's-head grin.

Hessler was suddenly growling like a dog, his face leaning closer. Saliva dripped from his mouth onto Danny's forehead.

Hessler reached out his hand and suddenly seared the glowing tip of the stubby cigarette against Danny's right nipple, pressing it firmly until it was snuffed out.

Danny screamed. He drew in a sharp breath through his gritted teeth, his eyes clamped shut. He felt a rush of blood to his head and grew dizzy for a moment. When he opened his eyes, they were blurry with tears.

*Oh, Jesus, it's Hessler!* Danny thought. Unless this was another one of his sadistic games. But why else would he burn him with the cigarette, unless it was him?

"It won't be very pleasant for you unless you talk," said Hessler. He unfastened the loop of rope keeping the left dowel in place, and gave it another wrenching half-twist before tying it off again.

"Don't kill me," Danny whispered.

"Why should I, if you tell me what I want to know?"

"All I know is what's in the papers."

Hessler gave the right dowel a half-twist and secured it back in place. Danny winced. Bones along his spine made a popping sound.

"Don't tell me that pretty detective of yours doesn't tell you anything. And don't ask me who I'm talking about. I've seen him come into the store for coffee. I've seen the way you look at each other. I've heard you making plans to meet. I know who he is, he's the one working the case. I believe you've known each other for some time. He's the one who suggested you come work here, isn't he?"

"No," said Danny amid rapid breaths. "He had no idea."

"I find that hard to believe."

"It's true. It was my idea, anyway . . . the job. I didn't know you were—"

"Well, maybe he knew but decided not to tell you about it."

"No, he couldn't have, he—"

For a moment, Danny wondered if Hessler was right. But no, if Hank had any idea Hessler was the killer, he would have arrested him. He never would have deliberately put Danny into such danger.

Hessler came out from behind the bed. He rubbed the ashes from Danny's red and swollen nipple, the touch of his fingers causing sharp pain to the burned flesh. Then, slowly, he withdrew his pack of Chesterfields and tapped out another cigarette. He placed it between Danny's lips and tried to light it, but the flame wouldn't catch.

"Suck it!" he ordered.

Danny was whimpering, terrified to breathe in. Hessler grabbed his burnt nipple and twisted it between his fingers. Tears sprang once more to Danny's eyes and he complied, taking a drag and causing the cigarette to glow warmly. He began coughing on the smoke. Hessler removed the cigarette from his mouth.

"I could turn you into a freak show attraction," said Hessler. "The Human Ashtray. How would you like that?"

"No," said Danny, shaking his head. "No."

"And don't yell for help or I'll cut off your head."

"Yes . . . sir," Danny whimpered.

"How close are they to catching me?" Hessler asked.

"They don't know anything," said Danny. It seemed best to tell him the truth.

He was a sitting duck. Hessler was going to kill him. Now that Danny knew his secret, it was all over. He would never get out of here alive, never be able to tell Hank. Hessler was going to cut off his head.

He had wanted so badly to help solve the case, and now here he was, bound like a character in a Conan tale and at the mercy of an evil sadist. Only there was no sword-wielding barbarian coming to save him. Hank may have visited him at work in the past, but he had no idea Danny spent any time with Hessler after hours, and never would have known he was in any danger.

"Have you ever heard of a stretching rack?" asked Hessler. "I admit mine is somewhat primitive."

*"Please!"*

"Please what? Please stretch you some more?"

*"No!"*

"In the old days," said Hessler, coming around to the left side and twisting the dowel another notch, "the Indians would kill a man by tying each of his limbs to one of four wild horses. They would send the horses charging off in all directions, and the man would be literally torn limb from limb, leaving behind a bloody torso."

Danny cried out from the pain; he felt as if his arm might pop out of its socket.

"Please, you don't have to do this." Danny was breathless. "I won't tell anybody, honest."

Hessler tied off the left dowel with the little loop of rope and went over to the right side.

"I just want to know about the investigation," said Hessler. "What do they know that they haven't put in the newspapers?"

"They know Frank Dolezal wasn't the killer," said Danny.

"And?" Hessler said, twisting Danny's burnt nipple.

*"Ow!"*

"What else?"

"I don't know."

"You don't know, or you won't tell."

"Please, I don't know anything. I'll do anything you want, just let me go."

"I've already got you doing everything I want. Right now I want you exactly as you are."

Hessler tapped his cigarette ashes onto Danny's chest.

"Where would you like it this time?"

Hessler held the cigarette inches away from the head of his cock.

*"No! Oh, God, no, please!"*

"Beg, Danny, beg."

*"Please, sir, no, not there! I'll do whatever you want, I promise!"*

"You're nothing but a spy," said Hessler.

"No."

Hessler made a lightning move toward the end of the bed and touched the tip of the cigarette against the sole of Danny's foot.

The pain made Danny cry out horribly. He squirmed upon the bed, although he had little room to move with his limbs stretched so tightly. All he could do was thrash his head from side to side. He clamped his teeth onto his bicep, biting down to try to fight off the excruciating burn to his foot.

If his body turned up somewhere, Hank ought to be able to identify it. That would lead him here to Hessler and the case would be solved. But it was little consolation for meeting his death at the hands of this madman.

"I'm only getting warmed up," said Hessler. "You'll have to bear with me quite a bit longer."

Danny's sobbing became uncontrollable, tears dripping down from his eyes, mucus building up in his nose. His entire body shook.

"See how finely that skin is stretched," Hessler said, running his fingertips along Danny's hairy chest. Then they found their way once more to Danny's armpits, and he began tickling him.

The feeling was so intense and so frightening that Danny all of a sudden shrieked very loudly. It was at this point that Hessler tied Danny's socks together and stuffed the knot in his mouth, tying the ends behind his head snugly, until Danny was firmly gagged, the large wad of smelly cloth depressing his tongue and preventing any but the most timid noise from escaping his lips; it also held his jaw painfully open and made breathing nearly impossible.

"That'll keep you quiet," said Hessler.

Danny tried making puppy-dog eyebrows at Hessler, but that only sent his captor into a fit of laughter.

"Oh, you are something! Look at you. What a whore!"

The telephone rang.

Hessler seemed not to notice at first, but then he seemed to shake himself out of his state and searched about him as if he didn't know where he kept the phone. On the fourth ring, he was at the bedside table, picking up the receiver.

"Yes?" he snapped.

Danny watched Hessler as he listened to the voice on the other end. Danny expelled air through his nose, blowing snot onto his face but clearing the way for air to pass through. His breathing after that was thin and wet, but at least he was breathing.

"Yes, Mrs. Cukrowicz, of course," Hessler said, grabbing a pencil and writing something down on a notepad.

Danny tried to breathe deeply and calm himself. If he were able to scream, he might try and hope that Mrs. Cukrowicz on the other end called the police. As it was, he could do nothing to save himself.

"Yes, 1309 Sumner, I know. I'll be right over." Hessler was tapping his pencil on Danny's forehead. He looked down at him and winked, as if they were still simply playing a game. "Of course it's no problem. . . . Well, thank you very much, Mrs. Cukrowicz."

Hessler hung up the receiver.

"Well," he said, and clapped his hands together once. "I have to go run a quick errand, but I'll be back. I'm sure you're not going anywhere."

Hessler grabbed his jacket from where he had dumped it in a nearby chair, and left the bedroom. Danny heard him taking the back stairs down into the pharmacy.

*Mrs. Cukrowicz. Another emergency prescription. Lives over on Sumner, that's only a few blocks away. Take him five, ten minutes.*

Danny tugged at his bonds, but quickly gave up, deciding it would only make the knots tighter.

Hessler would be below right now, compounding the prescription. It would take him no time at all, and then he would be out the door. Either by car or by foot, it would be only a matter of minutes before he would return.

Flexing his fingers, Danny found that with his left hand he could touch the dowel. In fact, poking the end of the dowel with his thumb, he managed to get his fingertips within reach of the small loop of rope that tied it off. Digging into it with his fingernails while holding the end of the dowel in place with his thumb, he managed to get the loop free, sending the dowel spinning back with the twisted rope. The disengaged dowel fell to the bed. Danny remained tied to the bedknob, yet the rope now held some slack and his arm had more freedom of movement.

*This is it. He comes back and sees me like this, I'm dead.*

Danny tried reaching the knots at his left wrist, but his fingers failed to stretch that far. The tip of his middle finger did manage to touch one of the knots, but this would do him no good at all.

He heard the rear door to the pharmacy slam shut. Hessler was on his way out. Distantly, he heard the sound of a car engine starting up; Hessler had chosen to drive rather than walk.

Danny tried pulling on the rope. With the added slack he had more leverage, and perhaps he could shake the bedknob loose. The rope was tied right at the base of the round wooden knob, and if it came off, he would be free. He jerked with all his might against the thing and allowed himself some time to see if it would work, but it would not budge.

That was it. He wasn't going to get out, and he could never pretend the dowel had sprung free all by itself.

*The dowel! Yes, that was it!*

His arms were suspended near the surface of the bed, and the dowel lay directly beneath his hand. He turned his fingers downward and was able to grip the end of it. He held the dowel firmly, fearing he might drop it and send it over the edge of the bed. But he was able to obtain a better hold of it, and at last held it tightly in his fist.

He positioned the dowel lengthwise in line with his arm and poked its end against the edge of the coiled rope around his wrist. The flesh of his inner wrist was soft, and he felt he could shove the dowel inside of the ropes and jimmy the bonds loose.

This was the kind of thing the characters in *Weird Tales* did when faced with a similar problem. People in Danny's favorite magazine were always getting bound and tortured. The heroes almost always managed to escape somehow.

*Almost always,* he reminded himself.

It was far more difficult than at first he had figured.

But at last he got the end of the dowel in between himself and the ropes, giving his flesh a good scrape in the process.

Blood was dripping out of the wound, though he hardly noticed the pain. His burnt nipple and foot were still throbbing with great intensity.

He poked the dowel down further until it was well past the last of the ropes. The dowel pressed firmly on his major blood vessels, and Danny could feel the flow of blood stopping to his hand. He cupped the other end of the dowel in his fingers and, using the pad of his thumb as the fulcrum, worked the dowel as a lever by moving his hand back and forth, trying to loosen the ropes.

It seemed slow going. Hessler was probably over at Mrs. Cukrowicz's flat by now, delivering the prescription. Perhaps she would offer him some tea or engage him in conversation. Certainly he would feel no urgency to return. He knew Danny was going nowhere.

He worked the dowel back and forth, pulling back on it with all his might, hoping to see the knot slip or some other such sign that it was going to work. The rope creaked a little under the pressure, but it was hard to tell if he was making any headway. He was unable at first to move his hand very far back, but now it went back a little further, and a little more, and a little more.

His wrists were small; he had to make the opening very wide if he hoped to get his hand through.

If he could somehow work the dowel around to the other side, behind his wrist, and loosen that side as well, he thought he might make it—but he had no way of manipulating the dowel around to the back of his hand.

*Well, here goes nothing.*

He had to remove the dowel before he could try getting his hand through. His fingers clutched its shaft and slowly pulled it out, being careful not to let go.

But once the dowel was free from the ropes, it snapped up into the air and spun a few circles before clattering to the floor.

*Shit, shit, shit!*

Danny folded his thumb into his palm, trying to shrink his hand down. He pulled down, trying to make it through the coiled rope. It was looser than before, at least. He got through down to the pads of his palm, but there he got stuck.

*Come on, come on, you son of a bitch!*

He wriggled his hand, trying to free it. The pain was great. The cut on his wrist from the dowel was bleeding in a trickle down his arm and onto the sheets. His hand was purple from the ropes up.

The rope rolled up a bit, toward the knuckles. Danny pulled hard, gritting his teeth. He had to get the rope past the first knuckle of his thumb. If he could manage that, he would be home free.

He heard the sound of a car engine pulling up in the alley, and his heart skipped a beat. The engine idled for a moment, and then he heard it move on.

Straining his muscles, he wrenched his arm downward and felt the rope give a little. He tried again, and at last, with a powerful yank, his hand was free.

He stared at it stupidly for a moment. It had no feeling, and he tried knocking it against the bed to shake some blood into it. He had done it. He couldn't believe it.

But now he had to get the rest of the knots undone.

He reached over to his right hand once the feeling returned to his left, first loosening the dowel and then fumbling with the knots for some time before they were undone and his hand was free.

He freed the gag easily, and then leaned forward and worked the knots at his feet. Having been tied down so long, his muscles were sore and he had a cramp in one of his calves. The knots were tight, but his fingers were nimble and he soon had them free.

Danny hopped to his feet and hurriedly threw his clothes on, but didn't bother with his socks or shoes. He had to get out of the apartment before Hessler came back, but first he needed to find some kind of evidence he could show Hank.

He went through Hessler's kitchen, looking for a blood-stained knife or something. But everything there was in order, and he found nothing extraordinary.

The newspapers last month had published a photo of the tattered quilt used to help cover up victim Number Eleven under the rock pile at the shore of Lake Erie. Perhaps if he could find the other half of that quilt . . .

He went back to the bedroom and started going through

the closet. He threw the clothes out, onto the floor and the bed. Hell, if Hessler caught him he would be dead anyway, so it didn't matter what kind of mess he made. If he was lucky, he would get out of here on time and escape with some kind of proof.

"Goddammit, where is it!" he demanded. He wanted something, anything.

He looked at his Mickey Mouse wristwatch, which told him nothing. He hadn't had the watch on while he was tied up, and had no idea what time Hessler had left.

He opened the drawers to Hessler's dresser, throwing everything out as he went. Socks, ties, underwear, pajamas, shirts, sweaters, scarves, handkerchiefs, mothballs. Nothing. Danny yanked the drawers full out of the dresser, letting them fall to the floor.

It was when he did this that he noticed the thickly padded envelope taped to the back of one of the drawers.

Danny ripped the envelope off the drawer and looked inside, expecting to find money. Instead, what he found were black-and-white pornographic photos of naked men.

As he rifled through them, he noticed to his surprise two photos of himself, taken three or four years ago. These were the photos Eddie had been trying to sell the last night Danny had seen him alive.

He heard the sound of Hessler's Auburn 851 Speedster pulling up in the alleyway. There was no mistaking the noise that big engine made.

He clutched the photos against his breast and went running to the back of the apartment, to the kitchen and dining area. He heard Hessler's footsteps coming up the back stairs, a mere door away from him.

Danny thrust up the window in the kitchen, which made a horrible rough scraping noise.

"Hey!" he heard Hessler shout from below. The footsteps increased rapidly, bounding up the stairs two at a time.

Danny climbed out the window and, barefoot, jumped out onto the iron fire escape in back of the building. He climbed over and grabbed onto the iron railing at its base, having to hang from the edge of the landing and drop to the alley below.

He landed on some broken glass, yet still continued running, down the alley and out to East Eighteenth Street. He continued running up East Eighteenth to Prospect, where a yellow DeSoto Sky-View cab with black fenders was heading straight for him. He saw no sign of Hessler following him. He stopped the cab and hopped inside, his feet smarting from the glass and the cigarette burn.

"Connor Hotel," he said. He would call Hank from the desk phone and have him meet him there.

# 13 October 1938

Mott Hessler was escorted into the hotel room at the Hollenden. He had been cooperative throughout the entire procedure, and Hank Lambert had found no reason to place him in handcuffs. Hessler had been working behind the prescription counter at his drugstore when Hank and Eliot Ness had gone and arranged a meeting. He had been all smiles, seemingly unconcerned about his being detained in regards to the slayings. He had stipulated, however, that he would only consent to the polygraph test if it were conducted in a setting outside of a police station, to avoid the press's finding out about it. Hank and Ness, having little choice, had agreed. Hessler had driven his own car to the hotel, with Hank and Ness on his tail.

"What a pretty room," said Hessler as he entered.

Hessler and Ness followed behind, along with Sergeant Boldebuck of the East Cleveland Police, who was present to operate their polygraph machine.

It was a modest room on the sixth floor of the Hollenden Hotel, with two twin beds and an arrangement of chairs around a sturdy oak table. One of the chairs had been turned

272

out from the table and the polygraph machine placed beside it on the tabletop.

"Please have a seat," said Hank, motioning toward the chair.

"Don't mind if I do," said Hessler, and seated himself squarely against the back, placing his arms along the wooden arms of the chair, his hands clutching the claw ends firmly. "Come on, gentlemen, let's get this nonsense over with."

Hank had been surprised by the cooperation Hessler had afforded them thus far. For someone who had supposedly killed and dismembered over twelve people, he was a decidedly cool customer.

Hank had been asleep in bed with Cathy last night when he had received Danny's frantic call. Danny had told him that he had been attacked by the Torso Slayer, and to meet him at the Connor. Hank had thrown his clothes on over his pajamas and gone out practically without a word to his wife. When he and Danny met, he questioned him thoroughly and was convinced his story was true. The kid had the marks on his body to prove it, the cigarette burns on his nipple and in the arch of his foot, the rope burns, the lacerations on his feet from running down the glass-strewn alleyway during his escape. Hank had had to hold him and talk to him at length to calm him down.

"Have you ever taken a lie-detector test before?" Hank asked Mott Hessler.

"No." Hessler shrugged. "Nothing to it, right?"

Hank was struck by Hessler's grin. His face was almost too perfect, his skin soft, his features angular. His black hair was slicked back from his forehead and his thick eyebrows were inquisitive. The bright cast of his eyes was disconcerting. Hank had never before seen eyes like these, like the glow of a wheat field at sunset. Even when relaxed, his face showed a slight smile framed by dimples. When Hessler smiled completely, his white teeth glistened and his entire countenance was endearing. He was perhaps ten years younger than either Hank or Ness, with the self-assurance and abundant energy that accompanied such an age. He wore a white shirt with red pinstripes, black suspenders, a wide black tie, and gray trousers.

Sergeant Boldebuck was rolling up Hessler's sleeves so that he could attach the wire sensors to the subject's flesh. Hessler's forearms were hairy and muscular. If he was equally muscular throughout his body, he would possess at least the physical strength necessary to have committed the torso murders.

The pornographic photographs Danny had discovered in Hessler's apartment would have no practical evidentiary value for the investigation, but all the same were enough to convince Hank. Danny maintained they were the same photos Eddie Andrassy had been intending to sell at the YMCA on the last night of his life. Unfortunately, the very fact that Danny had stolen the photographs from Hessler's apartment was enough to eliminate any value they might otherwise have had as evidence.

"This is the funniest thing I've ever heard," said Hessler, his eyebrows rising up in the middle of his brow. "My father's going to get quite a laugh out of this."

"Your father couldn't care less whether you lived or died," said Eliot Ness, uncharacteristically phlegmatic as he supervised Sergeant Boldebuck's operations.

"That's a risk you'll have to take." Hessler smirked, and then turned his attention to Sergeant Boldebuck affixing leads of wires to his skin with surgical tape. "I feel like I'm in the electric chair."

The file Hank had compiled during the wee hours of the morning was mostly of juvenile incidents and arrests. Hessler had never actually done any time in a juvenile home or been punished in any significant way by the criminal justice system, yet his record as a juvenile included sexual assault, battery, disorderly conduct, and under-age drinking. The sexual assaults had involved young males who had been sodomized while Hessler had attended an expensive local private middle school for boys. Hank assumed that the Hesslers were probably one of the "first families" of the school, and therefore although the school had reported the incidents, they punished Hessler with what amounted to a slap on the wrist, and somehow the justices in the court system must have been paid off or otherwise unduly influenced into being lenient. Hessler had faced few consequences as a result of his actions.

Among the incidents Hank had discovered were several of cruelty to animals, including occasions when Hessler had set off small firecrackers shoved up the sphincters of cats. He had also pulled out a cat's whiskers, chopped off a dog's tail with a hatchet, and baked a batch of kittens in an oven.

The reports were, of course, incomplete. Hessler had been shipped out east to prep school, and the Cleveland police would have had no record of incidents that had happened there. He was, however, questioned as a suspect in a sexual assault investigation some years later, shortly after he had returned to Cleveland. According to this report, no probable cause had existed to arrest Hessler, but it did provide other important information. Apparently, Hessler had been expelled from the prep school (no reason given) and forced to finish his education with a private tutor back home. Thereafter, he had enrolled in pharmacy school at Western Reserve University and been kicked out of the Hessler mansion on Euclid Avenue, for reasons unknown.

Early this morning, Hank had shown the file he had accumulated on Hessler to Eliot Ness, and Ness had looked visibly ill as he read through the pages. Together, they had been working on this thing all day. Based on the tip from Danny (whose identity Hank had kept secret from Ness, and who was too afraid of Hessler to file a complaint against him for last night's assault), as well as Hessler's case history, Ness had been enthusiastic about bringing Hessler in for a lie-detector test. The East Cleveland Police Department was the only local agency with a polygraph machine, but Ness had apparently had little trouble in making the arrangements, and their Sergeant Boldebuck had so far proven cooperative.

Hank turned to Ness and placed a hand on his shoulder. "Eliot, can you give me five minutes before we get started? I've got to make a phone call."

"Sure," said Ness. "But make it snappy, before Hessler changes his mind."

Hank gave Ness a friendly tap on the back, then left the room, going out into the hallway and down in the elevator to the plush lobby, always busy at this time of day with visiting businessmen going up to their rooms and townies heading for the hotel bars. People were criss-crossing the carpet in all directions. Hank spied a cute bellboy waiting next in line on a nearby bench for the bell captain to ring for him. His uniform was closely fitted, with little gold buttons in a V shape upon the red fabric of his coat.

Hank located a phone booth and closed the sliding door to give himself some privacy. He placed a nickel in the slot and heard the little bell ring. When the operator answered, he asked her to get him the Connor Hotel.

"All-righty," said the female voice. Her mouth was making smacking sounds—chewing gum?

A minute passed before an aged voice came over the phone: "Connor."

"Yes," said Hank, and cleared his throat. He was suddenly nervous. "I need to talk to Mr. Cottone in Room three oh five."

"I can take a message and have him call you back."

"Just go get him, will you? I'm a police officer."

"Yeah, and I'm the sheik of Araby."

"This is urgent. I need to talk to him right away."

"You and who else?"

"Tell him I said for him to give you two bucks."

"Wait."

Hank heard the old man drop the receiver on the desk, and the rest, for several minutes, was silence.

Hank had butterflies in his stomach. Time was wasting, and they needed all they could get if Danny was going to pull off this scheme without a hitch.

"Hank?" said Danny's anxious voice. Hank was relieved to hear him. He didn't know what he would do if something happened to him. Danny had had a close shave last night. If he hadn't been so clever, he would be dead.

"How you holding up, kid?"

"I'm OK. Don't worry about me."

"Listen," said Hank. He had to make the conversation short. Danny knew what he had to do. Hank only needed to give him the go-ahead. "We've got Hessler in custody right now. We're putting him through a lie detector test in a few minutes. It ought to last a couple hours. That should give you enough time."

"OK," said Danny.

"I don't expect you to find any body parts," Hank reminded him. "Just look for anything. Bloodstained clothing, surgical instruments, knives, maybe identification that doesn't belong to him."

"Or the other half of the quilt."

"Absolutely." That was the kind of conclusive evidence they needed. Hank was sure Hessler must have destroyed the rest of the quilt by now, the one he had used to wrap up the remains of Number Eleven, but he wanted to keep Danny's hopes up. "If you find anything, give me a call at the Hollenden, room six-eleven. We'll detain Hessler long enough to get a search warrant."

"OK."

"We've got Hessler here for the next few hours. Get yourself a cab and get over there. I've got to get back upstairs. Ness is probably getting all bent out of shape."

Danny laughed. "OK. 'Bye." Hank heard him make kissing sounds, which surprised him, since the old desk clerk was probably standing right next to him. But then, Danny wasn't exactly the easily embarrassed type, and the employees of the Connor were unlikely to ask questions.

"Good luck, kid," said Hank, and hung up the phone. He fumbled in his pockets for his cigarettes and quickly got one alight. He smoked part of it in the phone booth. The smoke filling the small space obscured his vision of the lobby. He opened the doors and stepped out into the hubbub, heading toward the elevators.

An elevator was standing open, waiting to go up. The blond kid operating the lever looked about eighteen and offered Hank a more than friendly smile. "Going up?" he asked, as if asking "Going my way, mister?"

"Sixth floor," Hank said, and the guy slammed back the lever, closing the doors and taking them up. Hank watched the brass dial above the doors marking their upward progress.

If Hank had his way, Hessler would never again see the light of day. Danny would be instrumental in helping put him away. Hank had spoken earlier with a county judge who would be all too eager to provide them with a search warrant, provided it was a sure thing. The judge didn't want the warrant to come flying back in his face, and this matter of Mott Hessler was sensitive, considering the collective weight his family could throw around. More than one judge was already in their pocket. Hank would have to be dead certain before he asked this one to go out on a limb. The judge had made it clear that he had to know *precisely* what they were looking for before a search warrant could be written up.

If everything went according to plan, even if the polygraph test turned up nothing, they would still get their man. Danny was bound to find something.

"Sixth floor," announced the elevator boy, his blue eyes twinkling. It was a blatant come-on.

Hank palmed him a nickel and gave him a wink. "And that's *all* you're going to get."

### 8:19 P.M.

"Are we ready?" Hessler asked. More and more he felt as if he were dealing with the Keystone Kops.

Mr. Safety Director Ness had been pacing back and forth awaiting the detective's return, while the sergeant from East Cleveland turned on the machine and began the preliminary testing.

"Is your name Mott David Hessler?" asked the sergeant.

"Yes." Hessler sighed, annoyed.

The sergeant examined the paper printout coming from the machine: a small line in blue ink, with a slight squiggle disrupting it at one point. The sergeant nodded his satisfaction.

"Good. Now, Mr. Hessler, I want you to give me a false answer, all right?"

Hessler nodded. Ness was looking at him funny. Hessler smiled warmly at him, as if oblivious to why he was here.

"Is your name Marie Antoinette?" asked the sergeant.

"Yes." This was going to get dull real fast.

The sergeant examined the readout and appeared satisfied with the larger squiggle Hessler's lie had produced.

"We're ready," the sergeant said.

Ness looked at his wristwatch.

Detective "Lucky" Lambert returned to the room, out of breath. Hessler wondered what he had been up to. A phone call, he had said. He was probably calling Danny-boy, the little slut. Those two faggots were up to something.

It didn't matter. Hessler would have the last laugh. They could never pin anything on him. They had no proof.

"Come on, gentlemen," Hessler said, "let's get on with it."

"It's hot in here," said Lambert, loosening his tie. He went across the room to the windows and threw them open. The breeze from outside was cool and damp. Rain had been predicted, but none had yet fallen. Noise came in from off the street: automobiles, people laughing, a woman screaming.

Hessler smiled.

"Let's not waste the man's time," said Ness. He grabbed a chair and sat before Hessler, elbows on knees, hands folded one over the other, eyes staring. Hessler stared back, trying to look like a sly fox.

Lambert sat in the chair next to Ness, while the sergeant stood by the machine. The device was a large gray box with lighted meter displays, silver toggle switches, and red flashing lights. The paper fed out of one end of the machine over a small rubber platen, while a flow of blue ink came out of the tip of a pen attached to a thin wire arm that rested upon the paper.

Hessler felt like standing up and ripping off the wires, teasing and taunting the policemen as if he were the Invisible Man, jumping up and dancing a jig, bouncing upon the beds, grabbing lamps and clocks and other objects in the room and throwing them at his inquisitors, spitting at them and insulting them as he escaped out the window and down the fire escape into the all-embracing night.

*Calm yourself,* he thought. Yes, that was the key. As long as he remained perfectly calm, none of this would mean anything. His answers would only register as lies if he allowed himself to be drawn in. He had to remain detached. He knew

how to beat the machine. They all thought they were so fucking smart.

"Mr. Hessler," Ness began, his manner serious. "May I
call you Mott?"

"No." Hessler was pleased to note the results registered
only a small squiggle: by all accounts an honest answer.

Lambert posed the first question: "Do you know why
we've brought you here?"

"For the room service?" Hessler affected a lilting and innocent voice.

"Mr. Hessler, please respond with a simple 'Yes' or 'No,' "
said Ness, clearly irritated.

"Did you know a man named Edward Andrassy?" Lambert asked.

"Not in the biblical sense, no," said Hessler.

"A simple 'Yes' or 'No,' " Ness reminded him.

"But you did know him," said Lambert.

"Yes." The blue line indicated he was telling the truth.
The police sergeant was making notations in pencil as the
printout rolled slowly forth from the gray metal box.

"Did you kill Edward Andrassy?"

"That depends on your point of view." The blue line registered practically nothing.

"I'm not going to tell you again—" Ness began.

"I know, a simple 'Yes' or 'No.' But need I remind you,
Mr. Safety Director, that I'm here of my own volition. If I
grow tired of your questions, I shall refuse to cooperate further, and then you'll be right back where you started."

"Maybe we should start somewhere else," said Ness, scanning some scribblings in his notebook. "You were accused in
five different instances of sexual assault while you were in
junior high school, isn't that so?"

"Yes," Hessler said, and chuckled. "*Accused* being the op-
erative word."

"Please, let me contin—"

"Those boys begged me to fuck them."

Ness reminded him once more to stick to simple "Yes" or
"No" answers, and not to expound upon them.

"Are you a homosexual?" asked Ness.

"No." Barely a squiggle.

"Are you a heterosexual?"

"No." Again, barely a squiggle.

"There was a family cat named Priscilla," Ness said. "You plucked out all her whiskers, am I right?"

"They were in her way," Hessler answered. "But what has this got to do with the torso slayings?"

"You cut off the tail of a dog, I believe, when you were eight years old, correct?"

"No, sir, I believe I was nine at the time."

"If you're going to play games, we'll just get down to cases."

"Which one?" Hessler inquired. "Number One, or Number Twelve, or one of the ones in between?"

"Start with Eddie Andrassy," said Lambert.

"Oh, Eddie, is it? Did you know him well?"

"We're the ones asking the questions. Did you kill Andrassy?" The detective, too, appeared bothered.

"That is a distinct possibility."

"What was the name of the second victim? Mustached man, mid-forties?"

"Laid out with Andrassy, wasn't he?"

"That's right."

"Don't waste my time. I might tell you a name, pluck one out of the air, but you'd have no way of proving it was him."

"Did you know Florence Polillo?" Lambert continued.

"She was a regular customer. I filled her prescriptions. Feminine complaints, you know. She was full of them. Big gal."

"Do you know what happened to her?"

"Murdered, wasn't she? Cut up into little pieces and set out in little picnic baskets. It was all over the papers."

"But you're the one who murdered her, aren't you?"

"What if I were?"

"Just answer the question."

"What if I say 'Yes'? It wouldn't make any difference. The court won't admit this as evidence. I could say anything I like and you still wouldn't have any proof."

"We'll try again. Did you kill Florence Polillo?"

"Let's say I did. Do you think I'd tell you?"

"OK, let's say you did. How would you go about it?"

"Trade secret. If I were the killer, how would I know you weren't going to steal my methods and strike out on your own?"

"So take out a patent," interjected Ness. "I thought you were going to cooperate with us."

Lambert pulled some photos out of a folder and began showing them one by one to Hessler.

The first one was a morgue photo of Pal Janssen's head.

"Do you recognize this man?"

"No." Hessler's lie failed to register on the readout.

"Recognize these?" Lambert showed him detail photos of Pal Janssen's corpse, shots of his different tattoos. Such lovely ones that boy had! Danny Cottone had a nice one, too.

"Very nice work," said Hessler, "but no, I've never seen them before."

"How about this?" It was a photo of a torn section of newspaper, the article he had left with Rosie Wallace's bones. The first two columns were a review of a show at the RKO-Palace, the next few a pen-and-ink illustration of up-and-coming Hollywood stars, featuring a rendering of Robert Young in some film called *Secret Agent*.

Hessler shook his head side to side, making his bottom lip curl. "Looks like a newspaper clipping."

"But do you recognize it?"

"Nope, sorry. Try again next time."

"How about something more recent." Lambert shuffled through his photos and came up with one of a woman's head—the one they counted as Number Eleven. It was even more decomposed than when Hessler had gotten rid of it, but then it had taken the fools three or four days to find her once he'd removed her from the Westinghouse. "Do you know this woman?"

"Yes," said Hessler, squinting his eyes and leaning forward sightly as if he recognized her. "Yes, I do believe that's Thelma Todd."

"He's lying," announced the East Cleveland sergeant, observing a pronounced jolt of blue scribblings.

"Of course I am. Everybody knows Thelma Todd was a blonde."

Hessler enjoyed playing this game with the policemen. He could keep it up for as long as he liked, providing them flippant answers intended to let them know that he was, in fact, the killer, but ones vague enough that they had no grounds to investigate further. They could never obtain a search warrant; they had nothing to go on.

"If you keep this up, we'll be here all night," Ness complained. Both lawmen looked dog tired and unhappy.

"Gentlemen," Hessler said, "I've got all the time in the world."

**8:39 P.M.**

Scattered drops fell upon the filthy brick pavement. The smell of rain was thick in the air, though the rain itself was a mere sprinkle. It had waited until the sky was fully dark before letting loose.

The Hessler's Drugs delivery truck was parked in back, a canary yellow Chevrolet panel van with bold red lettering on the side—but the sinister boat-tailed Auburn was gone.

Wearing the new pair of oxfords Hank had bought for him during the lunch hour, Danny sidestepped the broken glass along the alley behind Hessler's Drugs, but his feet still hurt. Normally, he would have been on duty at this hour behind the soda fountain. He had checked the front of the store and found that it was still open. Sam Kohler, one of the other pharmacists, was manning the store, but Danny had seen no one else in the place. He couldn't go in through the front; Sam would get nosy and fuck everything up.

He tried the service entrance at the rear, but it was locked. He was careful not to rattle it and attract Sam's attention. Breaking it down was out of the question, and he had no idea how to pick a lock, even though several boys at Parmadale had tried to teach him. Hessler had never entrusted Danny with a key, and now he understood why. But even if he could get in this way, he would have to break into the apartment from the back stairwell, and that was bound to attract Sam's attention.

The rain was pouring at last, getting Danny wet. He wore no jacket and the night was growing chilly. The drops themselves were cold, a real autumn rain.

Danny looked up, cursing the sky, and noticed the iron landing above him. It was too far to jump. But perhaps if he could get up there, he could enter the same way he had escaped, through the kitchen window.

A burst of lightning illuminated the sky, casting a brief shiny glow upon the roof of the Chevrolet delivery truck. It was parked slightly down from the iron landing, but if Danny could push it underneath he could climb on top and reach the bottom grate.

Naturally, the panel van was locked. He tried wrenching the driver's door open but only succeeded in rocking the car on its springs. Looking up and down the alley and seeing no one, he grabbed a loose brick from the pavement and sent it crashing through the window. He unlocked the door, reached in, released the emergency brake, stepped on the clutch and put the gear in neutral. Then, holding onto the door frame, he dug in his feet and pushed. At first he didn't think he could make it budge, but then it gave suddenly and he was able to slowly move it forward. The panel van veered slightly toward the building, and unexpectedly came to a stop as the fender rammed into the wall.

"Shit!"

Danny had hoped to get the roof of the truck directly under the landing, but the hood would have to do. He climbed atop the rain-slick fender and onto the hinged hood, making a dent in the metal and nearly losing his balance. From the hood it was still a reach to the lowermost part of the landing, and he couldn't quite make it.

Danny jumped and clutched onto the iron bar. Despite the rain his hands found a firm grip. His feet were now dangling above the delivery truck. He would have to get up before someone saw him.

Hanging from the bar, he brought his legs up, trying a few times before gaining a footing and managing to pull himself up over the railing, onto the landing.

Danny tried the dark kitchen window. It came open a few

inches and then stuck. He grabbed it from underneath and pulled upward, but he had to inch it from one side to the other before it finally loosened and came all the way up.

He peered into the darkness and climbed on through.

## 8:50 P.M.

Gusts of wind came in through the windows, catching the curtains and snapping them like laundry on a clothesline. A pale blue flash of lightning was followed by a sharp thunder crash, and the lights in the hotel room dimmed for a moment.

"What about this soda jerk you used to employ, a Ted somebody? What's become of him?" Hank asked.

During Hank and Danny's meeting the night before, Danny had revealed the nature of his relationship with Hessler, and what was expected of him in his role as soda jerk. Since Ted was no longer working there, Hank and Danny had put two and two together and were concerned about what might have happened to him.

"Ted Mauston?" Hessler said. "Oh, I had to let him go. Why don't you call him yourself? It's Main eight five seven three."

Hank wrote down the number on his notepad.

"We'll do just that," said Ness. "Tomorrow. Right now you just answer our questions."

"What about Danny, my new soda jerk? Aren't you worried about him?"

Hank looked up from his notes, startled by this new tack of Hessler's.

"What about him?" asked Ness.

"Why don't you ask Lucky here."

"Because I'm asking you."

"His name's Danny Cottone. Write that down, Herr Safety Direktor. C-O-T-T-O-N-E, that's right. He's a cheap hustler. You know the kind, sells his ass. Yes, that's right, a homosexual pervert. A sexual degenerate like you always accuse the Torso Slayer of being. Danny used to come in the store a lot, and I hired him on after Ted left, to keep him off the streets. No thanks to your detective here. Danny's his kept boy."

"That's a lie!" Hank snapped, jolting up from his seat.

"Sergeant?" Hessler asked.

Boldebuck examined the blue squiggles and said, "This says he's telling the truth."

Ness turned to face Hank. "Your informant?" he asked.

Hank said nothing. They would deal with this later.

Outside, the rain had crescendoed to a dull roar, and the lights of the city down below were obscured by a thin gray veil of water coming down. Numerous droplets were blowing in onto the exposed windowsills.

"Danny's a very . . . how shall I say . . . *imaginative* boy," said Hessler. "I imagine he's behind this whole charade. But I'm not in the least surprised that Lucky here would believe the word of a whore over mine."

"I'm a happily married man," said Hank, as if that would do any good. Ness might very well be prompted to look into this, and Hank ought to keep his big mouth shut.

"You ought to put Lucky in this chair, Mr. Safety Director, and find out just how happily married he really is."

"That'll be enough," said Ness.

"Ask him if he's a sexual degenerate."

"I'll advise you one mo—"

"Ask him if he's a killer."

"All I'm interested in is you." Ness was getting testy.

So far the questioning was not turning out in Hank's favor. Hessler had gone for a sucker punch, and Hank was still reeling from the blow. The lie detector had turned out to be a disaster. Even when Hank *knew* he was lying, Hessler somehow managed to beat the machine. And in cases where Hessler might find it difficult to lie, he offered deft answers that appeared to implicate him and yet fell short of a confession. No wonder he had consented. He *wanted* them to know he was a killer. He *wanted* them to realize they couldn't lay a finger on him.

Hank was damned if he would let him get away with it.

"You are the Torso Slayer, aren't you?" he asked.

"Objection!" said Hessler. "Counsel is leading the witness!" His eyes were aflame. An image flashed into Hank's head—of Hessler slitting Danny's throat. Thunder cracked from not far away.

"Are you or are you not the Torso Slayer?" Hank asked.

"That question is much too general."

"I'll rephrase it. Did you murder Eddie Andrassy?"

Sam Gerber would testify, with imminent authority, that whoever killed Andrassy killed the others. An admission of guilt in the Andrassy case would nail Hessler to the wall.

"'Eddie' again?" Hessler said. "You knew him, too, didn't you? He probably procured young boys to suck your dick."

"Leave him alone," Ness advised him. "Answer the question."

"Did I kill Andrassy?" Hessler stared off into space, considering. "Did I kill Andrassy? Did I kill Andrassy? Did I kill Andrassy?"

"Did you?" Hank prompted.

"Dear me, will you look at the time?" Hessler was casual as he removed the surgical tape and wires from his arms. "I'm sorry, gentlemen, but I really must be going. This has been most illuminating."

"Oh, no you don't," said Hank. "You stay right there. We have to decide what to do with you."

Hessler remained seated in the chair, looking annoyed.

Hank and Ness stood up. "Sergeant, keep an eye on him," said Hank. "Make sure he doesn't go anywhere. We'll be right outside. Come on, Eliot."

"Eliot!" Hessler mocked. *"El-i-ot!* That's right, follow him out like a little cocker spaniel. I thought you were in charge, here. You let this faggot order you around?"

"And sergeant," Hank added, "you'd better close those windows. The rain."

## 8:54 P.M.

Eliot Ness ignored Hessler's taunts and accompanied Hank Lambert out into the hall, closing the door behind them. He had no worry that Hessler would try to escape; Sergeant Boldebuck was armed with a .38, and Hessler had been patted down and found clean before the questioning began. Ness and Lambert would guard the door from out here, and Boldebuck would cover the window.

"What an asshole," Ness said. He thought of himself as a tolerant man, but Hessler had quickly gotten under his skin, and Ness had felt uncomfortable in his presence.

"I say we hold him," said Lambert, shifting his weight nervously from foot to foot.

"On what charge?" asked Ness. He wondered what Lambert expected of him.

"Come on, Eliot, can't you see he's the killer?"

"We've got no proof." Ness looked down at the decorative pattern on the hallway carpet—circles within circles within circles. He found it difficult to look Lambert straight in the eye. "I just don't know."

Either Hessler was innocent, or East Cleveland needed to buy themselves a new polygraph machine. But Ness had a feeling that Hessler was indeed their man.

"We don't have to charge him," said Lambert. "Just hold him." He lit up a cigarette, and Ness found himself breathing a cloud of smoke.

Ness shook his head. "Can't keep that up for long. Their lawyers will be breathing down our necks."

"Whose lawyers?"

"The Hesslers. Who do you think?"

"But they hardly even admit his existence."

"Oh, they'll admit it all right, once the press gets onto this." Ness spotted a tear in the carpeting and poked at it with the tip of his shoe.

"Well, fuck their lawyers! So they breathe down our necks, so what? We get a search warrant, find some evidence, charge the bastard with murder."

"We don't have enough for a search warrant, and you know it. If you want to charge Hessler, you're going to need a signed confession, and I don't think this cuckoo's ready to come out of the clock."

"Then let's take him down to the station for an interrogation. Pull out all the stops. Force it out of him."

"Lucky, that won't do a damn bit of good. If we get a confession out of him that way, his lawyers will say it was coerced. All they have to do is point to Frank Dolezal."

"But we had nothing to do with that."

"Doesn't matter."

Lambert was finished with his cigarette already and tapped out another. "Wait a minute," he said, the cigarette dangling from his lips as he flicked the flint of his lighter. "Just what exactly are you trying to tell me? Are you prepared to let him go?"

Ness looked Lambert directly in the eye. "We may have no other choice."

Lambert breathed out a cloud of smoke through his nose. "What if he goes out and kills somebody?"

"Like this Danny?" Ness pulled out his notepad, checked his notes. "Danny Cottone. Is that your informant?"

Lambert nodded, eyes closed as if he couldn't bear to admit it. "Yes."

"Then we'll assign an officer to protect Mr. Cottone, twenty-four hours. If he truly escaped from Hessler, he's the only witness we've got." Which basically meant that Ness could justify the use of officers to protect him, budgetwise.

Lambert nodded again, but said nothing. He tapped the gray ash from his cigarette onto the colorful carpeting. Ness smothered the ash with his shoe, just in case. The last thing he needed was the city's most famous hotel burning down while he, the safety director, fiddled.

"We have to let him go," Ness stated flatly.

"No," said Hank. "We don't have to. I'll talk to Danny, persuade him to press charges. As long as we can provide him with protection, I'm sure he'll cooperate. We can charge him with aggravated assault, false imprisonment—at the very least sodomy."

"If Hessler's to be believed," said Ness, "we could charge *you* with sodomy." He didn't enjoy playing this trump card on Lambert, but there was simply no way he could be persuaded to hold Hessler at this time. It would only ruin their case against him.

"Mr. Hessler is not what I would call a reliable source," said Lambert.

"Supposing he's right," Ness suggested. "How do you think that would affect our credibility if this made it to trial?

Supposing their side was able to prove that the primary detective on this case was a homosexual himself?"

Lambert was turning beet-red. "How dare—"

"I'm not accusing, just offering up a hypothetical. What do you think our chances would be if, say, their side claimed that you had a personal vendetta against Hessler because he was a rival for Danny's affections?"

"Why, you—" Lambert seemed to make an effort to hold his tongue.

"Easy," said Ness. "Easy. If we handle it my way, none of these . . . complications . . . will have to come up."

"And just how is that?"

"We let him go, keep him under round-the-clock surveillance. We'll arrange to have him checked out by Guy Williams and see if we can't get the family to commit him to the state hospital. We threaten them with a trial if they don't agree. We offer commitment to save them from scandal. Hessler gets put away. No more killings, and no possibility of an acquittal. Everybody's happy."

"And the case goes unsolved?" Lambert was steaming.

"Officially, yes. And Hessler can get some treatment for his homósexuality and psychotic behavior."

"Leopold and Loeb." Lambert whispered their names.

"What was that?"

"I get it," Lambert explained. "You've actually got sympathy for him. You'd rather put him in a hospital than send him to the electric chair."

"Now you wait a minute." Ness pointed a finger at him— something he couldn't recall ever having done to anybody. "You've got it all wrong. But you're right about Leopold and Loeb. That's exactly what I'm thinking of. Clarence Darrow tried to reason that they were insane at the time of the murder and therefore not guilty. It didn't fly. But the Hesslers can afford counsel of equal expertise, and they've got much more reason to try the same plea. Hell, we've already shot ourselves in the foot on that one. Every time we open our mouths, we're talking about an 'insane murderer' or a 'new type of insanity.' What jury in the world would possibly rule that he's sane? Whether we do it your way or mine, the outcome will be the same. Only your way, we'll suffer through worse publicity than you can possibly imagine—not only in this country but the world over. If the Leopold and Loeb case was the 'crime of the century,' what do you think this is?"

Lambert dropped his gaze. "So that's it, huh? You hang a sword over my head and we do it your way?"

"It's the only way." Ness placed a hand on Lambert's shoulder. He brushed it off, scowling. "Hank, listen, why don't you start our surveillance once we let him go. Tail him and see if anything comes of it."

"You bet I will."

Ness opened the door and found Sergeant Boldebuck and Mott Hessler engaged in animated conversation, the polygraph machine between them. Both men were smiling and laughing.

Hessler turned away to address Ness and Lambert: "What were you two lovebirds up to?"

"You can go," said Ness.

"Just like that?"

"That's right. But don't go out of town."

"Hey, I've got a business to run."

"We may want to talk to you some more."

"That's OK by me," Hessler said, then pointed to Lambert and said, "Only leave that one out of it. He gives me the creeps." Hessler rolled down his shirtsleeves, grabbed his coat, and walked past them toward the door.

"*Adiós,*" Hessler said to Lambert, giving him a vicious look. Lambert seemed ready to punch him in the face.

"Let me escort you to your car," said Lambert.

Hessler left with Lambert on his heels. Ness poked his head out into the hallway and watched them head toward the elevators together.

He felt awful the way he had treated Lambert, but a scandal had to be avoided at all costs, and he had landed upon a solution that seemed viable, if not ingenious—one that would mean an end to the killings while still salvaging his own career. If this could all be handled without any of it leaking into the papers, Mott Hessler could be quietly locked away in an insane asylum, and the citizens of

Cleveland would eventually forget the Torso Slayer ever existed.

### 9:01 P.M.

"After you," said Hank, thinking, *I ought to kill you right here.*

"No, after you," said Hessler.

But Hank stood his ground, and Hessler was the first into the elevator. The elevator boy was the same as before, the blond kid of the twinkly eye and rosy smile, a small snug cap atop his head. He sized them both up as they entered, beaming from ear to ear as if wondering which to choose.

The doors closed and Hank flattened himself against the side wall. Hessler took the one opposite. They stood there staring at each other.

"Going down?" asked the elevator boy.

"Yes," said Hessler, keeping his hands behind his back. The look on his face was smug.

Hank narrowed his eyes and gritted his teeth. He wondered exactly how much Hessler really knew about him and Danny.

Hessler's piercing stare was disconcerting. Although the actual descent took a matter of seconds, it felt an eternity to Hank. The elevator was quiet enough that Hank could hear his own heart pounding almost to the point of bursting.

At last the little bell rang, and the doors opened up at the lobby. Hessler squirmed past a group of conventioning Elks before they could get on, but Hank found himself trapped by the drunken lodgemen. He had to push his way through the fat middle-aged men, who were so drunk they didn't even know he was there. By the time he had squeezed past them, Hessler was running across the lobby and out the revolving doors, onto dark, rain-drenched Superior Avenue.

Hank took off in pursuit, but once he reached the sidewalk Hessler was already speeding off in his Auburn 851 Speedster. Hank's unmarked city-owned Ford Deluxe was parked nearby in a metered stall, but the door was locked and he became drenched from head to toe trying to open it. Checking his pockets for the keys, he suddenly realized Ness had been driving and must have them with him upstairs. A black-and-white Zone Cab sped past, headlights glaring, and struck a small puddle, soaking Hank from the knees down.

He hurried back through the revolving doors and into the foyer, across the lobby and to the elevators. The arrow on the brass dial above the doors moved slowly down.

"Come on, move your ass," he said.

An old woman in a flowery hat turned and gave him the evil eye, apparently believing he was addressing her. Hank ignored the old witch.

All he cared about was whether or not Danny had made it out of Hessler's apartment. Hank found himself staring at his own reflection in a fancy gilt-framed mirror on the wall opposite the elevators, and despised what he saw. He cursed himself for having allowed Hessler to get away. If anything happened to Danny before Hank could get there, he would never be able to live with himself.

### 9:01 P.M.

Danny peered out the kitchen window into the darkened alley, which was now the site of a minor flood, as water coursed down the center of the brick-paved passage following the path of ruts countless heavy trucks had left behind. The Hessler's Drugs panel truck remained crashed up against the wall, its fender slightly mangled. But looking up and down the alley, Danny saw no sign of Hessler's car.

He looked at his wristwatch and saw that his wrist was still marked with a coil of purplish bruises where it had been tied. Mickey Mouse's short hand was on the nine, his long hand on the twelve.

He still had plenty of time. Hank wouldn't be through with Hessler so soon.

Danny had examined every nook and cranny of Hessler's apartment but had found nothing, not even any more photos of naked men. He had found no machete, no bloodstained clothing, no nothing.

Which led Danny to believe that if Hessler was hiding something, it would be in the cellar. And as long as the coast remained clear, he was going to go check it out.

He had found a heavy iron crowbar among the items in Hessler's well-ordered broom closet. He carried this with him so that he might pry open the heavy padlock Hessler kept on the door to the cellar storeroom—and he could use it as a weapon, if need be.

He turned off the lights in Hessler's apartment and unlocked the deadbolt on the kitchen door, opening it onto the back stairwell. The hinges creaked, which made him nervous. Sam Kohler was still downstairs, and if Sam caught him, Danny would never see the basement. The stairs were unlighted, and Danny closed the door to Hessler's apartment, cutting off the last illumination he had. He feared turning on the lights, in case the sound of the switch would echo down the stairs and pique the interest of Sam Kohler.

Danny felt his way down the stairs, stepping with care and reaching the first floor landing without mishap. Here on one side stood the service entrance that opened onto the alley. If he needed to get out of here in a hurry, this was his best chance for an exit. On the other side, a broad swath of yellow light shone from underneath the door to the pharmacy. From behind the door, Danny could hear Sam shuffling around in the main storeroom, setting a porcelain jar on a countertop and whistling. All Sam had to do was open the door, and Danny would need to come up with some lame excuse as to why he was here. Sam might even try to detain him until Hessler came back.

He turned and started down the stairs to the cellar, stepping gingerly. He went slowly, hoping not to slip and go crashing down. The air as he went deeper was cooler and more damp, as if he were heading into a dank dungeon. He stepped out and down again, but the sole of his oxford met the resistance of gritty concrete. He lost his balance but caught himself against the wall. He had already reached the cellar.

Feeling his way around, he found the heavy padlock latching the thick hardwood door, and placed the crook of the crowbar inside the loop of the lock. The latch was at chest height. Danny knew breaking the lock would be difficult for him, he was such a weakling, so he positioned the crowbar with the bar end pointing up. Then, grabbing it with both hands, Danny pulled down. The lock gave no quarter, so he yanked firmly down on the bar and pulled himself up off the floor, hanging from it. Suddenly, the padlock gave way, springing open and falling to the ground along with Danny and the crowbar.

The crash was tremendous.

Danny's butt was sore where he had fallen, but he got up and dusted himself off. He looked up the darkened stairway, expecting to hear Sam Kohler ask "Who's there?" But Sam never came. He was probably at the front of the store helping a customer, or perhaps the jukebox was playing or he was listening to the radio and hadn't heard a thing.

He grabbed the crowbar off the ground and hefted it in his right hand. He turned the knob and opened the door, stepping inside and then closing it behind him. He could see nothing. He felt around on either side of the doorway for a light switch but found none. The air was filled with pungent odors. He took careful steps forward, holding out his hands to keep from running into something.

Something cold brushed his face. Danny gave a start and reached up to bat it away, but his hand got caught in it and suddenly a dim light bulb clicked on above his head, hanging from a cloth-insulated cord. He untangled his wrist from the cool metal chain and looked about the windowless room.

Near the door stood an industrial-size sink, and along the walls were stacked many cardboard boxes and burlap bags. Danny figured whatever was in those bags was making the room smell. A heavy butcher-block table stood in the center. On the far wall was an old cookstove, its black chimney pipe poking up through the floor. At one side stood another doorway, with letters stenciled in black paint reading BOILER. The cement floor sloped downward toward a rusty drain. Hessler never trusted anyone else to come down here, claiming he had had problems in the past with thieving employees.

*So this was where he did it!*

Danny made a quick search of the room, looking behind the larger objects, checking the sink and drain for bloodstains, and peering into the stove to look for bones. He examined the wood grain of the table and thought he found streaks of dark red, which he imagined were blood. There was no doubt in his mind this was where Hessler had slain all those people. The lock on the door, the drain, the sink, the stove, the table—it was all too convenient.

He had found the Torsos Slayer's workshop.

Danny decided to take a look in the boiler room before calling it quits.

The door was unlocked and not as heavy as the other. It opened easily, and Danny looked in upon the mostly dark interior. A few small windows were set high along the walls. Dim light entered, casting shadows from the iron grates covering the window wells above. Rain splattered against the windows, and from outside he could hear the steady drone of the storm.

Heat radiated from a massive boiler set in the middle of the room. Danny reached his hand out before him, searching for a light. He found another chain and gave it a pull, and a yellow low-wattage bulb came on. The room was practically bare, except for the gigantic boiler, the coal pile underneath the coal chute, and a refrigerator just inside the doorway.

Of all the things in the entire basement, the refrigerator was the most out of place. It was a White-Westinghouse model, with nothing particularly frightening about it, yet Danny's hand shook as he reached out and grasped the chrome-plated door handle.

He swallowed hard. *Here goes nothing.*

Danny pulled the door open, not knowing what to expect. The interior light illuminated several bundles neatly wrapped in brown butcher paper and tied with twine, in a variety of shapes and sizes. One was clearly in the shape of a head, lying on its side. Danny grasped the paper and tore it open with his fingernails—and found within the severed head of

Ted, the former soda jerk, his flesh tinted blue and dusted with a fine coating of ice crystals.

"Shit!" Danny said, slamming the door upon the ghastly discovery. All he wanted now was to get the hell out of there. He would find the nearest pay phone and ring Hank at the Hollenden, tell him he could get his fucking search warrant.

Danny closed the refrigerator door and caught a flint of light in his peripheral vision. He turned to see what it was.

"You little cunt."

In the doorway stood Mott Hessler, amber eyes agleam, both arms holding a machete, bringing the shiny blade down over Danny's head.

Danny ducked, swinging up the crook end of the crowbar and deflecting the blow. He took several hurried steps backward as Hessler lunged toward him. The crowbar must have taken him by surprise. Danny's only hope was to knock the machete from his hands. He couldn't allow Hessler to back him into a corner, as he was almost doing now.

Danny stood his ground, taking a firm grip with both hands around the straight end of the crowbar and holding it like a baseball bat. It was heavy and more difficult to swing than the machete, but if he lost his grip, he was dead.

"Cocksucker!" Hessler yelled, whipping his blade from the side as if to cut off Danny's head.

Danny met the steel with the crowbar, knocking the machete aside. He hoped he put a good nick in it. He hoped to find room in which to maneuver past Hessler. He had gained a few feet of ground, but he needed either to smash Hessler out of the way or knock him out cold before he could make a run for the door.

Hessler jabbed, trying to stab Danny in the gut, but Danny was able to step quickly out of his path, falling into the coal pile but hooking Hessler's arm with the crowbar. The machete blade met Danny's hand and cut him in between his thumb and forefinger, but he barely felt it. As Danny hooked him, Hessler lost his balance and fell headlong into the coal, plunging his weapon deep into the pile. Danny raked an armful of coal off the top onto Hessler's

head, and scrambled to his feet. Lumps of black fuel were
scattering all across the floor as Hessler flailed, trying to get
up.

"You little fuck, I'll get you!"

Danny made for the door, smashing the light bulb with the
crowbar as he went.

Hessler was on his feet and right behind him in the dark.

Danny swung the door to the boiler room shut, but as he
did, Hessler's machete blade broke through the rotten wood,
nearly striking Danny's face. Hessler swore on the other side
of the door as he withdrew the blade.

The heavy door to the storeroom was firmly shut. Before
Danny could open it, Hessler was in the storeroom and
nearly upon him. The machete blade came down again.
Danny swung up with the crowbar, but Hessler grabbed the
curved end with his free hand, yanking on it to pull Danny
closer.

Danny let go of the crowbar and Hessler went sprawling
backward, narrowly missing Danny with a swipe of his machete as he fell to the floor, toward the drain.

Danny pushed open the door and didn't bother to close it.
It was too heavy, and he had already broken the lock. It was
better for him to make a run for it.

The stairway was still in total darkness, but he found it
and took the steps two by two. He heard Hessler coming out
of the storeroom and up the stairs, right on his heels.

"I've got you, you little slut!"

Danny reached the first floor landing and tried opening the
service door that gave onto the alley, but it only opened
halfway. The Chevrolet delivery truck was blocking it. He
had no time to turn back, so he squeezed through and
climbed onto the mangled fender and hurtled over the rain-
slick hood, landing clumsily on the other side in the cold
stream of water flooding the alleyway.

Danny scrambled to his feet and looked back to see
Hessler trying to get through the doorway. Hessler was still
wielding his machete, but now Danny was weaponless.
Danny took off running along the edge of the alley, out of
the deeper water, heading for East Nineteenth Street. The
rain was torrential.

"Don't stop, Danny! Run! *Run!*" Hessler shouted from behind, laughing. Danny wondered if he'd made it past the truck, but he wasn't about to make the mistake of looking back to find out.

He turned the corner and headed south on East Nineteenth. The roar of the rain kept him from hearing any footsteps behind him. His drenched oxfords splashed through the puddles as he ran. Danny hoped his alley-cat surefootedness would help him through the water. The last thing he needed was to slip.

It was hard to see with the rain battering down on him. He saw no one out on the streets, not even any cars. Hessler was so close on his tail he couldn't stop anywhere to call for help. Before he could reach a phone, he would be dead. Most of the people in this neighborhood didn't even have a phone, and they would be suspicious of anyone screaming bloody murder.

"Help!" he yelled as he ran, but he was sure the rain drowned him out. "Help! Somebody!"

He crossed streets blindly, but there were no cars going through the intersections. He was running as fast and as hard as he could.

"Help!"

Danny heard Hessler laughing through the rain behind him. He crossed Carnegie, Central, Charity, and Scovill. He was going to keep south until he hit the railroad yard. He hoped to lose Hessler there. He was out of breath and freezing, yet his pace never flagged; he was too frightened. Adrenaline kept him going.

Orange Avenue and Broadway were dead. Cars were stalled in two feet of water, with no one inside them. The flooding on these streets slowed Danny down but presumably did the same for Hessler.

Once he was past Broadway, the railroad yard was simply over a small hill. The one thing he hadn't counted on was the mud. Near the top of the hill, he slipped and fell on his face.

He looked back behind him and saw Hessler was still slogging through the floodwaters on Broadway. Danny had put some distance between them.

He hurried to his feet and ran down the other side of the

hill, using the slippery mud to his advantage and sliding part of the way. The rain washed the mud from his face.

Danny saw a train down below through the sheets of rain, moving slowly north. He tried to get down the hill in time to hop on, but the caboose went past before he reached it. A freight train riding the tracks behind it was traveling in the opposite direction.

Danny looked behind him and saw Hessler heading down the hill. A forked lightning strike on the west side of the city illuminated the sky, and Hessler's machete shone white-hot for an instant as if it possessed a supernatural light of its own.

A deafening thunderclap followed.

Danny ran for the tracks. He crossed the first set and stood by the southbound freight as it rumbled past. It was going too fast for him to simply jump on, so he began running alongside it. It was the only way he could escape, as he was trapped between Hessler and the train.

The gravel alongside the tracks allowed Danny to run without slipping in the mud. He had never hopped a train before and was afraid he wouldn't make it. The cars were moving past him, faster than he could keep up, water spilling over them. He looked over his shoulder, but the bend in the tracks prevented him from seeing past the box-cars.

The cars each had rungs on their sides, and Danny figured his best bet was to grab hold of them. He saw an open boxcar coming his way and quickened his pace. He watched it over his shoulder as it came around, and when it reached him, he grabbed onto the highest rung he could reach and pulled himself up. The train was carrying him through the rain, his feet hanging off the ground. The rungs were slippery, but he held them in a virtual death grip.

Carefully, he pulled himself up the ladder until he was standing firmly upon it, feeling the rhythmic rocking and clattering of the boxcar from side to side as the train picked up its speed, passing through Kingsbury Run.

Danny had planned on riding the train for a bit and then dropping off, hoping to put a mile or two between him and

Hessler. But now the train was going too fast for him to safely jump off, and he couldn't hang on to the ladder forever.

The ladder was at one end of the boxcar, far from the open door at its middle. Somehow, Danny had to get to the door and get himself inside, out of the rain and into safety. But the side of the boxcar had no handholds. The only way he could get across was along the roof.

Danny climbed up the ladder. The cut on his hand was only superficial and did nothing to hinder his progress. Looking out upon the roof of the car, he saw it had a slope to it and wasn't entirely level. He inched out onto his stomach upon the roof and then brought his legs up. The rain washed over the top in rivulets, and he felt the car being buffeted back and forth by the uneven tracks. He crawled carefully along the roof, staying as close to the surface as possible, until he reached the middle. This part was going to be tricky.

Another burst of lightning lit up the sky, and in the flickering of blue light Danny saw the silhouette of a man walking along the top of the train many cars distant. As the darkness again took over, the image vanished.

Danny had nowhere else to go but into the boxcar.

He flattened himself against the roof, grabbed hold of its edge with a firm grip, and allowed his body to fall over the side so that he was dangling in the open boxcar door. The train shook to one side and tried to shake him off, but he held firm. From where he hung, he could see the dark interior of the car, which appeared to be empty.

Danny began swinging himself back and forth, building up some momentum. Looking down, he saw the train was traveling across a railroad bridge over the rain-swollen Cuyahoga; if he fell off the bridge, he would surely drown. When he had swung fully inside, he let go and fell tumbling along the wood floor. He flattened himself against it, preventing himself from rolling out the other side and over the bridge.

He lay there hugging the floor, his wet face pressed against the damp, gritty surface.

"Where on earth did you come from?" said a voice from

the darkness. It had a southern drawl and sounded nothing like Hessler, but still Danny rose to his feet and backed away from the voice, to the other end of the car.

"Who are you?" Danny asked.

A match was struck, lighting up both the man's cigarette and his face. He was a hobo, about twenty, with a few days' growth of beard and shadowed slits for eyes. He sat with his back against the far wall of the boxcar, one knee up, the other leg extended, resting one elbow on his pack. He blew out a cloud of smoke and shook the match out.

"Jim Teagarden," said the hobo. "Come set yourself down. Wanna smoke?"

Danny felt as if he were in a dream. He was chilled to the bone, drenched from head to toe. He'd just been running for his life and practically killed himself trying to get into the boxcar. Now this guy was offering him a cigarette.

"Sure," he said, and came closer. "Danny Cottone."

With both doors wide open the boxcar was not devoid of light. Danny's eyes adjusted as he found his way across the floor to where Jim sat. The floor of the boxcar was wet from rain that had blown in. He collapsed next to the hobo, clutching himself and shivering.

The smoke from Jim Teagarden's hand-rolled cigarette had the distinct odor of marijuana. Danny had smoked it before when customers had offered it to him.

"Here," said Jim, holding in a lungful of smoke and passing the marijuana to Danny.

Danny took the lumpy cigarette from Jim and sucked in smoke from the fiery hemp. It scorched its way down his gullet but soothed him and felt good. He held in the smoke and handed the cigarette back to Jim.

"Jesus," said Jim, touching Danny's soaked clothing. "We ought to build you a fire."

Danny exhaled, and then spat out, "There's a killer on this train." His teeth were clattering. He brought up his knees and hugged them.

"What say you?" Jim drawled.

"I saw him on the roof. He's coming after us."

"You're shittin' me!" Jim took another drag, making the orange tip glow and crackle.

"It's true, I swear. He's killed twelve people, and he tried to kill me. Don't tell me you've never heard of the Cleveland Torso Slayer!"

"No shit." Jim's dark face grew wide-eyed. "Here, on this train?" He breathed a cloud of smoke in Danny's face. Danny breathed it in, and grabbed the cigarette as Jim proffered it to him.

"No fooling," Danny said. "He chased me onto the train, and now he's looking for me." He took a larger drag than before and handed it back to Jim.

"Well, shit! What're we gonna do?"

Danny still couldn't tell whether Jim was taking him seriously or simply playing along. "I don't know."

Suddenly something landed on the roof with a dull thump, as if somebody had jumped the distance from the next car.

"Shh!" Danny whispered to Jim. "That's him!"

"What the—"

Danny clamped his hand over Jim's mouth. "Shh!"

Footsteps trod the roof of the boxcar, stopping at the middle. Danny watched the rain outside the boxcar doors, expecting to see Hessler come swinging through one of them any minute.

Danny whispered, "You got a gun?" and removed his hand from Jim's mouth.

"Nope," Jim whispered back. "Nothin'."

"Damn." Danny racked his brain, trying to think of a plan. "We got to get off."

"What! We'd be killed. Train's goin' too fast."

"Then we'll have to put up a fight. You ready to fight this bastard?"

"You really are serious," said Jim.

A hatch in the roof suddenly swung open, and Danny wondered why he hadn't noticed it when he was up top. Rain poured in through the opening.

"I know you're in there, cunt-boy," said Hessler's voice, followed by laughter.

Jim sprang to his feet and pulled Danny up with him. "Jesus Christ!"

A pair of legs dangled over the edge of the hatch, and then Hessler's silhouette was hanging by its arms. Hessler let go and fell to the floor of the boxcar, rising quickly to his feet. Rain fell down from the hatch onto his dark form and dripped down his body onto the floor.

"Careful," Danny warned Jim, "he's got a big knife."

This soon became evident as Hessler withdrew the long curved blade from behind him, where it must have been hanging from his belt. It shone dully in the darkness, held out in Hessler's hands.

"Jesus!" said Jim. "Stay back, mister! I'm warnin' you, I got a knife!"

Hessler's silhouette came closer, the blade outstretched before him, rainwater coursing down his figure.

"We could have been a great team," said Hessler. "The Torso Slayer and the Human Ashtray."

Danny clutched onto Jim. Trying to fight Hessler would be suicide. If they went anywhere near him, he would hack them to pieces.

"Where's your detective now?" Hessler asked. "He's left you out in the rain."

For a fleeting moment, Danny imagined Hank dropping in through the hatch and shooting Hessler in the back with his Colt .38. That would really be something.

The machete blade was only a few feet from Danny's face.

"You son of a bitch," Danny said, gritting his teeth.

He had to fight him; he had no choice, and he had nothing to lose by trying.

He ducked down and butted his head into Hessler's stomach, hoping to knock the wind out of him. Hessler keeled over, coughing, and Danny sprawled to the floor on his face, sliding across the rain-slick floorboards.

Lightning illuminated the boxcar, thunder rumbling after the loud *crack*.

Danny turned and saw Hessler on his knees above him, wheezing and trying to catch his breath, about to bring down his blade. Jim came at him from behind, grabbing hold of the hand holding the machete. Hessler elbowed Jim brutally in the ribs. Jim's grip faltered and he staggered back, clutching his side. Hessler swung the machete across backhanded and dug it deep into Jim's neck. Blood gushed out of the wound, spilling onto the floor of the boxcar before Jim's body fell with a *thud.* Gurgling noises came from Jim's throat as he clutched at his neck.

Danny screamed and tried to get to his feet, but then Hessler was upon him, wrenching his arm from its socket. Danny felt the bone pop and then the blade bite deep into his shoulder muscle.

He screamed in agony, his head thrashing from side to side in a pool of his own warm blood. As Hessler hacked away at his arm, Danny struggled and thought of Hank and wondered why he had failed to save his pony. . . .

# 31 October 1938

The darkened street along the docks was barren at this hour. A brisk wind swirled fallen leaves along the sidewalk.

At the corner, Hank Lambert met the wind head-on. He turned up the collar of his pea coat and tucked his hands into his pockets. He followed the length of the cobbled alleyway until he reached a nondescript black door. He rapped against the wood with bare knuckles. His breath came out as mist. He stood and waited.

A small window slid open, revealing two eyes staring out from behind a mask. "Yes?"

Hank uttered the password: "Tyrone Power."

The window slid shut, then came the sound of a heavy deadbolt being drawn back, and the door opened. Hank was greeted by a man in drag and a red wig, wearing a scarlet mask and a hat with peacock feathers. "Happy Halloween," said the doorman, closing and locking the door behind him.

Hank gave the doorman a tip and descended the rickety staircase into the cellar, where he was allowed in through a second door.

Within the tavern, the lightning was dim, so that at first what Hank saw were faces floating in smoky darkness, some

306

half-obscured by shadow. But as his eyes adjusted, he was able to make out more distinct shapes. The front room had sparse tables and chairs and a long bar. Against the far wall hung a dark purple drapery that led to the back room.

An unusual number of patrons had shown up in drag this evening. In fact, Hank recognized one as a professional female impersonator known as Johnny Magnum, who worked such legitimate Cleveland venues as the Torch Club on Euclid Avenue and specialized in Myrna Loy. But even on this night, most of the patrons had come as they were—rough dockworkers, athletic dancers, pale asthmatic youths, eccentric actors, and poets.

Hank sat at the only vacant seat at the bar.

"Hi, sweetie," said the bartender, a chubby effeminate man of about fifty known to all the regulars as "Toots." He had costumed himself only to the extent of wearing lipstick and rouge, with a pair of pipe-cleaner antennae sticking out of his white hair.

"Give me some tequila," said Hank, folding his arms on the grimy bartop.

"Can I interest you in our drink special?" Toots pursed his lips, dying to tell.

"What's that?"

"A Randy Martian." Toots's eyes lit up. He had been inspired by last night's Mercury Theater radio broadcast that had fooled some Americans into thinking that visitors from another planet were taking over New Jersey. "That's a vodka gimlet with cherry juice."

"I'll have my tequila."

"You're a real stick in the mud." Toots went to fetch his drink.

Hank preferred to keep to himself these days. Danny had been missing for over two weeks now. His landlord had sold his belongings and let his apartment. Hank wished he could believe Danny had skipped town out of fear, that perhaps he had gone nowhere near Hessler's that night. But the more likely possibility gnawed away at Hank's gut like an ulcer, that Danny was dead, that Hessler had caught him.

Hank had reached Hessler's Drugs too late that night because of the flooded streets; by the time he got there, both

Danny and Hessler were gone, although the Auburn was parked there in back. Hank had entered through the open service entrance looking for Danny. He went in armed with his revolver in case he met up with Hessler, and in searching the basement, had found the wrapped remains of Ted Mauston in the refrigerator. This discovery had led to a search warrant, and over the next several days the ensuing search unearthed the other half of the quilt used to wrap Number Eleven, as well as bloodstains on the concrete cellar floor. A search of the coal furnace in the boiler room revealed the brittle fragments of at least two human skulls. They had enough evidence to charge Hessler with several counts of murder—if they could ever find him. After that night, Hessler had failed to return to his store. The police closed up the shop and confiscated the Chevrolet panel van and the Auburn 851 Speedster, believing one or both of the vehicles had been used to transport torso victims.

"Your tequila, *señor!*"

"Thanks, Toots." Hank downed the shot. It warmed him up.

It was the agony of not knowing what had become of Danny that had led him to the tavern. Before, a visit here had been rare. Now it had become a nightly ritual. Despondent over Danny's disappearance, Hank had sought solace wherever he could find it—in a bottle, in a boy. Many of the men here were criminals, and if anyone ever found out about Hank's coming here, he could be fired on that alone, much less what it revealed about his sexuality. Yet even this no longer mattered. These days, he came in to work in the morning barely sober. He had lost interest in his job and only wanted Danny back.

"Hey, mister," a gruff voice whispered in his ear.

Hank paid no attention.

A stray hand reached around and groped his crotch. He allowed it to linger but did nothing to encourage it. At last the hand withdrew into the dark, and the disembodied voice grumbled its disappointment.

After several more shots of tequila and some conversation with Toots, Hank became less oblivious to those around him and sat with his back to the bar.

A burly laborer standing alone against the nearest wall caught Hank's eye and gave him a hard stare. Hank had never seen him here before. The man came away from the wall and approached him. The set of his face was angular and rigid.

Without a word passing between them, Hank offered him a cigarette and lit it for him. The man made a jerking motion with his head, indicating the back room behind the drapery, and grabbed Hank's arm in a firm grip. Hank got up off the barstool and was led through the dense smoke, beyond the heavy curtain, and into a room that was pitch-black and smelled of male sweat. The man behind pushed him through the crowd. Hank felt the naked flesh of more than one man as he made his way, until at last he was up against the farthest wall.

As Hank moved to turn around, the man kept him in place against the wall. Hank felt the man's crotch press against his ass. The man's fingers entered his mouth, and he sucked on them. With the other hand, the man unfastened Hank's trousers and yanked them down.

Pressed against the gritty stone wall, enveloped by the dark, Hank felt obliterated as the man forced his way in.

# 2 December 1938

Pittsburgh detectives led the Cleveland team across the frozen ground of the railroad yards. A bitter wind whipped their greatcoats. Hank, straggling behind, had to hold on to his hat. Ahead of him walked Eliot Ness, David Cowles, and Lloyd Trunk with his photographic gear, the three of them chatting with their Pittsburgh colleagues, who had already briefed them on the case over lunch.

"Here we are, gentlemen," said one of the Pittsburgh cops.

A string of abandoned boxcars was parked on an old hub at the far end of the yard. The Pittsburgh & Lake Erie Railroad had scheduled them for demolition. Yesterday afternoon, while conducting a routine inspection, three railroad dicks had come upon the bodies. The Pittsburgh authorities had sent Cleveland a wire, hoping the torso investigators might be able to lend some of their expertise, and asking them to come as soon as possible.

The crime scene was cordoned off with long yellow ribbons strung between wooden stakes and fluttering in the wind, guarded by uniformed railroad police. Old chemical-blackened wooden ties were stacked nearby, alongside a pile

310

of rusty torn-up tracks. The lawmen stepped over the ribbons and entered the area.

"This is where they found the first one," said Pittsburgh detective Tom O'Malley, pointing to an open boxcar in the middle of the line. He stepped up and into the opening, and the others followed. Hank gazed up at the cloud-blanketed sky. The wind screamed through the train yards. Hank climbed up the short stepladder and joined the rest inside.

The interior of the car was bare. The Pittsburgh cops had processed the scene yesterday and removed all the evidence. But the floor still showed bloodstains, which were by no means fresh.

"He was layin' down here," said O'Malley, "on his back near the wall, and away from the stains. His head was gone, right arm cut off and layin' beside him, here. We'll show him to you later at the morgue."

O'Malley led them to the far wall of the boxcar. The large rust-colored stains were closer to the center of the floor. Enough dried blood covered the floor that Hank imagined it had all come from the decapitation. Lloyd Trunk snapped photos of the stains, including broad spatters on the wall.

"He left his footprint, here," said O'Malley, pointing to a bloody tread mark. "Size twelve, from a rubber galosh. We also recovered a couple of pages of the *Youngstown Vindicator,* dated October fourteenth. Railroad says these cars pulled in here last week on a train from Youngstown. We think the murders were committed there. The railroad's records aren't so good. We can't trace the cars any further than that."

"That's only sixty miles from Cleveland," Hank said. "Close enough for me."

Even without having seen the bodies, Hank could tell this was the work of the Torso Slayer. From the gray barren boxcar came an aura of dread—a promise that things would get worse before they got better.

"We also found the butt of a hand-made stogy—probably marijuana," said O'Malley. "Didn't you guys think your killer was a dope fiend?"

"No, he's more of a sex fiend, like Leopold and Loeb."
Eliot Ness seemed unable to let go of this connection.

None of Pittsburgh's evidence collection was going to
matter, now. Cleveland police already knew who the murderer was, but they were keeping it secret from Pittsburgh, as
well as keeping it out of the press. It would be unwise to
break the story until they actually had Hessler in custody.

"Come on," said O'Malley. He breathed into his hands
and rubbed them together briskly. "I'll show you where we
found the other guy and the woman, and then we'll go back
to the morgue for some nice, warm coffee."

"I'll drink to that," said Hank.

## 1:49 P.M.

Three tables were set up in the lab at the Pittsburgh
morgue, covered with black plastic sheets. The Pittsburgh
and Cleveland lawmen encircled the tables, their attention
drawn to Dep. Coroner Anthony Sappo in the center. Sappo
carefully withdrew the sheet on the first table, revealing the
"other guy" who, O'Malley had informed them, had been
discovered in a burlap bag, his torso bisected and limbs cut
off, the head missing. Underneath the second sheet lay the
similarly dissected corpse of what had once been a woman,
but who was also *sans* head. The third sheet was lifted to reveal the heavily decomposed body of the young male from
the first boxcar.

The stench was overwhelming, but Hank observed that it
barely affected the men in the room. They were all hardened
pros. Hank and Ness were the youngest in attendance, yet
even they had seen their fair share of carnage during their respective tenures in law enforcement.

It was hard to believe that the body lying exposed on the
last table had once been a man. The head was missing, the
rest of him intact except for the severed arm, which lay by
his side—apparently the same manner in which he had been
found. But the flesh displayed splotches of color as varied
and diverse as a painter's palette. The feature most immediately striking, however, was the word carved in the victim's
chest:

# NA⊆I

The backward *Z* was incongruous. The word had been slashed into the skin rapidly and with a sharp blade. The wounds had spread and suppurated.

"*Nazi,*" said Ness. "What the hell does he mean by that?"

"You tell us," said Deputy Coroner Sappo. Wearing latex gloves, he grabbed the left arm and lifted it up so they could see the swollen, blackened fingertips. "Charred," he said. "Has your killer ever done that?"

"No," said Ness. "He usually doesn't give us the hands. If it is the same guy, he was probably trying to obliterate the prints to keep us from making an ID."

Hank was happy to let Ness do all the talking. He was too intent on examining the body. Yes, it was about Danny's height, but the flesh was so rotten it was impossible to identify him. The dick was purple and covered with death sores. The severed right arm lay with its hand palm-up. If it had any tattoos, they were presently hidden from view.

"Well, he didn't succeed," said Sappo. "Not entirely. Decomposition did more damage than the burning."

Sappo held up the fingertips for David Cowles, who examined them closely with a magnifying glass and then addressed Lloyd Trunk. "We can still get prints from this. They're distorted, but the feds might be able to do something with it."

"You may not have to go to all the trouble," said Sappo, reaching for the right arm and holding it up. "He left this hand alone."

"Probably ran out of time," said Ness.

Cowles examined the finger pads on the right hand, which showed no signs of charring. "These are pretty bad, too," Cowles said, "but we might get a good enough set to check against our own files. Lloyd, we'll ink them both, send the left to Washington and do the right ourselves."

"Gotcha," said Trunk. He went through a string of flash-bulbs taking photos of the corpse.

Hank was hesitant to ask Sappo to turn over the right arm.

If he did, all attention would be on him as he examined it, and if he found the tattoo, everybody would wonder how he knew about it. If worse came to worst, he would wait until they were through here and make sure he was the last man out, so he could sneak a peek.

"Coroner, could you turn that over so I can get a shot?" asked Lloyd Trunk.

"Sure," said Sappo, reaching for it with his gloved hands. "There's a tattoo here. It's faint, but—"

"Just turn it over," Hank snapped. He found Ness staring at him.

Sappo turned it carefully so that the hand was palm-down. The arm was as scabrous and growth-infested as the rest of the body, yet amid the bruises and discolorations Hank could discern a faded rose etched in red ink.

Hank stared at the hideous corpse and nearly burst into tears.

"Excuse me," he muttered, pushing his way through the Pittsburgh detectives and running from the room, down the main hall to the men's room, where he vomited his lunch into the toilet and sat on the floor of the private stall, crying.

# 12 December 1938

When Hank arrived at Eliot Ness's office as scheduled, Betty-Lou turned from her typewriter to greet him, but quickly withdrew her smile. Hank knew he looked a mess, but he didn't care. He had had a long, lost weekend, and he was sorry it was over. It was Monday morning, and he had been late for work, but at least he had shaved. Upon arriving, he had found a letter from Ness on his desk in a plain interdepartmental envelope, requesting a meeting at eleven o'clock. Well, here he was.

"You can go right in, Detective," said Betty-Lou. In her voice Hank read pity. But then she was privy to Ness's secrets. Ness probably pitied him, as well.

Hank opened the door and strode in. Ness looked decidedly unhappy to see him.

"Sit down," Ness said, motioning with his hand but failing to rise. "Get comfortable."

Oh boy, Hank thought, sitting in the overstuffed leather chair. This was going to be a hell of a meeting.

Behind Ness, the lake stretched to its northern horizon, the waters still and colorless.

Ness grabbed a file folder and opened it up before him on his blotter.

"Lucky, when I started this job three years ago, I began an investigation of the police and fire departments to root out deceit and corruption. I thought it would last a few months, but I failed to realize the scope of the problem. We had cops getting drunk on duty, even spending most of their shift holed up in a neighborhood bar. Citizen complaints led nowhere. We had several gambling dens operating with full knowledge of the police. Officers taking bribes. Officers getting involved in the policy racket, taking protection money. Officers turning a blind eye to narcotics, in the pay of the dope dealers. And not just patrolmen, but sergeants and lieutenants. Captain Harwood. Captain Lenahan."

"Jack Finnegan," Hank added sourly. "My partner."

"Now they're all gone, and we've replaced them with good men."

"None as good as Jack," Hank said. Now that he was done for, he may as well defend the honor of his one-time friend. Jack had moved out of the city, and Hank hadn't seen or heard from him in two years. He sure could have used his help on the torso case, which was clearly going to be his last.

"That may well be," Ness conceded. "Anyway, it's been three years and my investigation still isn't over. Some people in the department were able to hide their activities for a while and it took a little more legwork to weed them out. I set up a unit of 'Untouchables' working directly out of my office to investigate complaints. Bob Chamberlin heads it and they report to me and me alone."

"Don't pussyfoot around, Eliot," Hank complained. "Get to the point."

Ness sighed, absently turning over pages in the file folder, scanning its contents, avoiding eye contact with Hank.

Hank slumped into the chair and crossed his legs, but continued to stare directly at Ness.

"Remember that list of known perverts the postal inspector gave us? In case you hadn't noticed, you were on it."

"Really." Hank yawned.

"That was what first got me thinking, but I didn't act until later."

"It was Hessler," Hank said. "The goddamn Butcher."

"I treated it as a regular citizen complaint," Ness said in a calming voice. "And if there was any truth to what he said, I knew it would compromise our investigation, that it might even prevent the D.A. from prosecuting."

"Bullshit. You didn't give a damn about prosecution. You wanted Hessler in Guy Williams's nuthouse."

"I put my Untouchables onto it. They've had you under surveillance since October."

"You were spying on me?" Hank laughed. "I don't believe it."

"I know everything you've been up to, including your nightly visits to this seedy dockside tavern. But this matter of Danny Cottone was the last straw." Ness was condescending, as if speaking to a child. "You put this kid in danger and jeopardized our entire investigation."

"I never put him in danger," said Hank, though in his own mind he constantly debated whether or not he had. "I wanted to hold on to Hessler. You're the one who let him go. You're the one who killed Danny Cottone."

Hank had made the official identification of Danny based on his recognition of the rose tattoo. David Cowles and Lloyd Trunk had worked overtime on the fingerprints of the right hand to confirm the identification, and the prints had, indeed, been matched successfully against Danny's prints on file in the county jail. The meaning of this had not been lost on Eliot Ness, though he denied any culpability after having let Hessler go. Instead, he had reproached Hank for placing Danny in jeopardy in the first place.

"You had better retract that," said Ness. "I won't be insulted by one of my own detectives."

"Give me a break. You're about to fire me, anyway." Hank sat up in his seat and pointed his finger at Ness. "You're the one who wanted to avoid scandal. I wanted Hessler locked up. I was right, and you know it."

"Hindsight is always useful," Ness said. "Maybe I should have had Al Capone tried for murder, but what's the point?"

"The point is Danny's dead."

"No, Lucky," Ness lectured him, "the point is, you violated the public trust, and you lack a sense of duty. You've paid for the services of male prostitutes and participated in lewd acts in underworld speakeasies."

"You don't know the half of it," said Hank. All caution had been thrown to the wind. He didn't give a damn anymore.

"That's why you're fired, as of now."

"Then I'll be going." Hank rose to leave.

"Sit down, I'm not finished."

Hank sat. Hell, he had the time. These days, he was only home whenever he had no place else to sleep or sober up. He knew a divorce from Cathy was imminent, and he was ready to give it to her on the basis of his own gross neglect, even though he was liable to lose the kids. Over this he was heartbroken, but how could he remain a decent father to Becky and Luke after everything that had happened to him, and with such rancor between him and Cathy?

"Listen," said Ness, "I'm not a hard-ass. I think you know me better than that. I firmly believe that what people do in private is their own business."

"Sure, that's why you spied on me."

"But this is different. A man associating with pimps, prostitutes, hustlers, con men, junkies, and dope dealers has no business investigating a murder case in which our prime suspect is cut from the same cloth."

"Oh, come on."

"The bottom line is, you've got no business in this department. You're fired as of this moment, without pay, without pension, without appeal. And I suggest you talk to Dr. Williams and see about getting psychiatric help for your disorder. You go on like this, you're going to destroy yourself."

"I've had just about enough." Hank stood up. "By the time you're through with this department, there won't be a man left standing."

"Listen, Lucky, I'm sorry." Ness spread his hands, palms up. "I mean it. My hands are tied. What else do you expect me to do? I truly am sorry, believe me."

"Go ahead," Hank said, turning his back and walking out. "You go ahead. Be sorry all you like, because I couldn't care less."

He slammed the door behind him on his way out. Betty-

Lou jumped, startled by the noise, and gave him that same pitying look. Hank felt naked before her. She had probably typed the contents of Ness's file folder on him.

Hank looked her straight in the baby-browns and announced, "I'm going to go out and get stinko."

# 17 December 1938

"Whoopsy-daisy!" said Eliot Ness, catching Evaline McAndrew by the arm as she slipped on the black ice. They had left the Hollenden Hotel with the momentum of the revolving door at their backs, and both nearly fell flat on their collective ass. But Ness was able to catch his balance and save Evaline at the same time, purely by accident.

The doorman reached out to lend a hand, but Ness already had her. He waved his thanks.

"Goodness!" Evaline giggled, her hair caught in the bracing wind.

"I've got you!" Ness said, holding her tightly against him. The tight satin ball gown she wore under her coat prevented her from taking big steps, and that, coupled with her high heels, made Ness wonder how she managed to stay standing at all, icy sidewalks or no.

"Good night, Mr. Ness," said the doorman.

"I hope he doesn't expect a tip," whispered Ness in her ear, his words coming out slurred.

"Oh, don't be a poop." Evaline hiccuped. She'd been hiccuping since midnight.

Superior Avenue was quiet, but then the hour was late—or early, depending on how you looked at it.

"Now where is that car?" Ness wondered aloud, squinting his eyes as if his black '37 Buick would suddenly appear before them. He knew it was around here somewhere. They would just have to head on down the street until they found the damned thing.

"Maybe I should drive," said Evaline.

"You haven't got a license—"

"And you're drunk." She hiccuped again.

"And you can't drive," Ness added.

"I can so!"

"Of course you can sew."

"Ha, ha."

"The fresh air's sobering me up. I'm in better shape than you, anyway."

"There it is!" Evaline said as they rounded the corner of the hotel and faced the intersection.

Ness looked in every direction except straight ahead, where she was pointing.

"Across the street! There it is!" Evaline was jumping up and down with excitement, or perhaps from the cold.

Ness focused his eyes on the other side of the intersection and saw his car sitting there, parked right where he had left it seven hours earlier. The traffic signal turned green and allowed them to cross.

"Ooh, hurry!" said Evaline as they reached the car. The freezing wind howling down the street was coming straight off the lake.

Ness unlocked the passenger-side door and helped Evaline inside. He got in on the driver's side and started the engine, which turned over stubbornly after a few tries. He cracked the window a bit to keep the windshield from fogging up.

He ground the gears putting it into first. He hadn't done that in a long time. He depressed the clutch more firmly, and tried again.

"It's so cold!" Evaline said. "Turn up the heat."

"We'll have you home in no time," Ness said, and pulled out into the street. He would take the Detroit-Superior High-

Level Bridge across the Cuyahoga, and thence turn off onto West Lake Shore Boulevard and head toward the Lakewood neighborhood.

Ness had taken Evaline dancing at the Vogue Room that evening, their first date since the finalization of the divorce from Edna. They were also celebrating the acceptance of an article Ness had penned on "Radio-Directed Mobile Police" for *American City* magazine. He already had another one in mind on venereal diseases, which had become his new passion at the safety director's office, now that the torso case had practically played itself out.

After the dancing, they had joined another couple upstairs in a hotel room for further conversation and drinks. The time had slipped by rather quickly, and before he knew it, he had found himself utterly exhausted and decided they had better leave.

As they passed over the bridge, Evaline inquired, "Do people really jump off this thing?"

"Of course," Ness said. "All the time. It's more dangerous than it looks."

"How awful." Evaline hiccuped again, then giggled.

He hoped to become engaged to Evaline. She was a sweet girl. They had met years ago when they were both living in Chicago. Two years ago she found a new job in Cleveland, and they had renewed their acquaintance. She relished nights like this on the town, drinking and dancing like Fred and Ginger did in the movies, only less well on both counts.

On the other side of the river, Ness turned off the bridge and onto Lake Shore, accelerating to the greater speed allowed on the highway. The drive was lighted, but less bright than downtown. Patches of ice dotted the road, and the wind blew ghosts of snow flurries across his path. The occasional car passed by in the oncoming lane, and they all seemed to have their lights on bright. Ness kept having to squint as they went past, and watched carefully the yellow dividing line on his left. He had to make constant adjustments to keep the car driving straight.

"Damn suspension," he muttered.

Evaline had grown quiet. The heater was probably putting her to sleep.

Ness had needed a night like this after the week he'd had. The case of Hank Lambert preyed on his conscience. He was a good detective, the kind that was hard to come by, but his firing had been necessary and just. Ness could have been much harder on him. Lambert had gotten off easy.

He kept receiving notes signed "Your Paranoidal Nemesis," written in the almost illegible left-handed script, and he had come to realize they were indeed from Hessler. They were mostly insane babblings and would help little in finding him. The postmarks were always different, one from Youngstown, one from Chicago, one from Indianapolis. Ness had sent a description of their suspect to several such cities, but he knew only too well the chances of apprehending him were slim. Hessler knew they were after him. He would never screw up. He would continue sending these notes, taunting Ness perhaps for the rest of his life.

Suddenly a pair of headlights were heading straight for him. The bastard had crossed over into his lane.

Ness swerved sharply to the right and slammed on the brakes, but his left front fender struck the side of the oncoming car and sent both vehicles spinning in opposite directions upon the ice.

Evaline woke up and screamed.

Ness turned the wheel, trying to regain control of the car. He came to an abrupt stop on the shoulder, when the wheels met hard gravel. His engine had quit.

"Eliot!" Evaline said.

Ness had to put all his weight against his door before it would open. Getting out, he quickly surveyed the damage, which proved to be minor, especially for what could have been a catastrophic accident. His fender was twisted and the left headlight busted out. The driver's door was sprung.

"Eliot!"

"Wait here!" he said, crossing the highway and running along the pavement until he reached the other car.

The Chrysler he had struck had similar damage. The left front fender had come clean off, probably absorbing most of the blow, and they had been sent into a similar spin so that they were now facing the opposite direction from which they had come.

Ness approached the driver's side and peeked in.

"Are you all right?" Ness said.

"Give me your name," said the driver, an older man with gray hair and a mustache. His frumpy wife sitting next to him looked shaken, but unhurt.

"But are you all right?" Ness repeated. He could see his breath misting in front of him, and realized he was breathing right into the face of the driver, who could probably smell the alcohol on his breath. The last thing he needed was an arrest for drunk driving.

"Yes, yes, we're fine. But you must give me—"

Ness panicked. He turned and ran from the car. If he got away fast, no one would be the wiser. The driver would never know who had struck him, and Ness could avoid a messy scandal. SAFETY DIRECTOR ARRESTED. He could see the headlines now. DRUNKEN NESS CAUSES ACCIDENT.

He ran across the empty highway, watching for the ice, and got quickly into his car. The door wouldn't close.

"Eliot," said Evaline.

"Not now, Evaline."

"Eliot, I'm bleeding," she said, and showed him her red-stained hand and the blood in her hair. Looking beyond her shoulder, he observed a spider-web pattern in the passenger window where her head had struck.

"Oh, Christ," he said. "Are you OK?"

"I . . . I think so," she said, sounding confused. "At least it cured my hiccups."

Ness started up the engine, happy that it still worked. Looking in his rearview mirror, he saw the other car coming across the highway, heading in his direction. He gunned the engine and drove the car off the shoulder, onto the highway, wanting to put some distance between him and the other car as fast as possible.

"Hang on, honey. I'm taking you to the hospital."

The headlights of the other car trailed far behind. Ness

only hoped they had been unable to read his license plate before he had outrun them, or his career would be finished and he would never get elected mayor. He had a personalized plate reading EN-1, and it wouldn't take a genius to figure out to whom it belonged.

# 20 December 1938

4:37 P.M.

Hank stepped into the elevator along with a throng of women in stylish hats carrying Higbee's shopping bags and conversing in such high-pitched tones that he could barely make out a word they said.

"Next stop, the observation deck!" announced the elevator boy, who in this case was a short old man with a gray beard and no mustache who looked like an old salt. Elevator boys were always short, and Hank wondered if their vocation had anything to do with it, going up and down all day, three hundred days out of the year.

This elevator boy was part tour guide, expounding upon the history of the Terminal Tower, built by the famous (in Cleveland) Van Sweringen brothers during the late twenties, completed shortly before the stock market crash to become the tallest skyscraper in the world outside of New York, and so on and so on, the usual song-and-dance about the $x$ miles of steel girders, $x$ miles of plumbing, $x$ number of stone blocks, $x$ number of workers, and $x$ amount of dollars, all of which seemed very much to impress the ladies out doing their Christmas shopping, but none of which made the slight-

est impression on Hank. He had heard it all before, when he
had taken Becky and Luke up here.

He watched the lights illuminating floor numbers as they
rose ever upward. Unlike the ladies, he was not going up to
the observation deck for the "spectacular view."

Hank had received a letter in his mailbox yesterday, without a postmark and after the mailman had already come,
meaning someone had hand-delivered it. The linen envelope
was addressed in elegant calligraphic script and pitch-black
India ink to "Mr. Henri P. Lambert, Esq."

The letter within was written in the same careful hand,
with brilliant flourishes on the more exotic letters of the alphabet, and read:

December 19, 1938

Dear Lucky,
   I've got something you want, something near
and dear to your heart. You may call it a pony,
but I call it a torso. Semantics aside, I'm asking
you to come claim your property. I'll be waiting
for you on the observation deck of Danny's favorite
building tomorrow afternoon at 5:00 sharp. I'll
make you a trade—bring me the torso file from
your ex-employers and I'll give you back your pony.
No tricks. Come alone and on time or I'll toss
Ponyboy over the side, cunt and all. Make sure the
file is complete, and leave your gun at home if you
want your parcel undamaged.
   See you in the funny papers!

Yours truly,<br>[signed] X

At first when he received the note, Hank was utterly confused, so convinced was he that Danny was dead. But then
he phoned Vern Quast at Central Station and learned that the
FBI had come up with a positive match on the fingerprints
taken from the left hand of what they had thought was
Danny's corpse. The name they had come up with was one
James Teagarden of Charleston, South Carolina, twenty-one

years old, who had a criminal record for burglary in three states.

Only the severed right arm had belonged to Danny; all the rest to the unfortunate Mr. Teagarden, whose head had yet to be recovered.

All of which meant Danny might still be alive.

There was no mistaking the letter was from Hessler. Hank only hoped he wasn't walking into a trap.

"Twenty-first floor!" announced the elderly elevator boy with enthusiasm, as if barking a carnival attraction.

Obtaining the "torso file" had been easy. Hank had left the department without cleaning out his desk and went there this morning on the pretext of doing just that. The Detective Bureau was often empty, as the gumshoes were usually out pounding the pavement, and Hank had waited until just such a lull in business, while the secretaries and supervisors were out of the room, to head for the filing cabinet and retrieve the thick file.

It took up several folders and was over one thousand pages long, filled with witness statements, police reports regarding the finding of remains, gory eight-by-ten glossy photographs, copies of coroners' reports, and the assorted notes of several different detectives.

As Hank closed the file into his large leather satchel, he felt as if he were stealing the crown jewels. This was the biggest case in the history of the department, and with the file gone there would be no history of it, and no chance of prosecuting the case.

But that no longer concerned Hank. They had botched the case from the beginning, and he had nothing to be proud of. The one good thing that had come out of the whole ordeal was Danny Cottone.

Hank had lost his job and the respect of his peers. Word had gotten around the department fast, not only of his being fired, but also the reasons why. Cathy Lambert had a pipeline into the department through the other detectives' wives, and naturally she had wanted to know the real reason why her husband was eighty-sixed. They had lost no time in telling her, and Cathy had demanded an immediate divorce—the kind of divorce that had real teeth in it, with no chance of any visitation rights with the children. Cathy held all the cards; Hank had neglected her and he was a known sexual deviant, without a pension or any means of support.

Hank could no longer do anything about that sorry state of affairs, and he deeply regretted losing the kids, especially when Becky and Luke were so confused about what was going on. They would never know. Their father would simply disappear, and they would wonder if it was their fault.

"Fortieth floor, ladies and gentlemen!" the old man crowed, practically giddy.

Hank clutched his leather satchel. He had decided to trust Hessler completely and had told no one of their meeting. No cops were waiting downstairs, surrounding the building. Hank carried no gun, but then he had had to turn in his .38 along with his badge, and he had never owned a gun of his own. All he had with him was the torso file, which weighed a good many pounds and was wearing out his arm.

If Danny was indeed alive, he would be missing his own right arm. Hank could live with that. He would try to help Danny get used to using his left for everything, and naturally he would take care of him. Hank could find a job somewhere, but first they would have to hightail it out of Cleveland, perhaps go west to California.

He watched the numbered lights light up one after another on the overhead panel. His palm was sweaty, and he adjusted his grip on the satchel.

Hank had to be careful not to dream too much. For all he knew, it could be a trick and Danny might really be dead. In that case, Hank would never turn over the file. It was Danny or nothing, put up or shut up. Hank and Hessler wouldn't be the only ones on the observation deck, and he planned on keeping his distance, on the chance that Hessler wanted to try something.

But Hessler had already put Hank out of commission. His tattling about Danny to Eliot Ness had seen to that, and Hank had come to realize this had been no accident. It had produced the desired result, not only getting him off the case but destroying his career, if not his life. Hessler no longer had any reason for wanting to kill him.

"Here we are, the observation deck!" The old elevator boy climaxed. An orgasmic glow spread across his rosy cheeks, framed by his white fisherman whiskers.

The elevator doors opened on a hallway, and Hank stepped out of the car. The ladies followed behind him, honking like geese.

Hank stopped, staring at the arrow on the wall. The ladies passed him by and marched off in the direction of the arrow, down the long corridor toward the beckoning sunlight.

Hank looked at his watch and saw he was early. He wondered if Hessler was here already, and headed down the hall to see the famous view of the city that he had so grown to despise.

As the ladies pushed through the doors, a gust of arctic wind was let into the heated corridor; they squealed and giggled as they trundled forth, holding onto their carefully pinned hats. The last one held the door open for Hank. Her buck teeth reminded him of Eleanor Roosevelt.

They came out onto the north side of the building, facing the lake and downtown and the barren park of Public Square many stories below. The waist-high stone wall surrounding the deck was augmented by an iron fence to prevent dizzy tourists from falling, to a total height of about seven feet.

Hank looked to his left and to his right along the deck but saw no sign of Hessler or Danny. He crept to the edge and peered out past the bars, at the filthy city that looked, from up here, so insignificant—the city that had spawned a human monster.

His wristwatch was ticking toward five o'clock, and Hank decided he had better check out the rest of the deck, which wrapped around the building's outer edge. From the street, the observation deck would be the terminus of the pure vertical line of the tower before it began tapering off in a highly decorative pinnacle like an overblown church steeple constructed of gingerbread.

The deck was closing at five, it was now ten minutes to,

and most of the visitors had gone back down. Few people ventured up here at this time of year, anyway, with the wind so biting.

Hank found Hessler on the southern end of the observation deck, the side facing the snakelike Cuyahoga, Kingsbury Run, and the Flats, with its grimy steel factories spewing out thick black smoke. Hessler was standing near the edge in a black wool coat.

A figure in a similar coat was seated on a bench at Hessler's back, one arm folded in his lap, legs planted firmly on the cement, sitting rather stiffly and staring straight ahead. The two were still some distance away as Hank rounded the corner, and at first he thought the seated figure could not possibly be Danny. Nobody else stood at the southern view, probably because there was nothing to see.

"You're early," Hessler said.

The figure on the bench turned his head in Hank's direction but remained seated in the same position on the bench, his mouth shut.

Hank recognized the face.

"Danny!" he shouted.

Danny said nothing. Something about his face seemed strange, but from this distance Hank could make out little detail. He started closer.

"Stop right there," said Hessler. "Slide me the case."

"As long as I know it's Danny," said Hank. "And that he's all right."

"Go ahead," Hessler said with a wave of his hand. "Come on."

Hank approached, staring all the while into Danny's face, as if he were seeing a ghost. Deep red lines marred the olive skin in abstract criss-crosses. Hank saw no fresh blood. The wounds had healed into permanent disfiguring scars. Danny was no longer beautiful; Hessler had destroyed his face.

"Stop!" Hessler commanded before Hank could get too close. Hessler went over and stood behind Danny, placing his hands on the frightened kid's shoulders.

Hank could see his eyes now and saw that he was terrified,

especially as Hessler laid his hands on him. Yet he made no move to shrug Hessler away. He seemed too scared to move or even open his mouth.

"If you no longer want him, I'll understand. You just keep your satchel and I'll keep Ponyboy here. We've been together for some time now, hiding out. He's come to depend on me."

Life on the run had made Hessler the worse for wear. He was unshaven and his face gaunt. His eyes had lost their luster and appeared a gangrenous yellow.

"Let him go!" Hank shouted.

Hessler reached into the inner pocket of his coat, brought out a machete, and held the sharp blade against Danny's throat, pressing the tender scarred flesh. Danny tried to shrink away from the steel, but Hessler was holding him. His left hand remained casually folded in his lap.

It was then Hank noticed the right sleeve of the coat dangling at Danny's side, and he realized it was true; Hessler had chopped off Danny's arm.

"You bastard," Hank said. "Let him go!"

"Oh, come on, Lucky, let me put your pony out of his misery. He'll be better off dead, and surely you don't want him like this, looking like some carnival freak."

"Put the knife down," Hank said with force, as if he were covering Hessler with a gun.

"I'd rather finish the job," Hessler said, smiling.

"Please!" Hank begged. "Don't touch him."

"Why don't we let Danny choose for himself?" Hessler proposed, as if the idea had just then struck him. "If he tells you he loves you, you'll slide me the file and I'll let him go."

Danny kept his mouth shut, but a tear appeared on his cheek.

"I thought you were dead," Hank said to Danny. "I don't know what I'd do without you."

Still Danny said nothing.

"Try harder, Lucky," Hessler advised, pressing the machete against Danny's scarred flesh.

"Take the knife away from his throat, then maybe he'll talk."

"All right," Hessler said, and complied.

"Danny, I love you." Still no response. "Say something!"

Danny remained mute, as he stared at Hank, his face wet with tears.

"Here, Hessler, take it!"

Hank slid the satchel across the dirty cement, to Hessler's feet. Hessler snatched it up and opened the clasp, looking inside and rifling through its contents.

Without another word, he dropped the machete on the ground and went running toward the end of the deck, turning around the corner. Hank let him go.

Hank rushed to Danny's side and held on to him tightly.

The tears flowed down Danny's face, which was covered all over in scars. His face was pale, his eyes red-rimmed and bloodshot. His hair was greasy and unwashed, and his body exuded an unpleasant odor. At last he parted his mouth in a smile.

Hank kissed him and said, "Oh, Danny, Danny, Danny." His voice caught in his throat, and he began to cry himself.

He stood up, picking Danny up off the bench easily and holding his body against him. The right arm of Danny's coat flapped in the wind."

"You're safe," Hank said. "I've got you."

A piece of paper flew into Hank's face. Tearing it away, he saw that it was a report in his own handwriting, part of the torso file.

Somewhere, women were screaming.

Countless pages were blowing in swirls at the end of the deck, billowing up from beyond the railing, caught by fierce gusts of wind from below.

Carrying Danny in his arms, Hank ran along the deck and turned the corner, continuing along until he reached the north end, from where the screaming had come.

The ladies carrying Higbee's bags stood flat against the back wall, away from the railing, sobbing as a security guard approached.

"He . . . he climbed right up," one of them was blubbering, "and vaulted over. Oh, it was awful, *awful!*"

Distant voices like the squeals of mice rose up from the street below.

Hank poked his head through the bars and looked over the

edge, straight down. In the middle of the street, between the base of Terminal Tower and the statue of Moses Cleaveland in the snow-covered park, was a black speck surrounded by a pool of red.

Hank made sure Danny got a good look.

# 1 January 1939

"You want one?" Hank asked.

Danny nodded, grabbing the Lucky Strike from Hank with his left hand. Danny placed it in the corner of his mouth and lighted it. He smoked out of one side and breathed in through the other, like those pictures of Franklin Delano Roosevelt with his black cigarette holder, Hank thought.

"Want to stop in Cheyenne tonight?"

Danny shrugged.

"We could stop in Cheyenne or go on to Laramie. Guess it depends on when we get there, huh?"

Danny had spent the Christmas season under care of the nuns at St. Vincent's Charity Hospital. The doctor had been shocked that Danny was still alive at all. The right arm had been brutally severed and crudely cauterized. The doctor explained that the trauma must have been tremendous, and attributed Danny's survival to what had clearly been "a great will to live."

Hank had no idea what could have given Danny so much hope, but in selfish moments he liked to imagine he had something to do with it.

Danny's scars extended all over his entire body. Hessler

335

had mutilated the works from head to toe, leaving the genitals intact but lacing long sensitive pink scars all over the remainder of Danny's flesh.

With the help of Eliot Ness, who came to visit at the hospital, Hank had explained to the doctor exactly how Danny had ended up this way. Hank and Ness had spent a few hours together in the room watching Danny sleep and sharing a strained laugh over their misfortunes.

Ness had speedily resigned after it had become known throughout the city that he, the safety director himself, had caused a hit-and-run accident while reportedly intoxicated. No charges had been brought against him, yet Mayor Burton had forced him out of the administration, praising his record of past achievements in the process. Now Ness, too, was in need of a job.

"You want some music?" Hank reached toward the glowing car radio.

But Danny shook his head, offering Hank an apologetic smile. Danny had not spoken a word since being saved from Hessler.

"That's all right. I was just thinking maybe you'd like some music."

Danny puffed on his cigarette while Hank puffed on his.

Danny's color had been restored, underneath the scars. The nuns had seemingly worked a miracle. Danny had responded well to them, and also to Hank's almost constant presence at his bedside. Some sisters from the Parmadale Children's Village had come to visit him when they learned he was at St. Vincent's, and sang his praises to Hank. They said he'd been a "precocious" child and had always gotten himself into "mischief," but it was clear they had fond memories of his stay at the orphanage.

"Where should we go?" Hank asked for the millionth time. He had been unable to decide between two places: "San Francisco or Hollywood?"

Hollywood had a certain pull because of the movies and all the fascinating people who lived there. Yet Hank had read Dashiell Hammett's *The Maltese Falcon* and imagined himself setting up a private eye practice amid the hills of San Francisco. He would have to make a living somehow.

Danny made a sound in his throat, as if wanting to speak.

"What, Hollywood?" Hank asked.

Danny shook his head. "No," he croaked, his voice raspy from disuse. "San . . . Francisco."

"San Francisco it is!" Hank was thrilled to finally hear his voice again. Danny's recovery was the most important thing in Hank's life, and perhaps had given Hank something to live for, as well.


## 9:19 P.M.

Danny couldn't stop the tears from flowing. He had cried more in the last few weeks than he ever had before in his life. He had lost his mind during those weeks with Hessler, and it had taken heroic Hank Lambert and an army of nuns to restore it.

Torturing him with the knife, Hessler had made Danny confess all his secrets. Danny had fought him, withholding certain ones until Hessler again sliced his skin with the blade, but in the end Danny had had no more secrets left.

He had told all about his mother's tuberculosis, and about his fear of the Terminal Tower. He had told all about his adventures as a hustler on the streets. He had told all about Hank, and everything Hank had told him about the torso investigation. Hessler had drawn every last thought from Danny's brain, every last hope except for the desire to see Hank Lambert once more before he died.

But he had lived, and now here he was, a pampered passenger in Hank's old beat-up car, driving along the Lincoln Highway on the way to San Francisco, which Danny had seen destroyed by an earthquake in some movie. It seemed the best choice. The people there were survivors, like him. In Hollywood, Danny would be looked upon as a freak. He might make some money playing special parts in the movies, but he would rather live a quiet life at home with his wonderful detective.

Hank had told him his dreams many times during the course of their trip along the highway. San Francisco seemed the right place to become a private eye. The famous fog and abundant hills must be very romantic.

With his left hand, Danny removed the spent cigarette from his mouth, snuffing it out in the ashtray.

"Want another?" Hank asked.

Danny did not, and shook his head from side to side.

One question remained that he longed to ask, yet after confessing all his secrets to Hessler, he remained wary of speaking at all.

Danny looked over at Hank through his tears, examining Hank's profile glowing green in the light from the dashboard, and thought: *Do you love your little pony?*

# Author's Note

Although a work of fiction, this novel is based on the known historical facts in the case of the Cleveland Torso Slayer, who killed anywhere from twelve to forty people (depending on whom you believe) and who in reality was never apprehended.

Hank Lambert, Danny Cottone, and Mott Hessler are purely fictional characters. My fictionalized portrait of Eliot Ness is, I believe, closer to the truth than the popular myth that has come down to us. Ness certainly did much of what I have him doing, including the hit-and-run accident, which in reality took place in 1942. He did run for mayor of Cleveland in 1947 on the Republican ticket but lost handily.

The polygraph scene is based on Eliot Ness's own version of the story, which no one has yet corroborated. It has, however, become part of the myth of the Torso Slayer, and the character of my killer is based loosely on Ness's primary suspect. Ness claimed to have let the suspect go after the interview at the hotel (due to lack of evidence and the suspect's well-connected family) and maintained that the killer soon committed himself to an insane asylum, where he later died.

In some instances, the names of other actual persons have been appropriated for reasons of verisimilitude, yet their characters are wholly fabricated, used fictitiously, and must bear, at best, only a superficial resemblance to reality.

My researches consisted primarily of contemporary accounts in the Cleveland *Plain Dealer,* but also included the excellent article "Butcher's Dozen" by John Bartlow Martin (*Harper's,* November 1949), and Steven Nickel's *Torso: The Story of Eliot Ness and the Search for a Psychopathic Killer* (John F. Blair, Publisher, 1989). Among the other works consulted was *The Encyclopedia of Cleveland History,* edited by David D. Van Tassel and John J. Grabowski (Indiana University Press, 1987).

I also wish to thank Det. Sup. Mary Otterson of the Madison (Wisconsin) Police Department for her technical assistance; my editors, Otto Penzler and Bill Malloy in New York and Mike Bailey in London, and their assistants, for sound editorial advice all around; my agents, Owen Laster and Matt Bialer, for their support and encouragement; and Keng Kiew Leong for his faith in me.

JOHN PEYTON COOKE was born in 1967 in Amarillo, Texas. He is the author of two previous novels, *The Lake* (1989) and *Out for Blood* (1991). His short fiction has appeared in *Weird Tales* and *Christopher Street*. He lives in New York City.